SHAKESPEARE'S CONSPIRATOR

The Woman, The Writer, The Clues

Steve Weitzenkorn

ISBN: 1507856679
ISBN 13: 9781507856673
Cover illustration by Yuan Lee

For Bonnie, with love always

The courage and creativity of Amelia Bassano Lanier (1569-1645) inspired this novel. Like Shakespeare, much of her life is shrouded in mystery, but literary clues point to her as the author of many of his most famous plays. Several scholars speculate that she was the "Dark Lady" of Shakespeare's sonnets. Uncontested, is that she was the first female poet and fourth woman to be published in England. Her eloquent poetic treatise, *Salve Deus Rex Judæorum,* establishes her as one of the world's first feminists, centuries before the term was coined. Her pioneering volume is probably the first feminist literary work. This novel is a tribute to her.

ACT ONE

A PACT OF SECRECY

1

LONDON, APRIL 1587

B lood. Eighteen-year-old Amelia Bassano stared in horror at the red streaks on her white gloves. "No! What have I done?" she shrieked, her wound stinging. Her eyes shifted to the carriage window frame. A smudge of blood marked the spot where she'd struck her forehead as the carriage bucked onto cobblestones leading to Whitehall Palace. Again she touched the gash beneath her hairline, wincing from the sharp pain. "Of all times to be so careless!"

"Why stretch out your head? You can see well enough from inside," remarked Lady Susan Bertie, leaning from the other half of the bench and patting the cut with an embroidered handkerchief. "Hold this against your wound to stop the bleeding."

Amelia pressed the cloth to her forehead, triggering another stabbing burn. "I was trying to see who had disembarked from the carriages ahead of us." She again gazed through the window watching sunlight glisten off the palace's flint and white stone blocks, portrait medallions above the formal entrances, and the domed tower. "I can't meet the Queen looking like this!"

"You won't. It was never likely," replied the middle-aged aristocrat, tucking her strawberry-blond hair beneath a pearl-studded headdress, drawing attention to her almond eyes and aquiline nose. "We're here only to watch a play. You might see her from across the hall, but as a commoner, minor gentry at best, she'll have little interest in you."

"Then who will be interested in me?" murmured Amelia, not expecting a response. Thinking about it, a fleeting question crossed her mind: Might Will be here today? She had met Shakespeare two years earlier quite by accident, but he'd left London soon thereafter. She answered her own query: No, he's a fledging actor attempting to write his first script. He's probably still in Stratford-upon-Avon married to some enchantress.

"Many fine men have come courting but your haughtiness drove them away," chastised Lady Susan. "With whomever you meet today, act with greater dignity than you have with them."

Amelia tightened her lips to control her rage, only then seeing splatters of blood on the ruffles of her white silk sleeve and creamy satin gown. She felt like crying. The spots had spread, becoming scarlet blotches. She wiped her golden-brown eyes, swept strands of her coiled chestnut hair away from her face, and turned toward Lady Susan. "I want to fall in love, but those suitors lacked the courage to engage with a woman who sought her own success. I won't be the docile wife they seek, nor will I be bored." She disliked arguing with Lady Susan but disagreed with her characterization.

"I'm not haughty. Strong-willed. Tenacious. Passionate. Aspiring. Those fit better."

Lady Susan retained her serene demeanor, which Amelia admired but found irritating, for she had difficulty staying calm when their opinions clashed. "Still, you needn't challenge them with your quick-witted banter," Susan admonished, keeping her voice even. "Men dislike feeling inferior. Act like a lady as you've been taught."

Amelia had heard this lecture before and had tired of it. She turned to see the scolding look on Lady Susan's delicate features and disappointment in her eyes. The silent expression hurt more than her words, which Amelia knew rang true. Lady Susan could cut through her bluster. She knew her better than anyone, having raised her for the past eleven years. "Rest assured, I'll be courteous by necessity. I won't waste this chance to sway the powerful—be they nobles or dramatists."

As their carriage jostled closer to the imposing guard towers, Amelia removed the bloodstained handkerchief from her forehead. "How awful is it?"

"It's raw but not unsightly. Don't let it tarnish your confidence."

"How could it not? I spent hours preparing my hair, applying makeup, and dressing. Now all anyone will notice is my wound and none of my finery…or take much interest in me or my assertions."

"I doubt that. Your commentary rarely escapes notice."

Amelia shivered. Her ambitions filled her head. "I've dreamed since I was small of being a playwright and loved acting out stories, even when you were my only audience."

Lady Susan touched Amelia's arm. "And the most endearing were the tales you invented."

"Imagining and writing—that's what I do best."

Their carriage rolled to a stop. Lady Susan clutched Amelia's hand. "You look entrancing despite your injury."

Amelia swallowed, disbelieving. She didn't see herself that way even without the gash.

A palace guard helped Amelia and Lady Susan alight from the carriage. Amelia stumbled as her trembling legs reached the ground. She grabbed the guard's shoulder to steady herself. Embarrassed, she checked to see if other arriving guests had noticed, but nobody heading toward the grand entrance looked back at her. In the brisk April air, smelling of leather and horses, she admired a bed of yellow lilies bending with the breeze. She then brushed dirt from the hem of her long skirt and squeezed her fingers to regain her composure. Before turning toward the majestic door, she gazed across the expansive grounds cleaved by the long palace road and a procession of horse-drawn coaches. She inhaled and exhaled to stem her dismay. She wouldn't let it keep her from presenting a confident image.

Lady Susan grabbed Amelia's arm as they stepped through the massive gate and into the palace. "Bear in mind, if you act above your station, nobody will be the wiser."

Amelia knew her status well. It's a fact I can't change, she thought, but something to overcome, like my olive complexion that separates me from the fair-skinned English. She got it from her father who was a Venetian musician recruited by Henry VIII. He then played for Queen Elizabeth until his death in 1576. Amelia was seven when he passed but remembered his warning to conceal her Jewish faith, which also made her different. She wondered who knew or suspected, aware that many had been imprisoned or hanged for such an offense against English law. She worried that her skin tone would elicit unwanted questions.

The palace's opulent interior, which Amelia was seeing for the first time, struck her as a visual symphony—but her heart raced faster than the music she imagined. She scanned the royal portraits, tapestries, and elaborate chandeliers along the wide corridor. Vivid reds, blues, and silvers drew her eyes to the ceiling where paintings depicted English military victories—with each scene framed in gold leaf. It's intended to impress and intimidate, she thought, biting her lip to contain her excitement and maintain her poise.

She leaned toward Lady Susan. "Will Henry Carey be attending?"

"Most certainly, but refer to him as Lord Hunsdon. He is, after all, the Lord Chamberlain—responsible for palace protocol and royal events, like this one today."

"Indeed, I'll accord him all due respect."

"And do so for all Privy Council members you encounter, regardless of their reputation."

Amelia reveled being in the midst of power. It activated all her senses. These were people who could get her work published or performed. She'd curry their good will. She'd stoke their interest.

Amelia watched lavishly attired guests walking ahead of them and heard snippets of conversation echo off the stonewalls. Two men spoke of Queen Elizabeth's plans to establish a settlement in North America. An older woman, in a long ermine-trimmed gown with a full sapphire skirt, applauded the beheading of Mary, Queen of Scots a few months earlier, pleased it had stopped a treacherous Catholic plot.

Amelia frowned upon hearing the woman take pleasure from such a ghastly deed. She glanced at Lady Susan. "Nobody should be executed for devotion to a disfavored religion. Belief isn't treasonous."

One of the men in front turned and glared, stopping Amelia cold.

"Shh," admonished Lady Susan putting a finger to her lips. "Keep such opinions to yourself, especially here."

Amelia regretted her comment before she'd finished saying it. She had a habit of announcing whatever she thought without considering whom it might offend.

Amelia and Lady Susan glided through the Great Hall's marble-framed entrance. High mullioned windows accented each end, bathing the room in light. A long theatrical scaffold with an elaborate set dominated the far wall. Rows of gilt-trimmed chairs faced it, centered by the Queen's capacious throne. Amelia's eyes gleamed at the sight of the stage. This was a far cry from the theaters she frequented outside the city gate, with their rough-hewn benches and straw-covered pits. She felt brilliantly alive.

Many nobles had already settled into their seats as Lady Susan and Amelia strode forward. Amelia noticed one woman in a gray gown with fox trim waving her hands and twisting from the waist in exaggerated motions, no doubt a lower-ranking aristocrat striving to impress those above her station—something Amelia was loathe to do, but, she thought, I have my own devices.

Amelia nodded as Lady Susan introduced her to acquaintances while they navigated through the center aisle. A broad-shouldered man in a wide ruff and charcoal doublet leered at her—making Amelia self-conscious of her gash, bloodstained sleeve, and exotic complexion. Still, she bowed her head demurely, pleased her form-fitted bodice, tight corset, flowing skirt, and willowy grace garnered attention.

Upon reaching a row with vacant chairs, Amelia saw Henry Carey, an older man with a thin crooked nose, cinnamon-gray beard, and light brows curved over wary eyes. Amelia caught his gaze as he took his seat. He nodded with affection, pointed to his forehead, and mouthed, "What happened?"

She smiled back, recognizing his overtures had become more pronounced and less paternal. Nonetheless, Amelia arched her small breasts upward and kept eye contact until he turned to sit. She'd explain about her injury later if necessary.

A trumpeted fanfare announcing the Queen interrupted Amelia's reverie. She and the audience stood in unison as Queen Elizabeth paraded to her throne in a white gold-beaded gown in full royal regalia. Amelia beheld the Queen's white-painted face, which rumors claimed covered smallpox scars.

A master of ceremonies, dressed in bright blues and yellows, struck a dramatic pose at center stage. "My Queen, ladies and lords, and friends of the court, welcome to our encore performance of *Knight in the Burning Rock*. We first performed this tale of romance and chivalry eight years ago. By the gracious request of Her Majesty, we will reenact the drama with an entirely new cast. All the players are superb. I now turn the stage over to them, wishing you immense enjoyment."

Actors marched onto the stage with great flair in intricate brocade and velvet costumes, captivating Amelia from the start. Her eyes probed every nuance as she tried imagining how actors might bring her own fledging play to life. In one scene they created the illusion of fire with red and orange muslin strips, which Amelia considered excessive. When a hidden throne emerged from within a large boulder and roamed the stage, she thought the stunt had been added to draw attention away from the stilted dialogue. Regardless, the audience roared its approval and Queen Elizabeth cheered from her gilded throne.

At that moment, Amelia came to believe that she could write a better script, a more poetic one, a more personal one. She hugged herself to dispel the chill accompanying her epiphany. An instant later, doubts invaded her mind. She questioned her abilities. Can I credibly portray natural human inclinations, the honorable and the unscrupulous, in comedic or dramatic form? My skills must rise to the level of my ambitions. But how?

Amelia pushed these questions aside, resolving to contemplate them later, as she refocused on the drama. Her lips parted and her eyes widened upon hearing a familiar voice. Is that Will?

She leaned forward, studying a secondary character.

Could it be? She couldn't tell because a hat and collar obscured his features, but soon they became visible. Yes, that's him...his lithe movements, pear-shaped face, and bulging eyes.

For the remainder of the performance and through the applause for the last encore, she concentrated on her immediate desire. She whispered to Lady Susan, "I recognized one of the actors. How can I meet him?"

Lady Susan's bearing projected a sprightliness Amelia had long admired. "Performers usually greet their audience at the back of the Great Hall. Let's wait there." On the way, Susan asked, "Who is this gentleman?"

"Will Shakespeare. We met two years ago when he caught me secretly watching a rehearsal at Paul's Theater."

"I remember the trouble you caused," chided Lady Susan with a sly wink.

Amelia grinned while scanning the room for Will. She smoothed wrinkles from her cream-colored skirt, finger-brushed her burnished red hair, and shifted her weight from foot to foot. Suddenly, Lord Hunsdon emerged from the crowd in his regal midnight-blue doublet and cape. Oh dear, thought Amelia, he's not subtle and won't appreciate Will's flamboyance.

Lord Hunsdon strode toward them with a military gait. Only his thin gray hair and flecked beard hinted at his age. Amelia first met him at Duchess Katherine Willoughby's funeral seven years earlier and she liked that, even then, he had not treated her as a child.

"Amelia, you're exquisite today, even with your wound. Were you fending off a suitor?"

Amelia felt her cheeks warm at his clumsy attempt at humor and feigned compliment, uncharacteristic for the usually smooth man. "Lord Hunsdon, you're most kind. Alas, neither bravery nor self-defense caused my injury. I wounded myself."

"Henry, you know how to indulge the vanity of a blossoming young woman," remarked Lady Susan, touching her jeweled hat as she linked arms with Amelia.

Amelia realized Lord Hundson's flattery had an intention and, obviously, Lady Susan did too. While Amelia wished to cultivate his interest, some mystifying force drew her attention away as she craned her neck looking for Will. "I'm sorry, Lord, I don't intend to be rude. I'm searching for an actor and don't want to miss him."

Henry showed his normal aplomb. "Perfectly all right. I trust you'll introduce us."

She spied Will speaking with two young noblewomen dressed in gem-studded bodices, with their husbands standing nearby. Will appeared overly solicitous, and the men's bemused expressions told Amelia they found his animated attempts to impress entertaining and benign. At the first break in his monologue, they escorted their wives away.

"Let's go to him," suggested Amelia.

Will bowed as the trio neared. Amelia found herself drawn to his bold manner and dancing eyes, which radiated kindness and intelligence. His hair had thinned on top and he had grown a wispy beard since she last saw him. As they approached, his face brightened in recognition.

"Is that you…Amelia?"

Amelia grinned with delight as she lifted her hand. Will raised it to his lips with a sweeping flourish. Amelia loved the theatrical gesture and the attention it drew from other women. "Yes, Will, it is. Please meet Lord Hunsdon—the Lord Chamberlain—and Lady Susan Bertie. Lord Hunsdon is a great patron of the arts, especially theater. Lady Susan has embraced me as a daughter."

Will bowed again, spreading his arms wide. "I'm honored to meet you both. Lord Hunsdon, you're well regarded among actors. I'm delighted to make your acquaintance. I trust you enjoyed the performance."

Amelia interrupted, "My heart leapt upon seeing you on stage." She pinched herself for blurting so eagerly. She wished to project greater poise. "I looked for you at Paul's Theatre several weeks after we met, but Mr. Westcott, the owner, said you'd married and left for Stratford-upon-Avon."

Will seemed displeased to be reminded, looking down and squeezing his eyes shut. "Ah, yes, that's true. I vanished with the unexpected tides in my life. I've returned to London to find work and, fortunately, acquired this role."

"Did you finish your script about Henry VI?"

Will fluttered his eyelashes comically. "I've scrawled a lot of words...but not yet."

"You're a playwright and an actor?" asked Lord Hunsdon.

Will sobered at the question from a nobleman. "I'm working on it. It's a long play which I must prune."

"May I read your draft?" asked Amelia, dropping her eyes demurely. A momentary misgiving struck her. She had no intention of following through on her flirtations but realized her charm could enlist Will's help and that of Lord Hunsdon. When younger, her spirited intellect had been sufficient to persuade, but now she felt compelled to be bewitching as well.

Her flirtation apparently took Will by surprise. His eyes widened as he took a half-step back. When they had met, she was sixteen and not given to such dalliance. Will replied, "Let's arrange to meet and I'll show it to you, but promise kindness with your criticism."

Amelia held his gaze; flattered he'd offered her the opportunity. Although a commoner, like herself, he seemed worldlier. "I promise. My intention will be to help."

"Lady Susan said you're composing a script of your own," interjected Lord Hunsdon, touching Amelia's arm.

Amelia smiled, pleased Henry had raised the subject in Will's presence. She wished to impress both men with her project but worried they'd see it as folly. "I am. At one of Lady Susan's assemblies, I overheard a man telling a tale about two sets of identical twins, one of boys and one of girls in his town. He claimed they married one another and nobody could tell the couples apart, unless the twins identified themselves."

Will leaned in and Amelia felt his warm breath on her cheek, arousing her unexpectedly. Amelia's voice rose and her cadence quickened. "The man went on to explain how the pairs merrily pretended to be each other, creating confusion until a farmer accused one of the brothers of stealing a chicken. But the farmer didn't know which one and the twins wouldn't confess. So neither was arrested."

"Quite interesting," pronounced Lord Hunsdon, shifting his feet to crowd Will's space in a bit of manly competition. "You're turning it into a play for your own amusement?"

Amelia forced a smile while smoldering inside. "No, not that exact tale and not for my own amusement. I'm writing it to be performed, to entertain audiences, and to earn royalties."

Now she felt on stage, hoping her reaction wasn't too harsh and aware of Will absorbing every word. "The idea inspired me but I'm creating my own storyline. Today it's a raft of scribbles."

Lord Hunsdon raised his eyebrows and jutted his chin. Amelia recognized this skeptical grimace and braced herself for his comments, suspecting they'd be unfavorable.

"That's not the role of a woman, particularly one raised with privilege," he said with conviction.

Amelia burned, incensed, but kept her expression neutral. She had a polite rejoinder on her lips but Lady Susan spoke instead. "Henry, you surprise me. Why should such limitations be imposed? Are you defending them without knowing Amelia's abilities?"

Lord Hunsdon maintained a stoic expression as Amelia straightened her back. Her feet felt glued to the floor while awaiting his reply. He stood silently, apparently collecting his thoughts and she sensed a touch of flattery and humor might diffuse the tension. "Lord Hunsdon," she said affably, "I've long admired your wisdom, which I've taken to heart since my younger days." She inched closer to him. "Over the din in this hall, I wasn't sure if you said role or rule of a woman—for you've always spoken well of Queen Elizabeth's reign. I know you believe women can do more than cook meals, wash clothes, and look enchanting on a man's arm. Just as men can do more than plow fields, chop wood, and escort women." She cocked her head to the side watching for Lord Hunsdon's response as she lightened her tone. "Which would delight me literally and figuratively."

Lord Hunsdon's impassive expression gave way to a deep laugh. "You make compelling points and I admire your fire." He reached out and touched her arm. "Although I can't change English customs, I'd be pleased to read your script and render an opinion."

I swayed him, thought Amelia as Lord Hunsdon maneuvered his large frame to edge Will out of her view. "I'd be honored if you did," she replied, touching his sleeve with dainty fingertips.

Will leaned inward in an exaggerated manner, appearing from beside Lord Hunsdon's shoulder. "I trust you'll let me read it as well."

Amelia chuckled at his antic as a shiver of anticipation coursed through her. "But of course. We'll read each other's."

"Indeed. I'll see you soon, little theater spy." With a gleam in his eye he added, "Your gash—I trust it's not from other covert ventures." Without waiting for a reply, he bowed toward Lord Hunsdon and Lady Susan and cut toward the door.

Amelia felt her face flush and hoped her embarrassment didn't show.

Lady Susan frowned at her then turned toward Lord Hunsdon. "Henry, if you're serious about reading her script, come by Willoughby House. You and Amelia can gather in the drawing room."

Henry stroked his thin beard. "I am serious, but it must wait until after my trip to Essex. I'll send a messenger with possible dates upon my return."

Amelia nodded. "I'll be prepared."

"But, Amelia," warned Henry, "don't have fanciful expectations. I doubt theaters will accept anything composed by a woman, no matter my judgment."

Amelia's brief tinge of hope seeped away.

Lord Hunsdon turned, ensuring the actor had truly left. Then he asked, "Now, Amelia, what's this about being a theater spy?"

2

LONDON, MAY 1587

Amelia tapped her fingers on the windowsill. Thick rain pellets burst against the glass and off the stone courtyard at Willoughby House. She turned to check on Lord Hunsdon sitting at the round inlaid-walnut table in the drawing room pouring over her script. It seemed pointless, like lingering for an egg to hatch, but she couldn't help herself as she awaited his verdict. Still churning about his comments and the uphill struggles she'd face as a woman writer, she tried but could not decipher any hint of his opinion. Men, she thought, with their stone faces never reveal a clue. No matter, I'll prove myself...and that a woman can succeed even where men enforce their self-made rules.

Amelia circled the room, pausing by the black marble fireplace to gaze at the portrait of Lady Susan's mother, Katherine Willoughby, as a young lady. Amelia remembered the duchess as an elderly but stern woman who urged her to be strong when facing obstacles blocking her path. Amelia then recalled the recent afternoon at Whitehall Palace—her ugly gash now mostly healed, the drama, being among royalty, and the competition for her interest between Will and Lord Hunsdon. Each man intrigued and attracted her in his own way. Will projected youthful ambition and exuberance. He could help her penetrate London's tight-knit theatrical community. Henry was mature, steady, secure in his manner, and accomplished—and she sought his approval. He could exert influence in many quarters. Both stirred ardent feelings. But both were married!

Amelia settled on the harpsichord bench by a large window. She placed her hands on the keys and let them sit for a few seconds before playing an English madrigal while whispering the verses to herself.

Distracted, she climbed the curving stairway with polished wood banisters. The brooding framed faces of Willoughby ancestors stared from the walls. When the rain paused, she roamed outside, whirling around the garden bursting with daffodils, English primroses and bluebells. Water droplets glistened on their petals.

When she next peeked into the drawing room, Lord Hunsdon announced, "Amelia, I've finished."

She inhaled. "Is it praiseworthy?"

"It's clever. You have splendid ideas but it requires greater continuity."

Amelia's heart sank, fearing her script lacked merit. She assessed his sober expression. Was he being polite when he actually thought it was dreadful?

"Amelia, don't look so glum. It's good for someone who hasn't written a script before. Although it's disjointed, it can be fixed."

Overcoming her disappointment, Amelia explained how she'd started and stopped working on it several times over two years, got stuck, discarded parts she considered too juvenile, and tried sharpening the dialogue with puns and wordplays.

Lord Hunsdon gathered the manuscript sheets and patted them into a neat stack. "You have an appealing premise. The script in its current form, however, is only a series of scenes loosely linked together, rather than a fully joined plot. Each part is well presented and many are stories by themselves. What's missing is an overarching conflict or dilemma."

Amelia pressed her tension into her curled fingers. "You mean a problem introduced in the beginning that's not resolved until the end?"

"Exactly. Then connect the scenes to it, reconstructing them as needed, to craft a suspenseful story."

"Will you help me?"

Lord Hunsdon reached for her hand, pried her fingers open, and gently pressed her palm. "Harness your abundant imagination, compose the next iteration, and I'll provide further guidance."

He squeezed her hand and held it fast. Flesh communicating with flesh. Amelia caught her breath and considered Lord Hunsdon's elevated status: a Privy Council member and captain general—a powerful older man to whom she felt pulled. There wasn't a reason for him to be massaging her palm but his gesture kindled an unexpected sense of intimacy.

Amelia lowered her gaze to the pages between them then looked up at him. In his eyes she saw tenderness while his demeanor and bearing carried the force of authority—both thrilling and scaring her. She didn't wish to break her hypnotic attraction but realized her dignity required it. She tried easing her hand from Lord Hunsdon's hold while tugging gently on the gold hand-shaped pendant, called a hamsa, draped around her neck. It connected her to her father and secret Jewish heritage.

Lord Hunsdon did not relinquish his grip, which surprised Amelia and forced her eyes to back to his. "After you recompose and sew the scenes together, we'll discuss the entire plot and, if needed, how to strengthen it further. Now, let's review my notes…"

After a moment, Amelia eased her hand out from beneath his. She watched for a reaction but saw none. Maybe she had jumped to an erroneous conclusion but she thought not.

When they finished, Lord Hunsdon pushed back his chair and rose to his feet. Amelia stood with him and let her hand linger on his arm. "Thank you. You've been an enormous help."

He laughed and lifted her hand to kiss it. Every gesture, she noticed, concerned his touching her. She realized her young feminine charm, enticing glances, silky skin, and aspirations beckoned him. Yet his gravelly voice, wrinkled face, and the sags beneath his eyes made her hesitate. Despite his kindness. Despite his evident interest in her. Yet there was something seductive about him that enthralled deep into her core.

"What's The Horn? Where is it?" Amelia asked Lady Susan in the mansion courtyard while they cut spring flowers.

"It's a tavern in Shoreditch, east of London beyond Bishopsgate. It attracts an odd combination of laborers and artists. Why?"

Amelia showed Lady Susan the message she'd received from Will suggesting they meet there.

Lady Susan shook her head. "It's not a place I'd frequent. Propose a more genteel location, where a young woman will feel secure."

Amelia rejected that idea. She wanted to show she had the audacity to mix with working men. If that's where theater people imbibed, so would she. "Perhaps I should learn more about Will before agreeing."

"I have already," said Lady Susan. "I asked Lord Hunsdon to investigate, since Mr. Shakespeare showed such interest in you at the palace. Henry reported that Shakespeare performs at The Theatre, a playhouse in Shoreditch. He rents a cheap room near the sewage canal where the stench must be horrific. He hails from Stratford-upon-Avon, where his father is a disreputable tradesman."

Amelia placed the lilacs she'd cut into a basket as she contemplated. "Did he find anything suggesting Will is dishonorable?"

"No. But he learned Shakespeare finished grammar school at fourteen and hasn't had a day of formal education since. And his wife, Anne Hathaway, is nine years older and illiterate."

Amelia wrinkled her brow in surprise. She pondered why a man like Will, aspiring to be a playwright, would marry a woman who couldn't read. It made no sense to her. Lady Susan had taught her several languages, poetry, mathematics, science, philosophy, and Christianity. She prodded her to read classical Greek plays and Dante's works in the original Italian—all of which were in the mansion's library, where Amelia had spent countless hours. Amelia and Lady Susan had dissected many books together and debated the meaning of great passages. Amelia wondered how much Will knew.

A few days later Amelia, donning a white beaded French hood, passed beneath the swinging sign of a bugle and into The Horn's dim confines, letting in a stream of fresh daylight. Boisterous conversation bounced off the grubby stonewalls and vaulted ceilings. Two large iron wheels with thick candles planted around the rims cast weak yellow light and angled shadows in the narrow space. Several laborers lined a polished oak bar along the back, gesturing with heavy arms and large hands wrapped around mugs of ale. As Amelia searched for Will, other faces stared back.

She saw Will sitting at the window table with his hand resting on a thick manuscript bound by a rough cord.

"Few ladies walk through that door if those stares are any clue," she quipped approaching Will.

"At least not like you. They'll leave us alone."

He had spoken too soon. A drunken old man with gray stubble on his unshaven face waddled toward their table. "Buy you a lager?" he asked with slurred words, projecting fumes of ale.

Amelia replied, "Thank you kind sir, but my gentleman will purchase for me."

The old man shook his befuddled head and walked away.

"I trust you've been well," said Amelia.

"Not like you, attending events at Whitehall Palace with the aristocracy."

"I'm fortunate. They've been kind to me. Are you now living in London? Where's your family?"

Will raised a chalice to his lips, took a long sip of ale, and swallowed hard. "My family remains in Stratford. It's a chaotic household with three young children. I couldn't concentrate on writing, so I escaped to London."

"And what of your wife?" asked Amelia.

Will's grimace signaled that he didn't wish to discuss her. "She takes care of our children. Otherwise, we have little to discuss."

Amelia untied her hood and tucked loops of her wiry locks behind her ear. "How did you meet? What drew you to her?"

Will shifted in his chair. "She enticed me and flattered me. I was eighteen and I hadn't yet bedded a woman. She pulled me in and I succumbed willingly. A few months later, she declared her pregnancy and me as the father. We were forced to marry, to her delight and my chagrin."

Amelia reached across the table and tugged gently on Will's ruffled sleeve. "I can't imagine being married to someone who doesn't share my interests...but it could be material for a play."

Will burst into laughter, apparently taken by the notion. "My life is too ordinary for that."

Amelia tilted her head playfully to the side. "Didn't you tell me once that theater mirrors life?"

"I did. But I'm too close to this part of it."

Amelia appreciated Will's small disclosures as signs of trust. To encourage more, she revealed a few details about her life. The conversation then turned to scriptwriting. "Amelia," Will said, "I'm pleased you're interested in my work. I'd like your insights… And I'm interested in your script too," he hastened to add.

She'd been waiting for this—a sign that he'd value her opinion and also wished to help her—allowing them to forge a stronger bond.

"Lord Hunsdon, the Lord Chamberlain, read my scribbles and offered advice. I need to bind the overall storyline and much more." She rubbed the back of her neck then rushed her cadence. "It's not ready for presentation yet."

Will gripped his chalice with both hands. Amelia sensed his discomfort. He looked past her shoulder, not at her. Finally he pulled himself erect in his chair.

"Will, is there something you're not saying?

Will inhaled heavily. "You're devoting your efforts to a fruitless task, no matter how fine a writer you might be. Lord Hunsdon was right. Your project will not win favor."

Amelia fixed her eyes on him and set her jaw. "Will, you disappoint me. As a man, do you see no place for a woman colleague?"

"No. That's not what I meant."

"Then what? That you'd like me to help you but think it's pointless to reciprocate?"

Will blanched, evidently taken aback by the severity of Amelia's comment. "I meant only to state the challenge. You could set a precedent. Lord Hunsdon might give you an edge."

Amelia fingered her hamsa and spoke softly but with conviction. "Will, my goal is to succeed based on the merits of my work. Can Lord Hunsdon help my scripts get fair consideration? Perhaps, but I've not asked for that."

"Perhaps you should. He moves in powerful circles."

"He does and I intrigue him," Amelia said coyly, implying she could say more but chose not to.

Will leaned toward her. "Amelia, I'm also facing unfavorable odds. When I finish this script, I'll be competing with Christopher Marlowe who went to Cambridge. My education is paltry by comparison. My father, once a successful glover, is now an outcast. I earn a meager living as an actor. While our situations are not identical, we're both struggling to gain acceptance and get our work performed."

"That's a reason for helping each other. But first, tell me about your script."

Will tapped his fingers on the manuscript sitting on the table. "I'm wrestling with it. The first part is lengthy and weak. The middle section is more compelling. And I'm unhappy with the last portion. I'm stymied. I haven't written more than a few lines in months."

"What troubles you most about it?"

"Beyond its length, it's uneven and rambles, and I can't see how to fix it."

Will explained the storyline, how Henry VI assumed the crown as a baby, but regents ruled the country until he grew old enough to serve. He elaborated on the treachery of the period. "Even Henry VI's wife, Margaret of Anjou, became complicit. He had fits of insanity and she ruled England for a time, triggering a dynastic civil conflict called the War of the Roses."

"If I recall my history lessons," said Amelia, "it lasted thirty years."

"From 1455 to 1485. Henry V, the king's father, cast a long shadow over his son's rule. It's a fascinating piece of English history, especially since it launched the Tudor reign."

Will pushed his thick manuscript toward her and looked into her golden brown eyes. "Will you read it and offer a candid opinion?"

"Indeed. When would you like it back?"

"Is two weeks sufficient time?"

"It should be. Rather than meeting here, let's meet at Willoughby House where I reside. I can promise more comfortable chairs and better food."

Will nodded agreement, seemingly delighted with the idea. "Then will you show me your script?"

"I will, but understand I'm in the midst of revising it."

Amelia winced at the number of violent and bloody scenes in Will's six-hundred-page tome. But she saw how they could rivet audience attention. Will's propensity for dramatic action probably reflected his experience as an actor. His writing eloquence shone through more in the latter parts and places where he embedded sage observations, such as "Having nothing, nothing he can lose," and "And many strokes, though with a little axe/Hew down and fell the hardest-timbered oak." Will's ability to capture the essence of a scene through the turn of a phrase impressed her.

Still, she understood his frustration. The plot, though historically interesting, meandered confusingly. It took her several days to plow through it.

On the day Will was coming over, Amelia asked Enid Fletcher, the maid who had been attending to her since she joined the Willoughby household over a decade ago, to slice cheese, bread, fruit, and meats for his visit. She suspected he didn't eat well and would appreciate a meal. Over the years, Amelia had taught Enid to read and came to think of her more as a friend than a servant. They shared their innermost thoughts and sang together when Amelia played the lute or harpsichord.

Amelia organized her notes and placed them on the round table in the drawing room. Enid brought in the tray of food along with a plate of sweet cakes. She set two places with white china and silver chalices. There, Amelia thought, that should cushion the blow.

"Welcome," greeted Amelia opening the heavy door. The fresh air of May breezed in with Will. He entered with an easy gait, then paused as if unsure how to proceed in the stately manse. His hair was neatly combed and he wore a fresh white shirt. She smiled, believing he had done so for her.

"Come this way," said Amelia as she ushered him along a central hallway.

"Quite elegant," he commented, looking into the formal dining room as they passed.

"None of it is mine," said Amelia. "I'm a resident."

Will seemed baffled by the remark and Amelia realized he was curious about her living arrangement. She wondered how much to reveal.

The drawing room featured heavy walnut furniture and a marble-framed fireplace. A harpsichord, with its double rows of keys and an open wing-shaped case, stood by a window overlooking the courtyard garden.

"I'm glad I arrived hungry," Will joked, eyeing the tray.

Amelia touched his arm. "It will aid our concentration."

Will waited until she took her seat then settled into his own. "What did you think of my script?" he asked, getting straight to the point.

Amelia expected his question. She debated whether to lie, saying she loved it to spare his feelings or to be frank. She wouldn't want someone sweetening commentary on her work, as much as she'd like to hear it. She doubted Will would either.

She decided to approach her critique with delicacy, ensuring her voice conveyed kindness. "Will, I've read it and made copious notes. You have a muscular tale, but you're trying to accomplish too much in one play. I suspect you know that too."

"But I don't know what to cut without thinning the drama."

She lifted a page of notes. "Ready for ideas?"

Will nodded.

Amelia drew a deep breath. She wished to impress Will with her analysis without offending him.

"The middle section is the strongest. The dramatic tension is taut and the scenes well developed. It could be a play by itself."

He seemed struck by the idea. "Show me how."

Amelia leaned in, pleased by his reaction. She pointed in his manuscript where she thought the start and end points for that play should be. She explained her reasoning then surprised him again.

"Once audiences see the second part, they'll be eager to see the first. You'll create curiosity for it."

"Will hovered over the document and leafed through it, stopping at several points. When he finished, he bounced from his chair. Excitement filled his voice. "You're quite right! I'll segment the script accordingly."

Amelia beamed, delighted and relieved by his response. She had fretted that he'd reject such large-scale recommendations. If her comments had been paltry, he'd be disinterested in helping a girl with a privileged upbringing or think she was dabbling rather than writing a worthy script. She dashed those thoughts away. "Will, I'd like your insights now."

She explained Lord Hunsdon's critique of her script about the double set of twins. She reviewed the sequence of scenes, turning through pages of her draft.

"Lord Hunsdon believes I need an overarching dilemma. Can you suggest one?"

Will pursed his lips and rubbed his eyebrows. "I'm unsure. Your play is unlike any I've tried to write."

Amelia fingered her hamsa pendant, finding comfort in this amulet—her father's last gift before dying. She rubbed the ruby in the center of its gold-filigree palm then stretched toward Will. She summoned all her charms to make sure he'd say yes. "Dear Will, *Henry VI* is destined to be great. Never could I have composed such a work, and I ask you to extend some of your God-blessed talent to assist me."

Will appeared transfixed by her slender neck. In silken tones she continued. "We both know how lonely writing is, how much of a struggle it is to find compelling words or develop plot twists. Think of how good companionship would be with another writer who can offer unvarnished opinions and help find solutions when necessary. Could we create that together?"

Will's moist eyes softened as if overcome by her allure. "Indeed we can."

Amelia considered her notions about Will. She liked that he didn't pretend to be her better and saw merit in her suggestions. Despite eyes that seemed to big for his egg-shaped face and hair that swelled over his ears, she found his essence appealing. She reached over and touched his jaw line, intending to set off a tingling spark. "Will, we'll have fun. We'll elevate the quality of each other's work."

Will didn't respond in kind. Instead he chuckled. "Has anyone mentioned how enchanting and convincing you can be?"

Amelia warmed inside, pleased at her success. Setting her notes aside, she returned to her question. "Considering my storyline, what might be an overarching conflict?"

"Well, it mostly entails a comedy of errors…"

3

Amelia tossed another worn-down quill pen into the library fireplace and watched flames devour it. Lady Susan, knitting an afghan, looked up as Amelia grabbed a fresh one from the mantle.

"How many quills have you consumed this month?" asked Lady Susan.

"Twenty, I suppose."

Lady Susan grinned. "That's why there's a naked goose shivering in the garden.

"If you're worried, knit him a wrap. I must keep writing. Will should be here soon and I must first complete a scene."

Amelia dipped her quill into the inkwell, reflecting on ideas sparked by her conversation with Will. Although Lord Hunsdon's criticism had been useful, Will focused more on making the play fun for the audience. They laughed until tears rolled from their eyes while devising new schemes for the two sets of twins to sow confusion. Now she wanted to scratch out one last idea.

Lady Susan pointed her knitting needle toward Amelia. "Your dedication will be for naught if England goes to war with Spain. Sir Francis Drake sank twenty Spanish ships and King Philip is certain to seek revenge. A play, no matter how clever, will be of little import if we're invaded."

Amelia recalled the chatter in London's shops and on the streets about Drake's victory in the Bay of Cádiz and worry over Spain's reaction.

A loud rap at the front door saved Amelia from dreadful talk about soldiers and war.

"That must be Will."

She hurried to answer it. But rather than Will, a messenger stood on the portico, out of breath and drenched from rain.

"Milady, it's urgent. He paid me extra to bolt here," the messenger blurted, handing Amelia a soggy envelope.

Alarms struck. The message was not in Will's normal fluid script. Did he write it in haste?

> *Dear Amelia,*
> *I cannot meet today and perhaps not for some time.*
> *I received word my baby son, Hamnet, is feverish. I*
> *must return to Stratford with dispatch.*
> *With apologies,*
> *Will*

Amelia reread the note, gripping it with both hands while reeling to a chair. Disheartened, jumbled thoughts galloped through her mind: Is Will's note truthful or is he avoiding her? If his son is ill, may he fast recover...but she'd miss Will's mirthful collaboration. Would he miss her? She suddenly felt alone and adrift.

Amelia continued dwelling on the matter when she retired to bed. She closed her eyes and tugged her hamsa. She imagined seeing her play performed and created fresh scenes in her head. By degrees she started thinking of Will again, with her thoughts drifting to the time she first encountered him, thirty months earlier at Paul's Theatre.

After weeks of badgering her uncle John to let her see a rehearsal, he snuck her into Paul's Theater with a stern warning: "Stay hidden. Stay silent. If you're found, I'll lose my job as a theater musician. And you'll be arrested for trespassing."

Far back in the gallery and in shadows, she crouched on the floorboards between rows and peered down over the straw-covered pit to the scaffold that served as a stage. She watched how the actors turned scripts into performances. She marveled at how they brought the story to life and responded to the director's instructions and admonishments. She imagined writing her own plays and the delight of seeing them performed onstage.

Hours passed and Amelia itched to stretch her cramped legs but forced herself to keep still. Suddenly, she burst out laughing. Her adolescent cackle ripped through the theater to the stage below. She grabbed her mouth a moment too late and felt her eyes pop wide—all because a young actor muffed his line, turning it into a ribald proclamation. Other actors froze in place, listening and scanning the gallery.

"Who's there?" called the actor in a black archer's hood, agitated after botching his lines.

Amelia ducked lower and curled into ball. Her hands shook, her heart pounded, she could hardly breathe.

"Will, that blunder would surely arouse the audience more other lines in this tiresome play," one performer snickered.

But the director scolded, "Will, you should know your lines by now. And I'm paying musicians today so it's costing me money."

Jittery, Amelia peeked between the rough wooden chairs as Will brushed back his hood, squinting at a spot near her.

"What are you staring at?" asked the director.

"I heard something from behind the balustrade. It's probably nothing."

"Will," the director instructed, "concentrate on your lines. Think of nothing else. The timbers in this old structure rattle when buffeted by strong winds and a storm is brewing. Try it again and we'll finish for the day."

When the performers finally exited the stage, Amelia slithered nervously between rows to the nearest aisle, scraping her knees on rough floorboards. She heard someone charging up the steps and jerked in fright as scuffed black boots plunged before her eyes.

Startled, her path blocked, she looked up from hands and knees past dirty breeches into the eyes of the boy who'd butchered his lines. He peered down at her, his wavy brown hair mussed from the archer's hood. Sweat beaded on his forehead and a rip in his once-white shirt extended from wrist to elbow.

Amelia froze, embarrassed by his playful grin. His gleaming brown eyes seemed spread too far apart and his lips not long enough. She estimated Will was a few years older than her, perhaps nineteen or twenty.

Will scratched the back of his head, smirking. "Skulking through the rows are you? Whatever for?"

Trapped, desperate to leave, Amelia shook back her hair revealing her olive complexion. She stood and faced him. "Let me out," she pleaded, counting on a mischievous smile and rascally charm to persuade. "A gentleman would let me pass."

"Why are you here? Except for actors, musicians, and crew, the theater is closed."

She raised a finger to her lips with a touch of whimsy. "Shh. I know, but I came to see how a play is made. Don't disclose me. I'm doing no harm."

"That doesn't make sneaking into a theater and spying right."

"Oh, I suppose you've never done anything so naughty," she said teasingly, with more bravado than she felt. "Perhaps you haven't lived a very adventurous life."

"Don't leap to conclusions." Will paused, grinning, as he looked the girl over with an approving nod. "I'm jesting. Go on home, wherever that is."

Amelia suppressed a smile. Will's tone had softened. She sensed her spunk appealed to him—and that he found her attractive. More than once his eyes drank in her winsome figure. It occurred to her that he might be someone worth knowing. He could teach her about the theater from an actor's perspective.

"And where do you live?" she asked, since he wasn't rushing to leave. Some good may come from prolonging this conversation, she thought. He is, after all, inside a fascinating world she yearned to join.

From the stage a deep voice shouted, "Will, is that you up there?"

Amelia held her breath, standing stiff—except for her shaking knees and thumping heart.

Will again beheld Amelia then stroked his chin as if considering how to reply. A grin lifted his cheeks. "It is, Sebastian. I'm trying to pinpoint the noise I heard. But it'll remain a mystery."

"Will, the wind caused something to creak. That's all. I'm leaving before it rains. I left a cheese wedge and an apple on your table. Remember to repair the scaffolding and replace those frayed ropes."

"I will. Thanks for the victuals." Will waited for Sebastian to depart before turning toward Amelia. "Well, little theater spy, I didn't reveal your presence. Are you grateful?"

Amelia sighed, thankful for Will's gallantry although unsure about his motives. "I am. You're most kind. Why is he leaving you food?"

"I stay here when I'm in London. I hail from Stratford, and it's too far to travel back and forth each day. In exchange for a spot to sleep, eat, and write, I sweep floors, repair sets, and fix anything above or behind the stage."

Amelia glanced at his callused hands and noticed ink stains on his thumb and index finger.

"Well, if you'll let me pass, I'll be on my way. I'm late already."

Will stepped aside, letting her go.

"What's your name?"

"Amelia."

"Amelia, do come back. I'll keep your secret. And I like your laugh!" he said with an endearing smile, gladdening her heart.

Amelia hurried down the stairs and across the pit to a side gate. On the way she noticed a small room to the right of the stage. An oil lamp lit a scarred table laid with bread, cheese, an apple, and bottle of wine. Papers were stacked haphazardly on one corner near a quill and inkwell. This must be Will's room, probably a converted storage closet. She raced past it, through the exit, and into the windy afternoon to meet her Uncle John.

"What delayed you? I promised your cousins, Lucretia and Nicholas, that you'd arrive on time for your Sabbath dinner. Now, we're late," he complained as she climbed into his carriage."

"That young actor called Will came looking for whoever laughed when he uttered the wrong line. He stopped me while I tried sneaking out. I had to cajole him into keeping quiet." She noticed her uncle's concern. "Don't worry, he doesn't know how I got in."

"Will Shakespeare?"

"He didn't mention his surname."

The carriage weaved through narrow muddy streets. Workers trudged home from their jobs and merchants closed shops as shadows replaced the last vestiges of daylight.

Suddenly Amelia bolted upright screaming, "Wait! Stop!" She furiously ran her hands over the carriage seat and bent down to inspect the dark floor and feel around her feet.

"Uncle John! We must go back!"

"But why?"

"I can't find my satchel with my poetry, stories, plays, and... my personal diary. I must have left it in the balcony while crawling out."

"It's too late to return now. Besides, the theater will be closed. You'll get it another time."

Amelia saw no point in arguing further, but worried that if Will discovered her satchel he'd brazenly read her compositions and private thoughts. How would she overcome such humiliation?

Distressed, Amelia thrashed in bed all that night. She confronted her uncle upon seeing him in the morning.

"Uncle John, take me back to get my satchel. I suspect Will found it, and the curious fellow has probably read too much already."

She argued until she got her way, and that afternoon they entered the playhouse together while stagehands arranged the set and positioned props for the opening scene. Actors mingled in costumes as musicians tuned instruments before the stage.

John climbed onto the scaffold and called for Will.

"I'm backstage," a voice shouted back.

"Will, can I have a word?" John yelled.

Will appeared from stage left and spotted Amelia standing in the pit. "Ah, it's the theater spy. And you're dressed as a lady today. A vast improvement."

Amelia fingered the linen partlet covering her neck and shoulders and glanced down at the silvery skirt flowing beneath a snug gray bodice, accentuating her thin waist.

"What brings you back?" asked Will. "Oh, you're missing your satchel."

John said, "Yes, she wishes to recover it."

Will's lips quirked with amusement. "Come, it's in my room."

Amelia followed Will while John joined other musicians. Will lived in cramped quarters. Dust motes floated in the air and the space smelled of dirty clothes. Costumes, wigs, and hand props hung from iron hooks. A straw mattress covered with a wool blanket stretched along the back wall. On top rested a dog-eared script. A disorderly stack of papers, quills, and an inkwell littered a gouged table.

Will maneuvered around the table and lifted costume skirts. Behind one hung Amelia's satchel. She sighed with relief.

Will held out the grass-stained bag. "I found it on a chair after you disappeared down the balcony steps. I called out just as the gate slammed shut."

"Thank you. But—but did you read anything?" she stammered.

Will acted unfazed by her angst. "In searching for an address, I couldn't help but do so. I didn't open your diary, but I perused some of your stories and poetry...and enjoyed them."

Amelia glared, thinking how dare he, as Will continued. "You're an inventive writer, especially for someone so young. I liked best the story told from the servants' perspective— the one where they mockingly imitate the nobility they serve. Where did you get such insights?"

Stunned by his audacity, Amelia felt her cheeks burn. She composed herself. "You need only listen when they don't think others can hear..." Amelia cringed. "But did you read my personal quartos?" She knew they sounded like the ramblings of a lonely girl.

"I felt like a thief, but I did. They were obviously meant only for you."

Amelia wanted to sink through the floor. Will probably had a grand time laughing. "How much did you read?"

"More than necessary." He finally seemed to realize how much pain his indiscretion had caused. "I'm sorry if I took too many liberties. May I atone for it?"

"How? By allowing me to invade your privacy?"

Will laughed. "I thought you might like a backstage tour to see how everything works. You told me in the gallery that you wanted to learn how plays were produced. Would you like to see what audiences don't?"

Will's invitation struck the perfect chord. After all, he claimed he liked what she had written, and his praise felt wonderful. "I would. I'd like to see it all."

4

LONDON, SEPTEMBER 1587

Amelia broke into a cold sweat, hoping her Jewish heritage would not beset her. She'd heard rumors that Rodrigo Lopez, the Queen's physician, was a Jew posing as a Christian. Her Jewish cousins feared a witch-hunt for other hidden Jews if he were exposed. Amelia trembled at the thought. Was it only a matter of time? Imprisonment, torture, banishment, and accusations of treason all seemed possible. Horrifying stories about the Spanish and Portuguese inquisitions and Edward I's Edict of Expulsion were never far from her mind.

Amelia dreaded the risks of celebrating Jewish holidays. She plucked the folds of her skirt while waiting to be picked up by her Uncle John for Rosh Hashanah, the start of the Jewish New Year. Although Protestant, he knew her faith. He had played at the court with Amelia's father and had introduced Baptista to his sister, Margaret. The two had lived together and borne children but their religious differences kept them from marrying.

John delivered Amelia to the home of her father's niece—Amelia's cousin Lucretia. Twelve years older than Amelia, Lucretia had married Nicholas Lanier, a flautist, coronet player, and court musician recruited from the ensemble of the late Henry II of France.

Nicholas welcomed Amelia warmly and John departed. "*L'Shana Tova*—I wish you a good year," she whispered. Amelia sniffed the aroma of freshly baked challah, a sweet egg bread. A white embroidered cloth graced with fresh flowers in two slender vases adorned the dining table.

Ten-year-old Ellen ran to her older cousin, her pink floral dress streaming behind. She wrapped her arms around Amelia's neck. Ellen's older brother, Innocent, dressed neatly in gray wool breeches and white shirt, shook Amelia's hand like a gentleman. By contrast, fifteen-year-old Alphonso's white shirt hung loose from his brown trousers with a hole in one knee. He glared with an insolent expression and a shake of his wavy red hair.

Lucretia gathered everyone in a room at the rear of the house. She pulled heavy gray curtains closed on the lone window. "Nicholas, draw the drapes in the other rooms. See if anyone is lurking about."

After Nicholas left to check, Lucretia explained, "We have curious neighbors who I trust as much as I would a leaky boat on the North Sea."

Nicholas returned, reporting that he saw nothing unusual. Still, Amelia remained wary, listening for suspicious sounds.

Lucretia unrolled two towels until twin brass candlesticks sparkled in the low light. She inserted a white candle into each and lit them, waving her hands before her eyes and quietly singing the traditional blessing in Hebrew: *"Barukh atah Adonai Eloheinu Melekh ha'olam, asher kid'shanu b'mitzvotav v'tzivanu l'hadlik ner shel yom tov. Amein."* Blessed are You, Adonai, our God, King of the universe, Who has sanctified us with His commandments and commanded us to light the holiday candles.

With yellow candlelight bathing the room, Nicholas raised a silver Kiddush cup and whispered the blessing for wine. Then he lifted a plate holding a challah covered with a linen cloth. He placed it on the table as they softly recited the blessing. Upon finishing, Nicholas broke off a large piece and passed it around. Everyone tore a small portion to eat.

Lucretia gathered her children around, wrapping them in her arms and kissing each on the forehead. They turned toward their father, who placed his palms on their heads and whispered special blessings.

Tranquility permeated the home until Alphonso spoke in a voice shrill enough to alarm the entire neighborhood. "We're always tucked away like criminals to say Jewish prayers. Why should anyone be bothered?"

Everyone stiffened, twisting their necks toward the doors and windows, listening.

During the tension-filled quiet, a knot formed in Amelia's stomach as she considered all she put at stake by practicing her Judaic faith. While its rituals and philosophy had become more meaningful, she questioned the purpose of certain practices—especially those elevating men to a higher status than women. Her vision blurred as she focused on the fluctuating candle flames. *All my aspirations,* she thought, *will be crushed if I'm exposed. Lady Susan might* shunt me out the door. Lord Hunsdon would halt his assistance. And Will won't jeopardize his ambitions through association with a Jewess.

࿎

Still anxious two days later, a loud knock startled Amelia. Frightened, she approached the Willoughby House door with trepidation. She opened it a crack, relieved to see Lord Hunsdon dressed in a black doublet with a matching cape.

"I have an urgent question which requires an immediate response," he declared stone-faced.

Amelia's fears leapt like flames in a bonfire. "Wha... what's the matter?" Her mouth had gone dry, her heart raced. She gripped the door with all her might.

"Your lip is trembling. Are you all right?"

"You scared me. Is something wrong?" she managed to ask.

"Not at all." Lord Hunsdon grinned and Amelia saw the little boy in his etched face. "Would you like to see *Tamburlaine the Great,* a drama by the playwright Christopher Marlowe? It starts in two hours at the Curtain Theatre."

Amelia felt the tension drain from her body. She invited him inside. "I'd be delighted. It enthralled Lady Susan."

"Can you be ready within the hour?"

Amelia impulsively embraced him. "I'll rush. Wait in the drawing room."

In return, Henry wrapped his arms snugly around her, holding Amelia longer than she expected. The warmth of his solid chest pressed through her bodice. Her hug had been spontaneous, not meant to entice, but she liked the effect. She raised her hands to his shoulders, touching them lightly, and eased herself free.

"Enid! Enid, I need your help," she called.

Enid swept dangles of her limp dirty-blond hair away from her face as Amelia bounded up the curved stairway and into her bedchamber. From the armoire Enid selected an eggshell and crimson satin dress with brass ornamentation and a white ruffled collar. Amelia rubbed on the scent Lady Susan had imported from Florence and given her last Christmas, *Acqua di Melissa*. She loved the spicy-woodsy fragrance, made from oils extracted from sage, cloves, and cinnamon. She also liked that it attracted the notice of men.

"I'll wear this hat," said Amelia, lifting a black one with a long colorful feather from the armoire's top shelf.

"May I see the plume?" asked Enid as she rubbed sagging eyelid. Her troubled expression cleared as she handed it back. "It's fine. You can wear it."

"What were you inspecting?" asked Amelia, puzzled.

"That it wasn't a peacock plume."

"But why?"

"They're bad luck. There's an evil eye on them. Check the next time you see one."

Amelia held back a laugh. "Enid, that's another of your superstitions. But thanks for tending to my safety." Amelia smiled as she fitted the hat over her pinned-up hair.

"Ah, you look splendid," complimented Henry when she stepped into the drawing room.

Amelia curtsied fancifully, pulling her gown outward as she bowed. Lord Hunsdon laughed and nodded his approval.

Henry led her to his waiting carriage like a young gallant, even though he had long been married. He had twelve children with his wife, Ann Morgan. Amelia hadn't met Ann and Henry rarely mentioned her. Lady Susan once explained the two sides of Henry—the brusque military leader and court councilor on one and the solicitous gentleman on the other. Amelia imagined the combination kept his wife ensconced at their country estate.

Tonight Henry seemed eager to attend the theater with her. As the carriage rolled though London's streets, he slid closer until their shoulders brushed. Energy surged through her. She felt fully alert. He stretched his arm around her neck. He caressed her far cheek and nudged her to face toward him. "Amelia, you're an elegant young lady. I'm pleased to have you by my side." He touched the back of her hand and squeezed her wrist.

She leaned away to better see his narrow face, long gray-brown mustache, and thin lips. His glistening gray eyes stared back with admiration. When he helped her from the carriage, he held her hand and arm seconds longer than necessary. Again sparks passed between them and she wondered if he wanted tonight to be a juncture in their relationship.

Once seated inside, Amelia quickly became absorbed in *Tamburlaine the Great*. She leaned forward to study every detail of the sets and costumes, from the sumptuous palace and regal attire of a Persian emperor to the crude dwelling of the nomadic Tamburlaine—a Scythian shepherd and warrior, clad in a dull coat and the rough clothing of the Mongolian steppes. The play's violent battle scenes stirred her, but the intricacy of the plot and Marlowe's wordplay impressed her most. The style and structure of the verse was fresh and unique. He had elevated the art of prose and poetry, not relying on rhymes. The vivid and, at moments, shocking imagery created dramatic depth and tension unlike any play Amelia had seen. Between acts, she drifted to a quiet area with Lord Hunsdon and compared her writing to the virtuosity Marlowe displayed—and saw more of her shortcomings.

By play's end Amelia had set her mind on meeting this Christopher Marlowe. She liked Will, but he'd left London and she didn't know when he'd return. And he hadn't yet established himself as a playwright. Marlowe was celebrated everywhere and could connect her to the beating heart of London's theater community.

Amelia tugged Lord Hunsdon through the crowd to reach the playwright greeting his audience in the theatre's courtyard. Marlowe's baby face and wispy mustache fit her idea of a cherub grown into manhood, but with devilish eyes and untamed golden-brown hair. He looked every bit like a wild, unfettered young genius.

Henry wrapped his arm around Amelia's waist, pulling her close protectively as he introduced them both to Marlowe.

"Henry Carey, the Lord Chamberlain, I've heard much about you and your exploits. I'd say your family is worthy of a theatrical drama."

"Whatever do you mean?" replied Henry.

Marlowe waggled his finger at Henry mockingly. "You think I don't know about you? You're the son of Mary Boleyn, sister to the beheaded Anne. You come from tainted stock."

Amelia had never known anyone to address Henry with anything but respect. Marlowe's insolence repelled her, yet his audacity attracted her.

Henry drew himself up with full dignity. "Mr. Marlowe, you may be an excellent playwright, but you project more arrogance than I've seen in men twice as accomplished."

"Lord Hunsdon, you might be a Member of Parliament and knighted by the Queen, but dare I ask, *sir*, what of substance have you achieved in your *very* long career?"

Henry turned to Amelia. "I believe it's time to go."

"Departing with your young concubine?" taunted Marlowe, sweeping his hand in dismissal.

Marlowe's brazenness dumbfounded Amelia. She instinctively reached for her hamsa. He was rude and impertinent but highly perceptive.

"Mr. Marlowe, your crude comment cannot go unanswered. This young lady is not a concubine. Think what you may of me, but do not impugn her virtue."

Marlowe regarded them both with a skeptical eye and haughty silence.

"Let's take our leave," said Henry as he placed a hand on Amelia's shoulder and escorted her away.

Amelia looked back at Marlowe and his self-satisfied expression. He exuded sexual energy, transmitted though supple gestures, intense eyes, and full lower lip. An unbidden question sprang to her mind: What would it be like to kiss him? She imagined him rife with passion, quite unlike the sedate courtesy of Henry Carey.

Upon approaching the street, Amelia noticed a young aristocrat gaping at her on the arm of the elderly Lord Hunsdon. His look of astonishment stung and she turned to hide her embarrassment. Her distress grew upon considering Marlowe's similar reaction.

Unaware of Amelia's dismay, Henry asked if she would dine with him later that week. "There are matters I wish to discuss of a personal nature."

Another panicky jolt ripped through Amelia. She stayed outwardly calm, afraid of betraying herself. "Of course, Henry. Nothing too serious, I trust."

"You'll have to judge. Shall we sup at my London manor? My cook is superb."

Amelia fretted over what Henry wished to discuss. Her faith? She flinched at the thought. Surely, it wasn't her writing. Perhaps it concerned all his affectionate touches.

5

LONDON, MARCH 1588

After six months, Amelia still wondered about Lord Hunsdon's intentions. She thought he'd have revealed them long before now and her intuition, usually reliable, had not been true. He continued offering advice on her script and ideas sprang forth from her imagination with greater clarity. His linguistic mastery impressed her. While his suggestive gestures had become more loving, their lips never touched. An invisible line existed that neither he nor she would cross, but it had become thinner and her curiosity stronger. At the same time, Amelia felt the urge to garner the attention of younger men.

As she stepped down from Lady Susan's carriage in front of Hunsdon House, Amelia wondered if she should have refused Henry's invitation, but wished not to offend him or risk losing his help.

Hunsdon House, on King's Place in Hackney, a village three miles north of London, was modest compared to Willoughby House. After being ushered inside, Henry offered Amelia wine and asked the chef to complete preparations for the stewed pheasant. Henry escorted her to the library with its dark paneling and walnut bookcases. Amelia browsed the titles, impressed by Henry's collection, then settled on one of two cushioned chairs. Henry sat in the other.

"Amelia, we've been fond companions for months. Now I must ask a serious question."

His statement set her on edge, unsure what would follow.

He continued, "Have you considered your life beyond the shelter provided by Lady Susan, or when funds supporting you are consumed and you're truly on your own?"

Amelia did not expect questions about her finances. The topic touched a nerve. Why would he raise such a private matter? It was not something she'd ordinarily discuss, even with Henry who was among the wealthiest men in England. "I suspect the privileged lifestyle I now enjoy will end."

"Without a husband, how will you prosper?"

She winced. He had struck another vulnerable point. She worried about having passed the most desirable marrying age. Few nobles wanted a wife unable to bring property or title to a union. She also suffered from her impetuous tongue, being inclined to speak her mind even when advised to remain demure. Henry appeared undeterred by her and she chose to be forthright. "It's ridiculous that an unmarried woman cannot support herself like a man."

"It's difficult unless you're in a profession of the flesh."

"I intend to support myself as a playwright and poet, even though I'll be swimming against strong currents." As Amelia's declaration escaped her lips, she too doubted its feasibility, but the reminder served to strengthen her resolve.

Henry seemed dubious as well. "Indeed, you're correct about the resistance. May I be frank?"

"Please. It's a problem I'll soon face."

Henry stretched toward her and touched her hand. "Amelia, I favor you. You're acutely intelligent and willful. That's a daunting prospect for most male suitors. They want wives they can control."

"I was raised to assert my intellect. To use Saint Paul's phrase, I don't 'suffer fools gladly.'"

Henry laughed. "No, you don't. However, have you noticed how most men react to you?"

From the way he stared at her, she assumed he had moved on from talking about ambitions and acuity. "At times, but what do you mean?"

"They're attracted to you physically." He gazed into her eyes. "Then they hear your sallies and realize that you won't submit to their governance. So they turn their attentions to another lady."

Amelia nodded. She'd seen exactly those reactions as had Lady Susan. "Why should I capitulate to their will? I don't expect them to yield to mine if they disagree. What's wrong with deciding matters together, using both brains?"

Henry chuckled, leaning back. "Nothing."

Amelia stood, placing her hands on her hips, unsure whether Lord Hunsdon was laughing at her or amused by her insistence on men who would treat her as an equal. "I don't want to be dominated or to dominate. I want men to give my work and judgments comparable weight."

"Indeed. The man you marry will be fortunate, if he deems you a true partner."

Amelia's eyes locked on Henry's. "Why are we discussing this?"

Henry cleared his throat then raised his goblet. "Have another sip of wine. I'll expound over dinner."

As Henry rose, Amelia felt compelled to explain. "Henry, growing up in Willoughby House, I found myself in uncommon circumstances. The young men I met on social occasions were from aristocratic families and knew I was not. They and their parents sought girls with noble bloodlines—not someone with my lineage. And my self-governing nature and verbal jousting did not endear me to them. So when other girls were being courted and wed, I had nary a suitor. They desired a different sort of lady and few of them appealed to me."

Henry touched Amelia's arm and led her into the dining room. A fire shimmered in a white marble hearth. Carved lion claw feet supported the oval cherry-wood table. Two slender white candles glowed in tall ivory candlesticks. Steam rose from bowls of creamy soup placed on the table set for two.

Henry pulled out a chair for her. "Amelia, I enjoy your wit and that you view life from a different angle. I trust you enjoy our conversations."

"Henry, I take pleasure in your company and the wisdom you impart. I don't always agree, but I admire how you respond thoughtfully to my parries. If only more people would."

He did not reply until he had come around to the table's other side and seated himself. For the first time he seemed nervous.

"After our encounter with Mister Marlowe, I hope you'll consider my overture in the well-intentioned spirit in which I'm making it." Henry coughed. "Amelia...would you like to spend substantially more time together?"

"What are you suggesting?" Her fingers tightened around her spoon.

"I'm interested in your welfare, and yet your appeal to those seeking a young wife has diminished, especially as you've aged—not withstanding your exotic looks, which still intoxicate. Those parties who remain available for marriage are likely of poor quality and will be daunted by your intellect and strength—rendering you poor mates, as you've acknowledged. Your options have narrowed."

Amelia fidgeted, unsure how to respond. Nobody had declared this stark reality to her before, nor had she forced herself to confront it so blatantly. She drew into herself. Her mind grew numb. She forced herself to listen, knowing Henry would soon get to his point.

"Amelia, I'm sixty-two. You're nineteen. I have little reason to believe you'd be attracted to me other than intellectually. I, though, find you mesmerizing."

Conflicting voices erupted inside her. She prized Henry's friendship, but had he intimated that an affair with him, an older married man, might be among her few remaining choices? She wanted to cry, "But you're wrong!" She didn't want to compromise her future.

She masked her emotional turmoil with an impassive face. "Henry, you flatter me, but...but what about your wife?"

"She resides at our manor in Suffolk," he replied, dismissing the matter, "I don't see her for long stretches, especially when I'm in London or on military assignments."

"You're asking me to be your mistress?" Amelia felt her palms sweat. She could mount arguments in his favor. He could elevate her relationships and provide access to aristocratic circles in which she longed to belong. But should she degrade herself? What will people think, especially those she wished to impress?

"Indeed, I am."

Amelia stared at him, stunned, uncertain what to say. She'd never entertained such a possibility. She studied the folds in his neck, his gray and white streaked hair and beard, the deep lines in his forehead, and his narrow curved nose. Could she be carnal with this man? Would she find his naked body pleasurable or abhorrent?

Henry seemed to accept Amelia's uneasiness. "Before replying, may I elucidate?"

She nodded.

"Don't take my proposal as demeaning. To the contrary, it reflects my esteem for you."

Those were fine words, but Amelia wondered how aggressively he'd pursue his desire for sexual intimacy. She had toyed with him, but...

Henry continued, "I have no intention to regulate you. You'll have utmost freedom. You can go to the theater, meet friends, pursue your writing, and do whatever you desire without my permission. I'll help with your work as you wish. With such liberty, you'll have happiness and opportunity."

"What about your needs?" Amelia asked in a subdued voice.

"I ask for reciprocal kindness, affection, companionship, and that we spend nights together when I'm in London. I hope that intimacy comes naturally. However, I pledge to never force myself upon you or pressure you. If you're displeased or if you fear me, I'll be unhappy as well."

Henry sounded reasonable, as always. He had a distinguished bearing. He squared his broad shoulders in a slate gray doublet with long sleeves. His high white collar opened to his neck in the latest French style. He had shown her only kindness. He spoke with her not as a superior with a life-time of experience, or as a noble looking down on a lesser, but as a friend. She liked that, but could she share his bed?

"There's more. I'll ensure you have sufficient money now and in the future."

Amelia's conflicting thoughts narrowed to extreme concentration on his proffer. She felt blood rushing to her brain and the urgent need to think clearly.

"I'll demonstrate my gratitude in an enduring manner by granting an annual pension. I'll establish an account for you at the Royal Exchange. You'll be able to draw on it as you wish and I'll replenish it as necessary, assuming you're not extravagant—which seems not to be your nature. I'll also bequeath to you, or provide funds prior to my death sufficient for living as gentry throughout your life—unless it's spent frivolously."

Was Henry's proposition worthy of her? Two voices competed inside Amelia's head. One spouted reasons against it—Henry was old, he could take advantage of her, she'd be selling her soul to pleasure a wealthy and powerful man, she'd be disgraced, and when he pushed her away or died, she'd be shunned by the very people she sought to ingratiate. The other voice spoke to Henry's integrity, good nature, and intention to care for and protect her. He could open doors. If he made her financially secure, she'd never want for anything and have freedom to pursue her ambitions.

Her hands shook. Rarely was she so uncertain. Perspiration soaked her sleeves. "I must weigh thus carefully," she responded.

"I'd expect no less."

6

LONDON, MARCH 1588

Tormented. Plagued with indecision. Questions with no clear answers fogged Amelia's brain: If I accept Henry's proposition, will I despise what I've done? She wondered if Henry loved her or if she loved him. It wasn't the romantic love she imagined for herself or that she desired. Is it the only way to secure my future, to maintain a well-bred lifestyle—especially when English society views me otherwise? What will the nobility think of me? She paced. She stared through the window but could not focus. She tugged on her hamsa and twirled her hair, pulling it until it stretched from her scalp—but the pain gave her no greater sense of control. She felt trapped in her personal quandary: Becoming Henry's mistress will harm my marriage prospects. Other men will shun me long after it's over. Does accepting it repudiate all that I stand for? She had never felt so conflicted.

Amelia explained her predicament to Lady Susan as they surveyed the bare garden beds in Willoughby House's courtyard. Winter winds had swirled untidy piles of brown leaves into the corners. A springtime chill hung in the air.

"Lord Hunsdon intimated he might make such a proposal," said Lady Susan, while uprooting a dead plant.

"What's your opinion of it? And what if I refuse him?"

Lady Susan seemed to have anticipated her questions. "You may stay here for a time, but the funds your father provided are nearly depleted. It's common for wealthy men to have kept women, and Lord Hunsdon will treat you well."

Amelia stopped listening and focused on Lady Susan's oval lips coated in rouge. She watched them move—open and shut like tiny pillows pressing together. She felt overwrought, having slept little the prior night. Suddenly her concentration snapped back.

"We'll both have choices to make," the older woman continued. "If you decline, much will depend on whether you can support yourself or marry a man of means. If not, I could provide for you with my own resources for a while. But the first adjustment will be Enid."

"Adjustment?" Amelia asked. "Enid?"

"I like the girl, but she's an unnecessary expense," Lady Susan explained, absently playing with a loose thread on her dress.

Amelia panicked at the thought. Then what would become of Enid? She'd be forced to return to her family, and she once told Amelia that her father and brothers had abused her as a child—accounting for her permanently drooping eyelid. Could she find other work? Amelia loved Enid like a sister.

"Henry is being generous, more than I imagined. But who would marry you after being despoiled by him? Accepting Henry's offer could impair your future."

Lady Susan had reinforced Amelia's fears. She trembled considering the implications. Amelia had been raised by noblewomen but was not of them. For ordinary young women, especially the unlettered, becoming a nobleman's mistress could create a comfortable life. But for her, what would happen once she loses her youthful luster? Would she have suitable options after Henry dies?

"No. No! For God's sake, this is wrong." Enid shook her head vigorously. "You'll regret it for the rest of your days."

Amelia had sought Enid's advice on small matters but never of this import. She valued her sensible outlook, having grown up in a poor household. Her rough-hewn perspective borne from the harsh realities of her early life often cut to the quick.

"I can't become destitute. I won't survive," Amelia said with a sense of hopelessness. She stared longingly through the drawing room window at the dormant garden. She thought, perhaps, she had seen it bloom for the last time.

"You're too smart for that. But becoming Lord Hunsdon's mistress…Amelia, men can be very cruel. I know."

"But I trust him. He's always been kind."

"Men change. How will he be when the first blush wears off?"

Amelia put her head in her hands and felt moisture from her eyes spread to her cheeks. She looked halfway up at Enid. "But what about you?"

Enid rested a hand on Amelia's stooped shoulder. "Someone will hire me. Lady Susan will provide a good reference. You will too."

Amelia sat silently, brooding. She rose, hugged Enid, stepped into the hallway, and swept tears from her face. She'd made her decision.

❧

Amelia led Henry into the Willoughby House library to afford them privacy for what she expected would be a tense meeting.

"Henry, dear, you've put me in a quandary and I've sought advice from two women. One helped me weigh advantages and disadvantages of your proposal, and there are many of each—both short and long term. Another urged I refuse your offer, warning how it would harm my future. Accepting it will change my life, possibly in ways unanticipated today."

"That was wise. This is not a decision to make hastily," said Henry.

"I'll need to protect my future interests, notwithstanding our trust and mutual esteem."

Amelia tried to contain her nervousness but suspected Henry excelled at reading emotions. Her knees shook beneath the table inside her black wool skirt. Her leather boots tapped the floor, and she glided her hamsa back and forth on its gold chain.

"Henry, your proposal is part personal and part business."

"It is, indeed."

"They're intertwined. One cannot go forward without the other being confirmed. I imagine you conduct your own business that way, leaving little to chance."

"I protect my interests however I can."

"That's my intention. My objective is to mold our relationship in a way that's satisfactory for us both while ensuring my security."

Henry nodded.

She had reached the point of no return and allowed herself to plow forward. "I'll accept your proposition if you agree to three provisions.

He stared back, expressionless.

First, you must fund the lifelong account for me at the Royal Exchange beforehand, with an amount agreed upon by us both. You see, our arrangement could adversely affect my marriage prospects."

"And the second?" asked Henry stoically.

Amelia still could not read his reaction. "Before I proceed, will you accept my first stipulation?"

"I must hear everything before agreeing to anything. In the past, I've mistakenly not done so and regretted it. Please continue."

Amelia saw the sense in that. "Second, I'd like you to compose a letter describing your promises regarding our personal relationship—about only mutually agreed intimacy and the liberty I'll have to pursue my own interests and friends."

"And the third provision?"

"This one you might find unusual, however it's crucial."

"And it is?"

"Enid, my maid, comes with me. She's been serving me since I was seven, from my first day here. She's also my friend. She's to be paid a salary sufficient to meet her needs. Otherwise, I'd fear for her fate. Therefore, the amount deposited in the exchange must be enough to pay her salary over the course of her life, in addition to what you've promised me."

Henry, still stone-faced, asked, "Is that everything?"

Amelia fidgeted nervously, still unable to gauge his reaction. "It is."

"Your first two requests are unsurprising. I expected you'd want assurances. The one about Enid is more than I anticipated. Is it essential?"

"It is."

"Why must I pay her wages? Wouldn't room, board, and a small allowance be sufficient?"

Amelia felt her chest constrict. *Am I pushing him too far? Perhaps, but I won't relent.* "That's not much better than being enslaved. Would you agree to such conditions?"

"I'm not her. But your point is clear enough."

Henry paused, apparently thinking. "Amelia, I applaud your insistence. You're interested in more than yourself. But you're terms are expensive."

"I'm protecting my future, especially with over forty years separating us."

Henry rubbed the back of his neck and looked up at the chandelier. Amelia maintained a blank expression, believing he was contriving a show of reluctance. After several seconds he lowered his gaze until their eyes met.

"I see no point in resisting. We'll both get what we want." He stood and laughed. "But I doubt I'd enjoy being on the other side of an unfriendly negotiation with you."

He walked toward her. She willed herself not to stiffen as he came around and gently massaged her shoulders. Amelia leaned her head back until it touched his chest. She felt his fingers graze her neck as he fanned them through her curly hair. She shivered with the tingling sensation. She would become fully a woman at last.

7

LONDON, APRIL 1588

Amelia wiped unbidden tears from her eyes. Wistful, she peered into a wooden chest containing an archive of her eighteen years. It once carried her possessions when she moved to Willoughby House as a little girl and still held items from her father she would keep forever: childhood rhymes she made up and he wrote down, his journal and music sheets, his favorite wool shirt, letters received from his brother and cousins in Venice, a tattered Hebrew prayer book, and the note he wrote to for her prior to dying. They were all that remained, besides her memories, of her first seven years. She sniffed his shirt to see if it stilled carried his scent. It no longer did, but knowing he had worn it was enough.

That first chapter in her life was long over. Amelia remembered crying for days during the abrupt transition to the second, living with Lady Susan and her mother, Katherine. They were kind but stern. They cared for her but had little tolerance for self-pity. She closed her eyes as memories overtook her. She grew more nostalgic while sifting through her old drawings, poetry, stories, and mementoes collected during the past eleven years.

She caressed her father's letter; her most valuable possession stained from her childhood tears. Amelia lingered over parts she'd memorized long ago. She touched her hamsa as she read his narrative about it:

> *The hand-shaped filigree amulet tied to my music sheets was a gift from my parents, your grandparents, who dwelled in Venice. My father, Jeronimo, crafted and presented it to me in 1537, 33 years ago, upon my leaving Venice for England. He said a blessing, and then my mother, with tears rolling down her cheeks, fastened the gold chain around my neck. It's called a "hamsa," which comes from the Hebrew word "hamesh," meaning five. Some believe it stands for the Torah's five books of Moses; others call it the "Hand of Miriam," Moses' sister. I've worn it ever since, and it's thought to provide luck and protection for travelers. The ruby fashioned in the center of the gold palm represents the eye of God. This hamsa, which has been special to me, is now yours. May it keep you safe as you journey through life.*

Amelia's eyes moistened as she lay back on her bed, recalling pieces of her family history explained to her as an adolescent by her Jewish cousins. Her ancestors had lived in northern Africa on the Mediterranean Sea. Eventually they immigrated to the Murcia region of Spain, and lived for centuries in the town of Lorqui. When life became dangerous for Spanish Jews during the Inquisition, they moved again, first to Naples and then northward to Bassano del Grappa, a small town near Venice—and they adopted the town's name as their own—all well over one hundred years ago.

During a recent Jewish holiday, her older cousins explained that her father, Baptista, had been given a Christian name to ward off suspicion. He and his brothers had been recruited from Venice by one of King Henry VIII's emissaries. For decades her father had served as a court musician. Amelia recalled how he spoke to her in broken English but mostly in Vèneto, the language of the Venetian Republic, Italian, and Ladino—the private language of formerly Spanish Jews or *Sephardim*.

Lady Susan had often repeated the story of how her mother, the duchess Lady Katherine, met him. They became acquainted at the court when she turned twenty-six, after her first husband died. She liked Baptista's musical zeal and joviality, and they soon discovered shared literary interests. When a brash young lord sought to attack Lady Katherine in the dim courtyard outside Whitehall Palace's Great Hall, Baptista noticed the fear in her face and sauntered over as if nothing was amiss. He said, with jocularity, "Your Grace, I hate interrupting your amusement, but King Henry wants you to select the next few melodies for us. Would you kindly accompany me?" She remained grateful for his intervention and years later, as he lay dying, Baptista beseeched her to take in his daughter. Amelia's Christian mother was illiterate and incapable of educating her as Baptista wished. Katherine agreed, vowing that she and her daughter would see Amelia's promise fulfilled.

Amelia revered the story.

Her reflections dropped away as she gazed around her familiar bedchamber. She would be enjoying its comfort no longer, yet she felt ready to plunge into the next phase of her life—living with Henry and soon sharing his bed. She knew her father would disapprove but wondered if he'd have understood. She spoke aloud to him as if he were there. "Oh Papa, no man could replace you in my heart, no matter what he may bestow in affection or jewels. And don't worry, I'll never reveal our faith. Henry is the soul of reasonableness, but I won't take chances."

Then she thought about the risk she was taking. Once Henry despoiled her, she'd be utterly at his mercy.

Sunlight dappled Hunsdon House as it emerged on the horizon ensconced behind tall elms abundant with emerging spring leaves. Amelia waited for it to grow in stature as the carriage approached but her new home seemed smaller than when she only visited. Situated well beyond Cripplegate in London's northern wall, the three-story redbrick structure boasted a long portico along the garden side. Its public rooms were well appointed in walnut and cherry-wood furnishings. In the drawing room, cushioned couches and chairs with saber-back legs faced a large black marble fireplace. Upstairs, a four-poster bed dominated Henry's sleep chamber. Human figures had been carved into the oak headboard and medallions surrounded the canopy frame. Yet Henry gave her a separate chamber to start, permitting her time to become accustomed to the ways of the house.

Amelia perched on the side of her bed, confronting her new reality. She looked around the sunlit room, at her trunk on the floor, and Henry's large frame in the doorway. Neither seemed to know what to say.

Henry broke the awkward silence. "Content with your decision?"

Amelia unfolded her arms. His question and evident sensitivity comforted her. "I am now." She sprang to her feet with a lighthearted step convinced she could trust him. She kissed his bearded cheek. He leaned back, gazed into her eyes, and tucked a few stray hairs behind her ear.

That tender gesture told her all she needed to know.

Every week Henry escorted Amelia to the theater, palace social events, and concerts. Always courteous, he introduced her to nobility with pride, often commenting on her insightful remarks. She sought acceptance by the aristocracy, but worried they looked down on her. Being seen throughout London on Henry's arm did not alter that.

In close quarters Amelia saw that Henry was fit for a man of sixty-two. Still, weeks passed before they became physically intimate. He waited until she chose to give herself to him. Her readiness grew with each passing day until she truly wanted to please him.

On the night she entered his bedchamber dressed in a sheer camise, she stopped in the doorway to arouse him. She padded forward and leaned over him as he lay against the pillows. She placed a finger on his lips, smiled bewitchingly, and kissed him tenderly—anticipating the joy but also the pain women had warned her about. "Go slow, savor the moment," they advised, "don't let him be too rough. Even though it's your first time, guide the experience."

At first Henry was gentle and sensuous, but soon became overeager—as if he could not restrain himself. Amelia struggled to slow him down, but he pushed ahead, giving her little time to revel in the newfound sexual pleasures.

Then he mounted her and after a few thrusts it ended. She felt him shrinking with her own desires unfulfilled—and her curiosity short-lived.

Amelia lay beside Henry, feeling both aroused and disappointed. She curled her body, and when he drifted to sleep she sat in bed hugging her bended knees. *I've been deflowered and taken a path of no return.* She recalled the practical nature of their arrangement. If sexual relations with him became no more pleasing, she would accept it.

In bed, Amelia worked on learning what pleased him, but to her chagrin, he remained brisk about his business. Over time, she minded less, feeling she truly expressed her love and reverence for him when they were physically joined.

In July, Henry called Amelia to his study. His abrupt tone startled her. "I must go to war," he announced. "The Spanish Armada is sailing north toward England and we must repel it."

Amelia admired Henry's valor, but the news filled her with dread. "What does this mean?"

"The Queen has appointed me Principal Captain and Governor of the Army. I'll command thirty-six thousand men at Tilbury Fort on England's southern coast. We're to resist invasion and protect our Queen and country at all costs. I'll be away for an indeterminate period."

Henry's curt military manner unsettled Amelia. Whether it was for his sake or to protect her somehow, she would not permit his manly demeanor or her fears to come between them. She wanted only for this man she'd grown to love to return safely. She knew the Spanish empire's forces exceeded England's military might. At Henry's age, would he have the necessary stamina? Amelia realized how much she'd come to depend on him.

"How many Spanish warships are sailing for England?" she asked, her voice quavering as she considered the peril.

"Our intelligence reports describe over one hundred thirty vessels carrying more than twenty thousand soldiers and eight thousand sailors. They're coming from the Portuguese coast and we must defeat them at sea, and on land if necessary."

Alarmed, she asked, "When must you depart?"

"Tomorrow at first light. Rest assured, you'll be secure in London."

That night, Amelia curled into Henry, imparting her deep affection and love. She rubbed his shoulders and nuzzled the back of his neck as they lay in bed, but she knew his mind roamed elsewhere. He eventually responded but his lovemaking lacked its normal fervor. Amelia hoped it would not be the last time but feared it might. She wished him to remember her touch, scent, and how he felt being inside her. When he was spent, she spooned into his naked body, pressed her small breasts against his back, kissed his neck tenderly, and drifted to sleep.

Amelia awoke to Henry's kiss as he prepared to depart. As he donned his long red army coat with white and gold trim, his military bearing and hardened expression came to the fore. He strode down the stairs with pounding footfalls. She then heard the front door clap shut. His horse neighed and the patter of hoofs faded into the distance.

Amelia sat upright in the high four-poster bed with pillows propped behind her. As dawn light beamed through the opening between closed curtains, she realized that for the first time she was accountable only to herself. No one would ask where she was going or what she did each day. With the pension Henry had established, she had forty pounds sterling to spend each year—a veritable fortune to her.

Her thoughts turned to how she might occupy her time in Henry's absence. She needed to devote more time to her script. She'd been writing only in fits and starts in recent months, absorbed in the swirl of London's social life and Henry's easy company. As she considered where she had left off, a new idea sprang to mind.

Amelia wrapped herself in a robe and went downstairs. She walked past the kitchen, where Enid sat eating a bowl of porridge and honey. Though seduced by the aroma of freshly baked bread, she made her way to Henry's study.

Amelia entered the dark-paneled room, dominated by a carved oak desk. A portrait of Henry as a young military officer, fresh-faced with an earnest expression, hung above a black marble mantel. From the ledge Amelia pulled two tickets to Christopher Marlowe's latest play, *Tamburlaine the Great, Part 2*. Henry had acquired them the prior week.

Amelia slid the tickets between her fingers, considering whether to invite Lady Susan or Enid to join her. Images of cavalier, dashing Christopher Marlowe danced through her mind. She wished to gain his cooperation, and for that she'd need to be bold. Lady Susan's presence would restrain her and the discomfort might be too great for Enid. If I'm to present myself as a fellow playwright, she thought, I should be independent of society's usual fetters. I'll go alone.

She proceeded with her plans, undeterred that other theatergoers would find it unusual for a woman to arrive unaccompanied. Amelia swayed in her lush green and silver silk gown edged in white lace. She took her seat in the Curtain Theatre next to an empty one reserved for Henry in the balcony's first row.

Amelia writhed in horror as Tamburlaine viciously conquered foreign kingdoms, killed his oldest son upon finding him cowering in his tent after refusing to fight, defeated another seeking revenge, and hung enemies from city walls. Amelia continued shaking as the actors took their final bows. Still, she comforted herself; it's only a play. No one will be hanging from the walls as she strides to the courtyard to meet Marlowe.

Marlowe projected his typical arrogance mixed with a mercurial, dark manner. But she found herself drawn to him. If she could penetrate his shield of conceit and persuade him to meet her, she might benefit from his undeniable talent.

Amelia assumed she'd have fewer than thirty seconds of Marlowe's time as crowds formed around him. She'd prepared her overture, but her hands fluttered and her heart thumped. *Do I have sufficient courage to do this?*

Projecting an alluring pose, Amelia said, "Mr. Marlowe, we met briefly when Lord Hunsdon accompanied me to *Tamburlaine the Great, Part 1.*

Marlowe twisted his wispy moustache in apparent recognition. "Indeed, I accused you of being his concubine. Perhaps you weren't, but I saw the intent in his eyes."

"I'm not here to discuss Lord Hunsdon. He's at war, defending our nation. I'm here to introduce myself as a playwright. If I remember correctly, you wrote, 'Above our life we love a steadfast friend.' We could be that for each other.'"

Marlowe drew back, acting astonished by the proposition. "My, you're a bold young lady."

Amelia considered his theatrical reaction. Perhaps he expected women to pursue him, so he feigned disinterest—to see how vigorously they'd persist. "You're not the first to make that observation. I believe we could help each other."

"I doubt you can help me."

Amelia playfully wagged a finger at him. "You're quick to assume. You know nothing about me."

Marlowe sniffed at her presumption. "I know your Lord Hunsdon's consort. Now, while he's away, you're approaching me. I don't require such companionship or devotion."

"Can't you conceive that I might be my own person?"

Marlowe rolled his eyes to the overcast sky, apparently intrigued. "Even so, how could you help me?"

"That's for us to discuss. But not here."

"Only because you've piqued my curiosity. Meet me at The Horn on Tuesday at eleven o'clock."

Amelia caught Marlowe's challenge. *He expects me to object to meeting in a boisterous pub, but I've already done so with Will.* "The Horn on Tuesday," she repeated. "I'll be there."

Amelia retreated through the crowd. *I asserted my nerve and succeeded.* She had no doubt he could help her. Yet she could not deny another reason for her excitement. Marlowe exuded mystery and brilliance, with piercing eyes and long wild locks. She wondered what he'd be like if she penetrated his smug demeanor. That prospect stirred something visceral inside her.

❧

Amelia arrived early at The Horn and settled by the window. She watched working men slog by, some glancing at her sitting alone. Marlowe soon entered the dimly lit tavern, surprising her since she thought he might leave her waiting.

"I wasn't sure you'd come," said Marlowe.

"I had my doubts about you too."

"Are you normally as forward as you were at The Curtain?" he asked, sitting down.

"When necessary. I've been taught well."

Marlowe leaned back folding his hands behind his neck and pointing his elbows outward like wings. "Amelia Bassano, I've inquired about you."

"What did you learn?"

"You have influential friends including the Countess of Kent, Susan Bertie and Lord Hunsdon. You're his mistress."

She kept her tone light. "Call it what you will. He's a fine man. We're good companions. I won't divulge more."

Marlowe evidently took that as an admission. "So I was correct when I called you his concubine—only you're unmarried."

"You owe us both an apology for your crude remarks. Our relationship then was nothing of the sort."

"I apologize to no one," he said, not backing down. "You know the truth about yourself."

Amelia wished to veer away from this fruitless line of conversation. She couldn't permit Marlow to exert his verbal virtuosity to dominate her. "What's the truth about you?"

Marlowe's intense stare burned through her. "I'm the son of a shoe cobbler from Canterbury. I used my wits to get a scholarship to Corpus Christi College in Cambridge. I developed a few allies and used my skills and acuity from there."

"You're a brilliant playwright. I'll grant you that."

Marlowe acted as if he deserved the praise. "No one is better."

"That's a cocky boast."

"If it weren't true. Can you name someone better?"

Amelia stared back, stunned by his arrogance. "I haven't compared your work to Sophocles and Euripides, but perhaps I should."

"I'm impressed. You've actually read them?"

"I have, in the original Greek."

"Then you know how relationships power ambition. I make them and use them to get what I want."

Is he warning me? He's dangerous, manipulative, and intimidating—and delights in power. Her heart beat faster as she confronted him again. "Is that why you provoke people, as you did with Lord Huns—"

Marlowe waved his hand, cutting her off. "Enough of Hunsdon. Let's talk about you. I hear you're a writer, poet, and musician."

Startled by Marlowe's sudden change of topic, Amelia paused to regain her composure, pleased he had raised the topic she wanted most to discuss. "I intend to be an accomplished woman, much like you strive to be an accomplished man."

"That's very difficult for women. Are you willing to push that heavy boulder up a long steep hill?"

"Unlike Sisyphus in Greek mythology, I won't allow it to roll back down on me."

He nodded as if impressed she knew the reference, but his comment, like Henry's and Will's rankled. Each man at first discouraged her pursuit or surmised its futility. She wondered if every woman unaccepting of her preordained plight encountered similar reactions. Perhaps her quest need not be so lonely. She made a mental note to consider that thought further.

"You enjoy flaunting what you know," said Marlowe, apparently unaware that her mind had drifted. "What do you want from me?"

"I'm looking for a 'steadfast friend' with whom to discuss ideas, projects, and have invigorating conversations. And provide encouragement when needed. And possibly more."

She sensed he didn't know how to interpret that remark. "You think you can keep pace with me?"

"I've been wondering if you can match me," Amelia quipped.

Marlowe laughed. "Cocky, are you?"

"Not as much as you."

Amelia and Marlowe met weekly at The Horn. They discussed theater, writing, current events, politics, and challenged each other's thinking and beliefs. Amelia found the conversations intellectually exhilarating. She enjoyed counter posing Marlowe's pessimism with her more optimistic outlook.

"Christopher, you see everything in the bleakest light. Have you no faith in humanity?" Amelia challenged.

His disgust spewed forth. "Look at how people treat each other. The bad far outweighs the good. Even today, the English navy is clashing with the Spanish Armada. Men are killing each other for the Spanish king's greed and thirst for power."

"What about men sacrificing their lives to protect England? To protect us? Isn't that worthy? Doesn't that speak to people's goodness?"

He looked at her quizzically, affecting annoyance. "You're always quick with a rejoinder. Won't you accept my point just once?"

His rare compliment enlivened her. "When I agree. If you weren't so cynical, you might be happier."

"Happiness is ephemeral...an illusion. I'm a realist. That's essential to survival."

"But not to life's enjoyment," replied Amelia.

Marlowe shook his head, amused. "Try as you might, I'm unlikely to reassess my assumptions. But I admire the effort."

Amelia stretched her head over the table, grinning. "Is that another compliment from the esteemed Christopher Marlowe?"

He raised his wine chalice. With a glint in his eye, he gazed over its rim. "Perhaps."

The following week, the two met again over ale and wine in a tavern catering to the gentry. Marlowe showed Amelia sections of a poem about young lovers, called "Hero and Leander," on which he wanted a woman's perspective. For her part, she sought his advice on connecting storyline pieces. Upon leaving the establishment, they strolled past the gothic Guildhall and wound their way through London's streets to where Marlowe resided. All the while, Christopher explained how the handsome and charming Leandro overcame Hero's resistance to relinquishing her chastity and consummating their love.

Amelia wondered if by dwelling on this story, which seemed uncharacteristic for Marlowe, he was suggesting she respond like Hero. In so doing, she'd betray her loyalty to Henry. Although she saw through Marlowe's ruse, amorous feelings fermented inside her. So when he touched her back, tingles rippled down her spine. His hand pressed more warmly as they approached his rooming house and stepped indoors.

When they reached Marlowe's room, Amelia scanned the space in shock. He groomed and dressed meticulously, wearing the latest London styles, today with ruffled cuffs and a wide white collar. Yet dirt and debris and old spills coated the floor, discharging a gamy odor. Clothes were strewn and wrinkled garments piled haphazardly in corners. Tables shined with grime. Another Marlowe contradiction, she thought.

Wasting no time, Marlowe pulled Amelia's hand from her mouth and pressed his lips to hers. His passion seared through her. She yielded and responded in kind. Her modest breasts swelled against his chest and he led her to his bed. Thoughts of Henry raced through her with pangs of guilt. *I shouldn't be doing this. Henry's at war and I'm in another man's bed.* Marlowe drew her toward him, stopping all other thoughts. Where Henry was earnest, Christopher was sensual. Where lovemaking with Henry was mutual, Christopher sought control. Henry was forthright. Christopher was sultry and erotic. He made it thrilling and effervescent in a way the older man never had. Finally, when Amelia collapsed beside Christopher, in the calm following their exuberance, she closed her eyes. *I know not where this will lead, but I want more of it.*

Those doses were interrupted during days, and sometimes weeks, when Marlowe suddenly and mysteriously disappeared.

"I'm off for a time," he'd announce. When Amelia asked to where, he responded ambiguously. He'd say to research a play or visit friends or offer another vague reason. Occasionally, she'd show up at his room as previously arranged and he'd be gone. He never offered explanations and she never knew when he'd return.

Queen Elizabeth addressed soldiers at Tilbury Fort with Lord Hunsdon at her side: "We have defended our great nation. We repelled the Spanish Armada through a quirk of fate and the cunning of our great admirals. On July 25, our fleet confronted the Spanish Armada in the English Channel near the Isle of Wright. At first, the wind worked against us, giving the Spanish maneuvering superiority. But with God's grace, the wind shifted southerly, making the Armada vulnerable to an English attack."

The Queen walked back and forth on the platform, looking into the eyes of her soldiers—clearly proud and delighted by this story. "At midnight on July 28, we deceived them." She paused and smiled. "We drifted eight unmanned warships loaded with gunpowder, pitch, tar, and brimstone toward their anchored fleet. In the darkness, the Spanish might not have seen them or, if they had, were loading their cannons to attack them. Imagine their shock when our archers ignited those old ships. Fires erupted like hell at sea. You might have seen the orange glare from onshore—the flames set the night aglow—but not how the wind swept stream after stream of sparks into the Armada. Their sails caught fire. Their crews panicked. Many warships cut free their anchors and rushed to escape. Gale force winds forced them northward toward the west coasts of Scotland and Ireland but they found no safe harbor. The Armada's remnants limped back to Spain. They lost half their warships and five thousand men. We, though, lost fewer than one hundred sailors—may God bless their souls—and with the exception of the fireboats, no vessels. It was a great English victory!"

In early September, confident the Spanish were no longer a threat, Lord Hunsdon prepared to return to London and dispatched a messenger to inform Amelia.

Amelia prepared the manor for him, including his favorite supper of gosling, fennel, and sweetened carrots. But her throat seized with worry that he'd discover her affair with Marlowe, knowing it was a poorly disguised secret. She feared his reaction. He'd feel betrayed. Would he punish her for disloyalty? She considered disclosing it herself but struggled finding the words…words that might soften the impact. No matter, she couldn't do it on the day he returned or even the next. It would hurt him too much. It would be too soon and she lacked the courage. She couldn't fathom watching his face contort in anguish.

Upon arriving, Amelia embraced Henry with genuine affection, relieved he had come home safely. Wrapped in his arms, she realized the striking contrast between the young, volatile Marlowe and the mature, gentlemanly Lord Hunsdon. Marlowe exuded risk and peril. Henry emanated safety and security. She reflected on her foolhardy behavior: She'd endangered what she prized most by pursuing the ephemeral—Marlowe, a selfish man who would never be a genuine partner.

Amelia and Henry enjoyed a long, festive dinner and celebrated with fine wine. He inquired about her writing. She asked about life at the fort. That night they made love, this time with tenderness and passion. Now that she knew how heated sex could be, she found his heartfelt approach rewarding in its own way. But the dread of her secret kept her awake and she discovered her nightgown soaked with sweat the next morning.

During breakfast, Amelia steered the conversation toward a topic she hoped would take her mind away from her dilemma. She asked Henry if he knew the legend of Titus Andronicus, an ancient Roman army general. She didn't mention it, but she heard about him from Marlowe.

"That's an odd question," he remarked. "You've never shown much interest in military affairs."

"I've been studying the most popular plays. Many of them depict wars, spies, and military conflicts. This tale was mentioned to me and I thought it might make a compelling drama."

Henry obliged her with what he could remember. "Andronicus was a fabled Roman military leader, not a real one, who fought the Goths during the latter part of the Empire. In victory he captured and brought to Rome the Goths' queen and her two sons. I know few details but understand it's bloody and heinous story."

"Just the kind audiences love," said Amelia, smiling.

The two shared a smile. "I'm unsure what that says about people, but it's probably true."

"If I do the research and construct the plot, will you help with military details?"

"I will indeed," he said, still puzzled. "This topic, though, seems unlike you."

8

LONDON, MAY 1589

Will Shakespeare fingered the few coins in his pocket. With nothing more and desperate for work, he watched the rehearsal from the Curtain Theatre's gallery while waiting to meet its proprietor, Henry Lanman. The playhouse, on a parcel called Curtain Close in Shoreditch, sat two hundred yards from its rival, The Theater, run by James Burbage. Will rolled his eyes as a pompous young man strutted about the stage giving direction to actors, correcting pronunciations, and arguing over which words to emphasize. Will shook his head. *This fellow wants to control everything. He's fanatical.*

Lanman introduced himself to Will and they strode to his well-ordered office with scripts and ledgers stacked on a table behind the desk. An inkwell, quill, and candle lantern were arranged on a desk corner. The room smelled clean and Will saw nary a speck of dust.

"Who's that intense man dashing about the stage telling everyone what to do? I've never known such a director," said Will.

"He's not the director, he's the playwright. If he weren't so good, I wouldn't tolerate his insolence. He drives actors insane."

"Who is he? What's the play?"

"Christopher Marlowe. They're rehearsing his newest, *Dr. Faustus.*"

"So that's Marlowe," Will said. He'd heard rumors about the fellow's debauchery. Still, he merely added, "I heard his first two plays were immensely popular."

"They packed the house. He's king of this theater right now." Lanman looked askance toward the stage as Marlowe's bellowing echoed through the building. "Now then, how can I help you, Mr. Shakespeare?"

"I've returned to London and I'm seeking an acting position. I've also a written play and have two more in the works. I'm seeking a theater to stage them."

"I can help you with your first need but not the second," Lanman said briskly. "Our performance rotation is full. While we're closing a play next week, we'll be replacing it with *Dr. Faustus.* Plus, Marlowe has another script in the wings."

Will grimaced. "I won't earn enough from acting to support my family. I'll need income from my scripts too."

"I can't help you with that. Try James Burbage over at The Theatre or Sebastian Westcott at Paul's Theatre. I hate suggesting competitors, but I have nothing here."

Will reluctantly met with Burbage. Two years ago he'd left his acting job with The Theatre on a moment's notice when his son, Hamnet, became stricken. Will worried that he'd soured the relationship. However, Burbage, a hefty long-bearded man with a protruding belly, acted pleased to see him.

"How's that son of yours who fell ill?' asked Burbage as they shook hands inside his dingy cluttered office. Papers were piled in corners and on tables and chairs. Burbage lowered himself into his desk chair but Will stood, seeing nowhere else to sit.

"He's healthy now but he falls ill easily. I returned to London after the danger passed."

"I suppose you are looking for an acting job."

"I am. I'm also writing scripts and want a theater to stage them. Would you consider that?"

Burbage furrowed his wide brow in thought. "I knew you were scribbling before, but I didn't know how seriously. I'll look them over and let you know." Burbage rubbed his throat. "It's tough competing with Marlowe's plays at The Curtain."

"So I've heard," said Will, pulling a manuscript from his bag and handing it over. "My first script is about King Henry VI."

"I'll read it soon. In the meantime, I could use another actor. Auditions are tomorrow morning. Come by then."

Burbage tapped the top of his desk. He seemed struck by a notion. He brushed both hands through his coiled hair. "Remember the young lady you introduced to me when you were here last, the one with reddish-brown hair?"

"Amelia Bassano?"

"That's her. She's developed quite a reputation and people are talking."

Will didn't expect to hear that. "What's she done?"

"She's schemed her way into relationships with both Lord Hunsdon—the Lord Chamberlain—and Christopher Marlowe. She's overstepping her bounds everyplace she goes."

This didn't sound like the Amelia Will remembered. She never struck him as devious. He recalled the comedy they had discussed and her ideas for *Henry VI*. He felt a flicker of interest for they had enjoyed each other's company.

෪

The following week, Henry marched into Hunsdon House upon returning from meetings at Whitehall Palace. "Amelia, we must talk in my study."

Amelia's skin prickled. Henry's gruff tone alerted her to trouble.

After she settled into an armchair, Henry remained standing and declared in his blunt military manner, "I've heard rumors about your promiscuity. And that the object of your affection is the contemptible Christopher Marlowe."

Fear jolted Amelia's heart. Her body stiffened. Several times she had started to tell him, but could not find the courage. Now she regretted her timidity.

Her voice assumed an impenitent tone. "Promiscuous? That's an interesting word choice. If you mean that Marlowe and I have developed a friendship and spend time together, then yes, that term could be apt. If you mean I've indiscriminately bedded with him, then not."

Henry clenched his fists, trying mightily to control his fury. "He's been boasting about having sex with you. Is that true?"

Under his withering glare Amelia could not maintain the fiction they'd been merely friends. She wrung her hands and lowered her head. "Henry, I should have told you before someone else. I didn't have the heart, especially when you returned from the war bone weary."

"You've betrayed me," he thundered. "And what you do affects my standing at court."

To Amelia, it seemed the temperature in the study rose with each sentence. She pleaded for his compassion. "I didn't intend to hurt you or harm your reputation." Then she thought it best to appeal to reason. "Let's remember our understanding. You guaranteed me 'utmost freedom' so long as I spent nights with you when you're in London. I've not broken our agreement. We never agreed to an exclusive relationship."

Henry eyes pierced into her, which unnerved Amelia, but she kept her poise in defending herself—hoping to not cause further offense.

"As a young woman, you must expect me to pursue relationships with my contemporaries, and Marlowe is one. In the main, we're intellectual sparring partners. Have we spent private time together? Yes. Has he inspired my writing? Yes. Isn't that what you'd like for me?"

Henry's anger abated, but he shrunk like an abandoned old man, which wounded her even more. "Amelia, I don't want to imprison you, however I didn't expect you to seek other male partners while living with me. I grant your point, but it violates the spirit, if not the exact terms, of our agreement. And you've damaged my stature."

Amelia looked down, feeling contrite. "I should have been discreet. I should have known better."

Henry placed his hands on the wings of a chair and leaned toward Amelia, commanding her attention. "Now that I'm back, I forbid you from seeing Marlowe again privately. Or any other man. You may pursue ordinary friendships and professional associations if they're in the open—with nothing hidden behind closed doors. It's rumors and hear-say that scar the most."

Amelia confronted Marlowe backstage at The Curtain following an afternoon performance after all actors and stage-hands had departed.

"Christopher," she whispered, surveying the area to ensure they were alone, "Lord Hunsdon has returned and rumors about us are hurting him."

Marlowe tried pulling her into his arms, but she raised her hands to ward him off. He snarled, "Oh, so you're finished with me. It's his problem, not mine."

"Don't view it that way. He's a good man and dear to me."

Marlowe scoffed at such a tender sentiment. "He has power and wants to control you."

Amelia put her hands on her hips striking a defiant pose. "He controls me only as much as I permit."

"Don't deceive yourself. He can and he will."

Marlowe's face stiffened but Amelia saw pain in his eyes. "Why are you speaking this way?"

"Because you're rejecting me for him. That's plain."

"As a courtesy to Henry, I've only agreed to not see you privately."

Marlowe shot her a look of contempt. "That's all? What about my desires?"

"We'll see each other publicly and not raise suspicions."

"And my opinion means nothing?"

She paused, for now he had shown how much he feared losing her. "Christopher, there's no joy in this for me. I'll miss our rapture...our passion together...but it's best. We can make a collegial friendship work."

"To no end, I'm afraid."

"What do you mean?"

Marlowe rolled his script and shook it before Amelia's eyes. "You're under the illusion you can get your plays performed. But nobody will touch them. Theater owners won't invest in them because nobody cares about plays by women. I'd have explained this cold reality long ago, but then—"

Amelia snatched the scrolled script from Marlowe and jabbed it into his chest. "But then, what? I would've stopped having sex with you?"

Marlowe grabbed back the script. "You said it, Amelia. I didn't need you before we met. Why do you think I need you now?"

9

LONDON, MAY 1589

Alone in the drawing room of Lord Hunsdon's manor, Amelia pounded out a clamorous song on the harpsichord to relieve tension from her encounter with Marlowe, sending her fury through her fingers and into the keyboard. The jarring notes echoed her rage. How could she have been so foolish, selfish, and shortsighted? She hated herself for it.

Over the clash of notes, Amelia barely heard someone knocking. She rose swiftly, fearing Henry had returned.

Instead a messenger handed her a letter. "Mr. Shakespeare insisted I wait for a reply."

Amelia took the letter with both hands, recognizing Will's fluid handwriting. She unsealed it, pleased and relieved to hear from him.

> *Dear Amelia,*
>   *After two years, I'm back in London. Can we*
> *meet? I'll be at The Horn on Thursday at 10:00.*
> *Please hand your reply to the messenger.*
> *Yours,*
> *Will*

Amelia's gloom evaporated in a wink. *Yes, yes, I'll be there.* This was a welcome and timely surprise.

Will had two goblets of ale waiting on the table when Amelia arrived. Thin creases now lined his brow, his features were more angular, and his beard had thickened. Shallow crow's feet stemmed from his eyes. His lighthearted manner seemed a tad heavier and slightly forced. Amelia wondered if Will's once youthful exuberance had become burdened by a troubled home life.

Amelia realized how much she had missed Will. They had a natural rapport. Unlike Marlowe, so pompous and overconfident, Will appeared humble and unsure of his talent. Amelia believed her intellect and creativity would maintain his interest, while a little feminine appeal might add encouragement.

"Amelia, you're lovelier than ever."

At twenty, her tawny complexion and slim frame attracted men's' attention, especially when donning a snug black and silver bodice like today. The spicy scent of *Acqua di Melissa* added to her allure.

Amelia sipped her ale and felt the bitter liquid slide down her throat. "That's the charm I remember. How long will you be in London?"

He winced. "I have a history of coming and going, don't I? Barring an emergency, I'm making London my home for most of the year, returning occasionally to Stratford-upon-Avon."

"How's *Henry VI?*"

"That's one reason I invited you here." Will rubbed his palms together in glee. "Burbage has agreed to stage what I had formerly called Part Two and is interested in the other parts too."

Amelia raised her goblet. "Congratulations! To your achievement."

Will raised his goblet. "Burbage thinks they will draw as well as Marlowe's plays. And I'm indebted to you for recommending that I create three scripts from one."

"Will, I had faith in you and now Burbage does too."

Will bowed in a grandiloquent wave of acknowledgment. "I believe historical dramas are my forte and this is the beginning. After *Henry VI*, *Richard III* will soon follow." Will pointed to his head. "The plot is already entrenched."

Amelia delighted in his theatrical antics. How could she have ever demeaned herself with a man who thought himself so superior?

Will settled back down and nodded his goblet toward her. "How is your play about the two sets of twins?"

Amelia believed he already knew the answer. She cleared her throat. "Using your phrase, I'm calling it *A Comedy of Errors*, but...." Her lips turned downward as she continued. "I've gone to every theater owner, but none will look at it."

Tears welled in Amelia's eyes, and she dabbed them with a linen handkerchief.

"Do they say why?" asked Will.

"Some do, some don't. One claimed a play by a woman wouldn't attract audiences, which is curious since there's never been one. But there's also an unstated reason."

"Which is?"

Amelia stared through the rain-streaked window and gathered her courage to admit the truth. "I'm not well thought of among theater people. I shan't go into details but my reputation has been sullied."

"I won't inquire, but I've heard rumors…about another playwright."

Amelia swallowed hard; relieved he didn't mention names. She didn't wish to talk about Marlowe. An awkward silence filled the space between them. Yet she could tell Will's mind was working furiously.

"Will, what are you thinking?"

He coughed, making a dismissive wave. "It's nothing."

"Will, say it. You can be blunt."

"I'm searching for the right words so I don't offend you."

Amelia took another sip of ale. "I'll be more offended if you don't tell me."

Will still hesitated and when he spoke chose his words carefully. "There are certain barriers that aren't coming down. That means if you want your play performed, you'll need to make a reluctant choice."

"Will, what are you saying?"

Will shifted in his chair, grimacing as if struggling to broach his idea with her. "Amelia, I'll be plain. I doubt men's attitudes toward women will change. They're deeply implanted. So—and this was the mad thought that occurred to me—why not use a man's name as the author? Then your script would receive due consideration."

Amelia recoiled at the artifice. "You're suggesting I use a male alias like *Amiel* Bassano, or some other contrived appellation?"

"It could work."

"It might, but if every woman did we'd never be recognized for notable work. Our genders should not matter."

Will shrunk back in his seat, looking pained. "Everything you say is true, bringing me to the point I wished to make earlier, which would solve those practical problems but create other risks."

Amelia planted her elbows on the table. "And that is?"

"To get Burbage's true reaction, what if, with your assent, I showed him your script without any name on it? If he responds favorably, then we'll discuss our next moves."

Amelia saw the value of that approach. "That's an intriguing idea. But if he likes it, then what?"

"It will depend on his reaction," said Will.

Amelia fidgeted with uncertainty, reluctant to lose control over her work. "I have little to lose, I suppose."

"Amelia, it's worth trying. Can you bring the script here tomorrow?"

Amelia paused, assessing Will. She believed him to be sincere and fair-minded. He wasn't sinister like Marlowe, who would have a concealed motive. *I'll trust him and see. Only then will I know.* "I'll bring it, but I'll need it back."

"Indeed."

"If he likes it, will you reveal who wrote it?"

"I'll use my judgment, but won't risk having the play rejected."

"And I won't change my name to 'Amiel.'"

Will circled the block three times, passing in front of The Theatre, thinking through his discussion with Burbage. When he felt ready, he marched into the theater and found Burbage in his office. After opening pleasantries, Will began, "I have something different to show you— not a script about an English king—but one by a playwright wishing to remain anonymous. I'd like your frank opinion."

Burbage seemed both curious and pleased with his young writer. "That I can always render. What's it's called?"

"*A Comedy of Errors.*"

Burbage rocked back in his chair, chuckling. "A comedy of errors—that might describe the reigns of many English kings—if you have a sense of humor."

Will laughed along with him, trying to disguise his nervousness. *Burbage is in a good mood, but I should still be careful.* "I suppose so," he joked, "but a tragedy of errors could also be apt."

Burbage howled with laughter. "Point well taken. So what's it about if not a king like your first three scripts?"

"It's a comedy about two pairs of identical twins who were separated at birth, and through a series of satirical events and mistaken identities find each other in unexpected circumstances..."

Will summarized the script and explained plot twists. Burbage leaned over the pages, following Will's finger through the lines—his smile widening with each scene.

At the end, Burbage stacked the sheets with the title page facing upward. He stared at it, raising an eyebrow. "This is good. It'll draw an audience. But come, Will, have enough confidence to put your name on it."

Will stared, dumbstruck. *What dare I say?*

"Don't be so surprised. Although a comedy, it should do well. People need laughter."

Still shaken by this unexpected turn, Will stood to leave and turned toward the open door.

Burbage gestured for him to sit back down. "A week ago, you inquired about Amelia Bassano. Did you find her?"

Will swallowed hard. "I did. You were correct. She's living with Lord Hunsdon."

"Be careful around her," advised Burbage. "She doesn't know her place."

"How so?"

"She came here and saw Lanman at The Curtain too. She's peddling a script. I told her to keep it in her valise. I'll have nothing to do with her or anything by a woman." He stretched forward, imparting the wisdom of a man of experience. "I'm warning you. Don't associate with her."

Will retreated numbly, unable to believe his dilemma. Oh, that's sage advice, he thought ruefully. Truly the best I've received.

Outside Burbage's office he saw the shadow of a man racing away. When Will turned toward the street he saw him leaning against a stone building.

"You were listening outside Burbage's door?" asked Will accusingly as he approached the stocky bearded man

"I was and I heard most of it," the man declared.

He's about my age, Will thought, but with a bitter look more in keeping with someone who's had a difficult life.

The man stepped toward Will as if proud of his impropriety. "I watched you walk in. Aren't you the fellow who won Burbage's favor for three scripts about the same king? You fit the description a few actors gave me."

"I am, but what business is that of yours?"

"And now you're peddling a fourth one, and he likes it too?"

"So it seems. He appreciates good stories."

The man scoffed, "There must be more to it than that. He won't take mine and it's as good as any."

"I don't like what you're implying, mister..."

"Dekker, Thomas Dekker. I'll be keeping an eye on you. Something's not clean."

"Mr. Dekker, envy does not live well within anyone. It won't help you and doesn't worry me."

Amelia paced the streets near The Horn waiting for Will. Her leather chopines had rubbed her ankles sore. The two-inch wooden soles and heels were caked with crud from stepping off curbs into sloppy, potholed roads. Horses and carriages splattered mud on her black skirt. But Amelia thought only about Will's meeting with Burbage, paying little attention to where she walked. She passed The Horn again and then saw Will approaching from the opposite direction, looking downcast.

"Burbage wants *A Comedy of Errors*," he announced matter-of-factly.

Something's wrong, Amelia sensed. *Why isn't he pleased?*

"Let's talk inside," suggested Will.

They found a window table that two laborers had vacated. Will ordered ale for them both.

"Will, don't keep me in suspense."

"Burbage likes the novel theme and plot. He thinks it will draw sizeable audiences..."

Will's tone is flat, devoid of emotion. Something's not right. "Does he know who penned it?"

Will hung his head and put his fist to his mouth.

"What is it, Will?"

"Burbage assumed I wrote it. He said I should be confident enough to say so."

Oh no! Is Will stealing my work? "What did you say?"

"I didn't correct him."

Amelia jumped to her feet, folding her arms across her chest. *I didn't expect treachery!* "I trusted you! You didn't tell the truth?"

"Please, sit down," he said wearily. "I despise myself for offering it under false pretenses. But had I revealed the true author, he'd have rejected it."

"But he thought it was good!"

Will slumped in his seat, and she thought, *He's acting guilty but genuinely upset, like he failed me. And he has.*

In a regretful tone he said, "Yes, but only because he thought I wrote it."

Amelia lurched back, outraged. "Why are men so narrow-minded? Why won't they give women a chance?"

"Amelia, I admire your talent. I can't excuse Burbage and other men, but I believe everyone's work should be judged on its quality. It shouldn't matter whose it is. Unfortunately it does, and that's unlikely to change."

Amelia had no answer. Will asserted what they both knew. The natural window light had waned and yellow candlelight from the tavern's chandeliers and lanterns had gained strength.

Heartsick, thwarted, she didn't know what else to do. "So, my work is for naught."

"Not necessarily."

Amelia recognized the gleam in Will's eye, which meant he had an idea.

"Which is more important to you," he asked, "seeing your play be performed or having it attributed to you?"

She didn't understand why he'd try to parse the matter. "Oh, Will, part of the joy is the recognition. Let's not repeat our conversation from the other day."

"We needn't. Unfortunately, you have the same choice. Your script can gather dust on a shelf and never be performed, or it can be brought to life."

Amelia knew he had an alternative in mind. He wouldn't tread over ground they had already plowed. "What do you propose?"

"Suppose we form a business arrangement in which I submit your script under my name. Only you and I will know who actually penned it. I'll pay you most of the earnings, keeping a percentage for my work promoting it and working with actors to ensure the script is properly interpreted."

Will stopped short, waiting for Amelia's response.

She gritted her teeth, wanting mightily to resist. But she also wanted to hear him out. "But I'll still be unknown."

"True, but your creativity will flourish."

Amelia peered at the lantern flickering on their table. A candle glowed inside the glass cylinder as a wisp of silvery smoke floated upward, carrying the scent of melting wax mixed with that of the burning wick. A sick feeling settled in her stomach as she pondered her dilemma.

She rose slowly from her chair. "Will, stay here. This tavern is suffocating me. I must clear my thoughts and breathe cool air for a few minutes."

Will nodded and Amelia wandered into the gray night.

The streets were quieter. The calm helped her think. She drew into herself, wrestling with the implications of Will's proposal. Would she be giving up on the woman she wanted to be, along with her beliefs and dreams, or accommodating reality as well as she could? She had no clear answers. Down the block a horse neighed as two couples passed. *If I accept Will's proposition, will I remain always in the shadows, never known for my accomplishments? Who besides Will will know the truth? I'll know the truth. Is that enough?*

As Amelia wended her way back through dark narrow streets to the tavern, she thought about what she wanted and why she wanted it. The "what" seemed clear enough but the "why" remained elusive. The reasons went beyond the pursuit of entertaining and the recognition and praise that accompanied it. She believed this revelation would coalesce and inspire her, but not today. Then she thought of another idea—although far from satisfying, it might be something. She tucked it away, promising to return to it.

Once at The Horn, she watched Will sipping ale through the window. She tapped on the glass. Will looked out, his face pensive. She tried reading his eyes but the warped glass and candle shadows made that impossible. Yet she felt she could trust him.

"I've made a decision," she disclosed, once she reentered and retook her seat. "Will, I'll put my faith in you. I'll accept your proposition for *A Comedy of Errors*."

Will blinked nervously as if he couldn't believe it. He raised his goblet to her. "To our pact."

Amelia, with Henry and Lady Susan seated beside her, gazed from the first row of The Theatre's balcony at the set for *A Comedy of Errors*. The play began inside a duke's palace. Two double doors dominated center stage and boxes formed a staircase up to a wide platform for the duke and his entourage. Amelia scanned the room in her burgundy gown with a white lace collar and judged herself well dressed for her premiere. *This is the opening of my play, no matter who receives credit.*

Amelia watched intently, following the stage action and the audience's reactions. Will played Antipholus of Ephesus, the twin who had never met his father and was married to Andriana—a woman upset about her husband's infidelity. Although Amelia had written the scenes, she glowed seeing how the roles were portrayed. The interplay between the three women—Andriana, the indulging and clingy wife; her twin, Luciana, who advocates for women's independence; and Abbess Aemilia, a traditional wife—worked as Amelia had foreseen. Amelia delighted in the way Luciana's lines were delivered as a mocking, cynical tribute to men:

> Man, more divine, the master of all these,
> Lord of the wide world and wild wat'ry seas,
> Indued with intellectual sense and souls,
> Of more preeminence than fish and fowls,
> Are masters to their females, and their lords;
> Then let your will attend on their accords.

Twice, when Will spoke onstage, he searched for Amelia in the audience and delivered his lines to her. She loved their private exchange. And she thought of Will when another character said, "And now let's go hand in hand, not one before another." That captured the working relationship she sought.

During farcical scenes in which the audience roared with laughter, Amelia felt triumphant. *They delight in my puns and wordplays. I've succeeded in both entertaining and conveying a point.* Her heart fluttered when the abbess, whom she'd named for herself, was revealed as the long-missing wife of the character Egeon and mother of the long-separated identical male twins. Amelia smiled inwardly and straightened her posture at the secret self-acknowledgment that only she, Henry, Lady Susan, and Will understood.

Amelia's heart leapt at the thunderous applause at the end, only to feel it sink like a stone when Will appeared onstage to accept effusive accolades. She expected it. She didn't regret her decision, but it hurt nonetheless.

10

LONDON, APRIL 1592

"Would you like me to keep your secret?" asked Marlowe with the smug expression familiar to Amelia.

They sat in the dreary back of The Horn. Marlowe's smirking tone put her on edge. What does Marlowe know or think he knows?

"Secret? If the rumors are true about your mysterious life and frequent disappearances, I'd say you're the one keeping secrets," declared Amelia. "Are you spying on fellow citizens or foreigners?"

Marlowe jabbed a finger at Amelia. "Don't believe damnable rumors! Do you actually think I'm a spy? That's completely out of character."

Amelia didn't think so. "You're an enigma. You relish secrets. Does spying fit your character? That's a question worth considering."

"Back to your secret...and Mr. Shakespeare's. Do you want me to keep it?"

The mention of Will set her on guard. "Meaning?"

"I know who wrote *A Comedy of Errors*. It wasn't Shakespeare. But congratulations on a clever ruse and attracting steady audiences."

Amelia squirmed at this accusation. She had discussed the script with Marlowe frequently, especially during their first few meetings. "You extolled it," she said, attempting nonchalance. "Its success shouldn't be surprising."

"True, but how you got it performed was. You know Shakespeare and I are rivals. You betrayed me by becoming allies with him. And a frustrated writer named Thomas Dekker is asking questions about Will's brisk success. I feigned ignorance but that need not continue. Once again, should I keep your secret?"

"You know the answer. It's obvious," said Amelia, her voice quivering.

Marlowe stood to his full height and loomed over her. "I keep secrets but for a price."

This is the diabolical Marlowe I've feared, and he wants something...something steep, no doubt. His sneer chilled her to the bone. "You've stooped lower than even I expected."

"It's business. It's the way of the world. It's what I depict in my dramas."

"Like your despicable play *The Jew of Malta*? If Lord Hunsdon hadn't been with me, I'd have walked out."

"You found it offensive?"

"Is it not offensive to characterize a Jewish businessman as vengeful, villainous, and murderous—with nary a redeeming virtue—as if he represents them all? You're feeding people's ignorant biases, like throwing raw meat to lions."

"That's a simplistic analysis, especially from you," chided Marlowe.

"Now that I think about it, your 'Jew of Malta' seems a lot like you—ruthless, cunning, and mercenary. What do you want?"

"I want Amelia. The sex I had with you exceeded all expectations."

"No! I implore you. No."

Marlowe flashed his sinister smile. "Have you a choice?"

Amelia staggered from The Horn, her mind numb and her stomach in knots. *By submitting to Marlowe's blackmail, I'll be betraying myself. I'd have refused if only my integrity was at stake. But I can't expose Will, for his sake and mine.*

Amelia told no one. Disclosing Marlowe's blackmail to Henry, or Will, or Lady Susan would be too humiliating. *I'll find an escape. But how?*

Finding no recourse, two days after her encounter with Marlowe Amelia shambled to his rooms wearing a dowdy jumper and frayed blouse, dressed as unattractively as possible. She felt the walls close in as he shut the door behind her. He jammed the iron bar into its socket, locking the door with a clank. Panic seized her. She wanted to flee.

"Do you live with farm animals or is this mess yours alone?" asked Amelia, pointing to the floor strewn with dirty clothes, overturned mugs, and crumbled papers.

Marlowe contorted his face like a dog baring his teeth. "Aren't you the clever one? You expect me to be insulted?"

"I'm simply asking a question. This room is worse than usual."

Marlowe showed his broad sinister smile. "This, Amelia, is about power—getting someone to do what they hate doing. I hope it's not too high a price to pay."

Marlowe's breath reeked of whisky and Amelia detected the sweat of uncertainty. The boyhood features she once liked had hardened into a nasty mask.

"It's a very steep price. Your wicked game reveals more about your character than mine. Until now I hadn't believed in the devil, but you've convinced me otherwise."

He sneered back. "You think I'm the devil?"

Amelia jabbed two fingers into his chest. "You are Barabas, your own depraved character in *The Jew of Malta*—immoral and wicked. What was his line? Something like…

> *I walk abroad a-nights,*
> *And kill sick people groaning under walls.*
> *Sometimes I go about and poison wells—"*

Marlowe stiffened, growing angrier by the word. "Stop talking. Unlace your gown. Strip to your smock! I'll tell you when to go further. Act like you're enjoying yourself, like you desire me. Show me the lustful expressions you evinced when you did. Play your part—that of a strumpet."

Amelia itched to bolt from Marlowe's rooms. She suppressed her hostility, repugnance, and contempt. She made him climax quickly, performing the task like a farmer milks cows.

When he forced her onto the mattress, she closed her eyes, pretending to be elsewhere, but his groans, his sticky secretion, and the strong bleachy smell of semen returned her to reality. Amelia showed no passion, no affection, and prayed he'd soon tire of the routine.

Marlowe appeared not to notice. Indeed, he insisted they meet weekly as a condition of keeping her secret. He reiterated his threat as she redressed, as if she could forget it. She despised his display of malicious satisfaction. She knew not when or how this nightmare would end.

She staggered out his door, heaving, full of shame and remorse. She drifted through narrow streets until stopping in a dank alley. Alone, she leaned her back against the grimy brick wall and buried her face in her hands. The thin emotional membrane that had somehow contained the smoldering volcano inside her finally burst. She slid to the damp ground wailing in pain.

A month later, Amelia felt nauseous shortly after waking and as she dressed to see Marlowe. She asked the cook to make dry toast and tea to soothe her belly. Nonetheless, she vomited, emptying her stomach—attributing it to anxiety over complying with Marlowe's demands. An hour later, the feeling subsided and she crept away for her foul assignation.

The nausea returned the next morning and Amelia realized her dilemma. *When did I last menstruate? Am I pregnant? If so, whose baby is it? I've also made love with Henry.*

Amelia stewed for hours about whether to tell Henry or secretly abort the fetus. *I don't want a baby now. Should I have it and tell Henry the child is his, even if I'm uncertain? But Marlowe would suspect the truth and inflict more demands.* She wavered, crippled with indecision.

Amelia nibbled on a crumpet and played with mutton on her breakfast plate, too ashamed to look up at Henry sitting across the table. She believed he'd read her troubled expressions, but restrained himself from inquiring. *He knows I'll tell him but won't pry, but his patience has limits.*

At last Amelia lifted her glum face. She could no longer withstand the unspoken tension. "Henry," she said in a timid voice, "I'm afraid you'll be furious with me."

"The secret you're keeping must be distressing. You hardly slept last night."

She feared compounding her problem. Upon hearing her confession, he might evict her in a fit of rage. She gripped her lips, not wanting to say anything rash, and hoping he'd sympathize with her plight. After all, she'd been coerced into this nightmare. "I'm scared. I made a huge mistake. Please don't be too incensed."

"Amelia, you're shaking. What's wrong?"

Amelia put her hands on her belly. "I'm carrying a baby."

Henry beamed, pleased with this news. "You're sure?"

"Yes. I waited until certain before telling you."

"That's why you've been sleeping so poorly? The circles under your eyes keep growing wider and darker."

"I know."

"You're worried because we aren't married and don't know what will happen once the baby is born?"

"There's more," said Amelia, her eyes downcast.

Henry's smile evaporated. "More?"

"I don't know who the father is."

"You don't?"

She shuddered at the steely edge in his voice. "There's still more. I'm full of shame and regret. I've been crying for days. I've destroyed my dignity and much of my life."

"Amelia, just tell me. We'll find a solution."

"Remember the pact I made with Will to get *A Comedy of Errors* staged…" Amelia continued until she had recounted all the events leading to Marlowe's threats.

"That lout is blackmailing you?" charged Henry in his commanding voice.

"Henry, I don't know what to do. I—I need your help desperately and you must hate me for betraying you," Amelia stammered, collapsing into herself and sobbing.

He came around to her side of the table, gently caressed her shoulders, and said softly, "Amelia, you should have told me when he first threatened you."

"What could you have done? I'm so disgraced I couldn't tell anyone."

Henry's voice rose in anger, hostility dripping from every word, "I know a few secrets myself, secrets that bastard would never want revealed. You should have confided in me."

She rested her cheek against one of his hands. "Henry, I didn't know. I'm very sorry. I've been stupid."

"I'll visit Mr. Marlowe. You won't hear from him again. You'll never need to see him again unless you pass on the street. And he won't utter a word about your arrangement with Will Shakespeare after I confront him."

Amelia wept with relief. "Henry, thank you. A better friend I could never have."

"When is that knave next expecting you?"

෪

Marlowe pulled the window curtain back and peeked outside, looking for Amelia. She should have arrived by now. These weekly sessions were nothing like the times when she exalted him, but they bestowed a different form of satisfaction. He enjoyed watching her squirm as he forced her to pleasure him.

Marlowe let the heavy curtain fall back and gulped more wine. A minute later a light rap rattled his door. *Ah, she's here. I'll punish her for being tardy.*

He opened the door ready to castigate her but instead stared into the hard eyes of Lord Hunsdon.

"Expecting someone else? Were you about to say something?"

"No. No, not at all. To what do I owe this pleasure?" asked Marlowe, stepping back.

"I'm surprised you'd consider seeing me a pleasure."

Marlowe replied with a mocking contemptuous bow. "It's always a pleasure seeing you, Lord Hunsdon—the esteemed Lord Chamberlain."

"This might be an exception. Take three steps back and let me in. Now!"

Henry entered the dirty flat and shut the door, towering over the shorter man. He scanned the room, clearly disgusted by the filth and smell of spoiled food.

"Why are you here?" asked Marlowe, crossing the room and sensing a threat he'd be unable to subdue with offensive barbs.

Henry flung a rickety chair across the room. It crashed to the floor by Marlowe's feet. "Sit!"

Shaken, Marlowe lifted the chair upright and glared with malevolence. "What do you want?"

"Pretending you don't know?" asked Henry menacingly as he pushed Marlowe into the chair. "Amelia told me about your sick game. We frown on blackmail!'

"Blackmail? Whatever gave you that idea? I suspect you're jealous a younger man is enjoying your mistress," taunted Marlow, deploying his usual tack when confronted.

"Suspect all you want. Your sadistic escapade is over."

Marlowe's contempt boiled inside. *I must contain it to regain control.* "Did she reveal her secret?"

"She did. And if you disclose it, your life will be overcome by a wretched change."

"Will it?" asked Marlowe caustically.

The stiff older man continued unrelenting. "I'm aware of your secret activities, supposedly on the state's behalf. I know some went suspiciously wrong and I suspect you crippled them. I doubt you'd want such speculation known. Utter one word about Amelia or her secret—go near her, harm her in any way—and you could find yourself in the Tower of London for a brief stay."

"Brief?"

"Yes, brief because your fate could be the same as Mary, Queen of Scots. As you'll recall, Queen Elizabeth had her beheaded for treason."

11

LONDON, OCTOBER 1592

Amelia put down her quill and pulled a knitted afghan over her shoulders as Henry stepped inside Hunsdon House. A fire, crackling in the fireplace, had done little to settle her anxiety. She regretted being unfaithful and not turning to him earlier for help. She berated herself for not trusting him. Despite feeling betrayed, Henry came to her rescue.

Henry laid his fur-collared surcoat on a chair. His neutral expression turned to a smile upon seeing Amelia working on a manuscript. "Deep in thought?"

"Trying to write but mostly thinking about you and my plight. What happened with Marlowe?"

Henry placed his hands on Amelia's shoulders and she grasped them with hers.

"Mr. Marlowe disavows all knowledge or responsibility. He's truly a snake and the most lethal kind until he encounters a more dangerous force," he said. "Yet he won't bother you again. I made sure of that."

Amelia clutched Henry's hand, kissing it. "Thank you, how can I ever repay you?"

"There's no need."

She should have expected that he'd be stoic about doing what he regarded as his duty. Her thoughts, however, had already ranged ahead. She rubbed her belly. "Henry, what should we do about my condition?"

"Tell your family—your aunts, uncles or cousins. Whomever you trust. They'll help you follow your traditions."

Does he know I'm Jewish? "My traditions?"

He squeezed her hand. "I've known for years you're Hebraic and why you conceal it. That secret, too, is safe with me. Now your faith and family must provide guidance."

She tensed, worried about their judgment and what they'd say. She replied in a whisper, "Yes, I should talk to them"

"For my part," he announced, "I'll add sufficient funds to care for the baby until he or she is eighteen, including a worthy education."

"Amelia, there's no choice but to get married," declared Lucretia, her older cousin.

Amelia and Henry had gathered with Lucretia and her husband Nicholas in the Lanier's' cramped salon. Afternoon light filtered through the windows. Amelia, perched on a hard chair, had recounted her story.

Henry interjected, "There's no need to panic or force an unnatural arrangement. Marriage is one option, but there are others. The baby could be offered for adoption?"

Lucretia shot Nicholas a glance.

"Lord Hunsdon, with due respect, this isn't your problem to solve," Nicholas retorted.

"Nicholas, come with me to the kitchen," urged Lucretia, waving him along.

Amelia heard whispering but not the conversation itself.

She had hoped disclosing her predicament would be cleansing. Instead she felt dirtier and diminished. Her aunt and uncle's reactions exacerbated her worries. Her uncle had been rude to Henry. Now they were talking secretly in the kitchen. Why not in front of her? She wasn't a child. These were not good harbingers. She slumped in her chair, contrite over her circumstances. She didn't want Lucretia and Nicholas dictating her decision, but she'd fallen into a deep pit and couldn't climb out alone.

Lucretia and Nicolas returned, both with stern expressions.

"Amelia," Lucretia began. "We've always thought highly of you and enjoyed your company on holidays. We'll help if you'll permit."

Her tone is patronizing, thought Amelia, another disquieting sign. She tightened her jaw, fearing Lucretia would impose some horrible choice.

"Amelia, haste is required to preserve your reputation. You cannot have this baby out of wedlock. That will disgrace us all. Your father, bless his memory, would be severely disappointed."

The mention of her father felt like a punch to the gut. "What do you propose?"

"That you marry Alphonso," declared Nicholas.

Amelia's mind went numb. She could hardly breathe. To her, it seemed inconceivable that anyone could suggest marrying him. "Your son?"

"Yes, our son Alphonso."

"Slovenly Alphonso, the bully Alphonso, who has never uttered a kind word to me, or almost anyone else, and with whom I have little in common?"

"He's a superb lad once you know him, and a member of the Queen's recorder consort that once included your father," Lucretia proclaimed proudly.

No he's not, thought Amelia. He's imperious and rude. He plays for the court because his father acquired the job for him. "Why would he want to marry me? He's never shown any inkling he enjoys my company."

"That's not an obstacle," said Lucretia.

"Besides, what choice do you have?" asked Nicholas.

"This is quite a comeuppance, is it not?" crowed Alphonso as he met with Amelia in the Lanier home the following day for a private interview. "My parents never thought I'd do as well. Turns out I get a big prize for my bride after all."

Amelia listened to him with utter contempt. Nothing is going to work out well. He's despicable. "Are you delighting in my misfortune?" she replied. "Have you no compassion?"

Alphonso's ginger hair had darkened since boyhood and curled behind his ear. His pale face, squinty eyes, and pouty lower lip created a perpetual look of insolence.

"Why should I have compassion for the high and mighty one who has been brought low? And by your own conniving, no less. You've always been the one my parents compared me to. 'Why can't you be more like Amelia?' my mother would ask. Now I'm rescuing you from bearing a bastard?"

Alphonso's belligerence compounded her anguish. She could envision only a dark future with this man. *Why is he punishing me for comparisons made by his parents? I've not treated him poorly, just benignly to avoid his ill temper.* "The Germans have a word for deriving pleasure from the problems of others. It's *schadenfreude.* Should I expect that from my betrothed? Or should I expect better?"

"You always thought you were smarter than everyone else and you made the mistake of a fool. Now you resent being tethered to me. Come, where's your gratitude for my benevolence? Should I expect any?"

"It's obvious you enjoy rubbing salt into a wound," said Amelia, unable any longer to hold back tears. "Is there not an ounce of kindness in you?"

"It's what you deserve," he answered nastily. "I'm in control now."

To Amelia, the evening of Saturday, October 10, felt more like a sentence than a wedding. Lucretia and Nicholas insisted on two ceremonies: one at Saint Botolph's in Bishopsgate to satisfy Anglican religious authorities and a private Jewish ceremony at the unofficial rabbi's home.

Amelia had heard that the Jewish custom of breaking a glass at the end of wedding ceremonies had started as a superstition to ward off evil demons. *Maybe it will lessen Alphonso's contempt for me, make him kinder.* The glass breaking also reminded celebrants that even in the midst of joy, couples must possess sufficient strength to withstand life's pains together. Amelia felt the converse—heartbroken and alone with slim hopes for later marital happiness.

Amelia felt the disapproving stares of Will, Lord Hunsdon, and Lady Susan during the ceremony at Saint Botolph's, but Lucretia and Nicholas only invited members of the faith at the secret Jewish ceremony. A festive celebration followed neither.

Amelia had no explanation for Lady Susan after the ceremony at Saint Botolph's, but the sad look in her eyes cut through Amelia like a dagger, as if to say, "How could you harm yourself so severely?" Then Lady Susan took Amelia aside. "If you must escape this louse, come to Willoughby House. We're your family too."

Amelia gently rocked her newborn boy after giving birth in early March 1593. Joy and love swelled her heart as she had never before imagined. The likely circumstances of his conception seemed far away and unimportant now. He belonged to her. She admired his delicate fingers, lips, and eyes. "Your name is Henry. It's a good name. May you honor it always."

Alphonso swayed and staggered about the room, his normal condition after heavy gambling losses or when anger overcame him. "I'm the father in name only," he declared. "This infant is a Lanier but he's your burden."

"I expect little of you," returned Amelia with matching severity. "With or without your help, I'll give Henry the best life and the greatest love."

Amelia gazed at her baby lying peacefully against her chest. Despite her love, she felt the promise of her youth slipping away. After being impregnated, probably by a man who had raped her, and floundering through the emotional turmoil, she was shackled in marriage to a brute who ordered her around. Her life had changed and her dreams were tumbling from sight.

Yet she assuaged herself. She had written a popular play, and she and Will were working together on another. That was, she realized, the promise she must seize upon. She could not let the world outside dictate what she could be. She must do what she could on her own—for her newborn son and for herself.

ACT TWO

A TRAGEDY OF LOVE

12

Wails. Long shrill howls pierced the afternoon air. Amelia panicked. They're from a baby. *My baby!* She rushed through the street to her home—struggling to hold the sacks of fruit, vegetables, milk, cheese and bread weighing down her arms—then up the steep flight of stairs. She crashed through the door remembering Enid had the day off. Out of necessity, she'd left Henry in Alphonso's care while she bought food in the neighborhood Westminster district.

Amelia dropped her bundles upon entering their cramped three-room home, a far cry from the spacious mansions in which she'd been accustomed to living. Henry flailed in his crib, his face red from crying. She leaned over and picked him up, cradling him in her arms. Instantly she felt his soaked diaper and smelled his waste. Henry gulped for air as he settled down. Safe in his mother's arms, his cries descended into whimpers.

Alphonso flung open their bedroom door dressed in a rumpled shirt. He shot Amelia an annoyed look. "I couldn't get the little bastard to shut up."

"You were to watch him and change him. You've done neither."

Alphonso glowered. "I couldn't stand being in the same room with his bawling. The little heathen wouldn't stop."

Amelia tossed her head in anger. "He may not be your son by birth, but as my husband, we must raise him together. Won't you help?

"I didn't ask for him. I shouldn't suffer because you were Lord Hunsdon's harlot. It's he who discarded you!"

Alphonso barged out the door. As Amelia cleaned and changed her infant, she swore she'd find a way to escape her husband, for her sake and Henry's.

When Henry smiled again, she played a Venetian lullaby on her lute. She sang the sweet verses she'd learned as a small child when her father took her to Venice to visit cousins. As the song calmed her nerves and Henry drifted to sleep, she recalled running and giggling by the canals as Mediterranean sunlight shimmered on the water. Remembering more clearly her own childhood, she thought, is one benefit of having a baby. She also, in an age-old way, felt more connected to her traditions, to her father, and all he had left behind in Venice. She wanted, she realized, to visit the city again someday and take Henry with her.

Amelia's gloom darkened further. The Bubonic Plague had returned with a vengeance. She smelled the gruesome odor of death on the streets and saw fear lurking in everyone's eyes. She met fewer people in the market as many had fled to the countryside hoping to avoid contagion. All of London's theaters had been shuttered and Will said he planned to leave soon for Stratford-upon-Avon.

Will surprised her with a visit. As they sat in her cramped parlor, he made her laugh for the first time in weeks. His cheerfulness stood in sharp contrast to her mood and the deplorable conditions outside. He told stories using the exaggerated motions of an actor emphasizing a point. He comforted the baby while comically pretending he didn't know what to do. Although he had his own troubles, he acted as though he had none.

Amelia smiled while Enid laughed.

Will turned toward Enid. "May we leave Henry with you for a short time?"

Amelia held Henry in her arms and kissed his fuzzy head, delighting in the sweet bouquet of an infant. "We won't be long," she promised, handing the baby over.

Will and Amelia strolled to a nearby green. She laid a wool blanket between two trees. They sat a few feet apart facing each other. Greenfinches chirped above in an ash tree.

"*A Comedy of Errors* and *Titus Andronicus* doing well," began Will. "My latest play, *Richard III,* is drawing respectable audiences but not as large."

Amelia wondered: *Did Will notice that I named one character in* Titus *Bassianus and another Aemilius—Latinized versions of my names? I thought the association was obvious, but he hasn't mentioned it.*

Will broke her musing. "Have you heard about Marlowe?"

"Marlowe? Will, I want nothing to do with him."

"You needn't worry. He was stabbed to death last week."

Jarred, Amelia shot her hand to her mouth. "Killed? What happened?

"The particulars are shrouded in mystery, but I've been told three men, suspected of being Marlowe's fellow spies, double-crossed him."

"A spy! Then the rumors were true."

"There's much conjecture but little certainty. It's said he got into a fierce argument after imbibing too much, ripped a dagger from the belt of his compatriot and started a scuffle. One of the other spies, much stronger apparently, forced Marlowe's knife hand high above his head, then slammed the blade deep into his eye."

Amelia stammered in shock, "Oh-oh...how dreadful."

Will leaned toward Amelia as if sharing a confidence, touching her hand. "One man said he heard Marlowe squealed like a scared donkey. And his blood sprayed forth like a spouting whale, then he collapsed to the floor— wheezing his final gasp of air like the hiss of a dying snake."

Amelia careened backward, horrified. Will grabbed her wrists to pull her upright. She gently released his hands as she tried sorting her tangle of emotions. *Marlowe was a serpent, but I wouldn't wish such a fate on even him. But I feel no sorrow, only remorse and relief that he can do no more harm.*

With a plaintive tone, Amelia said, "Betrayal and malevolence can induce such a fate. The killers must have hated Marlowe. Not many trusted him."

"Perhaps," said Will, "but there's another supposition about his murder."

Amelia sat in silence waiting for Will to explain. His lower lip twitched as if he were nervous. Finally he continued, "Some actors are speculating that Marlowe was killed by Jews offended by his depiction of Barabas in *The Jew of Malta*—as a crafty, vengeful, Christian-despising man."

Amelia's mouth fell open, her neck tightened. She sensed danger lurking. "Is there any evidence?"

Will clenched his jaw, "None I know of, but it's as plausible as him being slain by a fellow spy." He picked up a long twig, tapped it on the ground, rolled it between his fingers, and snapped it in half.

"Will, why are you nervous? Your biggest competitor is dead. Otherwise, none of this should matter to you."

Will dropped the twig pieces. "The day before Marlowe was killed, Burbage persuaded me to write a script about a sly Jewish moneylender." Amelia heard a catch in Will's throat. "Now—"

"You're afraid for your life because Jews might kill you too." asserted Amelia, finishing his sentence while masking her own fears.

"That's a chilling prospect. Burbage has heard the same rumors but is undaunted. He's convinced such a drama will be extremely profitable. That's what matters to him."

Amelia's eyes locked on Will's. "Indeed, Burbage saw how much money Lanman at The Curtain made from *The Jew of Malta*—and the greedy man wants one like it. How ironic." She wagged her finger. "Will, don't let Burbage dictate. What matters to you?"

Amelia saw his discomfort with her blunt challenge. He looked down and a few awkward seconds later stared back at her. "But he is. I must stay in his good graces if I'm to earn enough to feed and shelter my family."

"Will, I doubt Jews had anything to do with Marlowe's murder. How many even live here? Have you met any?"

Will grabbed another twig and snapped it in half. "No, but their reputation is well known."

Getting rankled, Amelia jumped to her feet and gazed down at Will. "As vengeful killers?"

"Not here, but they did kill Christ. It's their greed and cunning that people know about."

Amelia fought to control her anger and disappointment. "And how do you know all this? It can't be from personal experience. And there's nothing about it in the Bible."

"It's implied in Matthew and priests profess it."

Inside Amelia seethed. She had to be careful but her argumentative nature compelled her forward. Her knees shook and she bent forward to steady them with her hands "Implied? Isn't it dubious that such an accusation is only implied when the New Testament contains unambiguous language about so much else? And since you've not met a Jew, one couldn't have cheated you. Why perpetuate such lore in a play?"

Will rose and replied in a hushed tone, as if trying to calm her. "I don't wish to argue these points. I'm here to ask for your help."

Amelia felt her throat constrict. "Will, I won't write a mean-spirited play."

Will touched her arm. "Nor will I. May I tell you about my father?"

She nodded, curious to hear what his father had to do with this.

Will began slowly and Amelia noticed a touch of sadness as he rubbed an eye. "My father loaned people money. At the time, his leather goods business was thriving. At first, he lent only to friends. Then strangers asked for loans. He charged a percentage to cover his risk, but lost almost everything when borrowers realized they needn't repay, because English law and Christianity prohibit levying interest. He had no recourse."

"What did he do?" asked Amelia, her curiosity aroused.

"He prayed and pled to no avail. Worse, constables arrested him for usury. He never recovered financially and became a pariah in Stratford." Will paused, looking forlorn. "So I appreciate the perils of moneylending. I don't want to portray a purely despicable villain."

But he and Burbage want the "villain" to be Jewish. Does he think I can provide a religionist's perspective? "Will, then wouldn't a tale about a Christian violating his religious doctrine be more dramatic? He'd experience more internal turmoil."

Will reached toward Amelia, pleading for understanding. "Perhaps, but that's not what Burbage is demanding and I can't defy him. He believes miserly Jews make good dramatic foils—ones that audiences like railing against."

"Obviously he does. Are you asking me to help write it and risk my safety too?"

"I'd like you to write all of it. Nobody will know. You'll be in no danger. By the time it's finished, the furor over Marlowe will be forgotten, and if there are any Jewish conspiracies, I'll know about them. And they'll have been defanged."

Amelia loathed this plan and Will's desire to shift his risk to her, although she didn't believe Jews were complicit in Marlowe's murder. She debated how strenuously to object. She swallowed hard, tasting bile. "But do we want to incite people's need to hate others so Burbage can reap greater profits?"

"That's—that's not my intention," stammered Will.

"But, indeed, that's what we'll be doing."

The sun broke through the clouds and Will removed his black coat, while appearing to gather his thoughts. "Not necessarily, the Jewish moneylender could possess complex motives and be more interested in protecting his interests than seeking revenge. When you craft the plot and create his character, you could give him two faces that conflict with each other: the humane and the repulsive."

"Humane and repulsive? That's quite a combination."

"Amelia, you can write it so audiences see something of themselves in both the moneylender and the borrower."

Amelia gazed up at the leafy trees filtering the sun's rays. She tried coming to terms with this dilemma and appreciated Will's desire to create nuanced characters. *Perhaps it's better if I write this drama rather than someone unsympathetic. If Will needs Burbage, so do I since I need Will. But am I selling my soul to the Devil?*

Amelia pressed her fingers to the hamsa draped around her neck. "Will, I'll do this if we promise to avoid defaming an individual or people."

Will sighed. His shoulders relaxed. "Agreed, we need not feed people's worst prejudices."

Will's comment did nothing to lessen Amelia's anxiety. She felt trapped. To satisfy Burbage, she would need to create an odious Jewish lender. To appease herself, the character must possess sympathetic, justifiable qualities so audiences understand his angst and his motives. This could not be a demeaning, repugnant tale like *The Jew of Malta*.

Now she noticed Will had a strange look in his eyes, as though, like Henry, he suspected her of being Jewish. She twirled strands of her coarse hair nervously. *Does he know about Alphonso's background and curious as to why I married him, of all people? Has he heard murmurs that several of the Queen's musicians are Jews, and Alphonso is among them, as was my father? If so, I can't allow him to dwell on them.*

"Do you have a working title?" she asked.

"'The Jewish Lender of London.' I like the sound of it."

Amelia recoiled then gathered her thoughts. "Let's not imitate Marlowe to that degree. I propose we shorten it to 'The Lender of London.'"

Amelia contemplated ideas for *Lender* over the next few days but a dramatic storyline eluded her. To jog her thinking, she strode to the River Thames with her lute and a satchel containing parchments, quills, and an ink jar. She settled on a boulder along the banks, watching river craft sail downstream. She rested her lute on her lap and strummed another Venetian melody from her childhood, believing lighthearted music could spell her sense of foreboding and grave misgivings.

When she finished a sweet song, she felt better but not inspired. She pulled several parchments from her satchel and stared at them blankly as the sun emerged from behind a cloud—its rays brightening the sheets before her eyes. Amelia squinted, seeing something she'd not observed before—tiny maroon flecks on the parchments, which were made from the hide of a lamb or goat. They must be blood specks not bleached out completely when the parchments were limed, she thought. How odd that they'd escaped her notice until now.

Suddenly, inspiration steamed through her. She wanted to escape Alphonso's clutches. She wished to show Henry his roots. She felt compelled to affirm her own heritage to write this play. She needed a dramatic way to keep audiences riveted. And, she thought, she knew exactly how to accomplish them all.

13

LONDON, JUNE 1593

Amelia contemplated the different parts of her plan. She'd contrived a clever twist for *Lender* to create dramatic tension. Persuading Will to agree should be easy. But how would he react to her announcement? She had to consider the best way to broach the subject. How would Enid respond? Lord Hunsdon? Would Alphonso explode at the news? That discussion she dreaded most. She'd find the right moment.

On Tuesday, June 22, the high noon sun brightened the city as Londoners enjoyed a rare cloudless day amidst the city's bleak conditions. In a red quilted jacket worn over a light blue frock and ivory underskirt, Amelia stepped from the resplendent sunlight into The Horn's dark interior. She saw only shadowy faces while her eyes adjusted to the dim light. She heard Will call her name before recognizing his features. He waved from a table near the rear where patrons still appeared as gray ghosts.

Amelia hung her valise on the chair and sat opposite him.

"I've barely slept," Will confessed, looking drawn. "I'm worried about my children, especially Hamnet, who's more vulnerable to the plague than his sisters."

"These are wretched times, especially for a parent," Amelia said.

Will sighed with resignation. "How will I support my family with the theaters closed? I'll be dependent on Anne's family, farmers who mock my poor husbandry skills. Still, I'm leaving for Stratford-upon-Avon tomorrow."

Amelia leaned across the table. She sniffed ale on his breath and thought he must have tippled several mugs before she arrived. His eyes looked heavy, weary with worry, and his shoulders slumped. "Will, are you all right?"

Will stretched taller in his seat, showing less of his worry and more of his intense curiosity. "I'll be fine. I see a fresh glow about you."

"I have ideas for *The Lender of...London*," she said.

"Tell me."

Amelia clasped her hands and placed them on the table. "However, to truly explore them, I'm going to Venice, perhaps for as long as two or three years."

Will's jaw dropped. "But why?"

"I must make a dramatic change. I must flee my miserable life with Alphonso. He drains the creativity from my soul." Then she rushed to add, "And I'll be far from danger should someone in London hear about *Lender* and take offense."

She noticed Will's apprehension. He had a way of bulging his eyes when something concerned him. But his reaction triggered a fresh burst of energy for her. Clearly, he valued their collaboration.

"Will, my work with you is vitally important. We inspire each other. Look what we did with *Titus Andronicus*. The Theatre has been overflowing for months."

"And we wrote it faster and enjoyed it more," added Will, pleased at the triumph of their combined work.

"I cherish our partnership, even though I'm behind the curtain. This need not stop because I'm going to Venice."

Will rubbed his eyes, obviously having doubts. "How can we collaborate when you'll be hundreds of miles away?"

"We'll use couriers. Since I'll be writing *Lender* by myself, I need only send the completed version. And I imagine Venice will inspire fresh ideas for new scripts, which we can send back and forth. We won't lose much time, especially with the theaters closed."

He still looked unconvinced, so she added, "Since you'll be in Stratford, we'll be apart regardless."

Will managed a smile that seemed forced to Amelia. "True, but I won't be staying there for years. I'll return when the plague has passed."

She saw in his eyes that his thoughts were racing ahead, and sure enough, he asked, "How can you afford to go to Venice?"

"I've saved some money, and with Lord Hunsdon's monthly beneficence I can pay for Henry and Enid. Will, I promise, this arrangement will work."

"Why Venice?"

"I have cousins there, whom I met when I visited with my father as a little girl. I'll stay with them."

"I see." Will looked forlorn, like being abandoned.

She felt a tinge of guilt, realizing he would miss discussing script ideas and projects with her. Nonetheless, she decided to press ahead with her thoughts about *Lender*. "I plan to change the venue of *The Lender of London* to Venice. Most Englishmen have never been outside the country. A play set in a foreign land will intrigue them."

Will finished her thought. "And you'll be able to create that foreign flavor because you'll be there."

"Yes. I'll be able to describe settings vividly, giving audiences greater insight into life in a different country."

Will's demeanor shifted, as though envisioning the possibilities. To move the conversation past this point, she explained about the faded blood specks on the parchment and how they triggered an emotion-laden idea for the play. Will acted puzzled at first, as if not seeing the connection. Then his face brightened.

"Aha, so the moneylender is due a pound of flesh if the loan is not repaid, and the judge allows it so long as he does not extract a drop of blood."

"Precisely. Imagine the lender's exuberance when the judge declares that he's won his due, then his horror when he hears the second part."

Will's eyes sparkled with excitement. He sprang to his feet, and with his posture and facial expressions portrayed the lender's emotional veer from joy to despair. "That's brilliant! The lender will realize in one dramatic moment that he's won and lost at the same time!"

Amelia met with Lord Hunsdon the next day. She entered Hunsdon House wearing an olive silk dress with wide sleeves and high neckline—a style that appealed to him. She brought her son so the Henrys could meet. They took their accustomed places in the large parlor she knew so well. The tall windows were open wide and a summer breeze wafted through. Upon sitting she realized she missed the rich feel of plush velvet fabrics and cool textured linen. He handed Amelia a chalice of a crisp, pale golden wine, then gently lifted Henry from her arms.

"He's a handsome lad," said Lord Hunsdon, raising the baby to eye level. The Henrys smiled at one another. "I see a resemblance. I think he has my eyes and mouth."

"I hope dearly that's true," said Amelia. "My fervent wish is that Henry is your son as well. May he become a good man like you."

She proceeded to tell him her plans. He asked what attracted her to Venice then added, "It's a beautiful city but there's an invisible undercurrent to its politics. It's a deceptive place. Be careful of entanglements with powerful people."

"Henry, it warms my heart that you remain interested in my welfare."

"I always will be. Is the money I have placed in your account sufficient to pay for your passage, and Enid's too?"

Amelia kissed him on his bearded cheek. "Henry, dear, it is. Your generosity has made this entire excursion possible."

When Amelia returned to her modest home, Enid jumped with delight when Amelia asked her to go. "I never thought I'd see anyplace beyond England. How long will we stay?"

"At least a year, perhaps longer. But there's something you must know."

Enid stood with serious expression as Amelia continued.

"I trust you. What I am about to say relies on that trust. If you come with me, you'd discover it in due course. So it's best you know beforehand since you may wish to reconsider."

Enid looked worried. "I don't know what that might be. But you can trust me."

"Enid, I have long kept a secret and so has Alphonso. We are Jews. We aren't Christian," she added, to emphasize the point. "No one else knows beyond our family and a few Jewish friends, except Lord Hunsdon. Not even Lady Susan, because Judaism is forbidden in England."

Enid appeared confused by this turn of events. "But weren't you and Henry baptized?"

"We were, but only to appear Christian."

"Do you believe in Jesus Christ?"

"I believe he was an extraordinary man but not the savior. He was Jewish, actually—and may have been a rabbi killed by the Romans. But that's all."

"I know nothing about Jews," said Enid. "But you've been kind to me. That's all I need to know."

Now that her conversations with Will, Henry, and Enid had gone well, Amelia braced to break the news to Alphonso. Contemplating it churned her stomach, because she knew it would trigger a confrontation. She would have to broach the topic when he was not drunk or hung-over. It couldn't be after a night of gambling losses. The best time would be after he won or the following morning, when he thought his luck had changed.

A few days later, Alphonso came home in a good mood, a rare event. He'd won more than he'd lost gambling and thought he'd found a method to boost his odds and future winnings. He explained it with glee, like a little boy. Amelia also saw the longing in his eyes for intimacy and knew obliging him would help her cause.

Amelia took his hand and led him into their bedroom. She splashed on her favorite woodland-spice fragrance. She lit candles and undressed seductively, staying within his reach. She saw Alphonso's eyes widen and his body react in anticipation. She knew what he liked even if reluctant to provide it. But tonight she would give the best performance of their marriage. She slipped her hand under his belt and reached for his already stiff member.

The next morning, Enid prepared breakfast for them and then took Henry outside for fresh air. Amelia and Alphonso ate together for the first time in weeks. They consumed heels of bread, cheese, and sardines in silence.

After he had his fill, Amelia said, "Alphonso, it's time we were truly honest with each other. We're married but have little in common. We don't share many interests or like the same pursuits. We have little to discuss. We don't suit each other, even when we try like last night."

Alphonso's body tensed as if expecting bad news. She couldn't read his impassive face but nonetheless went on, "Circumstances have joined us together. Neither of us likes it. The tension between us is often palpable. I need a break. You may as well."

Alphonso became surly. "Come out with it. What are you trying to say?"

"I'm going to visit my family in Venice. I don't know for how long." Relief descended on Amelia once she'd spoken the words. She believed he would welcome time free from her as well.

"What about *your* son, Henry?"

"I'll take him with me. Enid too."

Alphonso's face turned red. He leaned across the table until his face glared inches from Amelia's. His breath reeked of sour sardines. "You told her before me, your husband? You conspired behind my back!"

Amelia remained calm. It took all her nerve not to lean away but to stay composed. "I had to ensure this journey was possible. I didn't expect your approval."

"What about me? What am I to do?"

Amelia knew he'd loathe giving up the money she provided for his gambling, drinking, and other escapades.

"What do you mean, what about you? You're a musician for Queen Elizabeth's court."

Alphonso withdrew from the face-to-face confrontation. "When are you leaving?"

"In six weeks."

Flummoxed by this news, Alphonso reverted to habit. He stood abruptly, knocking over his chair. He stormed out the door, slamming it as he left—rattling dirty breakfast dishes still on the table.

Amelia expected this boorish behavior. Still, his naked hostility shook her. Perhaps, after an absence of a few years, his heart would grow fonder, but she doubted it.

14

DEBTFORD, ENGLAND, LATE SUMMER 1593

Departure day. Lord Hunsdon had made the arrangements and now they rode in his carriage across the River Thames to the port. Amelia's mood lightened; she was glad to be breaking free of her life in London and starting a long respite from Alphonso. But this lightheartedness mixed with her apprehension about the long voyage and what she might encounter in Venice.

Enid, holding baby Henry, sat opposite her and Lord Hunsdon. Soon Deptford Dockyard on the river's south bank came into view accompanied by the stench of spoiled fish. Deptford, once a small fishing village near London, became an important port when Henry VIII selected the site for royal shipbuilding, repairing, and provisioning. It grew in prominence in 1581 when Queen Elizabeth knighted Francis Drake, the legendary sea captain on his ship *Golden Hind*, after he had circumnavigated the world and returned with a bounty of spices and booty captured from the Spanish.

Today, Deptford was a busy mercantile port as well as a Royal Navy Dockyard. The summer heat and humidity hung in the air. Ominous clouds stretched to the horizon. Dock workers and seamen loaded huge bales of wool onto ships in berth. Other ships were under repair and hammer strikes echoed along the wharf. Vapors with the distinct odor of tar, used to create watertight seals in hull planks, carried in the wind. Workers scurried and foremen barked orders.

Lord Hunsdon had booked them passage on a Venetian merchant ship. In Venice, they would stay with Amelia's cousins, descendants of her uncle Jacomo. Jacomo's daughter, Orsetta Bassano, had died several years ago, as had her husband Santo, who inherited Jacomo's Venetian instrument-making business. Santo had worked with Jacomo for many years and learned the craft from him. Upon marrying Orsetta, to honor his father-in-law, Santo adopted the surname Bassano as his own and became a highly regarded instrument maker in his own right.

In 1582, Santo invented the bassonelli, a double-reed woodwind instrument. Nearing the end of his life, he arranged with the Doge, the chief magistrate and most powerful political leader in Venice, for the patent to be recorded in his son's name, Giovanni—whom everyone called Zuane. Zuane composed music and played for the Doge's *Serenita*.

Zuane and his wife, Miriam, in their early thirties, owned the Venetian instrument-making business now, but his real passion was composing, playing and directing. Miriam ran the shop. She, too, came from a musical family and played the flute, lute, and violetta, a forerunner of the violin with three strings instead of four. She learned the business and admired their artists' craftsmanship. She handled the business side and resolved problems rather than making instruments herself.

Before settling on a ship, Lord Hunsdon met with captains recommended to him and inspected their vessels to determine suitability for two women and a baby. He selected *La Fulvia* and Captain Natale because of his reputation for protecting women onboard and treating them with dignity.

En route to the port, Henry explained, "*La Fulvia* will sail east down the Thames to the English Channel, then head southwest skirting the English coast to the Atlantic Ocean."

Amelia listened to his descriptions while getting her last glimpses of London. She observed people in threadbare clothing trudging to jobs or to market and the well-dressed merchants and upper classes traveling on horses or in carriages. She glanced at the half-timbered buildings and stone Tudor mansions. She wrinkled her nose at the grimy cobblestone streets smelling of sludge and garbage. Looking the other way, she saw masted ships glide silently through the muddy Thames.

"The voyage will be about twenty-five days," said Henry. "Onboard you'll be living in cramped quarters. The cabins are spare. You will all share one with two cots and a rudimentary crib."

Flags of English, Dutch, and Portuguese vessels fluttered gently as ships were unloaded or prepared to sail. Amelia's eyes darted from one ship to another, marveling at their heft and the agility of their crews as they carried supplies, climbed masts, and checked rigging.

La Fulvia, an old galleon with three masts, appeared scarred and weathered from prior voyages. It flew the Venetian flag depicting a regal gold-winged lion on a red backdrop. A long oak beak protruded from the bow, tipped with a lion figurehead, as if to punctuate its prowess. Although built for trade, it carried seven cannons on the port and starboard sides. Amelia judged the ship to be one hundred and twenty feet long and twenty-five feet wide, and sturdier than expected.

Amelia treaded unsteadily over the boarding plank with her leather valise, loaded with books and writing materials, slung over her right shoulder. In her left hand she carried a large canvas bag. She hesitated twice when the plank shifted slightly. The ropes fastening *La Fulvia* to the dock crackled as the river current tugged the ship against its moorings. Amelia quickened her pace to get onboard before losing her balance. Enid followed carrying Henry and a small bag.

Amelia lowered her luggage to the deck and stood by the rail. She waved to Lord Hunsdon watching from the pier. He waved back and smiled. "Bon voyage."

Tears welled in Amelia's eyes. She projected her voice over the buzz of activity on the dock, "Goodbye, Henry. Thank you. You've been the kindest of anyone to me."

Once Enid stepped onboard, Henry turned and walked down the pier. Amelia watched until he disappeared from view. Of all her farewells, this was the hardest.

Wind whisked through Amelia's hair as she and Enid traversed the main deck. They were the only women onboard, a circumstance well noticed by crew members checking the rigging, preparing sails, and stowing supplies, including barrels of water and food, one piled high with bruised apples. Lord Hunsdon had paid Captain Natale to look after them and ensure safe passage. Natale introduced himself and showed them to their narrow cabin next to his, furnished with two cots and a crate nailed to a table to serve as Henry's crib. Then the captain introduced them to another passenger, Rafael Tolendano, a textile trader from Venice who traveled back and forth to London each season.

"Is it an easy voyage?" Enid, clearly nervous, asked Rafael.

"Most of it. But expect strong winds, hard rain, and rough seas when we sail through the Strait of Gibraltar."

Soon after, *La Fulvia*'s crew pulled in the ropes mooring the ship to the pier, lifted the anchor, and hoisted sails. The vessel drifted forward, swayed slightly, and slowly moved down river. Once in the open water, the sails billowed and waves slapped the bow as the ship moved south with the British island shrinking behind.

Amelia watched Enid squinting at the seemingly endless sea. All color had drained from her friend's face. Enid's lips quivered as she held Henry snug to her chest. Amelia eased the baby from Enid's arms. "You look stricken."

"I've not seen the sea before today. We're not going to sail to the edge, are we—or over it?"

Rafael, standing nearby replied, "Don't worry, there is no edge. The sea just goes on and on around the Earth until it washes onto more land."

Enid pointed to the horizon. "But...but I can see the edge. There's nothing beyond it. The Earth is flat like a pot lid."

"It only appears so," explained Rafael. "The Earth is more like an onion."

Without warning, Enid stumbled to the deck rail and heaved over the side. Amelia placed her hand on Enid's shoulder. When Enid raised her head, her blanched face resembled the gray storm clouds above.

A strong gust of wind made the ship surge forward and it leaned leeward.

"Oh! I'm going to retch again," cried Enid. She hung her head over the side and grasped Amelia's hand. "I've heard the stories and seen the awful drawings. We don't know what's out there."

"Enid, dear, this ship has sailed these waters many times. The crew wouldn't endanger themselves. We'll be safe."

After Enid recovered, Amelia remembered the envelope Will had given it her at their last meeting. His instructions were clear: Don't unseal it until the ship sails beyond the English coast. She retrieved it from her cabin uncertain what to expect:

> *Amelia, the joy I saw on your face as you played the*
> *harpsichord inspired this poem:*
> *With thy sweet fingers, when thou gently sway'st*
> *The wiry concord that mine ear confounds,*
> *Do I envy those jacks that nimble leap*
> *To kiss the tender inward of thy hand...*

Amelia pondered the sonnet by the dim light of the portal window. Questions streamed through her mind: What did Will mean by it? Was he jealous of the harpsichord keys because she caressed them with her fingers and he wanted her fingers to be touching him?

How should I reply? I wish not to hurt his feelings or lead him astray, nor do I wish to jeopardize our literary collaboration. I must consider this carefully.

Amelia stowed the sonnet deep inside her bag. She emerged from the dingy cabin onto the wind-swept deck. Enid, still looking pale, waited with Henry wrapped in a blanket. With thoughts of Will swirling in her mind, Amelia gently grasped Enid's arm. Together they walked toward the stern beneath full sails at mid-ship, feeling *La Fulvia* roll beneath their feet as the wind blew their long hair and full skirts from back to front, and ocean mist moistened their faces. Henry's eyes darted, watching the billowing sails. The clattering of ropes against the masts and wind's swoosh in the canvases seemed to mesmerize him.

The romance of this adventure, which had once swept through Amelia, began to recede. She'd left all she knew behind, thrown to the wind. She hoped everything she had spent so much time creating would be intact upon her return. But she had doubts.

The seas remained calm during the next two days and Amelia paced the deck, thinking about *The Lender of Venice*, making a few notes but little progress.

Gale-force winds and heavy rains rocked the ship as it traversed the Strait of Gibraltar. The masts seemed on the brink of snapping as the sails stretched to the bursting point until the crew scrambled to roll them in. *La Fulvia* pitched violently. The deck lurched as the ship plunged though the high, choppy waves.

Terror stabbed through Amelia like the lightning bolts overhead. She shook with the vibrating rumbles of thunder. Enid, her face ghastly, knelt on the cabin floor clutching a post, praying aloud. Amelia hugged Henry to her chest and whispered reassuring words to him. She watched his chest rise and fall with his breathing. He wailed and convulsed when thunder and lightning ripped the sky. Amelia discovered that swaying Henry in her arms and singing his name allayed her fears as well.

Eventually, they emerged into calmer Mediterranean waters and clear skies on the eastern side of the strait. Amelia sighed with relief when the crew again hoisted *La Fulvia*'s sails. Minutes later she watched a large seagull dive to the water, pluck a protesting fish from the sea, and carry it away in its curved orange beak.

La Fulvia enjoyed favorable winds as she neared the journey's end. She sailed into the Venetian Lagoon and the Basin of San Marco at the south end of Venice's Grand Canal. She passed warships anchored by the *Arsenale* on her way to the pier at *San Zaccaria* near Saint Mark's Square. Ships of all shapes and sizes crowded the wharfs. Seagulls flew alongside the galleon and cawed as if welcoming them.

Amelia with Henry and Enid gathered along the portside railing as the ship trolled toward its berth. Venice boasted three- and four-story light-colored *palazzos*, many with Moorish-influenced designs. The setting sun highlighted their grand facades with gold and silver washes. A tall redbrick clock tower with a band of white arches punctuated the skyline. The spires of Saint Mark's Cathedral rose to its right. The elegant *Palazzo Ducale,* or Doge's Palace, a large rectangular building featuring white Gothic loggias and lacy trim, dominated the waterfront. A sailor explained that it also housed the senate and courts—and was connected to a dreaded prison by the "Bridge of Sighs."

La Fulvia eased her way to the dock, slipping past an aging three-masted galley anchored offshore and smaller ones tied to the pier. Several men were moving crates and barrels off a galleon similar to *La Fulvia*.

Amelia turned to her voyage's companion as the ship's crew tossed docking lines to men on the pier. "Rafael, when is your next trip to London?"

"In three months. Why?"

"Could you courier materials to my colleague, Will Shakespeare?"

"Most certainly. I'll contact you a few days before departing."

With the ship calmed, wobbling in the gentle waves, Amelia scanned faces on the wharf, hoping to recognize her cousins. Nobody looked familiar. She studied everyone carefully. All appeared to be waiting for someone else. Off the other side of the deck, the sun was setting like a fiery red disc.

A brisk wind whipped Amelia's face as a momentary panic seized her. *What will I do? Where will we go if nobody meets us?*

She saw the same look of trepidation on Enid's face and realized she had to take charge. She had reached her father's boyhood homeland. She had family ready to welcome her.

"Enid, let's go ashore?"

15

"**A**melia's ship should have arrived three days ago," commented an uneasy Miriam Bassano to her husband Zuane.

She paced the rooftop garden perched in *Il Ghetto*, the Jewish enclave of Venice, clutching her hand and praying *La Fulvia* would arrive before sundown and the start of Rosh Hashanah, the Jewish New Year. Miriam's fervent wish was for Amelia to arrive safely and in time to join them for their holiday dinner.

"Delays are inevitable at sea. She'll be here soon enough," responded Zuane in his reassuring voice.

Miriam looked across the rooftop terrace where their fourteen-year-old adopted daughter, Julia, and her older brother, Zev, huddled with friends, other family, and members of their small synagogue. Julia and Zev's mother died after Julia was born and their father passed a year ago from influenza. Zev, now seventeen, inherited the family's wine-exporting business and Miriam and Zuane took in Julia.

For the third day, Miriam and Zuane sent their maid, Luisa, to the port at San Zaccaria to meet *La Fulvia*. This time, Miriam instructed her to wait on the wharf until the last ship docked, then report to her at the dinner. As each day passed without any sign, Miriam's fears grew that the ship had sunk or been victimized by pirates.

During this year's Rosh Hashanah, a newly published Jewish *Book of Customs*—the pride of the Venetian Jewish community—would be unveiled. *Venice Minhogimbukh* was a Yiddish translation of a scholarly version, *Sefer Minhagim,* first written in Hebrew two hundred years earlier. Although most Sephardic Jews—those descended from Spanish Jewry, like Miriam and Zuane—spoke Ladino, they and most others living in Il Ghetto were also fluent in Yiddish, the inside language of central and eastern European Jews.

La Fulvia was the last ship to dock that day. Men on the wharf secured mooring lines to iron bollards as the late afternoon sun cast the vessel's long shadow onto the pier. Luisa, unsure of Amelia's appearance, other than having rusty-brown hair and olive skin, which could describe many women in Venice, searched for a twenty-four year-old woman with a baby. She watched passengers disembark but saw no such combination. The closest were two women evidently traveling together, including a light-skinned woman carrying an infant. The description didn't quite fit. She waited for more people to disembark. Finally, when they were the only ones left, Luisa overcame her shyness and approached them. "Could you be Amelia Bassano?"

"I am. And this is my friend, Enid Fletcher."

Zuane recited the traditional blessings over the wine and bread then cut an apple into wedges. He passed around the slices, which everyone dipped into honey. They wished each other a sweet year and then bit into the crisp fruit. The diners watched a bright orange sun disappear in the western sky, its glow radiating from the heavens, creating a spiritual moment marking the close of one year and the beginning of another.

Miriam, her ears attuned to every sound, stretched her head forward upon hearing footfalls coming from the narrow bridge connecting Il Ghetto to the rest of Venice. She peeked over the rooftop railing, careful not to soil her coral gown, and squinted in the dark moonless night in hopes of seeing the plaza below. After a few moments, she pushed back from the edge, realizing nothing was discernable in the shadowy *Campo Ghetto Nuovo* or the passageway leading into it. A minute later, Luisa entered through the rooftop garden door. Behind her came Amelia carrying the baby along with a woman Miriam didn't know.

Miriam's anxiety turned to instant relief. A broad grin lit her angular face.

Amelia smiled back. Her windblown hair fell in tangles and the late evening light made the gray smudges under her drooping eyes appear darker.

"Welcome! We are so glad you're here!" beamed Miriam.

"As are we," said Amelia.

"To all of you, *L'shanah tovah*. I wish you a good new year," said Miriam.

"*L'shanah tovah*," responded Amelia.

Miriam swept her hand over Henry's feathery hair. "You look exhausted, except for your adorable baby. His eyes are shining in the moonlight."

Amelia scanned the garden and candlelit tables laden with abundant quantities of roasted goose, fennel, apples, challah, and wine. She drew in the fresh air filled with the succulent aroma of the well-prepared food.

Weepy emotions rose within her. For the first time she'd celebrate a Jewish holiday openly, and now joyously as a mother. She believed sailing to Venice had been the right choice.

Amelia awakened to the warmth of morning sun beaming through the arched windows of her bedchamber. Before even opening her eyes, she smelled artichoke frying. Rising from her bed, she encountered a horrifying sight in the mirror. Her curled wiry hair resembled an oversized bird's nest shredded in a windstorm. She brushed out knots and kinks, feeling the pain of hair stretching from her scalp. When she looked presentable, she changed into a long camel-colored gown and ruffled white blouse, and went downstairs.

Enid had already risen and was feeding Henry in the dining room. Amelia took the opportunity to go outside with Miriam to see the Bassano's home and studio in the morning light.

They lived on the second and third floors of a four-story building along the Grand Canal, north of the new Rialto Bridge near the canal Rio di Noale. The cream-hued building had four Moorish windows on the middle two floors. The center windows opened onto balconies overlooking the water. The Bassano instrument-making studio occupied the first floor, boasting a vaulted ceiling and thick stone columns.

The studio had entrances on the canal and landsides, as did the residence. Three moss-covered steps separated the studio entry from the Grand Canal. Grated iron gates guarded wide double doors. Through this entrance supplies were unloaded from transport boats and gondolas. The residence entrance was to the right of the industrial studio doors and two steps higher. Beyond a carved oak door, stairs led to the second-floor salon with twenty-foot ceilings. A round mosaic of a rabbit sitting behind a stylized lute over a background of yellow tiles adorned each side of the building, identifying the business both from the street and canal.

Miriam explained that the Bassanos were among a few Jewish families living in Venice prior to the establishment of Il Ghetto earlier in the century, when many Jews had emigrated from states to the north in central and eastern Europe. More recently it had attracted Jewish families originally from the Iberian Peninsula. Il Ghetto, occupying an island once known for its copper and cannon foundries, had been designated to house and manage this growing foreign Jewish population. Miriam told Amelia the term "ghetto" came from a Venetian word for "slag."

Venice included over one hundred small islands connected by nearly four hundred bridges, crossing one hundred and fifty canals. With the prominent exception of the new Rialto Bridge, most spans, like those connecting Il Ghetto to the rest of Venice, were set at street level and with wood plank surfaces. Horses could clatter over them, but boats could not go beneath. A political debate raged about raising the spans so boats could navigate the canals, but that might necessitate banning horses.

The Bassano's' position in Venetian society—as early immigrants, accomplished musicians, and successful business people providing instruments to the Doge and other aristocrats—afforded them the privilege of living in Venice proper. The Bassanos avoided drawing attention to their religious practices and few Venetians knew them as Jews.

Once back inside, Zuane explained, "We don't present ourselves as Jews to gentiles. Most assume we're Christian, which is best for business. The Doge pretends not to know. Some of our co-religionists in Il Ghetto are skeptical about our authenticity. But we know who we are."

At the dining table, Luisa served fried artichoke, fresh apples, and cheeses for breakfast. Amelia described the voyage and the rough weather and seas when they sailed through the Strait of Gibraltar.

She turned to Zuane. "I'm curious about the mosaic in each side of the studio. I understand how the lute represents the musical-instrument making business, but what's the point of the rabbit?"

"We're asked that occasionally. I have different explanations depending on who inquires. To some I say it's because our service is fast and nimble—like a rabbit. But the real reason is because the Jewish ghetto is shaped like a rabbit's foot. And we etch, in a discreet place, a rabbit's foot on each instrument we make. It's our signature."

Loud voices from outside startled Amelia and drew her attention toward the tall windows. Bright sun streamed in along with an argument.

"What do you mean, this lute is no good and you're not paying me?"

"The soundboard is too thin and the ribs are too thick. That affects the sound quality. If we can't sell it, I can't pay you."

Miriam informed Amelia, "That's our supervisor, Arturo Valiero, explaining our policy. The hot-headed man sounds like Guido, whom we hired last month."

"I want to hear what Signore Bassano has to say about this," demanded Guido.

"Signore Bassano doesn't run the studio. I do. My boss is Signora Bassano. Speak with her if you like."

"That wench? She won't fix this."

Amelia noticed Miriam's impassive expression as she rose. "Excuse me, Amelia, I better settle this matter. Join me if you wish."

They descended the stairs and stepped through the residence door onto the canal bank. A few gondolas plied the channel along the far shore. By the studio dock, Guido appeared ready to strike the older Arturo, who faced him with hands on his hips.

"The signora is here to back you, with an entourage," said Guido.

"You have it wrong, Guido," said Miriam. "Arturo doesn't need me to interfere. If he says your work is poor, then it is."

"Look at this lute. It's beautiful."

Miriam nodded graciously and seemed to smile with her eyes and lips. "It is beautiful. Our customers, who are expert musicians, want beautiful instruments..." Her tone and expression shifted, becoming serious. "But they won't buy them if the sound is bad. Everyone loses, including us. We lose because expensive materials are wasted and orders are delayed. That upsets customers. We aren't asking you to pay for those losses."

"I need money to feed my family."

Miriam kept her tone soft. "If you ordered a pushcart and it came with wheels that didn't turn, would you accept it? Would you pay for it?"

Guido crossed his muscular arms. "No, but that's not the point."

"What is the point?"

"Signora, my family is hungry. I have rent to pay."

"Arturo, how much rework will be necessary to fix this?" asked Miriam.

The supervisor waved his hand at her. "Too much to make it worth the time. We can re-use the neck. We might be able to salvage the shell. I won't know until I look closer at the ribbing. Maybe we could sell it to a student or beginner, but we'll need to disclose the flaws."

"If we did, what could we get for it?"

"Perhaps thirty percent of the normal price."

Miriam turned her attention back to the worker. "Guido, the best I can offer is thirty percent of your pay. If we can't sell this lute in a month, I'll deduct it from your wages."

"That's not fair."

"Do you want it or not?"

"What choice do I have?" he muttered.

Miriam kept her gaze steady as a breeze surged through her wavy brown hair. "If this happens again, we won't negotiate at all. This is the first and last time."

Guido took the money but looked back with a sneer as he stomped away.

"I doubt he'll show again for work," said Amelia.

Back in the residence, Amelia said, "You didn't yield to his demands but found a way to pay him something."

"Arturo found it. Workers won't respect you if you don't protect your interests, especially a woman. I don't want Guido or his family to starve, but I must safeguard the business. At stake are not just our livelihoods but those of our employees as well. If we don't make money, I can't retain them."

Miriam explained how she managed the Bassano instrument-making business and the joys and challenges of supervising craftsmen. She described her love of music and how enamored she had become with the process of designing and making the instruments. Miriam also described Zuane's passion for composing and orchestrating. They complemented each other's talents.

Amelia described memories of her father. She explained that, like Miriam, she wasn't a fine musician but enjoyed playing, and the melodic structures resonated with her poetic side.

Miriam said, "In two weeks, I'm travelling to Cremona to visit friends and fellow instrument makers. The Bassano studio doesn't compete with them because we have different specialties. In Cremona, I'll see two of the finest violinmakers. One is Amati, founded by Andrea Amati and since his death is run by his sons, Antonio and Girolamo. I'll also meet with Gasparo da Salò, who is another great violinmaker. Would you like to come along?"

Amelia glowed with delighted. "I'd love to."

"About halfway between Venice and Cremona is Verona—a beautiful city filled with old Roman buildings. And Bassano del Grappa is only a few miles from the main road between Venice and Verona. Would you like to see the town where your family lived and from which they took their surname?"

"I would indeed! Enid will care for Henry."

That evening Amelia walked to the Rialto Bridge and peered down the Grand Canal, watching people stroll along its banks and boats slip beneath. She continued at a leisurely pace to the Mercato Rialto, where fish sellers were cleaning stalls and packing their wares for the night. On the far side, she saw Julia pass under an arch and hurriedly look back, shaking the sandy curls that cascaded halfway down her back. To Amelia it seemed she was checking to see if anyone was following her. Julia then ducked down a narrow passageway.

Curious, Amelia hastened in the same direction. Upon reaching the street, she saw Julia disappear around a curve. When she reached it, Julia was nowhere to be seen. As Amelia walked on, a young man with black wavy hair and piercing blue eyes surged briskly past her, searching to the left and right. Amelia turned to see him pivot into an alley. She backtracked and saw Julia step from behind a wall, kiss him, and fall into his arms.

Amelia hesitated for a moment as she absorbed the scene—*a secret lover's rendezvous*—then strode away.

16

VENICE, OCTOBER 1593

Amelia appraised the unsteady craft powered by a tall gondolier slicing toward the Bassano studio dock. This flimsy boat would take her and Miriam to the port. It was only a short distance but strong winds were ruffling the canal waters and the wider basin could be treacherous.

Miriam seemed unfazed which Amelia found slightly reassuring. From the slippery stone steps they handed their bags to the gondolier who stowed them in front. The long boat teetered as they stepped inside. A crisp autumn chill pervaded the dawn air. The weak morning sun had emerged from behind buildings on the east side of the Grand Canal, casting long shadows into the water. Amelia shivered as the gondolier guided them under the Rialto Bridge, which spanned the waterway at its narrowest point. They wended around the next bend past elegant palazzos until entering the wide Basin of San Marco. Here the sun accented the water's silvery ripples. After passing the Doge's Palace they docked at San Zaccaria.

They boarded a waiting ferry, sailed west across the Venetian Lagoon to the mainland, and hired a carriage driver. Two sturdy chestnut-brown horses pulled them west toward Verona, and the sound of their hooves soon changed from clip clop over the cobblestones near the port to muffled beats pounding rural dirt roads.

They passed near the town of Bassano del Grappa. Amelia knew little about it except the connection to her surname. As they went by Miriam asked, "Amelia, how much do you know about your family's history?"

"Not very much. My father died when I was seven and his brothers in England, my uncles, either died before my birth or when I was quite young. So I never heard old family stories. And their children, born in England, rarely discussed it."

Miriam said, "I'll explain what I know, which I learned from Orsetta, my mother-in-law.

"Jeronimo, your grandfather and Zuane's great grandfather, was the last of the Bassanos to live in Bassano del Grappa as an adult. His father, also named Baptista, used the nickname 'Piva,' meaning bagpipe because that's what he played. His wife, Andrea de Crespano, was also a musician. Together they founded the Bassano musical instrument-making business. Many fine musicians took note of their craftsmanship and ordered their lutes and bagpipes. They taught their craft to Jeronimo and he inherited the business, eventually expanding into horns and other wind instruments—all over a hundred years ago."

Amelia listened closely, her eyes riveted on Miriam who sat opposite her in the carriage.

"Jeronimo was a natural salesman," explained Miriam. "He built trusting relationships and sold instruments in

Venice. Around 1506, the Doge invited him to play the piffero, a double-reed woodwind, and he became known as 'Maestro Jeronimo.' The job offered access to the best musicians in Venice. Their standards were high and Jeronimo's instruments were the best. And so the business grew even more rapidly. Soon he began making instruments for musicians in Florence, Verona, Rome, Vienna, and Prague."

Amelia pondered this as she glanced at the woods outside the carriage. She tried imagining what such a shop would have looked like in the remote town beyond her sightline.

Miriam picked up where she left off. "Hostility toward Jews in Bassano del Grappa grew in the early 1500s. It became so vehement Jeronimo moved his family and the business to Venice around 1509—fortunately before '1516' occurred, as Orsetta and Jacomo referred to it. That year all Jews were expelled from Bassano del Grappa, and many sold their homes at a loss.

"1516 was also when the Doge established Il Ghetto as Venice's Jewish enclave. At the time it was an abandoned industrial site known for its foundries. He ordered Jews to live in the slag-strewn wasteland and remain inside at night. Guards only permitted doctors out after dark if called for in an emergency."

Amelia leaned forward, captivated by the story and curious to learn more. "Why wasn't Jeronimo forced to move his family and the studio to Il Ghetto?"

"By then Jeronimo's instrument-making business was well established in the Cannaregio section, and he'd developed warm relationships with the Doge and members of the

Great Council. Well liked, he played at state dinners and social events and kept his religious beliefs to himself, although the Doge must have known."

"The Doge made an exception?"

"I only know they weren't forced to move and continued practicing Judaism quietly."

Amelia asked, "Why did my father and his brothers move to England?"

"That's a fascinating story too. Jeronimo's six sons became musicians, and some like your father also became excellent instrument makers. Your father was the youngest son by several years and seventeen years younger than Jacomo, the oldest son.

"In 1529, after your father turned sixteen, an emissary of King Henry VIII visited Venice. That same year the Jewish community dedicated Venice's first synagogue in Il Ghetto, *Sinagoga Tedesca*. Henry's emissary met with the Doge. He was mysterious about his reasons, but requested a meeting with Venice's chief rabbi and other Jewish scholars. The Doge arranged it and also invited Jeronimo, perhaps because he could bridge the gap between the insular rabbis and the world of politics and commerce. He also wanted someone in the meeting he could trust."

"What did the emissary want?" asked Amelia.

"Henry VIII sent him to Venice to acquire theological justification for annulling his marriage to Katherine of Aragon, so he could marry the much younger and alluring Anne Boleyn. Of course, papal or Catholic authorities would not offer such spiritual advice, so he sought out rabbis."

Amelia laughed. "I suppose he had no other choice."

Miriam went on. "There were no rabbis in England he knew of, but he'd heard of the Venetian Jewish community and thus sent his representative."

"So while the king forbade Jews from living in England, he sought their help when it suited his purposes," mused Amelia aloud.

"Indeed, and that was the first time anyone in the Bassano family had met someone from the English court. Jeronimo told the emissary that he was a musician who played for the Doge, as did his sons, and was there to foster communication—since as a Jew he could relate with all the parties."

"But how does that lead to the Bassano brothers going to England?"

"That's the next part. The Doge held a palace banquet to honor the emissary. The Bassano brothers played at the event. Impressed, the emissary asked Jeronimo if he could meet with them all afterward. Gathering in a private room inside the Doge's palace, he called them virtuosos; then explained that King Henry, as an amateur musician and composer, was dissatisfied with his court players.

"He then asked, 'Could I entice any or all of you to move to England and join us as court musicians. We want to make the music in King Henry's court the best anywhere. I believe his Majesty would make an attractive offer.'"

Two days later they entered Cremona, where Miriam would meet with renowned violinmaker, Gasparo da Salò. He built handcrafted violins, and in good weather, like today, he worked under a canopy behind his house. When Miriam and Amelia approached the residence, they heard a shrill voice coming from the back.

"Why must I wait until my sister weds before I do? Renaldo wants to marry me now."

"Your older sister, Nicola, must be married first," said Gasparo.

"Who would marry her?" replied Bianca, his youngest daughter. "She's mean and her looks are far from appealing. I'll be an old maid before a man sees redeeming qualities in her."

"Be patient, Bianca. Tazio may be interested."

"Tazio? He's no match for her foul temper. She'll stampede over him."

Miriam whispered to Amelia, "I don't want to listen, but I don't want to interrupt either. They were fighting over this last year too. Gasparo wishes to marry off his oldest daughter before his younger daughter, who is beautiful and generally cheerful—except at this moment."

The discussion had come to a halt, as if no one wanted to be the next to speak. Miriam knocked on the door, and Bianca answered in a huff. "Hello, Signora Bassano. My papa is in back. Follow me."

"Hello, Gasparo. Are we interrupting anything important?"

"No, nothing that we haven't discussed countless times," he said wearily. "Please, have a seat."

Gasparo removed his work apron. His tools and several violin parts were spread before them on his worktable: the polished upper and lower bout and waist comprising the instrument's body; the long fingerboard topped with its tuning pegs and scroll; and the bridge, tailpiece, fine tuners, and chin rest. All appeared ready for assembly.

"Gasparo, meet my cousin from England, Signora Amelia Bassano Lanier. She's a musician but not a violinist."

"You should try the violin. It's the most refined instrument."

"Signore da Salò, I may," said Amelia. "Though I'm still mastering the lute and the harpsichord."

While Miriam and Gasparo met, Amelia excused herself and explored the neighborhood. The argument she had overheard gave her the kernel of an idea. She pulled a writing journal from her valise while walking through narrow streets lined with two- and three-story buildings capped with red tile roofs. Soon she reached the plaza by the Torrazzo bell tower and the Cremona Cathedral, called the Duomo. A plaque on the tower claiming it ascended two hundred and fifty arms and two ounces amused her.

Amelia settled on steps at the base of the sienna brick belfry, beneath its enormous astronomical clock. She scribbled notes, imaging a story about a man with two daughters. The younger one is beautiful and personable. Men seek her. Her older sister is plain with a wicked disposition. She's sarcastic, caustic, selfish, and critical of everything. Men are repulsed. She has few friends.

Amelia strolled back through the plaza. Before entering the adjacent neighborhood, she gazed back at the Duomo di Cremona, admiring the huge stained-glass rose window that dominated the enormous sand-colored edifice.

When Miriam completed her meeting and they were inside the carriage heading out of Cremona, Amelia explained her idea, eager for Miriam's reaction.

"Imagine a father desperately wanting his unattractive daughter betrothed, like Gasparo. When a suitor pursuing his attractive younger daughter asks for her hand in marriage, her father refuses the request until his oldest daughter is married. Then a brazen man comes along who wants to marry this malevolent woman for access to her family's fortune—and he concocts a secret plan for taming her. I see it as a parody of the times and people pretending to be someone other than themselves to get what they want."

Miriam smiled. "Men love taming strong women. I'm lucky with Zuane. He appreciates me and my abilities."

"I'd never let a man 'tame' me—keep me from my dreams."

"Taming need not always be bad," said Miriam. "When a person is wild and angry, it probably means she's unhappy with her life. 'Taming' then might lead to greater contentment."

Throughout the journey, Miriam and Amelia talked continually about the "taming" play, as they affectionately called it. They laughed while conjuring absurd ideas and inserting them into the story, including how the "taming" male character pretends ridiculous things are true. They had sketched out much of the plot by the time they reached Verona, where they would spend the night and the following day. Amelia planned to enhance the satire and the underlying messages she wished to convey while Miriam held her meetings.

Before entering Verona, Amelia scrawled "The Taming of a Shrew" on top of her first page of notes. She showed it to Miriam.

A broad smile spread on her aunt's face. "That captures it."

17

When the specter of bubonic plague had receded, Will bade his family farewell and set off to pursue his profession once again. Burbage at The Theatre gladly took him back. While Will was fixing a trapdoor hinge in the stage floor, an unfamiliar voice with a thick accent interrupted him.

"Mr. William Shakespeare, is that you?"

A man, slightly out of breath, wearing a damp leather coat and holding a flat package stood in the rain beyond the lip of the stage in the open-air theater.

"'Tis I," said Will. "How may I help you?"

"I am Rafael Tolendano. I have come from Venice."

Will immediately warmed to that news. "Venice, did you say?"

"I did. I've a package from Amelia Bassano Lanier."

The mention of her name called up an image of Amelia. Will imagined her writing the script for *Lender*, with brownish-red curls framing her face.

"You have a script for me?" asked Will.

"I do. Amelia spent the month before I sailed back writing furiously so I could bring it."

"Yes, the *Lender of Venice*, as she is calling it," said Will, thinking Burbage will be exceedingly happy.

Rafael shifted uneasily. "No, that's not what I have. She sends her apologies."

"Apologies?"

"She said you might be expecting it. She's composed a letter explaining. She became enthralled with another idea. That's the script I am carrying."

That's not good news, thought Will. We agreed that she would write *Lender*. Will had, therefore, put it out of his mind, even though Burbage inquired often about its progress.

Rafael handed Will the package. "Amelia believes you will like it. She called it a 'serious comedy' entitled *The Taming of the Shrew*."

Will frowned as he untied the cord binding the package. A play about a shrew? He shook his head glancing at the opening lines of Amelia's note. "How shall I respond to her?" he asked.

"I leave in a week and will courier whatever you send back. When I return in a few months, I will bring any additional papers Amelia has for you."

"Most acceptable," said Will. "I'll review Amelia's script and prepare material for her."

When Raphael left, Will read Amelia's letter in the fading wintery light.

5 December 1593

My dear friend Will,

I trust this letter finds you well. I was touched by your expressive sonnet and truly appreciate the sentiments. Please be assured, I value our friend-ship and always think fondly of you.

I can imagine your chagrin upon learning this package does not contain The Lender of Venice. *I had hoped the city of Venice and its marine at-mosphere would inspire me. Yet, so far, only a few scenes have come forth.*

I will return to Lender *and send a draft when it's ready. I have considerable research to conduct and will spend more time in Venice's Jewish section called* Il Ghetto. *Inside is a vi-brant Jewish community with a beehive of mer-chants and traders. I'll pay close attention to daily interactions and customs. I plan to have a composition for my next dispatch. I dearly hope you are not too disappointed and Burbage does not react poorly.*

As I struggled with Lender, *serendipity in-spired another idea during a trip to Cremona. The fruit of that inspiration is* The Taming of the Shrew. *A quickly written first draft, still thin in a few parts, is enclosed.*

Remember the little tradition I began by naming a character Aemilia in A Comedy of Errors? *I am continuing my mischievous game by using names of people in my family and close friends, or variations of them, for certain characters. In* The Taming of the Shrew *I named a character for my father, Baptista, and one Katherine to honor Katherine Willoughby, Duchess of Suffolk. Another is named for my Uncle Nicholas. I trust you will indulge me.*

Please allow Lord Hunsdon to read The Taming of the Shrew *and other scripts I compose. He's a great friend with a deep interest in theater. He can help you and our plays.*

I hope the plague's specter has spared your family and all you love.

I am well and discovering that Venice suits me. It's what I need at this moment.

With warmth, sincerity, and best wishes,
Amelia

That evening, Will read *The Taming of the Shrew* under flickering candlelight. He drank hot cider and cupped the mug to allow the liquid's heat to warm his cold hands. It was past midnight when he finished. He read it again the next day, taking notes and identifying ways to refine it. He admired Amelia's clever storyline, especially how she portrayed Petruchio, the cocksure fortune seeker. With a few masculine refinements he'd become a vigorous fellow who would make audiences roar with laughter.

"You promised to bring your play about the Jewish moneylender, *The Lender of...Vienna*," was it?" growled Burbage from behind his cluttered desk.

"Venice," replied Will as he removed his wool coat, brushed a thin layer of snow from the shoulders, and hung it on a hook.

Winter daylight filtered through a smudged window and illuminated half of Burbage's face. Shadows darkened the other half but Will caught the snarl on his lips.

"Venice, that's right. I want my own *Jew of Malta*. The Curtain Theatre made barrels of money with Marlowe's play. That theme sells. When will I have it?"

Will sought to remain calm and confident. "It's taking longer to research than I anticipated. We'll be able to open the autumn season with it."

Even before Will finished his sentence, he regretted making the promise. He didn't know how long it would take Amelia to write it. If Burbage became too insistent, he might have to write it instead. "I have an alternative, however. It's a comedy that'll draw large audiences. After the plague and this dreary winter, people need to lift their spirits."

"Another farce, like *A Comedy of Errors*?" asked Burbage.

"Yes, but about marital relationships. A fortune hunter marries and cleverly tricks a demanding woman into becoming an obedient wife."

"You've aroused my curiosity, but I'll need to read it for myself. It's riskier than the Jewish moneylender play."

"Perhaps. Remember, making money is my goal too," said Will.

"I'll render my opinion when I finish it. But I want the *Lender of Venice* for September. Are we clear? No excuses, Will."

In the meantime, Rafael delivered Amelia's letter to Lord Hunsdon. He unsealed it in his study.

4 December 1593

My dear Henry,

Although it's been months since I left England for Venice, I carry you in my heart and head. My affection and gratitude for all you have done for me runs deep. Your profound kindness has softened my heart and made me wiser in my relationships. Your friendship is most dear and my thoughts turn to you daily.

I hope you will read materials I composed and sent to Mr. William Shakespeare. You showed me how to become a better writer and you'll see your influence in my latest script, The Taming of the Shrew.

I will be honored by your interest. Your insights and opinions are always taken to heart. I miss your wisdom and intellectual prodding. Our conversations and intimacy nurtured my being. I miss your deep voice, although it surfaces frequently in my memory and warms my heart.

My time in Venice has been wondrous and educational, and I feel close to my family and ancestral roots.

My dear Henry, I hope you are well and pursuing all that you love. I so appreciate how well you have nourished my life.

With love from your endearing friend,
Amelia

Lord Hunsdon re-read her letter. He missed Amelia. She had been a wonderful companion for an old man. He shook off that thought. He wasn't so old. Not so much that he couldn't continue helping her. He rose from his chair and gazed out the window toward the city of London. He would further his acquaintance with this William Shakespeare. He would support the cause of the young playwright—and Amelia as well.

18

Amelia stared at the script she'd been writing without seeing the words on the page. She sat in her chamber with a majestic view of the Grand Canal and across the water the thirteenth-century Turkish palace, *Fondaco dei Turchi*, with its Moorish design and rows of columned arches.

Julia interrupted Amelia's beleaguered trance. "Engrossed in deep thought?"

"I wish," replied Amelia. "It's more like a *tabula rasa*. I put quill to paper but write nothing. I've been gazing through the window as if ideas would float in and penetrate my brain. I've got to make progress on this script and send it to London, but I'm at an impasse."

"What it's about?" asked Julia.

"A Jewish businessman in Venice—a moneylender who imposes gruesome terms if not repaid. Ultimately, he becomes more obsessed with exacting justice—or what he perceives it to be—than repayment."

"Why must he be Jewish?"

"For two reasons. First, Christians aren't allowed to lend money and charge interest. Second, another play, called *The Jew of Malta,* attracted huge audiences in London. The theater owner insists a play about a Jewish businessman will too and he's demanding it."

"Perhaps he's the greedy one. What are you going to do?"

"Keep plowing forward," replied Amelia. "I should spend more time in Il Ghetto, since that's where the character would live. And I'd like to interview a moneylender. Will you go with me?"

"It's not a favorite place of mine," Julia said with distaste. "It's crowded, noisy, and smelly. People bump into you—not purposefully but it's hard to avoid. Zev likes it. It would be best if you went with him."

Amelia asked Zev when he arrived.

"I'd be delighted," he said, "but you must prepare for a unique cultural experience. When you were there for Rosh Hashanah and Yom Kippur, it was calm for the holyday observances. On a Friday like today, it will be crowded with people buying food and baked goods for their Shabbat dinners."

"Then I'll experience its full flavor," said Amelia, wondering how she'd feel surrounded by throngs of her own faith.

Turning to Julia, Zev said, "You should come too. It won't hurt to poke your head out of your cocoon and see how other Jews live."

"Why should I do what I dislike? You think I enjoy being in thick crowds of poor Jews, all crammed together in a confined space?" Julia asked, raising her long expressive eyebrows.

"Not all of them are poor," said Zev. "It's where they're required to live. We're fortunate that we are not."

Amelia noted the contrast between Julia's dour expression and her own excitement. "Please join us," said Amelia. "It's for my play and plays are about people. By observing their way of life, I can make it more authentic. And you may notice facets Zev and I do not."

Julia finally relented. "I will, but only because you insist."

Mid-morning, the three left on foot. Amelia shivered in a salmon frock—a snug bodice and long wool skirt—under a black coat for the ten-minute walk through Venice's labyrinth of streets. The sun gradually warmed the chilly city but the winter temperatures were still bitingly cold. They crossed a small canal and wended their way north through alleys until reaching the slender bridge and low gate separating the Jewish neighborhood from the rest of Venice.

Il Ghetto consumed a small island. Bridge gates were locked at night, guarded by Christian watchmen, paid by the Jewish residents. The system kept the Jews isolated and protected. Nearly five thousand Jews lived in this tightly packed area. As the population swelled, additions had been built on top of tenements. Most were five to seven stories, the highest in Venice. Synagogues occupied the uppermost floors of some buildings, because Jewish law prohibited anything from being constructed above one. The air above synagogues must be open to the sky—and building tops became the most practical places for *shuln*.

Amelia, Zev, and Julia strode across the Ponti di Ghetto Vecchio bridge into the hectic streets. People moved shoulder to shoulder in the overcrowded lanes. Laundry, hung to dry on ropes tied to windows, flapped in the cool air. Pushcarts loaded with barrels, flour, and vegetables made slow headway through the choked alleys. Some carts were stopped while being unloaded on the narrow streets, blocking others from getting by and inflaming tempers.

Women clustered five deep around street vendors. Both men and women argued about how fresh or how good were vegetables, breads, chicken, and cod. The cacophony echoed through the modest plaza called *Campo Ghetto Nuovo*. Flat-faced "Stucco Veneziano" tenements of varying heights painted ochre, burnt sienna, gray, and light maroon hemmed in the square. Amelia saw a wooden dome wedged precariously atop two buildings, which she believed was a synagogue roof connecting a corner of the public space.

The walk flooded Amelia with ideas for describing the environs of the play's Jewish moneylender. She absorbed the gritty feel and industrious energy. She listened to the bargaining for goods, complaining, storytelling, gossiping, insulting, and arguing. She watched people wildly waving their hands and arms to emphasize whatever points they were making, unlike anything she had seen in England. Here, if people thought it, they said it.

Amelia glanced at her cousins as she squeezed through the crowd past a fish stall. Julia seemed embarrassed by the interplay between merchants and their haggling customers. Zev seemed enlivened and he pointed to a sign down the way. Three spheres were suspended from a curved rod, one on each end of the bow with a third hanging straight down in the center. Above the symbol was the word "Lombard."

"What does that mean?" asked Amelia.

"That's a pawnbroker's symbol," explained Zev. "We call those shops 'lombard,' since they originated in the province of Lombardy. Some still call borrowing money from them 'lombard banking.'"

This regional terminology amused Amelia. "Let's go in," she said.

The lombard was crammed with merchandise. Jewelry cases beneath a long counter were secured with sturdy locks. Farm and woodworking tools hung on the walls along with well-used lutes and a violin. Brass candlesticks and silver platters were displayed on a table in the back. The store smelled like linseed oil.

"How may I be of service?" asked a burly bald man with a long raven-black beard.

"Signore, I'm interested in learning about your business," said Amelia confidently, hoping she didn't sound too bold.

"You are, are you?" replied the man with a hearty laugh. "Why should I explain my business? I've enough competitors. One just disbanded for which I'm grateful."

"Oh, I'm sorry. I did not explain my purpose. May I begin again?"

"By all means, signorina."

"I am a playwright. A man owning a lombard is a character in my script. So, I'd like to learn how the business works, not to compete with you."

"I see. And who might you be?"

Amelia considered whether she should use her maiden or married name. Perhaps it would be better to be anonymous. She didn't know if the proprietor had heard of the Bassanos and, if he had, what he thought of them.

"I'm Amelia Lanier. I'm pleased to meet you, Signore…"

"Perez. Samuel Perez.

"I know little about your business. Will you explain it?"

Perez remained behind the counter with his hands resting on a jewelry case. "It's simple. A customer who needs money comes to me for a loan. To secure the loan, I take something of value that the customer offers as collateral. It must have a worth sufficient to cover the amount borrowed plus interest. If the loan isn't repaid on time, and if I don't extend the loan, then I'm free to sell the customer's merchandise at a profit and keep the proceeds. If the customer repays the loan as agreed, then I return the item."

"Which do you prefer—selling the merchandise or collecting loan payments and interest?"

"I prefer the borrower to pay me back. I'm delighted to return the merchandise. It's better for business, for such customers are likely to return for another loan. And it's easier if I don't have to sell the collateral."

Amelia checked prices marked on jewelry inside the case and instruments hanging behind Perez. "Is it tricky appraising items and determining how much to ask to resell them quickly?"

"Sometimes, but I know my market well. Still, I'm wrong occasionally. I must anticipate how much buyers will attempt to negotiate and determine the lowest figure I'll accept."

"What worries you?" asked Amelia.

"I become suspicious when customers try to secure loans with articles that seem insignificant to them. That could be a sign that they may have no intention of repaying me. Then I could be stuck with hard-to-sell items which I eventually discount at a loss."

"Is that how you'd characterize the merchandise you have now?"

Perez pursed his lips in a regretful frown. "Most of these items will fetch a good price and sell within weeks. Some I purchased from customers who sold them for cash. There's a sad story behind almost everything in the shop. It's especially unfortunate when the item is a wedding ring or family heirloom. I get no joy from selling them."

"Where do you keep items you're holding as collateral?" asked Julia.

"They're in locked chests in a secure room. Each article is recorded in a ledger, labeled, and numbered so I can track which items are collateral for each loan."

"What happens if a customer doesn't have collateral— if they are so poor they have nothing valuable for you to hold?" asked Amelia.

"Then I ask if someone can offer collateral or guarantee the loan for them."

Ideas rushed through Amelia's head for use in the script. Then she thought about a remark he'd made earlier. "You said you were grateful one of your competitors disbanded. Why?"

"He was unscrupulous," Perez said flatly. "Lombard merchants don't enjoy a good reputation and he made the problem worse by being nasty and greedy. He made riskier loans, charged higher interest, and became brutal when he couldn't get his money back or if the collateral was insufficient. He'd send thugs after delinquent borrowers. I called him a *shallach*."

Amelia stopped writing. "Signore Perez, you called yourself a merchant, not a moneylender. Why?"

Perez gestured around the shop. "Look at these items for sale. This is a store. I sell merchandise as well as loans. Each has a price in the form of interest or collateral."

"You also called the disreputable lombard a *shallach.* Meaning?"

Zev put in, "Isn't that Hebrew for someone who's selfish?"

"Actually," said Perez, "it's someone worse than selfish. A *shallach* is extremely greedy, like a cormorant."

Amelia's mind hummed. *A shallach. A Hebrew word that could also be a name. Shallach…or Shall-lock…Shay-lock…No, they're not quite right for an English audience…Shy-lock…Shylock! That has an ominous ring.*

The trio left the lombard, weaved their way to the ghetto gate and crossed the bridge out of the crowded enclave. The once sunny day had become overcast and the mist-laden breeze penetrated their garments.

"I keep thinking about that lombard," said Julia. "How could anyone sell someone else's prized possessions?"

Amelia admonished her, "Julia, you never know the circumstances in which you might find yourself. He said that most people hope they're pledging an object temporarily."

Julia rolled her eyes. "I couldn't do it. Lombards are for poor people and their owners exploit them."

"You should be grateful you don't need one."

"I'll never be in that position," Julia scoffed, "and Marcello would never go into one of their stores."

"Marcello?" asked Amelia.

Zev stopped in mid-stride and pivoted toward Julia with a quizzical expression.

"He's a new friend," Julia replied, her neck and face flushing.

Zev asked sharply, "Are you talking about Marcello Caloprini?"

"Yes, yes I am," she said with her words trailing into a whisper.

"He's the boy you met by chance at the Doge's spring festival, at the masked dance," Zev remarked. "Do you know what his parents say about people like us?"

Julia turned petulant. "It wasn't by chance. He sought me out. His parents don't matter."

"But they do. Marcello's infatuation with Rosa Conti and her rejection of him are well known. Now he is pursuing you and such a union is impossible. Neither his nor our family will allow it. His intentions can't be serious."

"You don't know that. When we took off our masks, we both felt an immediate attraction."

Zev persisted, "That may be true, but Marcello's father is Sergio Caloprini. He hates Jews."

"What's important is that Marcello and I like each other."

"Sergio will make your life miserable. He's rude and intolerant of anyone who doesn't believe what he does. So is his wife, Carlotta. They once accused Uncle Zuane of being a heretic. And you want to be friends with a boy who comes from a family like that? His parents would rather spit on you than have a respectful conversation."

Julia's face turned redder. "But Marcello is not like that."

A few fat raindrops splattered in the ground as Zev went on, "Sergio can ruin our family's reputation, our businesses, and our safety if he chose. He's spiteful. You could be putting us all in danger."

"Zev, you don't understand."

They rushed toward the Bassano residence as the rain picked up. When they crossed the bridge from Via

Emanuele to Strada Nova, clouds burst and a heavy down-pour drenched them.

"Let's take cover in that storefront," suggested Amelia, pointing.

They huddled beneath an overhang and Zev grasped Julia's arm. "What about Parisse? He likes you and that's the match Uncle Zuane has arranged with his parents. It's just a matter of waiting until you're older."

Julia pulled herself away. "Oh, yes, everyone thinks I should marry Parisse because his parents and our family like each other. He comes from a respected *Jewish* family. But what about what I want? Nobody has asked that!"

Amelia worried silently about Julia's defiance and indignation along with Zev's strong displeasure—concerned they were moving toward a wider and more turbulent clash.

Zev crossed his arms and glared at his sister. "Julia, consider what's best for our family. Your interest in Marcello will lead to trouble."

19

VENICE, APRIL 1594

The crisis Amelia expected to consume the Bassano household stayed hidden beneath the surface. Julia kept quiet about her daily activities, mastering the art of evasion when asked about them. Zev chose to not raise the matter without a precipitating incident. Amelia believed it only appeared to be dormant and could erupt like a volcano without warning. Today it was far from her mind.

Cool breezes from the canal carried fresh spring scents and touches of welcome warmth. Amelia carried a basket containing ricotta and mascarpone cheese, fresh crusty bread, and red grapes through black-stone streets to the Bassano residence. She heard Henry laughing upon pushing open the residence door and scurried up to the salon, where Enid held Henry on her lap while singing nursery rhymes. He squirmed his way to the floor when Amelia entered.

"Mama," he shrieked as he toddled forward and hugged her legs.

Amelia picked Henry up and kissed his forehead. "I have fresh grapes from the market."

He kissed her cheek. "Grapes!"

"Once we remove the seeds, you can have some."

Enid handed two letters to Amelia. "Signore Rafael Tolendano delivered these."

Enid unseeded the grapes while Henry perched on Amelia's lap. She inspected her mail. One letter came from Will and the other from Henry Carey.

Amelia started with Will's message.

1 March 1594

Dear Amelia,

To my great delight, I poured over your script for The Taming of the Shrew. *It's as clever and entertaining as* A Comedy of Errors. *I've made minor revisions and thickened parts that were "thin," to use your word. I made some lines for Lucentio and Tranio more robust. You'll see my alterations in the enclosed manuscript. I believe it's ready for rehearsal and actors may have additional ideas, given their wont to improvise.*

I met with James Burbage and he informs me The Theatre *will reopen on the Ides of March, now that the plague has abated. I am relieved that none in my family were struck and hope you have been similarly spared.*

Mr. Burbage liked The Taming of the Shrew *and wants it staged as part of the opening week series along with* Titus, A Comedy of Errors, *and* Richard III. *Each will play on different days.*

Shrew *should draw favorably. I'm creating a copy for the bookmaker, who will retain the complete script for prompting actors. I'm also making a folio of each part for the performer portraying it.*

Mr. Burbage fumed when I told him The Lender of Venice *was unfinished. In response to his reprimand, I promised I'd have it for autumn. I presume you'll complete it by then.*

I see no harm in your giving characters names similar to those in your family, if that's your pleasure.

Lord Hunsdon is well and maintains an active interest in theater, especially our productions. He liked your script and wants to support our performances in his capacity as the Lord Chamberlain. He said he'd have more on that in the future. All because of you!

I eagerly await your response and reading your latest.

Your friend and writing companion,
Will

Amelia put down the letter with mixed feelings. The dreadful scenarios she'd imagined about Burbage's reaction to the delay on *Lender,* which she'd since re-titled *The Merchant of Venice* based on her conversation with the lombard, had not been borne out. But he'd given Will—her—a deadline. But she had no idea if she could meet it. Will's comments, though, about Lord Hunsdon warmed her heart. *If he became a strong patron of Shakespeare's plays, meaning mine as well, it would portend greater success. Does Henry say anything more specific in his letter?*

Little Henry's grapes were ready. Enid put several in a bowl and placed them on the table. "Shall I hold him in my lap while he eats?"

Amelia handed him over. "Henry, this letter is from the man for whom you are named. Someday, you'll meet him. He lives far away in another country, called England."

Henry stuffed grapes in his mouth. Soon the skin around his lips turned light purple.

> *Henry Carey, Lord Hunsdon*
> *London*
> *28 February 1594*

My dear Amelia,

Your endearing words warmed my heart and it is gratifying to know the esteem you have for me. It is mutual. I was moved that you thoughtfully enclosed Henry's handprint. I'd like to believe he is of my own blood, but I suppose that will remain unclear.

I swelled with pride upon reading the script Mr. Shakespeare showed me. I saw your distinct imprint, especially with the many musical references, which I don't recall in any of Shakespeare's prior plays. There are over a hundred lines in The Taming of the Shrew *with musical allusions of one form or another, some quite sophisticated—reflecting your family's deep musical heritage, and how much music has been part of your life.*

I expect audiences will enjoy the clever way you've woven the story together. Parts of the script made me recall our discussions about falconry, one of my passions. The parallels employed in the "taming" surprised me. I thought you were only half-listening at times, but clearly you absorbed everything. I also noticed how you drew on our discussions about court intrigue and deception to shape your plot. Only someone like me, who knows you well, would make these connections.

I am following your work and that of Mr. Shakespeare. I will soon be inviting him to the royal court.

I look ahead to hearing more about your experiences in Venice and reading whatever it may be you're writing now.

As always and with much affection,
Henry

Only Henry would be so astute to see my trail of clues, thought Amelia. Having him as a patron could only bode well for her fortunes.

Tears rolled down Amelia's cheeks as she erupted in laughter in one of Venice's ornate proscenium theaters. She and Miriam sat in the highest row by a marble column, watching a *commedia dell'arte*. Amelia paid close attention to the distinctive costumes and masks. One absurdly sinister character donned a colorful patched outfit with a cat-like mask. Another dressed as a fortune-teller, with an oversized purse dangling from his belt, wore a mask with heavy brows over beady eyes, suggesting a sly personality. Between pantomimes, characters reacted satirically to audience prompts and the troupe performed parodies of everyday conflicts among merchants and family members.

While most of the audience delighted in the antics on-stage, Amelia noticed two men several rows lower engrossed in serious conversation.

"Who are they?" whispered Amelia, pointing discreetly.

"The swarthy man with the large head and oily black hair is Sergio Caloprini. The one with the mottled skin and disfigured features is his partner, Vincente Ponti. They own the largest shipping and warehousing company in Venice."

During an intermission, Amelia noticed Caloprini and Ponti continued their tense exchanges, with Sergio waving his hands vehemently and Vincente looking discomfited.

"Zuane and I met Signore Caloprini at an event sponsored by the Doge," explained Miriam. "He is among the least liked and most feared men in Venice."

Amelia remembered Zev's comments about him. "What about Signore Ponti?"

"I've not met him, but I'm told he's more gracious."

When Ponti broke away and ventured outdoors, Miriam approached Caloprini. "Signore, do you remember me?"

"Ah, Signora Bassano. How is that little musical instrument shop that your husband runs?"

Caloprini's condescension did not escape Amelia's notice.

Miriam smiled coldly. "This is my cousin, Amelia, visiting from London."

"Signore Caloprini, I'm pleased to meet you. Are you enjoying the performance?"

"I've got more important matters on my mind than this drivel masquerading as comedy. But my partner insisted I come as a respite from business, which I surely don't need. Why are you here?"

"I'm a playwright and thought I'd not only enjoy Venice but learn from it—which I certainly have."

"I have little interest in the frivolous," he said, not seeming to care what she said.

Amelia started to respond when a zanni danced in blaring a horn, signaling that the performance was about to resume.

"Oh, that blast," said Miriam jokingly. "We'd never sell an instrument that harsh."

As they retook their seats, Miriam whispered to Amelia, "In addition to Caloprini's blunt nature, he dislikes Jews—especially those with the temerity to live outside of Il Ghetto."

Amelia, once again, was jarred by such an ugly description of the man. It spurred thoughts of the evening months earlier when she spotted Julia secretly kissing a boy, who she now believed was Marcello. Amelia had not considered intervening at the time since she deemed it beyond her place, but wondered now if she should. She had grown to like Julia. She would keep a closer eye on her. Perhaps she could steer her cousin away from hurt.

20

LONDON, JUNE 1594

"Traitor! Traitor! To the gallows, Jew!" howled the crowd lining the streets outside The Tower of London as horses dragged the hurdle carrying Rodrigo Lopez, once the Queen's court physician, to a public square. Will and Burbage watched the spectacle and followed the throngs. The guards pulled the bound Lopez from the wooden panel and pushed the staggering man in filthy clothes up to a platform where a noose dangled. The surrounding horde jeered and cheered as hangmen tightened the thick rope around his neck.

Will surveyed the rowdy crowd from the back. His eyes landed on Thomas Dekker, rocking and shouting near the front. Over the mass, he saw Dekker shaking his fist and hurling Jewish slurs.

The mob hushed as Lopez opened his mouth to speak. He licked his cracked lips and in a hoarse voice declared, "These are my final breaths, and with them I proclaim my innocence to all. I loved my Queen and still do, no matter my fate. And I love Jesus Christ."

"Jew! Traitor! Christ-killer!" shouted the crowd in reply, Dekker among the loudest.

With Lopez's body still suspended and jerking in its final death throes, and the executioners preparing to disembowel and quarter his body, Will and Burbage turned to leave.

"I can watch no more," said Will, "especially the gruesome conclusion."

"Gruesome it may be, but the crowd's retorts prove this is an ideal time for another play about a despicable Jew. I trust you'll have it for me soon."

21

LONDON, JULY 1594

England's royal carriage and its formal escorts approached The Theatre where Lord Hunsdon, Burbage, and Shakespeare waited. Will had to make the most of this day. Success or failure to impress the Queen would color the rest of his career, even though it was Amelia's play on trial.

The surrounding streets had been swept clean. Horse droppings had been shoveled away and the putrid odor no longer hung in the air. Walkway planks over the muddy road were neatly arranged to the side rather than askew and rickety. A red and gold banner over the theater entrance welcomed Queen Elizabeth.

Two royal guards assisted the Queen from her carriage. She looked resplendent in a black gown with embroidered red and gold scrolls, billowy sleeves, lacey neck and wrist ruffs, and white pointed leather shoes with a raised heel. Her curly red hair framed her white-painted face.

Lord Hunsdon, as the Lord Chamberlain, bowed. "Your Majesty, may I introduce Mr. James Burbage and Mr. William Shakespeare, the owner of The Theatre and the playwright respectively."

"Your Majesty, welcome to our humble playhouse," said Burbage, bowing.

"Your Majesty, I'm honored by your presence." said Shakespeare, bowing low with a flourish. "I fervently hope you enjoy my play." He backed away, feeling like an imposter.

"I could use a good laugh. I understand you're a gifted playwright."

"Thank you, Your Majesty. May our performance add levity to your day."

"I expect it will."

Turning to the Lord Chamberlain, Queen Elizabeth said, "Henry, shall we?"

The Queen settled in an oversized cushioned oak chair in the front row of the lower balcony, constructed specifically for her visit. The Lord Chamberlain sat on one side and Will on her other as the audience settled in the crowded theater. Two square pillars anchored each side of the stage, and a low burlap curtain was strung from one to the other. Rising behind it was a covered balcony with a wooden railing.

"What's the point of the makeshift curtain?" asked Elizabeth before the performance started.

"The play begins with an induction—a prologue— which introduces the play as a farce. *The Taming of the Shrew* is a play within a play and the opening scene dramatizes this," explained Will.

Throughout the performance, Queen Elizabeth smiled and chuckled as the actors performed with extra vigor. She laughed with delight when Petruchio tossed Katherine onto his shoulder and carried her away, and again when Petruchio called Katherine a wasp and she retorted, "Best beware of my sting." In a later scene, Petruchio had a weary tamed Katherine declare that the sun is the moon and the moon is the sun, an absurdity that the Queen found amusing and nobody believed, least of all Katherine.

When the play ended, the Queen said to Will and Henry, "Men and women may interpret this comedy quite differently. Men might believe it supports traditional roles. Women could view it as a parody of them, illustrating their ridiculousness. Taming indeed."

Will smiled. "Your Majesty, you're quite right. The play is open to varying interpretations. How one sees it may depend on one's predisposition. Perhaps it will compel some to reexamine their assumptions."

"It may, Mr. Shakespeare. Congratulations on an ingenious production."

Henry and Will escorted Queen Elizabeth to her carriage and bid her adieu. Will felt flush with success and moved quickly to spread the news to actors gathered in the now empty pit. Henry joined him a moment later.

"What did she think?" asked the male actor who played Katherine, the shrew. He had removed his wig and gown and stood shirtless and barefoot in black breeches.

As Will was about to answer a sturdy barrel-chested man interrupted. "Congratulations, Will, on another prodigious production. I'd heard much about it, but this is the first performance I've seen."

"Hello, Thomas, I'm honored." replied Will warily.

"Lord Hunsdon, meet Thomas Dekker. Thomas has written excellent prose, and I believe is working on a script."

"My lord, nice to make your acquaintance. I know of your interest in the arts and especially the works of Mr. Shakespeare," said Dekker.

"Quite true."

Dekker stroked his well-trimmed beard and shifted his beady eyes. "I've a question for you both that I hope neither will find impertinent."

Will didn't think kind remarks could come from a man with such a sneer.

"Does anyone besides me find it a bit odd, that you, Will, have suddenly gone from writing historical dramas about dead English kings to marital comedies set in Mediterranean climes?"

22

Amelia strolled with Miriam, Zuane, and Julia to the Rialto Bridge to watch *Regata Storica,* the annual rowing competition started by Doge Giovanni Soranzo in 1315 to celebrate Venetian military victories. But Amelia's thoughts stayed mired on her travails with *The Merchant of Venice.* Every sentence required more exertion than everything else she had penned.

For inspiration, Amelia had watched numerous Venetian plays to study plotlines, how the dramas unfolded, and how costumes were used to convey a character's nature. None of them invigorated her efforts with *Merchant.* Instead, the productions triggered new ideas and inflamed her imagination in ways that took her mind farther from it.

Recently, Amelia began writing a comedy about a king who, along with three lords, commits to three years of scholarship devoid of women. She had pages of witty notes, puns, and literary references for creating humorous dialogue and subplots, especially as the men encounter women and fall in love during their self-imposed hiatus. She called the script *Love's Labour's Lost* and, although she felt guilty, channeled her mental energy toward it.

Amelia's flowing coral skirt and white cloak fluttered in the breeze as she watched the first boats advance ceremoniously along the Grand Canal, rowed by colorfully dressed gondoliers. They carried the Doge, members of his feared Council of Ten and his six most powerful advisors. When they disappeared from view beneath the bridge, the competition began.

Venetians, massed along the banks, cheered for their favorites. Fathers held their sons up high to see over the heads of spectators in front of them. Others watched from windows and balconies of *palazzos* lining the canal, their boisterous voices echoing along the waterway as small sporting gondolas competed in the *Campioni su Gondolini* race. As the last of the heats rowed quickly by, the gallery followed the boats en masse down the canal to the finish line and floating stage in front of *Ca' Foscari Palace,* the headquarters of the Republic of Venice.

Amelia ambled along the wide canal, having lost interest in the ceremony after the winners were announced. Nearby, the Doge's musicians played festive songs and Zuane and Miriam pointed out instruments made by the Bassano studio. Venetians danced and sang until the sun dipped toward the horizon. Amelia, Zuane, and Miriam turned to head home.

"Wait, I need to see something," announced Julia, breaking into the crowd.

In her yellow frock, Julia slid through the crowd toward a handsome dark-haired young man huddled with several others on the *Riva Ferro,* the street along the Grand Canal.

She casually passed him without saying a word, like they were strangers, but Amelia saw the boy slip something into Julia's palm. Marcello? A note? She couldn't tell in the late afternoon shadows. Julia looked at something in a shop then ran back.

Julia suppressed a smirk as she rejoined them. Amelia didn't ask and Julia did not comment about her brief excursion. They strolled together toward the Bassano home for dinner, recounting the day's events. Julia surprised Amelia with clever wordplays and puns in Italian and English about the "stream of events," the "splash of music," and the "battle of the paddles." Amelia liked her wit and sense of humor, which contrasted with her dour moments and sharp judgments. Although heartened, Amelia knew what had enlivened the teenager.

Nearing the residence, Amelia spotted Rafael lifting the brass lion-head knocker on the landside door. She hurried to greet him.

"I have two letters," he said, handing them to Amelia. "I'll be sailing back to England in a few weeks. Will you be sending more papers?"

Amelia smiled. "I will. Thank you for delivering these."

One came from Will and the other from Lord Hunsdon. What news would they have? How did Will and Burbage respond to the delay with *Merchant*? What did they think of *Shrew*? She wanted to tear herself away but stayed composed, inquiring about Rafael's trip.

When Rafael left, she raced up to the residence.

As Amelia entered the salon, Julia rushed in from her bedchamber, wearing a flowing dusty-rose dress with a gold-ruffled neckline and fitted bodice.

"You're dressed to bedazzle," said Miriam, coming up from the studio. "Where are you going?"

"To meet a friend and I'm late," said Julia as she dashed for the stairway to the ground floor.

She's rendezvousing with Marcello, Amelia thought. That was the purpose of the message handed to her by the Grand Canal.

"Wait! Wait, come back," shouted Miriam.

The abrupt slamming of the door reverberated up into the salon.

Amelia rushed to her bedchamber and opened Will's letter.

2 August 1594

Dear Amelia,

Queen Elizabeth came to The Theater to see The Taming of the Shrew! *She laughed throughout, completely enthralled. After witnessing her reaction, my nervousness turned to exuberance. The Queen looked resplendent, the playhouse never appeared so grand, and the performance dazzled.*

Her Majesty wants to see more of our productions—possibly staged in Whitehall Palace. That's Lord Hunsdon's doing. He's a good friend to us. He thinks the best choices for such performances would be A Comedy of Errors *and* Titus Andronicus. *I'm disappointed he did not mention* Richard III.

Burbage is pushing hard for The Merchant of Venice, *especially after seeing the frenzy at the hanging of Rodrigo Lopez. The secret Jew was convicted of plotting to poison the Queen and conspiracy against the crown. Has the script been sent? He wanted it for autumn. My excuses are getting thinner and his questions are starting to drip with suspicion.*

I am working on a new script about King Richard II. I hope to finish early next year.

I must close now. Rafael will be coming to retrieve this letter shortly and I am about to meet with Lord Hunsdon.

Yours sincerely,

Will

Anxiety spread through Amelia like rushing whitewater. The news about Rodrigo Lopez frightened her to the core. She wondered if she should ever return to England. She worried about missing Burbage's deadline for *Merchant* and putting Will in a precarious position. Would he understand? Would he forgive her? All she had striven to accomplish seemed in jeopardy. Her heart pumped madly. Never had she been under such pressure or so stymied. She detested this project and would fulfill her obligation, but didn't know how much time she'd need. Her only saving grace was Lord Hunsdon's beneficence. Only he could have enticed the Queen to see *Shrew.*

Amelia put Will's letter down and unsealed the one from Henry Carey.

Henry Carey, Lord Hunsdon
The Lord Chamberlain
1 August 1594

Dear Amelia,

I spoke eloquently about The Taming of the Shrew *with the Queen. I did not need to invite her to see it; she instructed me to schedule it. She came to* The Theatre *with great fanfare on 28 July. She was quite impressed and enjoyed it immensely. As the Lord Chamberlain, and responsible for ceremonial events and orchestrating court functions, she's instructed me to arrange other performances of your plays—or should I say "Shakespeare's plays"—at the palace.*

Given the Queen's interest, I'll take an increasingly active role regarding Mr. Shakespeare's theatrical company. The risk of error or misjudgment is too great for a man inexperienced in the ways of the court. I'll put my imprimatur on his troupe, in my capacity as the Lord Chamberlain, in a way he welcomes and which bestows honor on it.

A cloud is gathering over your clandestine arrangement with Shakespeare in the form of Thomas Dekker. He's an aspiring playwright asking challenging questions, such as how it could be that Shakespeare is writing marital comedies set in foreign lands when all he had previously composed were plays about English monarchs. He's suspicious but I'm unsure of his motives.

For now, dear Amelia, keep writing great scripts. Although Will is frustrated over The Merchant of Venice, *my advice is to take your time and do it well.*
With my most affectionate love,
Henry

The two letters inflamed a twinge of longing for her native land. She wanted to see *Shrew* performed onstage. Yet her new adopted city enchanted her. She wasn't finished exploring it—and expanding what she could do. So she would have to be content with writing letters for a while longer.

But a pang of worry crept into her consciousness. Will doesn't write a word about Thomas Dekker but Henry expresses concern. *Should this bother me?*

23

T his will be the most romantic night of my life, thought Julia. For the first time I have a true love for *Festa del Bocolo*, the Festival of the Blooming Rose. Perhaps Marcello and I will plan our future together.

Julia knew well the legend behind this Venetian holiday—a tale of love between a woman of nobility, Maria Partecipazio, and her troubadour lover, Trancredi. A romantic, he composed heartfelt poems to her. As a commoner, though, he felt the need to prove himself to her social class. To do so, he joined the army of Charles the Great. Mortally wounded in battle, he knelt over a bed of white roses. His blood turned the blooms red. He plucked a blood-drenched flower from a thorny branch and handed it to his friend, Orlando. With his last gasps Trancredi pleaded, "Take this rose to my beloved in Venice as the final token of my devotion and love. Tell her that her name was on my lips as I breathed my last." Upon returning to Venice, Orlando gave Maria the rose with Trancredi's message. The next morning, April 25, Saint Marks Day, Maria lay dead with the blood red rose resting on her heart.

Julia sneaked from the house to meet Marcello at their secret rendezvous on the *Fondamente Nuove*, a walkway along the Venetian Lagoon on the northern edge of the city— where they'd be unlikely to be recognized. Her heart leapt upon seeing Marcello in a black surcoat and white shirt, beaming and holding a long-stemmed red rose. Julia loved the way his cheeks dimpled with the slightest smile and she danced into his open arms.

Julia looked around to ensure nobody saw. "Marcello, my love, my passion, my joy." She tightened her arms around him in the twilight breeze, feeling safe in his arms. She loved the feel of his strong body against hers. Then she leaned her head back, gazed into his eyes and kissed him passionately.

They walked along the lagoon until reaching a quiet canal. No one hovered nearby. They saw candelabras and flickering candlelight inside windows. In darkness, they strolled farther and settled on the lagoon bank, dangling their feet and listening to the water slap beneath them.

Julia held her rose while leaning lovingly against Marcello, who wrapped his arm tenderly around her shoulders. Together they gazed at the open water. Occasionally, they'd see the lanterns on boats sailing toward the tip of Santa Elena Island, perhaps destined for the Basin of San Marco and the Grand Canal. Julia relished the tranquility, saltwater scent, and moonlit whitecaps on the gentle waves.

Julia's thoughts alternated from her feelings for Marcello to hard reality. Their families would never accept their love. She held his hands in hers, stared into his shining blue eyes, and admired his gently upturned nose. His wavy black hair swept over his ears. His fair smooth skin glistened in the moonlight. His deep-set eyes and broad smile melted her heart.

"Let's stroll along the lagoon," she suggested.

They ambled quietly, each within their own thoughts.

"Marcello, we've seen each other secretly since last January, and I wish never to stop."

"I love you, Julia. I've never said so to a girl before."

Julia's heart fluttered, glowing deep inside from his words. She kissed him, wanting her feelings to be drawn into him through the passion of their lips.

When their lips parted, Julia said, "What will we do when our families find out? Eventually they will. It keeps me awake at night."

"My father will fly into a rage, but I'll confess my love."

"My aunt and uncle could sever me from the family. They want me to marry a Jewish boy who is as interesting as stale bread."

Julia stopped and faced Marcello, admiring his button nose and combing her fingers through his dark hair. "I'm scared. I don't want to lose you."

Julia again looked around and Marcello did too, checking if anyone had followed.

They glided down a narrow alleyway and into a plaza anchored by an old gothic church. The neighborhoods of Venice looked different at night. They were dark and shadowy, almost melancholy. Scattered lanterns dimly illuminated narrow pathways. They heard boots echoing off the stone streets and buildings but saw no one. They turned a corner as a man up ahead disappeared around the side of a building. When they followed, he was gone. The empty alley was eerily quiet.

Julia wrapped her arms around Marcello, shivering against his chest.

As they were about to kiss one last time before going their separate ways, a deep male voice startled them. "Marcello?"

They jumped at the sound and pivoted to see a tall man roughly fifty years old dressed in a long black-velvet embroidered stole.

"It is," said Marcello, a slight quake in his voice, apparently recognizing the man with deformed facial features and dappled skin, seemingly the result of a fire from long ago.

"Good evening, Signore Ponti," said Marcello as Julia stepped backward to recede into the night shadows, clutching the rose behind her back.

"Marcello," Ponti projected, "why are you here? Who is this young lady?"

"We're enjoying the night air," said Marcello, not introducing Julia.

"And you are?" Ponti asked Julia after an awkward silence.

"I'm Marcello's friend, Julia."

"I…I apologize for my poor manners," stuttered Marcello. "Julia, this is my father's business partner, Signore Vincente Ponti."

"I'm pleased to meet you, Julia, but I must be on my way," said Ponti. He turned abruptly, headed across the small plaza, and disappeared into the night.

"We've been caught. Oh my lord, we have been caught," said Marcello.

"He doesn't know who I am, only my given name," said Julia.

"He'll find out. When he tells my father, the result won't be pleasant."

"We can't be afraid," Julia cried. "We love each other. When we tell our parents how much, they'll want us together. They'll see how stupid they've been," though she hardly believed her own wishful thinking.

Marcello frowned, downcast. "Julia, I wish you were right, but I fear you are not. Kiss me one last time. I don't know when we'll see each other again, but it can't be soon enough."

Marcello enfolded Julia in his arms. She felt his heart pounding as her chest pressed against his. She kissed him gently, then passionately, not wanting it to end.

Marcello leaned back, looking into Julia's eyes while keeping his arms around her waist.

Her eyes welled with tears. She felt one trickle down her cheek.

Marcello kissed Julia once again. "I must go. I love you. I adore you."

With that, Marcello raced toward his home and Julia meandered slowly back to hers, troubled and lost in thought.

Marcello's family dwelled in a palazzo facing Rio di San Lorenzo canal. Byzantine-style windows and surmounted sculptures highlighted the edifice. Tall windows opened to a long second-floor balcony. Sergio Caloprini could afford it. The shipping and warehousing business he operated with Vicente Ponti generated large profits. Their vessels plied the seas between Venice, Spain, Greece, Constantinople, and Egypt, carrying Venetian products to distant lands and returning with exotic goods for the Italian peninsula.

Marcello slept little that night. He kept wondering what Ponti would say and how his father would react. He remained on a knife's edge while eating breakfast with him, nibbling to create an appearance of normalcy. His anxiety grew throughout the day.

Sergio returned from work early that evening. His booming voice rattled the walls. "Marcello! I must speak with you!"

Marcello quaked at the fury edging every word. He trudged to his father's office. Sergio loomed behind his heavy, ornately carved desk. His burly physique dominated the room. His thick black hair, dense mustache, and hard-set eyes projected an intense anger.

"Signore Ponti said he saw you with a girl last night near *Campo dei Gesuiti*. Who was she and why?"

"We were enjoying the night air and talking," replied Marcello nervously.

"Who is she? Julia somebody according to Signore Ponti."

"A friend I met at the spring festival."

"A friend? Don't lie. I'm not a fool. That's not how it looked to him."

Marcello's face warmed with fright. His lip trembled. "We like each other. What's wrong with that?"

"You were hugging and about to kiss when Signore Ponti interrupted. That's more than friendly affection."

"We love each other."

"Do you know what love is?" Sergio roared. "What about Rosa? That's who your mother and I favor!"

Marcello scowled at his father, sick of his hostility and his way of mocking rather than helping his son.

"Again, who is this Julia? Who is her family?"

"You won't approve. You'll probably denounce them," said Marcello sullenly.

"Then I demand to know. Tell me. Now!" Sergio bellowed, his nostrils flaring.

"You hate her family."

"Julia...Julia," Sergio said aloud, as if sorting through women with that name. "Bassano? Bassano!" Spit sprayed from his mouth. "Are you mad?"

Marcello glared at the veins pulsating in Sergio's temples and along his neck. "How can you disapprove when you've never met her?"

"That family is despicable. They're Jews—*Ebrei*—who pretend not to be. They're unworthy of us, of you. It's their kind that killed our Lord Jesus Christ. Do you want to dishonor our family?"

"But I love her..."

Sergio swept his arm in a wide scything motion to stop Marcello from saying more. "I forbid you from seeing her. Ever! I'll stop it."

"But we're in love."

"You can't love someone whose clan is responsible for the death of our Savior. They can't be trusted!"

Marcello glared at his father, not moving a muscle.

"Now leave my sight while I deal with this disgrace. And don't leave this house!"

Julia, twitching nervously, found Amelia writing in her bed-chamber. Two candles cast a wavering yellow light over her composition.

"What's wrong? Your face is phantom gray."

Julia gripped the stem of her wilting rose, which had lost several petals. "Marcello's father is about to learn about us. We thought we were alone but were caught by his business partner," she said, distracted by worry. "Marcello's father will explode and forbid him from seeing me. What should I do?"

Amelia believed the time had come for plain speaking. She said softly, holding both of Julia's hands in hers, "You've taken many risks to see him, but your love might not be enough. The hate of others can be overpowering."

Julia mopped her tear-streaked face. Her light brown hair hung limply over her shoulders.

Amelia continued, "Julia, as your friend and someone who loves you, I may say things you don't wish to hear."

"I suppose. What should I do?"

"First, wait to see how Marcello's father reacts. We also don't know how Miriam and Zuane will respond should they learn about this. This state of not knowing is the hardest."

"I'm so afraid and scared of what Miriam and Zuane will say."

"However they react, listen and digest their opinions, even if you disagree."

"But I love Marcello. He's my life, my future."

"Miriam and Zuane also love you and want the best for you, although their ideas may differ from yours. Whatever they say, show you understand their viewpoint rather than try to win an argument. I know from experience that doesn't work well. Focus on finding solutions, which may be the best way to preserve your relationship with Marcello."

Julia rubbed her bloodshot eyes, looking miserable. "Amelia, can I stay with you tonight?"

"Of course."

Julia went on, her voice cracking, "I like everyone to think I'm strong and confident, but I'm not. I'm always pretending."

"We all do at times. Yet facing our fears makes us stronger."

Amelia looked deeply into Julia's eyes, seeing the hurt in them. "Come, lie on my bed. Let me hold you. I'll share whatever strength I have."

✑

The morning sun slanted through the shutters into Amelia's bedroom but did not wake Julia sleeping beside her.

Poor dear, thought Amelia, She'd only fallen asleep an hour ago.

Amelia pondered their conversation. She couldn't see a pleasant ending to Julia's infatuation with Marcello. Was Julia being foolish? Probably. Was she following her heart? Indeed. Who could fault her for that? She's dreading what might come next, what others might try to impose. As am I. But will she do something rash?

24

VENICE, APRIL 1595

S ergio stormed into his office early the next morning, dispatching a messenger to the Bassano musical-instrument studio with a note for Zuane. Ciro, one of Marcello's friends who worked for the company, overheard the messenger tell a co-worker, "The boss gave me a message for Bassano. I thought they despised each other."

Ciro raced to inform Marcello.

Upon arriving, the messenger interrupted a meeting between Arturo, the studio supervisor, and Miriam. She questioned the urgency at first, but then was stunned to learn the message came from Caloprini. She could not imagine the purpose.

"I'm permitted to hand this note only to Signore Zuane Bassano or Signora Bassano," the messenger declared.

Miriam introduced herself.

"Sign here," he said presenting her with a ledger. "I'm instructed to wait for a reply and take it directly to Signore Caloprini."

Miriam unsealed the message, read it twice, and grimaced.

For Zuane Bassano:

We are anything but friends, but we have a mutual problem involving my son and your niece. I suspect you will be as unhappy as I upon learning about it. Can you come to my office by the Arsenale wharf today at noon? If not, suggest an alternate location and time today. This urgent matter must be settled.

Sergio Caloprini

Miriam told the messenger to wait. She climbed upstairs to the residence, finding Zuane in his office. She handed him the note and waited for his reaction. Zuane looked at her with a puzzled expression. "What can this be about?"

"I don't know, but there is much Julia hides from us.

He took paper from his desk and agreed to meet Sergio as proposed. He ran various scenarios through his mind. What kind of trouble could Julia be in?

An hour later, Zuane boarded a gondola moored to the studio dock. An employee rowed him through the serpentine course of the Grand Canal to Caloprini's business in the Arsenale.

At the time Sergio and Zuane were meeting, another messenger delivered a letter to Julia. Her hands shook as she read.

Julia, my love,

Words are insufficient for expressing my love for you. I want us to create a life together. As I feared, Signore Ponti informed my father about us. He's furious and has forbidden me from ever seeing you. I love you too much to comply and know you love me. Nothing else matters.

We must escape together. I have a friend in Verona and believe his family will take us in temporarily, until we make permanent arrangements. We must leave tonight before we are stopped. If you truly love me, deep in your heart as I love you, meet me tonight after sundown at the campo where we first kissed.

Also beware, my father sent a message to your uncle. I believe they're planning to meet, but I don't know when or where.

Your eternal love,

Marcello

Julia read the letter again, weighing its significance. *What will I sacrifice by leaving my family and the security of my home?* Yet she gave it only a fleeting thought. Her most pressing question was, "*How could I live without Marcello?*"

Julia strode toward her chamber. She removed a large quilted bag from her armoire and packed clothes. She selected carefully, taking practical items. The bag could not be too heavy, for she didn't know how long or far she'd need to carry it.

When she finished, she stole into the kitchen and took dried beef, bread, and fruit, not knowing when she'd have her next meal once she left. She wrapped these foodstuffs in a cloth and shoved them into her bag.

Now she had to wait until nightfall, a few hours away. She meandered through the house, imprinting the look of every room in her brain. She roamed the neighborhood and along the Grand Canal. Finally, she returned to her room and waited for sunset.

As Julia reclined on her bed, she closed her eyes and drifted off. Her uncle's booming voice startled her awake. "Julia! Julia! Come here at once."

The butterflies that had settled temporarily in Julia's stomach were set a-flutter once again.

Zuane and Miriam, both with stern expressions, were waiting in her uncle's office.

Amelia heard the shouts and rushed there as well, afraid matters had taken another unhappy turn.

"Julia, what's happening between you and this Marcello?" asked Zuane, his arms crossed.

Julia confessed their love for each other, choking on her words. When she finished she added, "The only problem is that our families loathe each other. That's why I didn't tell you. I can't help where my heart takes me and it's taken me to him."

"Loathing?" questioned Zuane, waving the message from Sergio. "We don't hate them. If Sergio hates us, it's because he despises all Jews, and perhaps us in particular because we don't live in Il Ghetto. He resents that we are respected by the Doge, Senate members, and most of the Council of Ten. Those relationships preserve what we have."

Miriam said, "You're Jewish, he's Catholic. We don't mix. It's too dangerous. That's why we won't allow you to see Marcello. You mustn't do something you'll always regret."

"How do you know what I'll regret? This is my life." Julia pivoted on her heel, ready to storm out of the room, and found Amelia standing in the doorway.

Amelia raised her hands. "Julia, wait. Listen a moment longer."

"What for? I've heard enough," she protested, trying to squeeze past Amelia.

"We are not your enemy, just the contrary," Amelia said kindly. "What you do has an effect on us all. Your aunt and uncle may well know what's best for you, as difficult as that is to hear and accept."

"Oh?" snarled Julia. "I thought you were my friend!"

Amelia gaped, obviously stung by Julia's barb. After a moment of stunned silence, she replied, "I am, and what I've said, I've said as a friend. We can wish for a different world, but we must live in the one we have."

"I don't believe that twaddle. I don't think you do either," retorted Julia, pointing an accusing finger.

Amelia waited until Julia lowered her arm. "How much are you willing to sacrifice to make a point or pursue your relationship with Marcello?"

"We are talking about love, Amelia. Love! Not some arranged courtship."

"Darling," Miriam said calmly, "we know this seems unfair to you. Yet pursuing a relationship with a young man with completely different beliefs, and who comes from a family that harbors antipathy toward us, won't lead to happiness, only strife and hardship you cannot imagine at your age."

"You don't know that. We love each other—"

"Julia, dear, there are certain rules we must live with even if we dislike them. One is that Catholics marry Catholics and Jews marry Jews. We don't merge, and those that do are shunned."

"That's stupid," Julia cried.

Zuane said, "Julia, Marcello's father has forbidden it too. I met him earlier today. He has someone watching Marcello's every step. It's over."

Julia pleaded, "Allow me to see him once more to say goodbye."

Miriam said, "Forget about Marcello. That's final."

Julia knew her uncle and aunt would not budge. Silently weeping, she retired to her room, her mind racing. Above all other thoughts, one question repeated itself over and over: *How can I sneak away now that dusk has come?*

Marcello tracked the moves of his father's human watchdog while plotting how he'd escape from the palazzo. His canal-side chamber occupied a corner of the third floor. A wrought iron railing outside spanned two high windows that swung inward on hinges. He planned to tie a rope to the railing and climb down. Again he checked his sightline to the water below. He'd need to be careful not to swing into the window beneath his and to land on the ledge above the waterline. Then he could work his way along the ledge to the narrow alley next to the building. He'd never done it before but the width made it possible.

Before heading for his chamber, he told his guard he would eat then go to bed. After a meal of mozzarella, bread, and a small capon breast, Marcello secretly stuffed a rope and knife into his pants, bid good night to the watchman, and returned upstairs.

Dressed in dark clothing, Marcello packed a small bag and leaned out the window. He cut the rope into two pieces of the same length. He tied the bag to one end and lowered it to the ledge, securing the other end to the railing. He waited quietly, alone in his dark room for thirty minutes, before putting his plan in motion. He lowered himself more easily than he expected but had a start when the wrought iron railing creaked from his weight. He willed it not to break away, then descended as hastily as he dared. He missed the window on the way down but caught the ledge above the canal with only the toes of one foot. The other dipped into the murky water. Had he not been gripping the rope firmly, he'd have fallen in.

Marcello pulled himself up until he could place his other foot on the ledge. He steadied himself and grabbed the bag tied to the other rope. He unknotted the sack and swung it around the building into the alley, careful to keep his balance. It landed with a thud. Then he inched his way along the ledge, his hands flat against the stone building until reaching the corner. He leapt into the narrow passageway, snatched his bag, and raced toward *Campo Bandiera e Morro*.

Marcello planned to wait for Julia by the round wellhead that capped the water cistern in the square's center, near the church of San Giovanni Battista in Bragora.

Julia waited long hours, fretting, before making her move. She heard Miriam and Zuane walk to their chamber, whispering, no doubt about her. When she thought they had fallen asleep, she grabbed her bag and quietly opened her door. She tiptoed along the hall, down stairs, then through another hall, across the salon, and descended the dark stairway to the landside door. She paused in the foyer, listening before unlocking it. She eased open the heavy door, ready to slip out, when it slammed shut. She screamed.

Her uncle loomed from the shadows, his hand pressing the door closed. She saw deep disappointment in his drawn face.

"Where are you going?" he demanded.

"To see Marcello one last time. Let me go."

"Do you take me for a fool? I suspect that bag is packed with clothes. Where is he taking you?"

Julia slumped against the door weeping, not saying another word.

Zuane said, "It doesn't matter, I don't expect the truth from you. You're not going anywhere."

Amelia, alerted by the commotion, descended halfway down the flight of stairs. "Julia, you can't win this battle. Stay with me tonight. Running away will worsen matters."

"Why should I listen to you? You're on their side."

Amelia knew the blindness of passion only too well. "We're all on your side, even if you don't realize it."

Julia put her face in her hands. Then she looked at Amelia through her tears.

"I don't know what to do. I'm confused, trapped. I'm being forced to betray my love, to break my solemn promise."

"Dear Julia, there's nothing else you can do tonight."

"Julia," her uncle said, "I am not moving from this spot."

Julia slumped on the stairs, awash in misery, and giving in to the inevitable. With downcast eyes she climbed the few steps toward Amelia. Amelia put her arm around Julia's waist and escorted her to her bedchamber.

Marcello circled the dark campo restlessly, looking for any sign of Julia. *She won't forsake me. I've risked everything for her.* He waited and worried, paced and wondered where she could be—certain of her love. He could not imagine what had caused her delay, but there must a good reason. *Julia's smart and clever; surely she could sneak from her home.*

He pulled her reply to his letter from his pocket, reading again her brief message in the faint light.

> *Marcello, my love,*
>   *You are my world and we will create our own paradise free of the hatred our parents have for each other. I will come as soon after dusk as possible. Wait for me. If I get there first, you can be sure I'll wait for you.*
> *Your love,*
> *Julia*

Strong winds whirled through the campo in the moonless night. Marcello shielded his eyes from swirling dust. It began raining—first as a sweeping drizzle, then as a downpour. It stormed for several minutes then slowed momentarily before drenching sheets started again.

Hours passed and Julia had not come. Cold and damp, Marcello listened to the rhythm of his deep husky breaths as his despondency grew. *Should I continue waiting? Has Julia betrayed me?*

When Marcello could not stand waiting any longer, he found a sharp stone and etched on the side of the well:

> *J, I waited hours for you. I'll return at dawn.*
> *Always in love, M*

Marcello slogged through the pouring rain with his bag slung over his shoulder. He trudged along tributary canals until he could go no farther then turned aimlessly down dark passageways. Some were only four feet wide. Walls and buildings rose eerily on either side. He heard muffled voices seep through dimly lit windows of tiny homes.

He felt faint, lost, alone. His sodden leather coat weighed heavily on his shoulders. His cold hands shook. He wove side to side through narrow alleys that seemed to close in on him. He spread his arms, letting his knuckles graze buildings on each side as he staggered along, scraping the skin off. He didn't care.

His pain and foreboding grew. The emptiness in his gut expanded and the dull ache inside sharpened. He felt hollow, like everything he'd once believed had been sucked from his soul.

Marcello's continued his erratic wandering until hearing footsteps behind him. He swung around but saw nothing in the black night. *Phantoms?* He pushed himself off a rough brick wall and wobbled from one side to the other. He stumbled on a raised paving stone and stepped into puddles while catching his balance. Water oozed into his boot. He heard distant voices. More footsteps tramped behind him— or were they ahead of him?

Marcello didn't know why, but he started to run. The streets no longer looked familiar. He saw nothing he recognized. He darted through one narrow alley and zigzagged down another. He couldn't see any landmarks above the buildings. The streets were unmarked. He relied on his intuition and sense of direction to navigate through the maze.

Finally, he recognized a building. He bolted down a pitch-black alley only three feet wide, expecting it to connect with a bridge. From there he'd find his way to *Riva degli Schiavoni* and the waters of San Marco's Basin. He careened past dark windows and banged his head on an unlit sconce. Dazed, he saw the alley's end and lurched ahead, moving as fast as he could toward the bridge.

The line of buildings ended but the bridge was an illusion. He sprinted into open space with nothing beneath his feet and plunged into the dark canal. The cold, foul water shocked him. Inky concentric ripples emerged in the rain-splattered water, but Marcello did not surface inside them. The canal resumed its black and silvery sheen. Marcello's bag bobbed near the bank. Nobody was nearby to rescue a young man too stunned to swim.

25

A gondolier discovered Marcello when dawn's first rays cast a serene light over the canal. His body had floated downstream and lodged beneath a bridge. The gondolier pulled the cold gray corpse from beneath the span and laid him on the bank. Canal water trickled from Marcello's mouth. Another gondolier retrieved Marcello's waterlogged bag and laid it beside him. It had drifted along the surface until snagging on a building crevice.

Authorities identified Marcello immediately and dispatched messengers to Sergio Caloprini's home and business.

Sergio and his wife, Carlotta, raced to the canal in the brisk spring air. Carlotta heaved in long guttural breaths upon seeing her lifeless son. Her fleshy hand clutched her heart. She bent deeply and wailed. Sergio glared in shock, anger, and humiliation. How could this happen to his son? How did he escape the palazzo unnoticed? His watchman would be punished severely.

Carlotta pounded her fists into Sergio's chest. "You turned him into a caged animal and he escaped! Now he's dead. Dead!" Carlotta screeched. She gasped for air, and her words came out thickly amid her wracking sobs.

"This is not my fault," Sergio retorted, his anger coming to a boil. "The Bassanos are to blame. Those Jews sent their girl, Julia, to tempt him. She, the entire family, and that woman from England will all pay."

Carlotta pushed herself away. "Your hatred blinded you to your impact on our son...*our* son! Marcello rebelled against your control. You didn't reason with him. You sought to impose your will. We don't know if Julia Bassano or her family had anything to do with this. They may detest us, but I doubt they'd wish such a terrible fate to befall our son. And revenge won't bring him back!"

"No! No, it can't be true," raged Julia, overcome with grief upon hearing of Marcello's drowning. She could hardly breathe between strangled cries of pain. She yelled at her aunt and uncle. "You've done this!"

Amelia, Miriam, and Zuane gaped silently.

"Are you satisfied now that Marcello is dead and my life is ruined? He thought I betrayed his love. Because you stopped me!"

"Julia, we're all upset," said Amelia. "No one could have predicted this tragedy."

"You're as much at fault as they," cried Julia.

Miriam said softly, "Julia, Amelia only wanted to help."

"Help who? She didn't hold the door shut, but she made me feel it was futile to force myself past Uncle Zuane."

Amelia handed Julia a white handkerchief. "Marcello's death is horrible, an accident. We thought you were being reckless. We do care for you."

Julia's lips trembled. "Isn't that nice," she said sarcastically. "Aunt and uncle, your problem is solved. Are you happy?"

"We thought Marcello would simply return home, disappointed, when you didn't meet him," said Miriam.

Julia dropped onto a leather chair with a blank expression, turning her turmoil inward. Her stomach churned, her head pounded. She knew her life would never be the same.

Miriam stepped over to Julia and placed her hand gently on her shoulder. Julia shoved her away, shouting, "Don't touch me! Leave me alone." She jumped up and ran to her bedchamber.

Julia's keening sobs reverberated for hours through the house. When the wailing subsided, followed by a long bout of deathly silence, Amelia peeked in. Julia, sitting forlornly on the edge of her bed looked up and then away. Amelia asked if she could come in. Julia nodded. Amelia hugged her. Julia leaned into her cousin, weeping as Amelia's white blouse absorbed her tears.

A few minutes later, Julia fell into a fitful, exhausted slumber. Amelia lowered her to the bed, waited for her breathing to steady, and slipped from the room.

26

LONDON, APRIL 1595

Will headed to The Theatre, repeating in his mind his last conversation with Burbage, which resembled those they'd had several times before. Burbage had pounded his fist bellowing, "Where is it, Will? You promised I'd have my *Jew of Malta* by now. What are you calling it? Oh, yes, *The Lender of* Vienna or somewhere?"

Will recalled squirming in Burbage's dingy office, watching a vein bulge on the little man's forehead. Today he'd try a more conciliatory approach. After Burbage's bellicose inquiry, he said, "I'm progressing but keep hitting snags. I never thought this script would be so hard to write."

"Will, I have a business to run. I'm only selling half the seats for *Richard III*. I'll have to close it soon and replace it with something new. What have you got for me?"

"But *Titus Andronicus, The Taming of the Shrew,* and *Two Gentlemen of Verona* are doing well. They are attracting full houses." The latter play Amelia had dispatched several months ago.

"Most of the time," Burbage retorted. "The audience is thinning for them too. It's just a matter of time before we'll need to stage something else in their stead."

"I'm well along drafting *Richard II*," Will pointed out hopefully. To distract Burbage, he summarized its plot. "It dramatizes the king's fall from power and the ascension of Henry IV. It's a tragic tale about the cost of excessive greed and poor stewardship—and sure to draw audiences."

"Is it ready now? Now is what I need!"

Will frowned, shaking his head. "No, there's still much work to do. I have, though, laid out the plot for a play about King John, but—"

Burbage thumped his fist on a stack of papers. "Will! I can't wait. What can we start rehearsing today?"

Will thought about another script he'd received from Amelia, *Love's Labour's Lost*. He wasn't sure what to make of it. It had all the clever hallmarks of an Amelia script—word-plays, double entendres, puns, and a play within a play. It was an implausible comedy about nobles choosing to give up women but who then face alluring temptations. But it was not what Burbage wanted.

Without preamble, Will extracted the script from his case and pushed it across the desk. "It's still a little rough, but we can stage it within a month. I'll make refinements, then get parts to the players so they can learn their lines and rehearse."

Burbage leafed through the manuscript. Will couldn't read his expression but felt awkward in the silence. When the theater owner spoke at last, he sounded optimistic.

"Will, this might be a good one for spring and summer. Could we open it in May?"

Following Burbage's assent, Will rushed to rewrite some rough spots and begin rehearsals for *Love's Labour's Lost*. While explaining the plot and characters to the performers, Lord Hunsdon sauntered into the theater carrying the script Will had loaned him days earlier.

"Lord Hunsdon, it's good to see you," said Will.

Turning to the actors, he instructed, "Gentlemen, read and practice your lines. I'll return in a few minutes."

Will led the way to a dusty room filled with crates, old scenery, curtains, spare ropes, and other supplies. They stopped in a narrow aisle among boxes.

"Lord, meeting in this storeroom is not befitting a man of your stature, but I don't wish to have our discussion overheard."

"What is it?" asked Henry.

"First, what's your opinion of *Love's Labour's Lost?*"

"Ah, it's another masterpiece by Amelia. It's original and quick. The dialogue is smart and nimble. It will be quite successful."

"I believe so," said Will. "Burbage is less confident. He's pushing for a serious drama—one in particular that Amelia is writing—about a Jewish moneylender. Evidently she's wrestling with it and given other scripts, like the one in your hand, greater priority. I'm not complaining but…"

"But because Burbage is clamoring for it, you're worried about being exposed, especially since you can't predict when she'll finish it."

"Exactly," said Will. "I doubt I can mollify him much longer."

"Amelia has not written to me about that script or problems she's having," said Henry, "but I can probably relieve some of the pressure."

"How?"

"When Burbage acted, before building The Theatre, he was a member of the Earl of Leicester's Men. That theatrical association conferred a certain status upon him. He may think it still gives him greater authority than he actually possesses. I suspect he needs you as much as you need him, but he's not revealing his hand."

Will wanted to believe that was so but didn't see how it resolved his predicament. "How does that relieve pressure?"

"It doesn't. We must equalize the pressure," said Henry.

"But how?"

"I could become your patron, conferring status on your company. It might be called 'Lord Chamberlain's Men.' I'll create more opportunities to perform for the court. Burbage will then need to deal with me as well when he's unhappy about scripts or not getting ones he demands."

Will liked this idea, and knew it came about only because of their mutual relationship with Amelia. "I'd be honored if you bestowed such a designation, making my dealings with Burbage more evenhanded. I'm very grateful."

"Shall I proceed?"

"Without question and, please, with haste."

27

VENICE, APRIL 1595

Amelia read poetry aloud to allay her own fears and calm Julia as little Henry played with wooden blocks and a toy horse. Still in her nightgown, Julia sat listlessly with Henry—her face pale and her eyes red. Amelia wondered what would happen next.

Julia slept for much of the next few days, going to bed early, waking late, and napping in mid-afternoon. The morning after hearing the news of Marcello's death, Amelia discussed her sense of foreboding with Zev, Miriam, Zuane, and Enid, who held Henry in her lap. They conferred in the privacy of Zuane's office. Tall windows offered access to a narrow balcony overlooking the Grand Canal. Concerto pages were spread on an oak music stand. A lute and violin rested on Zuane's desk atop music sheets.

Zuane's news supplemented Amelia's fears. "Sergio was livid when I met with him the afternoon before Marcello's drowning. He blamed Julia for enticing his son. He called her a fortune seeker intent on improving her status, claiming she used her youthful sexuality to attract Marcello then manipulated him into proposing to her."

Amelia didn't believe a word. "Julia can be stubborn and underhanded at times, but she's truly grieving for Marcello."

Zev asked, "What will Sergio do?"

Zuane replied, "In business, he's vengeful and strives to destroy those he considers a threat."

"That's what's disturbs me," said Amelia. "He'll probably react as he has in the past. What do we know about him? Where is he vulnerable?"

"How is that useful?" asked Miriam.

"If he is seeking revenge on Julia and this family, we must identify what will compel him to reconsider or withdraw. If he sees the risk isn't worth taking—"

Miriam interrupted, "But he's far more powerful than us."

"True, but he has more at stake." Amelia looked into the eyes of everyone else in the room, trying to assess each one's resolve and willingness to act before being trapped by Sergio's aggression. "A small advantage we have is that few people in Venice know Enid and me."

"So you can be clandestine?"

"Exactly," replied Amelia. "And we can deploy my knowledge of drama. I know how to put on a performance, perhaps for Signore Ponti. He did not seem to like Sergio when I saw them talking at the theater. To my eyes, his anguished expressions bordered on hatred."

Zuane understood where her thoughts were leading. "Now that we're considering the matter, I have a cousin that works for their shipping business. He could be helpful. He hides his Jewish heritage, of course, but he's a manager. I'll ask him to report anything he hears."

Amelia felt heartened by this news. Yet she still believed exploiting Ponti's antipathy could be pivotal. If Sergio disgraced the company they jointly owned, he'd be harmed too. And Ponti might wish to be rid of Sergio all together.

"Enid, we'll dress like ladies of the night, but not as seductively," said Amelia.

"But I've nothing to wear like that and neither do you."

"But you can sew. I have dresses from England that are unstylish here. We can re-fashion them," suggested Amelia. Her mind fired with ideas. A strategy had come together in her head. She felt engaged, driven. Rather than writing a plot, she was executing one—with urgency and purpose— feeling alive, thrilled, and confident.

Enid smiled, intrigued by the idea, as Amelia had suspected. "Then an actress I shall be."

They climbed to Amelia's bedchamber, where her trunks were stored, while Miriam cared for Henry.

Enid flipped a latch, opened the lid, and pawed through the dresses.

"What about this one?" asked Enid, pressing a dull brown and black smock with a scoop neck against her body.

"We need something more prosperous-looking and colorful," said Amelia.

Next, Enid withdrew a red velvet gown with a thick belt, wide scored sleeves, and cream lining.

"That's closer to the image I want," said Amelia. "Can you make the neckline more revealing?

Enid held it up and inspected it. "That should be easy."

"Isn't there a headdress that goes with it?"

"It's here," said Enid as she lifted the hat with an attached veil.

Amelia nodded in satisfaction. "That's perfect for your sandy hair. What else do we have?"

Enid sifted through the next layer of dresses and produced a sky-blue gown with a white bodice and lavish draping sleeves. "I can tailor the gown so it hangs off the shoulder and reveals your upper chest."

Amelia held it against her. "Making it suggestive?"

"Indeed. It'll be easy," said Enid.

"I'll put it on so you can get started."

When Enid completed the alterations, they chose accessories and assessed themselves in the mirror. Amelia hid her coppery hair curls beneath a linen whitework cap with a sheer veil. Enid then put on the red hat, which drew attention to her pale skin and green eyes.

"You look elegant," said Amelia as she adjusted the fashionable headdress. "Do I look like a harlot?"

"As much as you can."

"For the final touch, let's paint our lips red."

Amelia's skin prickled, her earlier confidence dissipating as she and Enid walked to the Restaurante Ferro near the Rialto Bridge, where wealthy businessmen drank and dined. She questioned whether their audacity, amateur acting, and costumes would fool anyone, especially someone as savvy as Ponti. She saw no point, though, in turning back. They had to do something and she could think of nothing better.

She noticed Enid's trepidation in the tightness of her lips, her clinched fists, and hesitant stride. More than once Enid had asked what would happen if someone punctured their charade. Amelia didn't know, except they'd need to invent a story on the spot and escape quickly.

Restaurante Ferro was among the safest and most lucrative hunting grounds for ladies of the night. The strumpets were discreet and well known to regulars. New faces were instantly noticed and, if attractive, captured the clientele's curiosity.

Before entering, Amelia showed her most confident face.

Inside, candles and oil lamps set on dining tables and a carved walnut bar cast shadowy yellow light. Men were gathered in huddles, speaking in hushed voices. Heads turned when the door opened, shooting a bright shaft into the dimly lit room. Amelia and Enid stood in its beam in their low-cut dresses. Amelia's eyes adjusted as she scanned the room. She strutted to the bar and spoke to the bartender in intentionally stilted Vèneto. "I'm looking for Signore Ponti. Is he here?"

All the eyes shifted toward Ponti sitting at the opposite end of the bar. "Who might you be?" he demanded in a deep voice.

"Signore, we've never met. May we speak privately, perhaps at that table in the corner?" Amelia suggested, getting a closer look at his burn-scarred face and white-streaked hair.

"Anything can be said before my friends."

"Perhaps so, however, it might be better if we didn't," Enid said in a confidential tone. She handed him a short note.

Ponti grimaced as he perused the message. When he looked up, he nodded in agreement. "Perhaps we should talk privately."

Sitting down, Ponti said, "You still haven't told me who you are."

"I'm Simona and this is Nicola," offered Amelia. "We were Marcello's friends. Not like girlfriends, just friends. We're originally from London, but my father grew up here. He hated English weather, so when he moved back, I invited my friend Nicola. We're not too fluent at Vèneto yet, so excuse our poor grammar."

"All right," said Ponti, seemingly curious about this odd background. "Why are you meeting with me?"

Enid put her arm on Amelia's bare shoulder. "Marcello told us that he feared his father. We weren't to tell anyone, but now that he's dead—"

"Sergio loved him."

Amelia explained, "He may have, but Signore Caloprini threatened Marcello. That was how he forced his son to follow his commands. And the punishment was severe if he did not."

Ponti's face remained impassive, but Amelia thought he well understood his partner's temperament. "Simona, what's your purpose?" he asked.

"When Marcello met Julia, he wished to follow his heart and not his father's orders."

"So? How does this tie to his drowning in the canal?"

Enid leaned over the table, providing an ample view as she said sotto voce, "He told us his father would kill him if he discovered his love for Julia. Marcello made us promise that if anything strange happened to him, we would tell you or his mother. He said he trusted you to take the correct course." She drew back, as though just noticing where his eyes had strayed. "We can't see his mother. She's grieving and, we hear, not speaking to anyone, including Signore Caloprini."

Ponti's eyes darted around the restaurant, checking if anyone was observing. "What is the message Marcello swore you to deliver?"

Amelia took over the conspiratorial lead. "He believed his father would blame Julia or her family, and he hoped you would stop any plots to harm them," she whispered. "He said you were tough but fair-minded."

"Why come to me and not the authorities?"

"Marcello knew about his father's bribes," said Amelia. "They're beholden to him."

Ponti nodded knowingly. "I'll investigate and see what I learn."

"That's what Marcello would want," said Enid.

Ponti paused, clearly thinking through the matter as a new expression crossed his face. Amelia recognized the signs of naked greed. "Simone and Nicola," he said slowly, "you were right to come to me."

After meeting with Ponti, Amelia and Enid headed through the *Campo San Bartolomio* in the exact opposite direction from the Bassano residence. When nobody followed, they crossed a canal and stopped in a church to pray—or pretend to—for a few minutes. The tranquility and vanilla smell of devotional candles calmed Amelia's racing heart. When no one suspicious entered, they left through another exit and darted through the narrow streets.

Miriam greeted them in the salon when they arrived at the Bassano residence while Henry slept in his cradle.

Enid reported breathlessly, "I think the meeting went well. We performed better than I expected."

Miriam asked, "What's Ponti thinking?"

"I suspect he's wondering how to exploit this situation for his own purposes," Amelia speculated.

"He and Caloprini are business partners but not friends," Miriam noted. "Do you think Ponti will betray him?"

"We planted a seed. We'll see what grows," replied Amelia.

Ponti began plotting the moment Amelia and Enid left. He shifted his eyes around the restaurant. Now that Simona and Nicola had left, no one took further notice of him. He assessed the opportunity their damning information presented. How could he use it to maneuver Sergio out of the business? He knew the man well. Seeking revenge fit his modus operandi. Destroying Bassano's business would be his first inclination. Yet the crime could redound upon their shipping business unfavorably, especially if the Doge suspects the truth. He then could be tarred by the same brush as Sergio and lose everything. A plan took shape in his head, and it required catching Sergio or his goons in the act.

Ponti ordered another drink. He considered who he could trust, who hated Sergio, and who would spy for him. He needed them for allies.

Amelia, Miriam and Zuane were shaken when Zuane's cousin at the shipping company reported he had heard whispers that Caloprini wanted to torch the studio after Marcello's funeral. Once workmen left for the day, they met in the still space.

His account sent chills down Amelia's spine as she envisioned the horrifying hanging, drawing, and quartering of Rodrigo Lopez—and feared something just as awful could happen to her and her cousins, as the Inquisition had done to Jews in Spain and Portugal. She drew in a deep breath and worked to stay calm and think rationally. "How can we stop Caloprini? If he succeeds in burning the studio, the residence will be destroyed too."

Miriam answered, "Our calculations must surpass his."

"How can we do that?" asked Zuane.

Miriam, always practical, replied, "Let's begin by protecting what we have. Let's pack our inventory and move from the studio. Zev, can you investigate storage and workplace options?"

"I start today."

Along the walls of the well-organized studio were shelves and cubbyholes containing materials and parts for building musical instruments. Each wall was dedicated to a type of instrument. To the right, upon entering the studio from the landward side, were supplies for wind instruments. Metals and wood planks for instrument bodies were set along the first section, and smaller parts were arranged within slots and bins, all neatly labeled. The other side housed materials for lutes. Partially assembled parts were stored on both sides of the door. Mounted to one side of the massive canal-side double door was a large board listing orders and the status of various projects. Tools were lined in racks on the other side.

In the center were well-worn worktables with instruments in varying stages of completion, including a partially finished lute and crumhorn. One table was dedicated to creating the fine ornamentation and detailed etching for the most expensive instruments such as pivas and bassonellas. Each table featured side slots for tools and small parts.

As Amelia surveyed the workspace, she realized that packing it would be a significant undertaking. She asked Miriam, "What's the best way to do this, so everything can be put back in order later?"

The next day, Miriam met with Arturo, the studio supervisor and lead craftsman. They constructed a plan in which materials and supplies along each wall would be packed in well-labeled crates. Instruments-in-progress would be placed in special protective cases. Arturo described how each crate should be organized so its contents could be accessed efficiently. He met with his apprentices and workers, giving instructions and stressing the need for secrecy.

Three hours later, amid swirling dust motes and packing confusion, Amelia spotted a tall well-dressed but hard-looking figure silhouetted in the canal-side door. When he stepped inside she recognized his marred face. *It's Ponti! Does he recognize me?* She drew back into the shadows, but his gaze did not follow her. *He shows no signs of it. Today my face and hair are uncovered. And my lips are natural.*

The studio appeared like organized chaos with shelves half emptied and crates spread everywhere as workers feverously packed them.

The man glanced from one end to the other, seemingly appraising the state of affairs. Then he looked from Amelia to Miriam. "Is one of you Senora Bassano?"

"I am, Signore Ponti. What brings you here?"

28

The black-draped funeral gondola carrying Marcello's casket moved through the Grand Canal into San Marco's Basin. Julia and Amelia watched from their gondola trailing well behind. It docked east of San Zaccaria by a byzantine-style palazzo. Sergio and Carlotta, waiting on the broad *Riva degli Schiavoni*, stood apart from each other as if total strangers. When Sergio edged closer to his wife, she stepped farther away. Marcello's parents followed the pall-bearers through the narrow *Calle del Doce* to *Campo Bandiera e Morro* and into the church of *San Giovanni Battista* (Saint John the Baptist) in *Bragora*. Amelia and Julia watched them disappear inside before entering the *campo*.

Amelia's mind alternated between two places—here with Julia, who wore an elegant black gown with lace trim, and the Bassano studio, where she feared terrible events were about to unfold.

"This square is where we first kissed," cried Julia, gripping Amelia's arm with one hand while pointing with the other, "right under that albero tree. Our heads barely cleared its branches."

The funeral mass would begin in thirty minutes. Julia and Amelia waited in the warmth of the sunny square for the bells to toll. They walked slowly around the wellhead where Marcello had waited for Julia that fateful night.

"Oh, no!" screamed Julia, pointing at the message scraped onto the side of the cistern: *J, I waited hours for you. Will be back at dawn. Always in love, M.*

Amelia read it and enfolded Julia lovingly in her arms. Her cousin's wrenching sobs heaved deeply into her own soul. She knew words could never capture the sorrow they both felt but she had to try. "Julia, this proves he waited for you. He loved you."

"And he drowned. He never saw the dawn," Julia sputtered through tears. "His last thoughts were of me." Her eyes turned glassy. In a faraway voice she said, "Amelia, I thought of ending my life last night. I don't know what stopped me. I should have."

Amelia hugged Julia, desperately wanting to ease her trauma while believing her cousin's throes were essential to discharging her grief. "You're devastated. I would be too," she whispered in Julia's ear. "I'm grateful you're here and alive. Although Marcello's death is tragic, and he cannot be replaced, you can have a wondrous life. I think he'd want that."

"I couldn't love another man like I loved Marcello."

"That may be true, but you'll love another man in a different way, a way that will also be special." Amelia thought of Lord Hunsdon, the one man she truly loved and respected, compared to her misfortune in marrying Alphonso. Her heart felt heavier.

"I don't think so. Marcello was my true soul mate."

"You have much to live for, and you don't know who you will meet."

Julia circled to the far side of the well and leaned against it, her eyes puffy and red. "My parents are gone. I have only my brother."

Stunned by Julia's claim of isolation, Amelia swallowed hard. "What about Aunt Miriam and Uncle Zuane?"

"I hate them. I can barely tolerate being in the same room as they."

Amelia remembered her adolescence and how unforgiving she could be—but not with Julia's vehemence. "They love and care for you. You may dislike their decisions, but they acted as they thought best."

"It doesn't matter. I can't forgive them." As Amelia thought of her own role, Julia turned on her. "I thought you were my friend, but you sided with them. Why weren't you on my side?"

"Julia, true friends don't always agree with you," she said softly, "but they want what's good for you. They will challenge to you when they think you're going astray. That's what I tried to do."

"I know, but still…"

Amelia stepped around the wellhead and coupled her arm inside Julia's. "You may not realize it now, but Miriam and Zuane are the same way. They love you and wish you only happiness."

All the while, black-dressed mourners trickled into the square from three streets that emptied into it. They disappeared into the church either silently or speaking softly.

Amelia, in a low voice, told Julia about her young head-strong days, moving the conversation away from Julia's troubles. She told stories of growing up in England. She talked about the theater, how she met Will Shakespeare, became friends, and began working on plays together. She disclosed how she grew from a selfish girl who thought she knew better than others to a woman who learned from foolish mistakes. She concluded, "My father, in his wisdom, wanted a thorough education for me. He believed I could become an accomplished woman. So can you."

Julia smiled weakly. "Nobody before has said anything like that to me."

Amelia blinked tears away, at once saddened by Julia's admission and touched that her young cousin was realizing that Amelia saw her potential.

Together they watched larger groups crossing the square to the church. Amelia wondered who wasn't coming—and might be doing Caloprini's dirty work.

Bells clanged in the church tower and they headed toward the arched entryway of the eighth-century structure. The service had just begun as they stepped into the hushed nave, lit by candles and natural light from windows up high. They settled in the last pew next to an elderly couple.

Amelia's mind wandered throughout the Mass of the Resurrection. She surveyed the vast church interior with its tall red columns trimmed in gold, holding aloft soaring arches and the cross-beamed ceiling. The backdrop to the white marble high altar, embellished with gold, featured a huge painting of the Baptism of Christ by Giambattista Cima. As angelic choir voices flowed through the church, she recalled the sequence of events since first hearing Julia blurt Marcello's name a year earlier. Little could she imagine Julia's budding romance would end so tragically. Tragedy, she thought, not too unlike the story Miriam told on their return from Cremona. The tale by Luigi da Porto revolved around two young noble lovers—Romeus and Giulietta. She committed to learning more about it. She saw the parallels…a melancholy romance, a drama with a profound message…

The priest swung a censor over the casket spreading aromas of burning incense. He prayed for Marcello's soul to rise up to God with the vapors.

Julia wailed at the sound of Marcello's name, breaking the service's dignified solemnity. Everyone on their side of the church and across the aisle turned to gape, but Julia's eyes were locked only on the casket about to disappear forever.

Three gondolas approached the Bassano studio. On each, one man rowed and two others crouched on either side of a peaked wood cabin in the center. Some of the men wore black toques—round hats with narrow brims—while others were hooded.

Inside the studio, forty water buckets lined the walls and another twenty were clustered around the center of the large room. The space stood empty with the exception of wall-mounted shelves and two battered worktables not worth saving. Zuane and four other men hid inside watching the approaching gondolas through the wide door. Miriam, Zev and two of Ponti's men observed from the residence windows above, standing among many more water buckets. Enid hustled with Henry across the street to safety.

Arturo Valiero, the studio supervisor, paced in a white shirt with full sleeves and lace closure, black breeches, black cloak, and round white cap rather than his work clothes. Behind him were muscular men hand-selected by Ponti, all poised and ready for action.

The boats closed to the dock. Zuane stepped outside as a man in the lead gondola lit a torch. He held it aloft as it burst to life. Masked men in the boats behind him ignited several more like pickets of flame, their orange glows reflecting in the water.

"Stop before making the biggest mistake of your life!" shouted Zuane.

The leader waved his torch. "I think not, Bassano. I'd hate to see you burn to death along with your business, but it's not because you're undeserving."

"Why are you here? What harm have I done you?"

A man in the second boat pointed his torch at Zuane and yelled, "Don't act like you're unaware. We're here to incinerate your business and more if we can!"

"But why? A man should know before he dies or loses everything."

The same man shouted again, "It's your niece, you fool. She lured Signore Caloprini's son to his death."

Zuane shouted back, "So you're working for Caloprini! He's paying you enough?"

"We're here to avenge Marcello's death and exact justice."

Arturo stepped through the studio door onto the landing. "I've heard everything. Stop before doing something you'll regret."

"Who are you, old man? Stand clear before you burn with the building," howled a big man waving his torch.

"You need not know my name, only that I represent the Doge."

"You expect me to believe that?"

"Believe what you will. Even if you murder me and Signore Bassano, it's too late."

"I think not!"

"Look behind you."

The leader turned while the other assailants kept a steady eye on Zuane and Arturo.

Arturo continued, "See that gondola rowing south? It's heading for the Doge's Palace after lingering on the far bank. My appearance was the gondolier's signal to depart. He'll report to the Doge, and Caloprini will be arrested later today—the same day he buries his son. A double tragedy."

The leader remained silent for a few seconds, apparently undecided. He looked over the men in the gondolas holding their torches high.

Ponti's men marched from inside the studio onto the stone landing flanking Zuane and Arturo.

"I know you! Why are you here?" demanded a man in the third gondola.

"Yes, you do, Torre. I recognize your voice. And you know for whom I work. That should tell you something."

"It tells me you're a traitor."

"Think twice about what you're about to—"

A thunderous boom reverberated through the studio, rattling the canal-side doors.

"We've got them now!" shouted Torre. "We caught them from behind."

"Now!" shouted the leader as he cocked his arm and threw his torch in a high arc. It skidded on the half-open studio door, falling inside. Other burning torches flew overhead and skittered through the opening while the gondolier across the canal paddled faster downstream.

Another rumble tore through the building. Zuane rushed through the canal-side door, jumping over flames, as four men crashed a thick battering ram through the locked landside entrance. Two others pitched torches through the opening. More fiery brands quickly followed. The attackers dropped their battering ram in the open doorway, preventing the hatches from shutting. They ran inside, grabbed torches that had landed on the floor and ignited the wooden shelves and old worktables—all of which burst into flames.

Ponti's men bolted toward them as more torches sailed through the canal-side doors before being slammed shut. Inside, they tackled one arsonist, beating him raw until he stopped moving. His torch fell to the floor as flames licked the walls. Other attackers lit what they could before dashing back to the street. The three attack gondolas pushed downstream.

Zuane, Arturo, and Ponti's men furiously hurled buckets of water on the blazing walls. Thick, black suffocating smoke filled the studio. Miriam and Zev with two Ponti guards in the residence raced down to help.

They fought to douse the fire, while inhaling the hot, smoldering air. Sweat rolled into their eyes. They swept it away with sooty hands as jagged flames relentlessly climbed the walls, seeking the ceiling.

Julia, with tear-stained cheeks, hunched in the rear of the gondola. When the boat rounded a bend on the Grand Canal, Amelia screamed at the sight of thick black smoke pluming upward in the studio's direction. "Caloprini, that bastard!" she yelled, shaking her fist as Julia's jaw dropped in horror.

"Paddle faster. Don't let up," Amelia urged the gondolier as she stood up to see better, seething in fury.

The gondolier turned casting a poisonous stare, swung back, then pivoted quickly slamming his long oar into Amelia's face. As she fought to regain her footing, he stabbed the oar into her midriff. She stumbled backward. He stabbed again, pressing the oar hard into her gut, pushing her to the side until she fell into the canal.

Julia screamed and rushed the gondolier, catching him off balance. He glared in surprise while trying to steady himself with the oar and clutching her with his other arm. She rocked back beyond his grasp and charged him again, smashing her head into his jaw. He dropped the oar and with all her might she shoved him until he buckled overboard with his arms flailing wildly.

Julia searched the water for Amelia and saw her swimming to catch up with the gondola. She ran to the bow, grabbed the oar, and raced back to the stern. She extended the oar toward Amelia, who surged until finally grasping it. Julia pulled Amelia to the side, grabbed her wrists and lifted her into the swaying boat. Out of breath in her dripping bodice and skirt, Amelia collapsed onto a seat.

Without warning, the gondola pitched down steeply toward the front. They heard the heavy breaths of the gondolier and saw his hands gripping the side as he tried pulling himself back in. Julia seized the oar and crushed it into his knuckles. He roared in pain. She smashed them again until one of his hands lost its grip. Then she speared it into his chest until he fell back into the water.

Taking turns rowing, they swept the gondola down the length of the canal, peering ahead at the blaze. Flames leapt through the fumes. The acrid smell of smoke grew stronger.

Long black streaks marred the building's exterior. Scorch marks rose to the balcony above the charred remains of the studio's canal-side doors and below broken second-floor windows. Ponti's men filled water buckets with canal water and hauled them inside. Amelia noticed a brutish-looking man bound to the dock. His head hung to one side. Bloody welts protruded from his bruised face and around his swollen eye.

Upon reaching the dock, Amelia heard a piercing shriek erupt from inside. Miriam streaked out with her skirt and sleeves ablaze. Amelia leapt from the gondola and hurtled toward her, hastened her to the ground, and rolled on top. Amelia breathed in relief upon hearing the steamy hiss of flames being extinguished by her still-soaked wool gown.

Vincente Ponti waited for the gondola to reach the landing by *Piazza San Marco* and the *Palazzo Ducale*—the Doge's Palace. He'd seen the smoke rise in the distance behind rows of buildings while the sun shone in the western sky and cool breezes blew in from the basin. Soon the gondolier, paddling swiftly, came into view. Ponti, expecting to confirm his suspicions, knew his next step. He had to ensure he'd be unseen at two critical moments.

"What did you witness?" asked Ponti as the gondolier tied up at the dock.

The boatman wiped sweat from his brow. "Three gondolas, each with three men, paddled to the Bassano dock. Torches were lit and Bassano spoke with them. Then a man in the white shirt emerged, signaling that Caloprini's name had been mentioned. Seconds later your men came onto the landing. Two loud booms followed. Then torches were hurled into the building. Others might have been thrown from the street side too. The plan to implicate Caloprini worked but not the part to scare them off. I don't know what's left of the building."

"Thank you. Now disappear and forget all you saw."

Ponti marched toward the main entrance of the Doge's Palace. He stopped beneath the colonnade, ducking behind a pillar to avoid being seen by guards a few paces away. He pulled two notes from his coat pocket and reread them. He checked to ensure his handwriting was well disguised. No one could know they came from him.

Ponti returned the messages to his pocket and strode confidently to the palace entrance. "I'm meeting fellow senators in the Upper Chancellor's offices."

"Proceed, signore," replied one guard.

Ponti walked into the palace and through the grand inner courtyard. Colonnades ran along the sides. A four-story white edifice dominated the far end, topped with corner steeples and a higher one in the center, each with statues of legendary figures. Other statues graced the alcoves. To his right, the grand *Scala dei Giganti*—Stairway of Giants ascended. Ponti glanced up the wide steps to the imposing statues of Mars and Neptune, checking for anyone watching from the second-level loggia. Satisfied, he headed casually to a stone lion's head jutting from the wall. Through its open jaws one could drop anonymous accusations against others. Although one of several in Venice, its location inside the Doge's Palace signified the informer had access and denunciations would receive immediate attention. Ponti slipped the first of his two notes through the lion's mouth.

On the wall's other side, an investigator read the message:

> *I accuse Sig. Sergio Caloprini of dispatching arson-*
> *ists to burn the Bassano instrument-making build-*
> *ing. Sig. Z. Bassano and his supervisor can verify.*

Ponti once again checked to see that no eyes were following him as he sneaked over to another "Mouth of Truth." This protruding human face had been sculpted with a fierce expression, large bulging eyes topped with thick brows, and a stern open mouth. The inscription beneath the head indicated it was for allegations against those hiding income from the government. Ponti secretly dropped his second message inside the mouth:

> *Sig. Sergio Caloprini is evading taxes due the*
> *Republic of Venice. Investigate to find the evidence.*

After the funeral, the Caloprinis gathered with friends in their spacious salon adorned with naval tapestries and heavy furniture. Carlotta and Sergio told stories about Marcello and acknowledged expressions of sorrow from their friends. Weary, Carlotta desired a good night's rest after several traumatic days, but Sergio vowed to wait until receiving details about the burning of the Bassano studio.

Several guests were saying goodbye and repeating condolences when jarring knocks rattled the front door. Everyone turned as the door burst open. Three broad-shouldered, black-hooded guards blocked the entry, each with an intimidating scowl. The guard in charge demanded that Sergio step forward.

Unfazed by the man's arrogance, Sergio swaggered through his guests. "What's the meaning of this? How dare you barge into my home, especially at a time of mourning!"

"Signore Caloprini, by order of the Doge and as emissaries of the *Consiglio Maggiore*, we are here to arrest you. Come with us or we'll forcibly apprehend you."

"On what charges?" demanded Sergio, planting his hands on his hips.

Carlotta stepped away, covering her mouth.

"One, conspiracy to commit arson. Two, tax fraud."

The guards seized Caloprini and marched him through the night, past the looming facade of Saint Mark's Cathedral to the wide Piazza San Marco, around to the prison adjacent to the Doge's Palace. Thick iron bars covered the windows of this house of horror. It would be his final lodging.

29

VENICE, APRIL 1595

Amelia's anger had turned to seething rage. Devastation had struck everywhere. For Marcello. For Julia. For the studio, business, and craftsmen who would have no work. Heartsick, she couldn't grasp how they could climb out of such calamity. Her despair over her struggles with *The Merchant of Venice*, and how it might be destroying her relationship with Will, seemed insignificant by comparison, but it too weighed on her mind like an iron shackle she could not throw off.

Amelia surveyed the scorched Bassano studio with Zuane, Miriam, Zev, Julia, Arturo, and Enid. The inside surfaces were smudged with soot. Clouds of thick smoke lingered in the air. The exterior was charred black. This had once been a thriving workplace. The path back would be long and steep.

Julia said, "Aunt Miriam and Uncle Zuane, I'm very sorry I brought this upon you. All because I loved Marcello."

Miriam consoled her, "Dear Julia, nobody could have predicted this catastrophe. Fortunately, we're all uninjured. We can repair the studio and clear the fumes from the residence. It will just take time and work and money."

Julia hugged her aunt. "I'm overcome with guilt. This has been the worst week of my life."

"This episode contains lessons for us all," said Miriam.

Amelia scanned the charred walls and ceiling, the burned remains of the thick doors, and her own soot-covered hands. This is the damage hatred and prejudice can inflict, she thought. Marcello's death was tragic enough. A workplace once filled with the clamor of instrument making—tapping, sawing, fastening, assembling, and sound-testing objects for enlivening life—had become eerily silent. This arson arose from malevolence and spite.

Amelia exited the landside door to examine damage from the street. The Bassano studio mosaic of a lute and rabbit had been begrimed with soot. She ran a finger over the emblem, uncovering a streak of yellow, brown, and white tiles as grit caked her fingertip. She had begun wiping it with a rag when a figure called in a deep voice, "Have you a few minutes?"

Vincente Ponti strode toward her. "Are Signora and Signore Bassano available?"

"They're inside. Prepare yourself. It's a disaster."

Ponti inspected the fire debris, scorched stone columns, and soot-coated vaulted ceiling. "This vile act will not go unpunished. But I have other matters to discuss. Let's go onto the landing where the air is clean."

Zuane said, "Of course. I am, however, surprised to see you."

Once beyond the charred remains of the canal-side door, Ponti said, "My men explained about yesterday's events. You must be shaken from this horrific loss."

"We'll recover," said Miriam glumly.

"Has anything happened with Caloprini?" asked Amelia. She struggled to keep her animosity contained, but her voice betrayed her.

"Soldiers arrested Sergio last night. The charges against him are serious. The man captured during the arson has accused him of plotting this attack. He's trying to save his own hide and fears spending the rest of his life in the Doge's prison."

Amelia considered Ponti's manner, business-like with traces of compassion. He liked being in control. "Did you get what you wanted from this?" she asked.

"I'll know soon but I believe so. But you have much to recoup. I regret my men could not prevent Caloprini's gang from burning your studio. They failed to anticipate an attack from both sides of the building. I'm here to discuss that matter."

"What's to discuss?" asked Zuane.

"I told Miriam that I could be trusted, but trust doesn't guarantee results. Nonetheless I'll benefit from your tragedy. That's not moral."

"You stood to gain no matter the outcome. You knew that from the start," said Amelia tersely.

"I cannot undo what has been done," replied Ponti. "Yet I can help you recover. I'll supply men and materials for restoring your studio and home. You manage the reconstruction and they'll do the work. I'll pay for it."

Miriam stared at Ponti in disbelief. "No one's helped us like that before. We don't ask for charity."

"It's not charity. Without Caloprini, I'll become wealthier and more powerful. For me, your suffering is not a financial debt. It is, rather, a debt on my soul."

Zuane stepped forward and extended his hand. "You're an honorable, generous man. We appreciate and accept your offer."

Ponti gripped Zuane's hand firmly and cupped it with the other. "Now you know who I am. However, I'm not finished."

"Is there something you want in exchange?" asked Amelia, unable to overcome her skepticism.

"No. I am a businessman. If one of my buildings burned, it would not only be a huge cost to replace, but would interfere with my ability to do business until I did. That's why I'm offering you warehouse space for a temporary studio until this one has been restored. It won't be ideal but perhaps better than whatever alternative you're considering."

"What will you charge for rent?" asked Miriam.

"Nothing. I'm not using the space. When my business grows, I'll need it, but not now. Just leave it in the condition you find it."

"We will," said Miriam, overwhelmed by his generosity. "We will not forget."

Fatigue. Drive. Hope. Cohesion. Amelia experienced them all at once. Just when she thought she could push herself no further during the long days of clearing debris and cleaning the residence, then setting up the temporary studio in an empty warehouse near the wharf, she exerted herself further. Her muscles and back ached, her hands were raw, and at times she could hardly stay on her weary legs and calloused feet. Yet she felt renewed. They all labored together, reminding her of La Fulvia's crew—the ship that brought her to Venice. Miriam, Zuane, Julia, Zev, Autoro, and the Bassano craftsmen worked feverishly. Everyone took pride in their combined progress and helped each other. Every crate they emptied and every worktable they set up added to her gratification—and that of the others as well. She noticed how Julia had begun to ascend from her despair and strive with purpose. Amelia marveled at it all. She had not known such fraternity before.

While the physical work required little thinking, Amelia had trouble turning her mind away from *Merchant*. She started seeing a path through the mental barriers impeding her progress. She more clearly saw Shylock, like Miriam, Zuane and Julia, as a victim of animosity toward Jews. She knew better the emotional stress and indignation that he and real people who were treated similarly endured. How could they not resent being the object of enmity simply because of their faith? She thought there must be a way to dramatize Shylock's story and also rebut misconceptions about Jews. But how, while still satisfying Burbage?

Amelia composed speeches in her head for Shylock while organizing tools and shelving supplies. She watched Bassano employees work in her midst. All were Catholic and probably unaware they worked for Jews. But what if they did know? How might some react? What might they say about their Jewish employers in private conversations, especially if they felt mistreated?

A speech for Launcelot Gobbo, a character employed by Shylock but contemplating a job elsewhere, took shape in Amelia's mind. She could hear him rail against his Jewish boss—call him a fiend and the devil incarnate.

She watched as wind gusts rocked ships anchored in the harbor. Large three- and four-masted galleons strained against anchor chains and the ropes holding them fast to the pier. Amelia's thought pattern shifted, considering the prejudice that stained this affair in a new light.

Julia's voice jarred Amelia from her reverie. "Has your mind gone off to sea?"

"In a way. I've been watching those ships and, oddly enough, they make me think about the plight of women, and how man-made rules constrain us."

"How could ships in port bring that to mind?" Julia asked.

"Women are born into unfavorable circumstances. Men make it difficult for us to flourish and break from restrictions they've created." Amelia pointed toward the water. "I think we're like those ships anchored or lashed to the pier. Women must have extraordinary strength and good fortune to break free from the ties holding them in place—the place where men have tethered us."

"But it can be done," said Julia. "Look at Miriam. And you."

"Miriam has the benefit of Zuane's liberal outlook. As for me, I've tried but not been very successful. I haven't yet made peace with my circumstances. I've compromised my identity so I can express my creativity. I live with that decision."

"But—"

"There are no 'buts," interrupted Amelia. "When those ships to go to sea, they'll be rigged with sails which will propel them to faraway destinations. In England and here too, I assume, most girls grow up illiterate. They're like ships without sails and cannot go far…and you're a victim too."

"How so? I can read, write, and compute."

"I don't mean to open a sore that's yet to heal, but who created the rule that it's impermissible for a Jewess to love a Catholic man and marry him?"

Julia frowned at this reminder. "I don't know. Isn't that why Zuane and Miriam and Marcello's father were so angry?"

"There's nothing in Torah or the Bible that prohibits it," Amelia asserted. "Rabbis and priests created that rule. All men. Then they instilled that belief in their followers."

Julia appeared to see the connection. "Are you implying that men and their religious teaching kept Marcello and me from courting openly and marrying?"

"I am. It's religious dogma that impeded your ability to follow your heart."

Julia wiped tears from her eyes.

"I'm sorry, Julia. I shouldn't have said anything. I didn't mean to upset you."

"Amelia, you helped me understand. Now I should get back to work."

Sergio Caloprini's leg irons clanged on the narrow stone steps as guards led him from the richly-paneled courtroom in the Doge's Palace, where he had been sentenced, to the prison dungeon across the *Rio di Palazzo*. He'd been betrayed, but could not exact revenge. The evidence presented had been damning. His life had been shattered.

The guards marched Caloprini to the enclosed *Ponte dei Sospiri*, the Bridge of Sighs, which arched high above the canal. They gave him the final courtesy of pausing to peer from its stone-barred windows. He looked one last time at San Marco's Basin and the island of San Giorgio Maggiore. He inhaled and exhaled deeply before being pushed onward, down a steep flight to the dreary dungeon. The noxious prison air, a mix of foul body odor and human excrement, assaulted Caloprini as he reached the constricted passageway below. Cells on either side resembled stone manmade caves. Most warehoused several convicts. The thick iron-reinforced cell doors were only shoulder height. One guard unlocked a heavy portal while the other pressed Caloprini's head down, shoving him forcefully inside. He staggered into the darkness. The cell door slammed behind him with a clang of finality. He heard the bolts slide and smack ominously into place confirming his fate—trapped in a windowless pitch-black cell. He couldn't see the walls or judge its size. He heard moans from other inmates. He breathed in the stench of unwashed men, urine, and feces. He crouched confined in a pit of filth.

A weak voice from deep inside the darkness called to him. "I don't who you are or what you've done, but if you're here it matters no more. Your life is all but over. Don't waste your vigor thinking of how to escape. Nobody has. No guard will let you get close enough, because if an inmate escapes on his watch, he must serve the rest of that man's sentence."

Caloprini sank to the stone floor and pressed his back against the cold wall. A wave of utter fatigue surged through him. For the first time he could remember, he was powerless.

30

Lord Hunsdon, serving as the Lord Chamberlain, half-listened to the Privy Council discussions in Whitehall Palace. The aging William Cecil, Lord Burghley, droned on about the poor harvest of 1594 and resulting winter starvation among the farmers, especially in northern Cumbria County. He worried that the dearth of seed for spring planting would make matters worse this year, but he had no remedies.

Peregrine Bertie, the Baron Willoughby de Eresby and brother of Lady Susan Bertie, spoke next. Having served as England's ambassador to Denmark, he described how the Danes had upheld agreements permitting the free passage of English merchant ships—allowing trade to proceed peacefully.

When the discussion turned to Lord Hunsdon, the matter he wished to discuss seemed trivial by comparison. "Your Majesty, as the chief minister of your royal household and commissioner of the court, I bring to this table a lighter matter. You've enjoyed the plays of your subject William Shakespeare, and I recommend we distinguish his fine theatrical troupe."

"How would you suggest?" asked the Queen with a touch of skepticism.

"By designating them the 'Lord Chamberlain's Men.'"

The Queen raised her eyebrows. "We've not done anything of this sort before. Why now?"

"His plays are exceptional, exceeding those of Christopher Marlowe."

The Queen turned visibly disdainful. "Henry, that's a name I wish not to hear again. Raising it will not help your cause."

"My apologies, Your Majesty. You opined how much you enjoyed *The Taming of the Shrew*, and Shakespeare's other plays have been well received, including *A Comedy of Errors* and *Titus Andronicus*."

"It's not those plays that trouble me. His plays about Henry VI and Richard III did not portray the monarchy favorably. They make my predecessors look petty and vengeful. My subjects could lose respect for the crown if he pens more like them."

"Your Majesty, those kings ruled well over a hundred years ago, and their wisdom cannot compare to your enlightened leadership. Shakespeare merely humanizes them. He helps people understand their history."

"Henry, that may be, but I won't tolerate anything more current, and certainly no such dramas about me. That said, I think his comedies are vastly entertaining and thought provoking."

"Then may I bestow this honor, accepting your caveats?"

"So long as Shakespeare complies."

With a flourish Will jumped from The Theatre's stage to the pit. "Lord Hunsdon, to what do I owe this pleasure?"

"Where may we have a private discussion?"

Will's eyes betrayed his uneasiness. "No one will hear us in the back of the upper gallery."

After climbing to the top, Lord Hunsdon signaled for Will to sit while he stood in the aisle facing him. "I have favorable news along with a word of caution."

Will blinked with fear. "Caution...in what regard? I'm not a reckless man."

"I've spoken with the Queen. She appreciates your plays but does not wish to experience the wrath of your pen—as have two prior monarchs and perhaps more to come. She doesn't believe those scripts demonstrate sufficient deference for the crown."

Will surged from his seat, his eyes bulging. "She doesn't, does she? I'm only bringing their reigns to life...and those kings didn't show great respect for their subjects."

"Calm down, Will. She thinks you're a superb playwright and she is especially enamored with the comedies. But she doesn't want a rebellion. Her father, Henry VIII, while popular early in his reign, was reviled at the end. And don't forget he ordered her mother and my aunt, Anne Boleyn, beheaded for treason in the Tower of London."

"The Queen has nothing to fear from me," replied Will, adopting a more humble stance. "My objective is to entertain, not incite."

"I understand," Henry said. "But when monarchs feel threatened, they can be vicious. While Queen Elizabeth's manner is unlike that of her half-sister Queen Mary, who had nearly three hundred Protestants burned at the stake, her tolerance for dishonoring England's historical sovereigns has limits."

Will shifted his weight from foot to foot, unsure how to interpret Lord Hunsdon's message. "I have an historical drama about Richard II nearing completion and I'm planning one on King John I. Should I abandon them?"

"I don't think that's necessary. They ruled hundreds of years ago and were not Tudors. But don't write about her."

"I won't. You may assure the Queen. You said you had favorable information as well?"

"With the understanding we've just reached, I wish to honor your theatrical company and become its patron, If you accept, you'll be known as the 'Lord Chamberlain's Men.'"

Will relaxed his jaw and revealed his slightly crooked teeth. "I am most honored. I humbly accept."

Burbage slammed a script onto a stack, scattering dust motes into the air of his cramped office. Will tried fanning the particles away as he entered. "I have superb news."

"Finally, "The Jew of Venice" is done?"

"No, that's not why I'm here."

Burbage glared, curling a script and pointing it at Will, "You disappoint once again. This cannot continue. I have no more patience. So what other matter is of such great import?"

Will stared back, not wanting to show his worry. His business with Burbage was vital. He needed it to maintain his room and board in London and support his family in Stratford. His wife complained constantly that the money he sent back was insufficient.

When Burbage seemed a bit calmer, Will continued, "Lord Hunsdon, the Lord Chamberlain, will be sponsoring my troupe—lending prestige to your theater as well."

"Prestige! How will prestige earn me more money? That's done with great plays that draw big and steady audiences. Will I soon hear that you're performing more at the palace? I'll get nothing for those shows. Nothing. This patronage could cost me money."

Burbage's reaction caught Will by surprise. He held up his hands. "No, it won't. You'll earn more because I'll enshrine you as one of the sharers. You'll get a portion of the profits, plus what you make as The Theatre's owner."

"But I'll also be liable for a share of any debts. I'll have to bear that risk along with risks I shoulder running The Theatre."

The man was refusing a gift, and Will did not intend to offer it twice. He turned on his heel to leave.

Burbage cried, "Wait!" Then in a quiet but controlled tone he said, "I accept. I'll be a sharer, but permit me to direct the company's business affairs."

31

B y the time Amelia and the Bassano family moved back into the residence, the tension and anxiety caused by the arson had subsided but not disappeared. Each night Amelia went to bed with her ears tuned to every stray noise. Loud voices from the canal put her on high alert. She sat bolt upright in bed and listened until the sounds faded. During the day, studio renovation continued and construction clamor reverberated into their living quarters. It was necessary but unsettling. They all worried about further repercussions.

Amelia had been working diligently on *Romeo and Juliet*—her new title—amidst the distractions of moving, packing, and unpacking. She had drafted several scenes. As compelled as she was to portray a clash between Jewish and Christian families, as Julia had experienced, she chose not to. She feared drawing attention so explicitly to her own faith. Her bitterness spiked, though, when she worked on parts reminding her of Caloprini. At other times it festered like an open wound. She could not fathom how religious prejudices destroyed the desires of two young hearts—leading to the death of one and emotional turmoil in the other. She channeled her sentiments into the script, always considering the lessons she wanted to convey while driving toward a sharper conclusion.

The redecorated salon resembled a music room. Lutes, viols, pfeifes, cornets, recorders and other woodwinds, including the family's latest invention, the bassanello, hung from the walls. Music sheets lined the shelves. A circle of chairs with music stands occupied the center. When Amelia entered the room, sunlight streamed through windows, lighting Julia's face, sandy hair, shoulders, and the long neck of her theorbo. She sang softly, her voice barely audible over the notes of her instrument. While the song was melancholy, Julia smiled upon seeing Amelia.

She then strummed a madrigal by Claudio Monteverdi, and Amelia joined in with her lute. Next Julia started a dance song on her pfeife, which Amelia hadn't heard her play since before Marcello's death. Amelia smiled inwardly, sensing Julia's emergence from her emotional abyss. The energetic melody drew Enid, Henry, and Zev to the room. Henry ran to Amelia and she scooped him into her arms. They danced merrily around the furniture and Henry squealed with delight.

Julia switched back to the theorbo, also known as a chitarrone, a large lute with a long neck extension and two pegboxes. An ornate carving surrounded the sound hole. The instrument, one of the newer ones made at the Bassano studio, had a broad bass range and a powerful sound. Julia picked it up for the first time since Marcello's drowning.

They continued strumming and singing, each song livelier than the preceding one. Zev joined in with the bassanello and Enid harmonized. Their voices carried throughout the house. The events of the past three months seemed to disappear with the rise of their voices and the promise of a new future.

When they stopped playing, Amelia watched Julia's mood darken. Despondency seemed to creep back into her soul. She wanted to cry out to Julia: No, don't slip back, fight the gloom, create music for your life. Amelia understood, though, that such exclamations would not alter Julia's drift toward despondency and could antagonize her. She needed to divert Julia's thoughts and hope her tender emotions would follow.

In a light tone, Amelia suggested, "Julia, let's stroll outside. Zev, will you join us? It is a beautiful night."

The full moon reflected off the glassy canal and they were each lost in their own thoughts while meandering along the banks. Amelia held Julia's hand. Zev gazed at the constellation Sagittarius and bright stars in the summer sky. He asked, "Have you ever experienced something and afterward thought you had dreamed it?"

Julia replied forlornly, "Like my romance with Marcello? I didn't dream it but I still see him in my dreams. I won't let him vanish from my memory."

Amelia said, "You'll always remember him as special in your life. I'm married to a man I neither love nor respect. Before him, I'd been intimate with two men I admired, at least for a time, but only one did I come to love. Sometimes I dream about what I could have had but never will."

Julia said, "It sounds like there's much you regret."

"And I'm burdened by it."

Amelia didn't want them to stray too far from the original drift of their conversation. "Zev, I am still thinking about your question about past reality sometimes seeming like a dream."

Julia waved her hands in a burst of playfulness. "Imagine if fairies could dance by, sprinkle magic dust on our eyes, change reality, and bring us new love."

"Yes, imagine how they could spring from a mountain and do just that," mused Amelia.

"Zev laughed. "What if they made a mistake and we ended up loving the wrong person?"

"That's a devious thought," jested Julia.

"It could be farcical. It could create chaos," chimed Amelia.

"Or tragic," said Zev. "Think of the people who would be hurt. How would matters ever get straightened?"

Amelia pondered the question. "Could the fairies undo what they do? While it lasts, the mass confusion could be comedic and magical for people watching it unfold."

Julia tugged Amelia's hand, "I believe an idea is germinating in your brain."

"I suppose it is."

"This could be fun…a play about fairies, dreams and magic potions. Love potions!" Julia exclaimed, smiling whimsically.

Hmm, Amelia thought, love potions—that makes the idea both romantic and fanciful, especially if the wrong person got the wrong one.

Julia turned to Amelia with a spring in her step. "Could we write something together? Something jovial. Something mischievous. Imagine if we discussed plots and characters, speeches and dialogue, and composed while walking along the canals or wherever we'll be inspired. We could even explore the woods on the mainland and envision fairies for the new script. What do you think?"

This notion intrigued Amelia. Working on scripts could be the best cure for Julia's mourning for Marcello. Her youthful energy and schemes might generate rafts of creative and unconventional ideas, especially for a novel play about summer dreams and fairies.

"Yes!" Amelia replied, "That's a splendid idea."

1 July 1595

My dear friend Will,

It's been an eventful spring and early summer. There is too much to explain in a brief letter, so I am describing only a few highlights.

Enclosed are my suggestions for Richard II. *Writing plays about monarchs is truly your forte.*

I've been working on a new script inspired by problems my family has experienced here, especially my fifteen-year-old cousin, Julia. I've coupled it with two stories by Venetian authors—Luigi da Porto and Masuccio Salernitano. The original one was written over 100 years ago and the other was published fifty years later. I have blended the tales.

*All the prose and poetry is original. The drama con-
cerns two star-crossed lovers from feuding families.
It's a tragic love story. Although the calamity in the
drama differs from what actually happened here,
it's similar to the climax in the Venetian literature.*

I'm calling it Romeo and Juliet. *I switched
the venue from Padua to Verona, which I visited
last year. The family surnames are variations of the
two real feuding families, Montecchi and Cappelo.
Rough drafts of the first and fifth acts are complete
as are outlines of the middle three. I'm confident
this play will appeal to a large audience and hope
the theme appeals to you. After receiving your reactions and suggestions, I'll complete it.*

*I hope this partial script satisfies Burbage for
a time. If he wants a tragedy, this promises to be a
momentous one.*

*I've become enamored with the Italian and
Vèneto languages. They have different cadences
than English. Their common sentence structures
diverge from those employed most often by English
speakers. This has affected my writing style, since
I am speaking these languages daily and then
writing in English. I've also discovered that when
I'm composing verses in iambic pentameter, as I
am in* Romeo and Juliet, *using the syntax of
romance languages is easier and facilitates the
flow.*

I know you're eager for a draft of The
Merchant of Venice, *and I wish I had it ready.*

Unfortunately, there is still much work to do. I'll get my heart back into it this fall.

I hope you and your loved ones are well.

Your "Theater Spy,"

Amelia

32

Amelia and Julia rambled around Venice seeking inspiration and finding it while gliding through narrow streets, slipping down shadowy passageways, crossing canal bridges, and watching gondolas traverse the waterways. They wrote in small *campos* and visited magnificent Gothic churches.

The "dreams" play was the perfect script for Amelia and Julia to write together. Julia's idea about love potions helped crystalize plot themes for Amelia. The project belonged to them both.

Amelia and Julia changed the working title frequently. One afternoon they stood on the Rialto Bridge discussing it while watching Venetians return from *Rialto Mercato* with fresh fish and vegetables.

Amelia said, "We both want 'dream' in the title."

"Yes," agreed Julia. "The entire play can be viewed as one long dream that Robin Goodfellow has in the summer woodland."

"What about 'Dreams within Dreams?'" asked Amelia. "It resonates because the lovers' dreams include dreams of waking up and remembering dreams of fairies conniving in the woods and switching love potions."

"But the play is also about love," said Julia.

Amelia admired the Moorish and Byzantine inspired palazzos lining the Grand Canal as she pondered. "Our story brims with comic confusion. There's also the dream in which a character believes the queen of the fairies is falling in love with him. This play is about the ridiculous."

"But are we getting any closer to a title?" asked Julia.

"It will come to us," said Amelia. "Let's put it aside for now."

The more Amelia and Julia crafted the play, the more they laughed, which led them to conceive even crazier scenarios. They walked to a fountain in a small campo, sat on the ledge encircling it, and scribbled everything down as a gentle breeze ruffled their papers and streamed their hair.

Before leaving, Julia asked, "What about 'Dreams of Lovers on a Summer Night?'"

"That's the best title so far but—"

"Not quite right yet," said Julia, finishing Amelia's sentence.

Amelia suggested, "What about 'A Midsummer Night's Dream?'"

Julia beamed as her eyes widened. "It has an exotic and mysterious ring…and implies romance."

As they strolled back to the residence, Julia said, "You once explained how you embed clues in your scripts alluding to your authorship—in part by inserting content and descriptions that Mr. Shakespeare could not, since he lacks the personal knowledge and expertise. You cited musical allegories and metaphors as an example."

"I also use feminine imagery like flowers, gardens, songs, and clothing. I portray how women think and depict strong women."

Julia gestured as they entered a small *campo*. "And your plays are set outside of England."

"Will has never traveled beyond its shores."

"Have you inserted Judaic references?"

Amelia understood immediately why she asked. "Not yet, but that's an intriguing thought. Our ideas for *A Midsummers Night's Dream* include a web of disguised allegories, some connected to religion and the history of faith. Alluding to Jewish sources might add nicely to the allegorical confusion."

Julia agreed, "We're hiding secrets inside the script. It's like a masked ball where you don't know who others really are. But in the play, we never remove the masks. The audience will see only what we choose to reveal."

"When we complete the first draft, let's test how good we are. Let's show it to a rabbi to see what he perceives, and if he finds any allegories."

Julia said, "Rabbi Aryeh would be a good choice. He's about your age and runs the yeshiva, the Jewish school in Il Ghetto. When we finish, let's show it to him."

A few months later, after the rabbi sent them a message saying he had read the script, Amelia and Julia visited the yeshiva in the Spanish Synagogue. They peeked into a large classroom furnished with long wooden tables. Boys wearing black skullcaps called *yarmulkes* or *kippahs* sat across from each other reading Hebrew texts. All boys! thought Amelia. Don't these rabbis believe in educating girls too? Are we not deserving?

They waited until the class ended and Rabbi Aryeh emerged with his hands gripping a book behind his back. His long rusty brown beard and black suit appeared more suited for an older man.

"What did you think of our comedy?" Amelia asked.

"I liked it far more than I expected," he allowed. "I had to put it down to mull over certain parts. It's fascinating and subject to many interpretations. Is there a message you're attempting to impart?"

"Ah, that's an excellent question and one we've chosen not to answer. We believe an intriguing feature of this play is that it can have different meanings for different people. Some might regard it only as an entertaining comedy without deeper significance. Those who scratch beneath the surface will interpret it in their own way. We choose not to influence that."

Julia said, "Two people have read it twice. They both said it meant something different to them the second time than the first. We didn't expect that, but it reinforces our decision to be ambiguous about our intentions."

Rabbi Aryeh pointed to the manuscript on his desk. "Perhaps that's a sign of good storytelling. Every Torah portion can be interpreted in different ways, and the lessons extracted might vary significantly depending on the reader's perspective, and where he...or she...may be in life."

Amelia said, "I wouldn't put this script in that category. It's simply a creative work. What meaning did you get from it?"

"It demonstrates the challenges of love and reciprocity, or the lack of them, and the effects on people who feel their love is unreturned. There is also an important message about mishandling something powerful." Rabbi Aryeh tapped on the script. "It's conveyed when the consequences of the misused magic and love potions become apparent. You do it with satire but the repercussions of real misuse or abuse of power can be serious. If audiences get that from the play, a profound lesson will be learned."

Amelia smiled. "I'm pleased you believe there's more to it than fantasy."

Rabbi Aryeh had not quite finished. "Finally, the play within a play in the final act shows if people look at their own behavior from the outside, they'll see themselves in ways they might find surprising."

"Are there any Jewish concepts you suggest we implant?"

"There are. First, though, may I inquire about an allegory I detected? I can't conceive it's coincidental."

"To what do you refer?" asked Amelia.

"Does the character Titania symbolically represent Titus Flavius Caesar Vespasianus Augustus, the Roman emperor who ransacked and destroyed Jerusalem's temple in A.D. 70?" Rabbi Aryeh asked, pronouncing each syllable of Titus' name with distain.

Amelia smiled at his astute observation. "She does."

"Ah, then I suppose the humble-bees in the story symbolize the rebellious Jewish Maccabees?"

"Our imaginations could not help but be influenced by Jewish history."

Rabbi Aryeh stroked his thick beard. "Very shrewd. Subtle. I wonder who else might discern such nuance."

"Only the perceptive who have studied history and literature, like you. Are there other ways we can weave in Jewish dimensions?" asked Amelia.

"I reflected upon reading about Helena and her father, Nedar, who was missing. In Hebrew, 'nedar' has two meanings. When used as an adjective, it means absent, just like her father. That was clever. As a noun, 'nedar' means vow. This brought to mind the *Mishnah*, the written form of Jewish oral traditions from centuries ago. You could draw a parallel from the tractate *Nedarim*, or the "Book of Vows," after the mix-up with love potions. This might occur when Helena, insecure about her appearance and envious of beautiful Hermia, compares herself to Hermia. Helena could list the same qualities and in the same order as those in 'The Book of Vows' concerning marriage annulment. They're beauty, skin tone, and height."

Amelia exchanged a glance with Julia. The rabbi's suggestion would be easy to incorporate.

"Another place where you might add a distinctly Jewish flavor is in the first scene of Act Five," he went on. "You could draw from the *Zohar*, which means splendor or radiance. It's about Jewish mysticism known as *Kabbalah*. In descriptions of the apocalypse, it describes how God 'revives the dead and showers them with dew from his hair.' Wonderful imagery. You could borrow from it when characters emerge from sleep. Oberon, king of the fairies, could consecrate them with dew."

Amelia and Julia danced out of Il Ghetto like school children. The rabbi had given them two subtle clues to embed. Someday, someone with knowledge of Jewish texts would notice them, and wonder how they had been inserted. They might at first consider them curious coincidences, but if more Jewish allusions were discovered in other scripts, they'd realize it was intentional. That realization, Amelia believed, would lead to the conclusion that only a playwright, or in this case playwrights, knowledgeable about Judaism could have written the script.

33

VENICE, MAY 1596

A melia received two letters that altered her life's course once again. Intuitively, she sensed misfortune had struck upon seeing the senders' names. She unsealed the message from Lord Hunsdon first.

> *Somerset House, London*
> *17 April 1596*
>
> My dear Amelia,
>
> *I'm proud to be a patron of Shakespeare's company and seeing the warm receptions of its plays. I picture how your face would glow if you saw the favorable responses. I can imagine already the uproarious reaction A* Midsummer Night's Dream *will garner when it's staged. I'm amazed at the invention that spins from your mind.*
>
> *The Queen has extended her grace by inviting me to live this final stage of my life at her Somerset*

House. This is where I'll be for the purposes of future correspondence and when you return to England.

I am cheered when I think of you and imagine your gorgeous face before me. It's been over three years since you left for Venice. I hope you're ready to come home soon. I say that selfishly since you would bring added joy to my life.

Yours always,
Henry

Amelia grimaced, surmising Henry must be ill or weakening. He was seventy and facing his own mortality.

With a heavy heart she opened Susan Bertie's letter.

London
15 April 1596

Dear Amelia,

I hope my prodigy is well. Your respite in Venice must be rejuvenating since you remain there. I look forward to when we can sit together and discuss it.

I must convey lamentable news about Lord Hunsdon, which I doubt he'll divulge himself. The Queen declined naming him Earl of Wiltshire, an honor once bestowed upon his father. It's a designation that Henry had long sought. Since then he's become despondent and lacks his former confidence. With his mood and health abating, the Queen tried compensating by inviting Henry to live in Somerset House, where he resides today.

We see Henry less frequently at the court. Yesterday, he looked dreadful. He lacked vigor. His

*usual meticulous appearance was less so. His face
was slack and his skin pale, almost gray and deeply
etched. He seems in a perpetual decline.*

*I know Henry played an important role in your
life and you hold great affection for him. If you're
contemplating a return to the country of your birth,
this may be a good time. It would raise Henry's spirits considerably.*

Endearingly,
Susan

Amelia put Susan's letter down and reread Henry's. She
knew Henry had too much pride to say what he wanted
directly, but it was all there. Lady Susan put the exclama-
tion point on it. Her heart sank with the news. She resolved
to return to London immediately. Her gratitude for all he
had done and meant to her required it. She had completed
her draft of *The Merchant of Venice* and would take it with
her.

That evening, Amelia announced her decision. Miriam
and Zuane reacted with empathy and understanding,
stressing how much they would miss her. Julia squinted
back tears, breaking Amelia's heart and reminding her of
Marcello drowning.

Julia flashed a weak smile. "Amelia, you've been my tru-
est friend. When you leave, I'll feel alone and lost."

"Julia, I, too, have enjoyed our conversations and our
work together. I think you're ready to compose on your own."

From Julia's forlorn and puzzled expression, Amelia
gathered that that had not occurred to her. "Amelia, it's not
the work I'm sad about. It's us. I'll miss our relationship."

"Julia, you've touched my heart. Yet I fear my dear friend, Lord Hunsdon, is near death, and I must see him before he passes."

Miriam said, "Amelia, if Julia is willing, could she travel to England with you? She's welcome to come back anytime."

"Oh Amelia," beamed Julia. "Could I?"

"It would be my dearest pleasure."

Despite her desire to make haste, Amelia had to arrange for passage on a ship bound for London. Finally, with the necessary bookings made, the day came. With gladness in her heart that she'd be returning home, she pulled on her buskins, loose knee-high leather boots, under a full-length chemise and long gray skirt. The voyage to London would take several weeks. Since the ship would stop for a few days in the old port of Civitavecchia, about forty-five miles from Rome, Miriam asked her to deliver a letter to her cousin in the ancient city's Jewish Quarter.

At the port of San Zaccaria, within sight of the Doge's Palace and the prison confining Sergio Caloprini, Amelia, Henry, Enid, and Julia boarded a three-masted galleon much like *La Fulvia*, the ship that brought Amelia to Venice three years earlier. It, too, flew the red Venetian flag emblazoned with a gold-winged lion—the republic's regal symbol.

Seagulls squawking overhead followed the vessel through San Marco Basin and into the Adriatic Sea. The sails billowed, catching brisk winds, and the coast of Venice shrank in the distance.

Amelia leaned against a railing on the main deck in the shadow of the huge tan sails. The constant rise and fall of the waves, the orchestrated work of the crew, and the ship's fluid movement instilled introspection and wonder.

The group spent their days on deck watching the rocky coast, green hills, and sheer cliffs slip by as undulating waves swayed the ship. The seas were calm and lazy clouds drifted overhead, casting shadows on the landscape. Small villages hugged the rugged bluffs. At night, through the blackness, street torches flickered in the distance.

After rounding the peninsula's tip, they sailed past Naples, where white and apricot-shaded buildings climbed the hillside rising from the waterfront, and where the massive double humps of Mount Vesuvius dominated the background. Days later, Civitavecchia and the imposing stone turrets of Fort Michelangelo emerged from across the Tyrrhenian Sea. In the port, fishermen unloaded their catches and the smell of raw fish carried in the salty breeze.

They hired a carriage to transport them to Rome and reached it by evening. As they neared the Jewish Quarter, the *Teatro di Marcello*, the great theater Julius Caesar had begun and Augustus completed, came into view. They descended a hill and passed through narrow streets lined with four- and five-story buildings until they entered a small bustling plaza. There they found the residence of Miriam's sister and her husband, Laila and Avi Abenezra.

Miriam had explained that they lived on the second floor, and Amelia looked up at the high rounded and squared windows fronting the faded orange structure. "Hail to Rome" was chiseled in Latin between the first and second stories.

After mounting the stairs, they were invited into a plain room with a cross-beamed ceiling and tall windows framed with inward-swinging green shutters. The aromas from Laila's fagioli bean soup and fried artichokes welcomed them. "I have a letter from your sister," Amelia said, withdrawing it from her satchel. "She was very happy we could visit you."

The following morning, Amelia and Julia set out with Laila to see the Roman ruins.

"What happened to the great city ancient Romans built?" asked Amelia, her curiosity aroused, as they climbed Capitoline Hill toward the remains of the Roman Forum.

Laila explained that during the centuries of invasions and turmoil, the grand buildings constructed during the Roman Empire crumbled and decayed, especially during barbarian conflicts in the sixth century. Parts of Rome were abandoned, falling into disrepair. Drainage systems were neglected and low-lying areas became marshes. The great aqueducts deteriorated, leaving sections of the city without water. Residents abandoned those areas and the shrinking population huddled near the banks of the Tiber River.

The marble facades, columns, and other feature of great Roman buildings, including the Coliseum and the structures comprising the Forum, had been plundered and re-used, often in constructing Catholic churches.

Weather and nature exacted a toll as well, burying some remains. Looters destroyed and removed monuments. They carted away much of the grand exterior of the Coliseum, known as the Flavian Amphitheatre, leaving only the supporting inner wall or substructure pocked with holes from where marble was originally attached.

Laila's descriptions ignited Amelia's vivid imagination—bringing these ruins to life. She envisioned emperors, senators, generals, and citizens walking though the Roman Forum deep in conversation. How did the city look when Julius Caesar walked across its great promenades? In her mind, she transported herself back in time to the height of Roman glory.

Laila continued her running narrative as they navigated among ancient ruins. Amelia asked question after question: "What was life like for the ruling class back then? What did the average citizen see, hear, and experience?" When visiting the Coliseum, she remarked on the contrast within the Roman culture of designing majestic buildings and the barbarity of gladiator fights. The Coliseum even had a special gate for removing slaughtered contestants.

The Arch of Titus, on a rise southeast of the Roman Forum, impressed her with its grandeur. "Stop!" cried Laila as Julia stepped under the arch.

Julia halted in mid-stride, pivoting back toward Laila. "Stop? But why?"

"Jews should never pass beneath it because it depicts the Roman plunder of Jerusalem—a crime against our heritage."

Julia retraced her steps as Amelia circled the arch, studying the bas-reliefs on its sides. One portrayed Emperor Titus triumphantly returning to Rome in his chariot, accompanied by Nike, the winged Greek goddess of victory. The other side memorialized Titus' siege of Jerusalem in 70 A.D., with soldiers carrying to Rome the spoils of victory, including a huge menorah. Amelia grimaced at the stone display and beheld another irony.

Romans were proud of conquering and enslaving other peoples but demanded justice for themselves.

Amelia wondered how such a vicious, militaristic culture could spawn a Senate for making laws and a court system balancing the emperor's power. Brutality and brilliance operated side by side, she thought. She drew paper, ink, and a quill from her valise and jotted notes. She could hardly record her thoughts fast enough.

The next day, Amelia searched for inspiring places to write. Near the remains of the Roman Forum, embedded in the rocky slope of Capitoline Hill, she found a bench tucked in an alcove backed with a beautiful mosaic fresco of three women in flowing gowns. It overlooked the rubble and tall weeds, once the Roman seat of power and conquest. Amelia scanned broken marble columns, some cut to the ground resembling chopped tree trunks. Others stood tall, rising to where they once supported ancient roofs and majestic porticos. Rows of arches fitted into ancient foundations provided passage to underground rooms. Her eyes kept returning to the remaining columns of the Temple of Saturn, still holding aloft connected pediment fragments, with the Latin inscription proclaiming "The Senate and People of Rome Restored What Fire Had Consumed." She visualized a robust political community laced with intrigue, pursuit of power, and deception amidst the grand architecture. This is fodder for a discussion with Will, she thought. With my newfound knowledge combined with his interest in political theater, this could be the genesis of a remarkable play.

These ideas lingered inside Amelia's head as they travelled back to Civitavecchia and sailed onward to London. Soon she would again be working closely with Will, creating great dramatic works together. She would see her plays performed and hear the audience applause—relishing the fruits of her labor. She would keep the company of the nobility who had shaped much of what she had become. With that thought, her mind returned to Lord Hunsdon, the reason she had left Venice in the first place. She feared for his health. For her, the ship could not sail back fast enough.

ACT THREE

PURSUITS OF AMBITION

34

LONDON, JULY 1596

Amelia could not stop brooding. She wrung her hands and paced on the ship. She fought to dispel her pessimism but could not shake it. "Henry, Henry," she said to the endless sea, "please don't die before I can say farewell or proclaim again my love for you." The uncertainty knotted her stomach and got worse the moment she saw the coast of England.

She had only known the vigorous Henry, not the weak and bedridden man she resigned herself to finding. He had helped her through her life's worst moments. What had she done for him? She had not even been with him when he needed her most. That she had taken the first ship back upon learning of his condition was not enough. She should have anticipated his demise. "I've been selfish for staying so long in Venice," she declared to the wind. Although she recognized the fallacy of her logic, it did not assuage her remorse.

"Oh, how good it is to walk on solid ground," Amelia said to Julia and Enid as they gathered their luggage. But the firmness of the land did not steady her nerves. It was her son's small hand holding her hand as they walked toward awaiting carriages that brought a sense of calm.

From the carriage window, curious three-year-old Henry scanned the city. When they rode through the South Tower of the London Bridge, built over the River Thames in medieval times, Henry's questions flowed as fast as the river: "Mama, where are the gondolas?" "What's that big castle with jagged towers and big clock?" "Why are streets so dirty and smelly?"

They navigated through Westminster past courtly buildings and churches. They rode through fashionable Canon Row, lined with mansions, to an adjacent neighborhood crowded with small three-story residential structures, their pitched roofs nearly touching. The carriage slowed to a stop.

Henry scrambled out. "Is this my new-old home, Mama?"

The child's enthusiasm warmed Amelia's heart. "It is."

Henry peered up at the red brick building. "All ours?"

"No, honey. We live on the second floor."

Amelia smiled, glad to be home, although the thought of seeing Alphonso again rattled her frayed nerves. She did not expect a warm reception.

She glanced around the neighborhood. Little had changed since she had last lived here, although the buildings seemed dingier. Most windows were open and black paint flaked off louvered shutters. The thick air carried the pungent scent of horse dung.

As soon as Amelia opened the door, the odor of perspiration-soaked clothes assaulted her. Strewn in a corner were dirty breeches along with sweat-stained undershirts and codpieces. Chairs and tables were approximately where she remembered, but grime layered every surface. A chicken bone lay on the floor beneath the square dining table. Dirty dishes and pans were piled on a counter. Music sheets, weighted down by ink jars, angled out from haphazard stacks on the stone mantel. Their edges flapped with the wind gusts flowing through the open windows. In her bedchamber, the unmade bed reeked of bodily excretions and sweat. Soiled sheets and blankets had been heaped on the floor. She wanted to retch.

Amelia dropped her valise with a thud. She wanted to scream at Alphonso: How could you live in such filth? Did you care for anything at all?

Amelia reluctantly called for him, and breathed a sigh of relief when only silence reigned. Her discovery of the unkempt rooms reminded her of all she disliked about Alphonso and that she had come home to a man she'd never love. As this unpleasant thought echoed in her mind, a new one struck her: *I must find happiness elsewhere, somehow, with someone.*

The next day, Sunday, Amelia woke early to find the other half of her double bed still unoccupied. Alphonso had not returned. Is he sleeping with whores? Has he contracted something dastardly?

Amelia pushed Alphonso from her thoughts as she dressed in an amber gown with billowed sleeves and a tailored bodice. She wished to look her best for visiting Lord Hunsdon at Somerset House, and fitted a feathered hat with an upturned brim over her burnished red curls. There, she knew, she'd be welcomed.

When Amelia arrived, Lord Hunsdon's nurse, a dour middle-aged woman in a gray uniform, answered the door. "He's sleeping and doesn't want visitors. You should leave."

Amelia pressed her, "I've just arrived from Venice. I came back especially to see him. I'll wait until he awakes. I'm sure he'll see me."

The nurse recoiled, apparently taken aback by such assurance from a stranger. "I doubt that's a good idea. I'd ask his wife, Lady Anne, but she's praying for him at Westminster Abbey. Go. I'll send for you if he so wishes."

"I'm sorry, I won't. If he awakes and refuses to see me, I'll leave. Until then, I'll stay. Tell him his visitor is Amelia."

Amelia barged past the nurse into the salon and settled on a wide chair upholstered in a red and gold speckled print. The nurse glared at her presumption and Amelia stared back. "I'll keep myself busy."

Amelia spent the next two hours reminiscing about her years with Lord Hunsdon. She could not once remember him being ill. She fidgeted, worrying his condition had worsened.

At last, the nurse returned. "Lord Hunsdon awoke. I told him you were waiting. Are you Amelia Bassano Lanier?"

"I am."

"Keep your visit short. He has little strength and getting him ready consumed considerable energy. But he smiled for the first time in days knowing you're here."

Upon entering Lord Hunsdon's bedchamber, Amelia masked her shock at the smell of sickness and seeing Henry buried under mounds of blankets on a warm day. His face was gaunt and ghostly. His hair was thinner and gray had overtaken its once reddish tint. His eyes had lost their sparkle. He looked resigned. Only his gentlemanly smile seemed the same.

Belying her feelings of dread, Amelia said cheerily, "My dear Henry, I'm very happy to see you." She leaned over and kissed him on the cheek. Then she lifted his hand to her lips and kissed it too.

"Dear Amelia, seeing you has buoyed my spirits higher than they've been in months. My prayers have been answered."

Amelia pulled a chair to the side of Henry's bed, held his hand, and caressed his arm. "Henry, I've missed you. I've missed our love, which I carried with me in Venice."

"And what of your husband?"

"I have never loved him. It is you whom I grew to love, in spite of our vast differences. I love your kindness, your wisdom, your counsel, and the way you cared for me, especially when you could have abandoned me. I love who you are."

"I am truly honored. Thoughts of you have kept me alive. Thank you for coming back."

Choked with emotion, Amelia could hardly breathe. She massaged his hand, feeling the bond of their devotion. "You showed me what love meant. I wish I had done more to show my love. It's a regret I'll always have. Now that I'm here, I will stay with you for as long as you desire."

Henry squinted at her through filmy eyes. "You look vibrant while I've deteriorated in body and spirit. I need not tell you, for you see for yourself. I'm a proud man who has been humbled by the course of life's events. My days of pretense and status seeking are over. I only wished for some final moments of happiness and you're bestowing them on me."

"I heard Queen Elizabeth honored you with a visit"

Henry grimaced weakly. "She came more because of guilt than care, but it was thoughtful nonetheless."

"What gave you that impression?"

"I had hoped the Queen would honor me with the title Earl of Wiltshire, like my father. When I would have been truly honored, she declined. Yesterday, standing beside this bed she offered it, I believe out of contrition or pity. So I could not accept. In my hoarse voice I told her, 'Your Majesty, you did not consider me worthy in healthy life, so I shall account myself unworthy as I near death.'"

Amelia's heart sank. This man had refused to compromise his dignity even in a weakened state. "You made an honorable decision and I hold you in highest regard." She then sat on the bedside, kissed his forehead, and laid her head on his chest.

"Amelia, dear, I relish your affection. I missed it. And now I'm unable to reciprocate. I'll never be whole again."

Indeed, Henry's once muscular chest had become soft. It felt fleshy and fragile, which Amelia hadn't anticipated, and that compounded her sense of impending doom. "Henry, you need not worry about that."

"But I do."

Sorrow overtook Henry's face. His eyelids drooped and his lips turned downward sadly.

"Henry, think of the wondrous parts of your life. My years with you were like a brilliant summer day. I shall always be enlightened by them."

A single tear flowed down Henry's sallow cheek. He closed his eyes and drifted to sleep. Amelia listened to his labored breathing. A few years ago he had remarkable energy, even as an older gentleman. Now, weary of life, his once robust vitality was nearly drained.

Amelia's heart ached as she left Somerset House. The vital Henry Carey had withered. She plodded down the street as if her chopines—open-toed platform shoes that she'd purchased in Venice—were weighted with lead. She promised to return in the morning.

She proceeded to The Theatre, intending to find Will. As she neared the playhouse her pace became brisker and her mood lightened, buoyed by the prospect of seeing him and finally delivering the script for *The Merchant of Venice.* She hugged the cord-bound manuscript to her chest, confident it was her best work yet, even though the most difficult and emotionally wrenching to compose.

Amelia looped around a filth-filled horse pond, the stench from which she detected well before reaching it. Soon The Theatre's circular timber and brick structure rose before her. She cracked open its large gate and peered in, listening from the shadows beyond the open-air pit. Actors perched on the stage ledge like birds on a chimney top. Will faced them in the pit with his feet planted wide on the matted straw, meting out directions for scenes in *A Midsummers Night's Dream.*

A blond actor playing Puck shook his long curly hair. "What's the point of these lines? Why am I saying them to the audience and not to characters onstage?

> *If we shadows have offended,*
> *Think but this, and all is mended…"*

"Well, err…consider it for a minute," Will fumbled.

Amelia chose that moment to step into the open, making her presence known. "Hello, Will. May I answer that question?" She turned toward the actor. "You wondered why those lines are spoken directly to the audience?"

The actor screwed up his face at this interruption. "It seems out of character to me."

Shakespeare hurried to greet her, his white shirt open halfway down his chest and his arms flapping like wings. "Amelia, what are you doing here? When did you return to England?"

Will's hair was thinner on top and longer and thicker on the sides. His auburn beard was sparse on his cheeks and jawline and denser on his chin. His eyes sparkled, but beneath them were dark smudges and thickening bags.

"I left Venice on short notice. I had hoped my letter would arrive first. Today, I only want to deliver this package." She handed over the script. "Let's meet later this week when you have time."

"Yes. We have much to discuss," said Will, beaming with joy to see her again.

Veering toward the blond-haired actor who had asked the question, Amelia said, "I was privileged to read an earlier version of the script, and that speech puzzled me at first too. I believe it's intended to tell the audience that what they had witnessed may all be a dream, a dream shared with the characters, as if they too were asleep and just aroused. So if anyone watching felt offended, remember, it's only a dream and by pardoning us they are free of it."

The actor nodded, acknowledging this interpretation. "Do you think I should deliver the speech in a friendly tone without flourish, to set it apart from the dramatic conclusion?"

"That would be suitable," replied Amelia. "You might also deliver it in a confidential tone, as if sharing a secret with the audience. What's your opinion, Will?"

Will winked slyly at Amelia. "Either would work. You've explained the purpose well."

"Thank you, Will. Now I must go."

Amelia took little Henry with her to Somerset House early the next morning, still mystified about the continued absence of Alphonso. The overcast summer day carried the smell of impending rain. She navigated the streets in a midnight blue satin dress, cloak, and matching hat. Henry's pageboy haircut bounced playfully as he shook his head and pranced in a crimson young boy's skirt.

Approaching the manse, Amelia saw men in long black coats dismount from a funeral carriage and walk solemnly inside. Her heart sank. She ran toward the door but a guard stopped her. The nurse stepped outside.

"He didn't awake after you left," she informed Amelia. "Your image was the last he saw and your voice the last he heard before slipping from this Earth."

Amelia raised her hands to her face and began sobbing, again full of regret. *I should have brought Henry yesterday to meet his namesake again. Lord Hunsdon would have been so touched. Now it's too late. My son was too young to remember the first time. And this sorrowful scene is not the memory I want him to have.*

She lifted little Henry into her arms as tears streamed down her cheeks.

Henry asked, "Mama, where's the man you wanted me to meet?"

Amelia said softly, "We cannot meet with him now. God has taken him."

Amelia didn't expect Henry to understand, and he didn't.

"Mama, why would God take him away? Didn't he want me to see him?"

"When you're older, I'll tell you about this special man and dear friend."

Upon arriving home, Amelia had barely removed her cloak when Alphonso barged in with a scowl. His tousled dark red curly hair fell nearly to his shoulders. His green eyes radiated contempt.

"Well, my whorish wife has returned from Venice. And you visited Lord Hunsdon, the man who impregnated you, before seeing me. Remember me, your husband—who you don't like to whore with?"

Amelia gaped; stunned that Alphonso make such accusations in front of Henry, Julia, and Enid. Henry started crying, frightened by the wild-haired man, and Amelia picked him up.

"You're worried about your son," shouted Alphonso, "after abandoning me for three years. Are you still expecting me to be his pretend father?"

Humiliation and anger churned inside Amelia, rising like steam through her chest until a stinging sensation lodged behind her eyes. How much did Henry understand? Alphonso's drunken words cut through her like a knife. All the mistakes she'd made in the past, the scars that had healed while she lived in Venice, were again open sores.

Alphonso continued with his stream of filth. "How many men did you whore with in Venice?"

Amelia, dazed by his animosity, sputtered to Enid, "P...P...Please take Henry outside. This conversation isn't for his ears."

After handing Henry over and hearing Enid's footsteps fade, Amelia ripped the hat from her head and tossed it on a chair. She wouldn't tolerate any more drunken accusations. "I'm the wife you agreed to marry, no doubt for money, much of which you've squandered gambling. But since saying our vows, I've been faithful, your lewd conjectures notwithstanding."

Amelia stepped closer to Alphonso until she spoke directly into his face. "You're correct, I visited Lord Hunsdon yesterday. Did you forget you weren't here? I won't try guessing where you were." His guilty flinching confirmed the worst. "Lord Hunsdon died last night. He was a far better man than you'll ever be."

Alphonso pushed Amelia away. "Get away from me bitch!"

"Think what you will. Now, I'll go find my son."

Amelia walked around Alphonso with a determined gait and then turned to Julia, "Will you accompany me?"

Amelia opened the door, spun around, and shot Alphonso a withering glance. The two women thumped down the stairs to the street. The overcast skies had darkened and thunder boomed in the distance. Although Amelia put little stock in superstitions, she couldn't help wondering if this was an omen foretelling her future with a man she could not abide.

35

Amelia joined three thousand mourners in Westminster Abbey for Lord Hunsdon's funeral, along with Lady Susan Bertie, now forty-six, her second husband Sir John Wingfield, and her brother, Lord Peregrine Bertie. Peregrine held the title Baron Willoughby de Eresby and served as the Queen's ambassador to Denmark.

In a long black silk Venetian gown, Amelia stood shoulder-to-shoulder with Lady Susan, who radiated in a beaded black gown with a high ruffled neckline, befitting the somber occasion. The duchess' skin remained smooth, if paler, and her oval green eyes sparkled. Only her diminished energy and flecks of gray hinted at her age. In Venice, Amelia had fondly described Lady Susan as "the noble guide of my ungoverned days," and still valued her wisdom.

"Tell me about Venice," asked Lady Susan. "Is it as romantic as the stories?"

"It is that and more. I fell in love with the city, with its palazzo-lined canals and Moorish architecture."

"And what is the 'more'?"

Amelia brushed back a few strands that had fallen over her face. "Intrigue flows through Venice like water through the canals, thrust by a deceptive undercurrent."

Lord Peregrine joined in, "It sounds like our royal court, where everyone possesses a hidden agenda."

"Politics and the pursuit of power are everywhere," added Lady Susan.

Amelia smiled, relishing the company of nobility. She wished to belong to their circle, their class, but by birth could never truly be a part.

Lady Susan clasped Amelia's hand, squeezing it warmly. "Did Venice spark that vivid imagination of yours?"

"For that, the entire region is fertile ground," Amelia said brightly. "Ideas sprang up faster than I could gather them. And I came to more than a few realizations, which I'd like to make subjects of future conversations."

Inside regal Westminster Abbey, where English monarchs had been crowned and entombed for centuries, Amelia gazed upward. Her eyes followed rows of towering columns to the high vaulted ribbed ceiling. To her side, light streamed through a stained glass window with a likeness of King Edward, the Confessor, in a white and blue robe holding a ring in his left hand and a scepter in his right. She scanned the gothic lines through the transept to the majestic high altar with its golden glow. Priests and mourners were dwarfed by its magnificence.

The dignified service, music, and eulogies honoring Henry's public life and valor echoed eerily off stonewalls and columns. But to Amelia, they didn't capture the essence of the man she had known. His public and private sides differed. If she could address the mourners, she'd speak of Henry's kindness, integrity, sensitivity, and forgiveness.

They filed out of the massive cathedral and proceeded to Willoughby House. The three-story redbrick Tudor manse with dark-paneled rooms featured an interior courtyard. A large black-marble fireplace complemented the grand salon's white and golden-brown marble floor. Large chairs upholstered in red velvet encircled a heavy round table.

As the drinks had their effect, conversation loosened. Lord Peregrine regaled them with stories of Denmark. He described the town of Elsinore, situated on Zealand Island off the northeast coast. Established in the early 1400s by King Eric of Pomerania, Peregrine considered this isolated hamlet a poor choice for the seat of Danish power. Its strategic placement on the narrow strait connecting the Baltic Sea and Atlantic Ocean, separating Denmark from Sweden to the east, could also put the monarch in harm's way.

As Lord Peregrine retold Danish legends, mesmerizing his small audience, one especially resonated with Amelia. It involved a young fictional prince intent on avenging his father's murder. He wanted justice but was paralyzed by indecision—because he believed his father's murderer now sat on the throne. A script idea lodged in Amelia's mind. She would discuss it with Will. He liked this type of stirring tale.

Before leaving, Lady Susan pulled Amelia into the library. Amelia knew this room with floor-to-ceiling books well, for she had spent countless days reading in it as a young girl.

Lady Susan closed the door; further arousing Amelia's curiosity. The duchess then explained, "Shortly before you returned, Queen Elizabeth inquired about you. She wants me to arrange a meeting now that you're back."

Amelia felt her heart quicken. "But why?"

"I know not, but the Queen said she likes your 'turn of phrase.' Interpret that as you will."

"I'd be honored," said Amelia, wondering what Lord Hunsdon might have said about her scriptwriting. A trickle of perspiration rolled from under her arm. "When will this meeting take place?"

"Soon, I suspect. She called me aside especially to tell you."

36

LONDON, JULY 1596

Amelia and Julia set out in oppressive humidity to meet Will at The Theatre. Amelia wished to introduce Julia as her writing partner and to resume a close working relationship with him. She no longer considered herself Will's junior partner, having written several plays that drew sizeable audiences, received favorable commentary, and earned money. She also sought an accounting of royalties due to her.

Amelia debated whether to tell Will that Queen Elizabeth sought a meeting with her. After weighing reasons each way, she decided against. She could only speculate as to why the Queen extended the invitation, and she didn't want to worry him unnecessarily.

"Julia, you'll like Will. He's flamboyant, talented, and knows intuitively what works theatrically and what will not."

Upon approaching the brick and timber playhouse, the two women batted away gnats swarming along the banks of the horse pond. Once inside, Amelia squeezed through costume racks lining a narrow corridor, trying not to snag her long gray skirt. Julia followed in a golden-brown dress with layered shoulder rolls. The costumes smelled of dried perspiration, a sign they'd been recently worn and not washed. The racks were labeled for plays currently being performed by Lord Chamberlain's Men: *Love's Labour's Lost, Richard II,* and *Two Gentleman of Verona*. One half-filled rack awaited the opening of *A Midsummer Night's Dream*.

Will greeted them from behind his writing table, waving them into his tiny workroom. The sleeves of his white shirt were pushed up to his elbows. His mustache overlapped his upper lip and his thick eyelids called attention to his large eyes. Two battered guest chairs blocked the door, keeping it from swinging shut. "Ah, you've maneuvered successfully through our costume corridor. We're cramped for space," he said apologetically, "and this is the only spot to store them."

Amelia squeezed into a chair, scraping it against the floor to create legroom. "Will, this is my cousin, Julia Bassano."

Will extended his hand. "I'm delighted to meet you. Amelia wrote of your contributions."

Julia put down her valise and shook Will's hand. "I'm pleased to meet you, Mr. Shakespeare, and eager to see the plays, especially *A Midsummer Night's Dream*."

"You'll appreciate how the players bring scripts to life. It's a magical process."

Amelia noticed the buoyancy in Will's voice. Was he trying to impress Julia?

"We had a zany time dreaming up *Midsummer*—if you'll excuse the expression," said Julia.

"It's a complicated show and the actors are requiring extra time to master it, but it will be the most unique play ever performed on this island." Will turned to address Amelia directly. "Every rehearsal I hear something I didn't fully appreciate before, leading to a slightly different interpretation. It's layered with nuance."

Amelia twisted around, looking at the costume racks. "Where are the costumes for *Romeo and Juliet*? Has it closed?"

"No, it's popular, but being performed at The Rose Theater. The stage here lacks sufficient height for the balcony."

Amelia's thoughts jumped immediately to the impact on royalties. "But The Rose is smaller."

"Not now. Philip Henslowe, the owner, enlarged it to accommodate bigger troupes and more elaborate productions. He added five hundred seats to compete with The Curtain and The Theatre."

"How did Burbage react?" asked Amelia.

"He caterwauled at first. He urged me to change the balcony scene. 'Why can't it be a first floor window?' he asked. 'It won't make any difference.' But he knew better. The balcony is far more dramatic."

Amelia could tell Will had enjoyed winning this battle with Burbage, and learning that two theater owners had vied to stage one of her plays gave her a measure of satisfaction. "He now knows you have options."

"Indeed. He didn't like Henslowe welcoming us with open arms."

Amelia pointed to the stacks on his table. "What have you been writing?"

Will lifted the edge of one. "This script is *The Life and Death of King John*. It's ready for casting. I'm now working on a series about Henry IV."

Amelia smiled. "You like King Henrys, Will. This time you only had to reverse the Roman numerals for a new story."

Will laughed. "I managed to slip in a couple of King Richards as well, and I've added a John."

Now that she had inquired about Will's work, Amelia segued into the question she had been waiting to ask. "Have you read *The Merchant of Venice*?"

"It's excellent and, to me, worth the wait."

Amelia discharged her held-back breath, relieved and pleased with his reaction. "Will, I'm glad you like it, and glad I didn't settle for earlier drafts. Still, I worried about your assessment, especially after all the delays. Has Burbage seen it?"

"He has. He's impressed by the deep, and at times subtle character development. He liked the agonizing emotional pulls and unexpected plot twists. While it exceeded his expectations," Will added wryly, "he reminded me he wanted it long ago. He won't let me forget that."

Amelia understood his implicit meaning. "When will you stage it?"

"This autumn after I return from Kent."

"Kent?" asked Amelia. "Isn't it sixty or seventy miles southeast of London?"

"Part of the company will be performing there for a month. Burbage is displeased, but actors will earn extra money. We'll shorten our play rotation here, but otherwise everything remains the same; and understudies will have more opportunities to perform."

Amelia realized that, in her absence, Will had built an impressive following.

"Let's return to *Merchant*," he said. "I noticed you named a character Bassanio. Without the 'I,' it's your family name."

The two shared a smile. "I'm continuing the pattern we discussed before going to Venice. No one will notice. And it sounds indigenous to Venice."

Amelia glanced at Julia as if for agreement but her true intention was to signal that they shared a secret. If Will only knew about other clues she embedded in *Merchant, Midsummer,* and those that preceded them. He may see the outside layers, but not the hearts beating inside. And it seems Shylock's rhetorical questions have not raised objections. He asks, as a Jew, am I not "fed with the same food, hurt with the same weapons, subject to the same diseases, healed by the same means, warmed and cooled by the same winter and summer, as a Christian is?"

"You appear deep in thought," observed Will.

Her contemplation interrupted, Amelia jerked her head back. "Just reflecting on the work required to pen *Merchant.* It's different from everything else I've written. But we have business to discuss."

Will grimaced, as if bracing for a difficult issue. "Such as?"

"Money. My royalties. I've not received anything since leaving for Venice."

"Ah, yes," Will said smoothly. "I have most of it in The Theatre's safe."

"Not all of it?" asked Amelia, her voice rising.

"Burbage has been slow paying me," Will protested. "He still owes for May and June's performances. And Philip

Henslowe at The Rose hasn't paid for June yet. But I have everything else, including a ledger listing all performances, royalties received, and each of our shares."

She felt relieved to hear of his probity, for it should be a sizable sum after three years. "Thank you, Will. I'll take it upon leaving."

Will nodded then pointed to the thin sheaf of papers on Julia's lap. "What have you there?"

Julia said, "Amelia and I have outlined ideas for a new romantic comedy."

"About?"

"About nothing." Julia giggled, covering her mouth.

"How can it be about nothing?" asked Will, apparently charmed by the young woman.

"Amelia would say it's much ado about nothing."

"I don't understand."

Amelia inserted herself into the conversation. "It concerns how the absence of certain matters affects courtships and how deception creates impressions when nothing actually exists. The word 'nothing' also plays on the word 'noting'—pronounced similarly—referring to innuendo, gossip, and hearsay."

Julia added, "We'd like to show you our outline before going further."

"Julia has contributed many ideas," Amelia noted. "She has a flair for them."

Julia smiled. "I've had a good teacher."

Upon completing their discussions, Will explained his royalty ledger to Amelia and handed her a purse heavy with coins. She held it in both hands, impressed by its weight, and then packed it in her valise. Walking from The Theatre and onto Shoreditch's grimy streets, she gripped its handles tightly and watched for unsavory characters—intent on getting home safely. Yet even there she would have to hide her earnings from Alphonso. If he knew, he'd spend it recklessly.

37

LONDON, SEPTEMBER 1596

Amelia pulled the sheet up to her neck, gazing at the morning light angling through her chamber window. She and Alphonso did not share the same bed. She heard his raucous voice coming from the other room, and to avoid encountering him waited until hearing the front door creak open and bang shut. Then she rose to the muffled chatter of Julia, Enid and Henry.

Amelia's wrinkled white cotton smock draped to her feet as she padded from bed. She peered into a tall oak-framed mirror, horrified at the sight of her tangled tresses and weary face after a restless night. She brushed her shock of curly hair, slipped into a scarlet satin robe, and entered the parlor.

"G'morning, Mama," screeched Henry, running to her.

Amelia lifted her son and kissed his rosy cheek. She glanced at Enid. "Is he gone?" Enid nodded as if she'd been reprieved. Henry wiggled from Amelia's hands to play with a wooden hoop and rolled it across the floor.

Suddenly, the door crashed open. Alphonso barged in. "Where's my flute?" he barked.

"I hung the case on a wall peg," explained Enid, pointing. "I didn't want Henry playing with it."

"You imbecile, you should've told me! Now I'll be late to the court," he inveighed. "They dislike me already. I better not lose my job!"

Alphonso ripped the case from the peg and rushed out the door, slamming it on the way.

Alphonso's boorish behavior continued, stopping only several days later when Amelia told him she would be meeting the Queen with Lady Susan.

"What? How have you earned that honor?" he asked, disbelieving.

Amelia sensed his jealousy. "When I lived at Willoughby House, Lady Susan encouraged her to invite me to palace events when appropriate—and we had some brief conversations."

"Does the Queen like you?"

"She's only extending a courtesy," replied Amelia, attempting to make light of it.

Her worries over his petulance vanished when he asked, "Will you do me a favor?"

Oh no, here it comes, she thought. Will he ask me to do his bidding?

Alphonso pleaded, "This is hard to ask. If you say no, I'll understand."

"Alphonso, we're husband and wife. Why are you dancing around with me?"

With the way eased, Alphonso came to the point. "I deserve a promotion within the recorder and flute consorts at the court. I've been stuck in the lowest rank for years. They claim other musicians are better, but I'm as good as most. Can you tell the Queen I'm worthy?"

For the first time since she'd returned, Alphonso's antagonism had receded. He was acting friendly only because he wanted something. "I haven't heard you play recently, but I'll raise the subject with her."

The offer did not cheer him as she hoped. Instead he lamented, "It's not my musical proficiency that's a problem. It's my likeability."

"That you can improve," she assured him. "You can practice with me. And speaking of improvement, I'd like to raise a sensitive subject: our finances."

Alphonso's legs twitched, knocking into the table. "What about them?"

"We're spending far more than you earn as a court musician and that I receive in royalties. We're steadily depleting the hundred pounds sterling my father willed for when I married and the funds Lord Hunsdon provided."

Alphonso frowned. His jaw tightened. He clenched his fists. Amelia sensed that he was holding himself back from becoming openly hostile. She wished to defang the retort she believed was poised on the tip of his tongue. "You might consider Lord Hunsdon's money illicit, but it reflects his regard for me. It pays for our rooms and Enid. He provided funds specifically for her."

Rather than argue as Amelia expected, he pressed his request for her to advocate for him. "If I'm promoted, I'll be paid more. A good word from you to the Queen could make the difference."

She stared at him disbelieving. Everything came back to what he wanted. He has no intention of stopping his reckless spending and gambling. He'll keep resisting no matter the impact on our family—if he sees it at all. But if he continues, our savings will be whittled to nothing.

"That's not the point. You're spending too much," she told him. "I live frugally but you're bringing home only a portion of your wages. Where's the rest going?"

"Are you accusing me of squandering it?"

"That's a good way to put it. Are you?"

Alphonso's face reddened. He slammed his fist on the table. "You bitch! You're not running my life."

She refused to permit his usual bluster. "Alphonso, you've lost control with your spending. Can nobody reason with you?"

He swung his arm to strike her, freezing it just before hitting her cheek—leaving his hand quiver in midair.

In a controlled tone, barely above a whisper, she declared, "Be glad you stopped short of striking me."

"And if I hadn't?"

"I might raise the topic with the Queen."

Alphonso grabbed his hat and stormed out, leaving the door swinging on its hinges.

Amelia awoke drenched in sweat, anxious about meeting the Queen. Uncertain about the purpose, her mind swam all night from one scenario to another. Early morning rays beamed through cracks in the thin curtains, creating slender lines of sunlight across her bed. She stepped over to her oaken dry sink and submerged a washcloth into the ceramic basin sitting on top. The moist towel cooled her clammy hands and she rinsed her face until sleepiness drained from her eyes.

Enid helped Amelia wash and dress. They selected an ivory gown with golden-brown leaf designs over a white bodice. Enid then swept up Amelia's coppery hair and fixed it in place with pearl-beaded pins. They completed the outfit with a white ruff around Amelia's thin neck.

Before Whitehall Palace's wide arched entry, Lady Susan waited for Amelia in a gold-spun gown—appearing tiny against the massive white stone building with rounded and steepled roofs.

Inside, Whitehall Palace inspired awe. Ceremonial guards stood at attention in scarlet silk and black velvet uniforms as the two women passed, their full skirts swaying in harmony. Large tapestries and royal portraits adorned the walls. Tall gold-rimmed porcelain vases sprouted bouquets of red and white roses, adding to the splendor.

They were ushered into the richly decorated throne room where several others also waited. Long red velvet curtains framed soaring windows. Moments later, Queen Elizabeth, breathing heavily through her mouth, entered from double doors in a beige dress with a scarlet underskirt, simple bodice and sleeves, a cloak, and high leather boots that clopped on the stone floor. She handed a lady-in-waiting her riding gloves. Her cheeks were free of the white makeup she often wore, revealing facial scars from smallpox.

Elizabeth, catching her breath, joked, "My six-mile canters through the palace grounds make my councilors delirious. They think their Queen will get thrown from her horse and crack her royal head. Why, at sixty-three I'm a better horseman than nearly all of them."

Elizabeth swept beads of perspiration from her brow and then singled out the newcomer in court for attention. "Amelia, I've heard much about you—from our late Lord Hunsdon, the Lord Chamberlain, and of course from Lady Susan."

Amelia performed a deep curtsey. "Your Majesty, thank you. I'm honored to be in your presence."

The Queen perched on her lofty gilded chair under a gold brocade canopy, casually draping one hand over the armrest. "You're a woman now," she noted, "and more becoming than ever."

"You're most kind, Your Majesty. I'm grateful to be home. Although I'm saddened by the death of Lord Hunsdon."

"He was superb. I valued his loyalty and integrity. What occupies you now?"

Amelia had expected that question. "I'm caring for my son and composing poetry. I'm also acquainting my cousin, who returned with me from Venice, with England's rich traditions."

Elizabeth signaled for Amelia and Lady Susan to step forward and ordered all others to step out so she might have a private discussion. Still she spoke in hushed tones, ensuring only the two of them could hear. "Amelia, I understand you have a collegial relationship with Mr. Shakespeare, who is enjoying great theatrical success."

Amelia tried to remain calm. "Your Majesty, I am one of his admirers and impressed by his playwriting range. We've had conversations and I've furnished some assistance."

"Aren't you being too modest?"

"Your Majesty, I'm unsure what you mean."

Queen Elizabeth had held the reins of power for too long to be duped. "I believe you do but are reluctant to reveal your contributions. Often lords and ladies selfishly promote themselves to win my favor. Rather than exaggerating, you seem to be claiming too little. Are you protecting Mr. Shakespeare?"

Amelia's nervousness grew. She feared saying something wrong and chose caution. "Your Majesty, why would you have such suspicions?"

"The plays performed under Mr. Shakespeare's name generally fall into two categories: historical dramas about English kings and comedies set elsewhere, often with prominent roles for women. The monarchal productions are rife with political intrigue. The comedies portray the complexity of human, family, and marital relationships. It's seems unlikely the two would be written by the same hand."

Amelia felt her knees weakening. "That does seem improbable, Your Majesty. But Mr. Shakespeare is a keen observer of humanity."

The Queen regarded Amelia in apparent disappointment. "I am your Queen. If anyone can keep a secret, it is I. And I believe I know your secret."

Lady Susan gripped Amelia's arm, willing her to remain silent. "Your Majesty, forgive her. She's concerned about Mr. Shakespeare's reputation. She's being less than forthcoming for that reason only, not to mislead you. Amelia is unaware of discussions the late Lord Hunsdon and I have had with you."

"Well, Amelia," said Queen Elizabeth, "is it more than a coincidence that during the time you were in Venice two plays set in that region debuted: *The Taming of the Shrew* and *Two Gentlemen of Verona?* And a tragic romance called *Romeo and Juliet*, set in Verona, is now playing at The Rose."

Amelia's legs shook beneath her long black skirt. She clasped her hands to steady her nerves. She wondered how the Queen knew about *Romeo and Juliet*. She had not written to Lord Hunsdon about it. No matter, now she needed to be contrite and forthright with the Queen. "Your Majesty, please be assured I meant no disrespect. I hold you in the highest esteem. You are indeed correct. Those are not coincidences."

"Well, then. What shall we do about it?"

"Your Majesty, as much as I would like having my name attached to those works, theater owners would not have staged them if they had known the playwright was a woman." Amelia heard her voice quake, but continued with as much composure as she could muster. "They turned me away time and again. Now I have a pact with Mr. Shakespeare, who is not, I assure you, treating me unfavorably."

When the Queen concluded the discussion, guards opened the doors for the others to reenter the grand room and Lady Susan introduced Amelia to various courtiers. Amelia noticed a man in his forties with dark eyes, unruly eyebrows, and a dense beard. He did not strike her as nobility, yet a countess seemed utterly entranced by him.

Amelia nudged Lady Susan, "Who is that beguiling fellow that has Countess Rutherford under his spell?"

"Simon Forman."

"Who is he?"

"He's a renowned herbalist, occultist, and astrologer. He has helped many people."

"A mystic? I don't believe in fortunetellers."

"Forman advises both nobility and commoners. He's made many accurate predictions. Like you, he straddles both worlds."

"Perhaps he could predict if I'll be trapped forever in my sorrowful marriage."

She meant it partly as a joke, but Lady Susan seemed serious. "If you see him," she warned, "stick to business. He's an oily character."

Amelia nodded, knowing what Lady Susan meant. The countess appeared to be one breath away from inviting him to leave with her for a secluded rendezvous.

As Amelia watched, she could understand why. She too found herself attracted to the man. What an opportune solution, she thought, for a married woman saddled with a repulsive husband.

"You seem intrigued by him," Lady Susan observed.

"Oh, no," Amelia said, laughing lightly, "I'm merely confirming my beliefs about charlatans. They first need to mesmerize their prey."

38

LONDON, OCTOBER 1596

Amelia shuddered thinking about the opening performance of *The Merchant of Venice*. How will the audience react? How will Alphonso, Julia, and Enid who will accompany her? Will they absorb the nuances or consider it an anti-Jewish treatise? Will they recoil at the portrayal of Shylock or view him as a tormented and sympathetic figure? Will it trigger the audience's worst prejudices or provoke understanding?

Enid watched Amelia pace nervously in the parlor. "You're shaking. What's wrong?"

"I'm scared and the chilly autumn air isn't helping. I fear judgment, especially from my family, who know I wrote this play. Will they hate me?"

"We love you. We know how tortured you were while writing it."

Amelia rubbed the gold hamsa dangling from her neck. "Enid, I'd like to be invisible tonight. What if the audience reacts in horror?"

"Amelia, you are invisible to them. They don't know you wrote the script."

Amelia ruefully acknowledged the accuracy of this observation. For once she felt grateful for having to resort to subterfuge for her plays to be produced.

"Enid, will you help me dress in my raspberry gown with ruffled sleeves? It's in the armoire. I'll wear my pearl choker too. My velvet chopines with mother of pearl will go well with that ensemble as will my French hood. Then I'll splash on *Acqua di Melissa.*"

They joined a large crowd streaming into The Theatre and climbed to the seats Will had reserved for them in the balcony's first row. Three platforms rested on the hardwood stage, each a foot higher than the one below. Amelia rubbed her hands to keep them from trembling. Julia, sitting beside her, placed her hand atop Amelia's. "Everything will go well. You'll see."

As the performance began, Amelia examined faces in the audience. When Antonio promised to guarantee Shylock's loan of three thousand ducats to Bassanio, Amelia studied the expressions of Julia and Alphonso as the moneylender recounted his past mistreatment, the borrowers' despicable slurs against Jews, and the irony of now seeking his help. They watched with rapt attention. Did they identify with Shylock's angst? She turned her attention back to the stage in time to hear Shylock say:

> If you repay me not on such a day,
> In such a place, such sum or sums as are
> Express'd in the condition, let the forfeit
> Be nominated for an equal pound

> Of your fair flesh, to be cut off and taken
> In what part of your body pleaseth me.

The audience gasped, Julia and Alphonso among them. "Barbaric," Amelia heard someone opine from behind her. Amelia held her breath and gripped her knees, waiting to hear the assembly's sentiments as the story unfolded. She expected more horrified reactions.

When Act IV began, Amelia's anxiety peaked. The harsh court scene was unfolding. The loan hadn't been repaid and Shylock refused an offer for three times the sum owed in lieu of a pound of flesh. He sought revenge for the slights he'd endured. Portia—a clever, affluent heiress disguised as the judge—announced the verdict: Shylock was indeed due his pound of flesh. The audience roared its disapproval.

Alphonso covered his mouth in shock and lowered his head. Julia squeezed Amelia's hand. Enid wiped away tears with a handkerchief.

Then Portia continued as a tense silence filled the theater:

> Tarry a little; there is something else.
> This bond doth give thee here no jot of blood;
> The words expressly are 'a pound of flesh:'
> Take then thy bond, take thou thy pound of flesh;
> But, in the cutting it, if thou dost shed
> One drop of Christian blood, thy lands and goods
> Are, by the laws of Venice, confiscate
> Unto the state of Venice.

The audience sighed with enormous relief. But how did they view Shylock? Did he make them distrust Jews all the more? Or did they empathize with Shylock's anguish and quest for revenge? Amelia had struggled to write this scene. Now they'd witness Shylock pay for his vengefulness rather than his greed. It would haunt him the rest of his days. Would the audience believe he got what he deserved? Would they feel the consequences were too great or too life altering? These questions plagued her.

After actors took their final bows to thunderous applause and the theater quieted, Amelia's family gathered around her.

Julia said, "Seeing this play performed is very different from reading it. Now I see how the audience reaction depends on how actors portray their roles, emphasize lines, and project their characters' attitudes. I had difficulty watching it, but you've depicted conflicting sides of humanity."

Alphonso said, "Amelia, as a Jew, I heard the messages you implanted. Some Jews will sympathize with Shylock, but others will be aghast."

Alphonso's comment took Amelia by surprise. It was the most astute observation she'd heard from him. "That's what gives me nightmares."

"And rightfully so," said Alphonso. "Many Jews will think it further stigmatizes them as greedy. Christians, too, may draw mistaken conclusions, using them to justify hostility toward Jews."

Amelia replied, "Alphonso, I appreciate your honesty. I worry about that too."

Julia said, "Amelia, in anyone else's hands, this play would have been far more skewed, and the depiction of Jews more brutal. Shylock would not have been humanized. His rancor would not have been portrayed as an understandable reaction to historic mistreatment. Don't cry for what you have written. Take solace knowing you did your best."

Listening to Julia, Amelia realized how much her cousin had grown since the first day they met in Venice. Julia was now seeking to console her, which warmed her heart.

Enid lifted Amelia's hands and held them gently. "I know well the sleepless nights you've had over this script. Now you should stop lugging around your guilt like a bag of coal."

Amelia's worst fears came true when Alphonso's parents summoned her to their home. Like many others, they had heard the uproar about the play and saw it themselves.

"Shame! Shame on you!" excoriated Lucretia. "Alphonso told us you wrote that libel. How could you malign your own people?"

Mortified, her face burning with humiliation, Amelia glowered in stunned silence in the Lanier's' salon—where she had celebrated Jewish holidays as a girl. Lucretia and Nicholas glared from across the room along with their daughter, Ellen, now a young adult and their son, Innocent, in his late twenties. Gray streaked Lucretia's wavy shoulder-length hair. She appeared older, Amelia thought, than her forty-one years. Nicholas, in his midsixties with thin gray hair combed back, projected sheer hostility.

"What you've done is a *shanda!*" he accused her. "You've given cause for Christians to hate and reject us even more. You've added misery to every Jew's life."

A *shanda*—the Yiddish word for an outrage and terribly shameful act—cut through Amelia like a knife. She instinctively folded her arms across her tightening chest, feeling her heart thump and her hamsa press into her skin. She thought of her father: Would he understand? Would he be outraged?

Lucretia answered Amelia's unspoken questions. "You've disgraced your father's memory. He'd renounce you if he were alive. That's what we're doing. We're disavowing you," she added with a burst of malice. "You're a blot on our entire family."

"Disavow me? When have you vowed for me? I'm the niece who loved you. The niece you called 'endearing.' I'm also your daughter-in-law. And you ask for not a word of explanation?" cried Amelia, her face burning with fury.

"Amelia, don't joust over semantics," declared Nicholas. "From this day on, you're no longer part of this family. Innocent and Ellen are forbidden to see you. As for Alphonso, he'll have to decide what's most important to him. How he'll stay married to you is beyond my ken. If he does, he's renounced as well."

Amelia walked toward the door, doing her best to maintain a semblance of dignity. Her insides churned. She should have known that such straightforward folk would not understand the play's subtlety.

Nicholas followed Amelia across the salon. In a determined voice he commanded, "Don't return. To us, you no longer exist. You're dead in our eyes and expunged from our lives forever. I will not utter your name again."

Amelia staggered away. Feeling hollow, she pulled her wool coat tight to stave off autumn chills. Her legs moved by themselves, for she had no awareness of trudging through the road muck, soiling her leather boots and long buff skirt. Her head pounded as if being struck by a hammer. She narrowly missed colliding with a horse and wagon loaded with barrels—although the back corner struck her arm as it turned. Urgent voices called for her to jump away, but they barely penetrated her consciousness.

Amelia slogged ahead aimlessly. Her distress seeped deeply into her soul. She leaned against a post and closed her eyes.

"Amelia? Amelia! Are you all right?"

She knew that clarion voice. Will. He carried a basket with fresh vegetables. "Amelia, you look stricken. Come with me."

He wrapped his free arm about her waist, escorting her around the corner to his room.

Amelia shivered. "Will, how did you find me?"

"I was returning from the market. What are you doing so far away from your Westminster home?"

"I don't know…I didn't know where I was."

Will studied curiously the undignified sight before him. "You must get out of your muddy clothes. I'll find a blanket to wrap around you."

Amelia settled on a hard chair in his small parlor. Costumes, hats, and masks hung from wall pegs. Scripts and papers were piled haphazardly on a crude wooden table beside an empty ink jar with a well-worn quill inside. In a corner she noticed a stack of the letters she had sent him from Venice. She wondered why he kept them, especially where he'd see them every day.

Amelia trembled still from her dismissal by Lucretia and Nicholas. All her fears about reactions to *Merchant* had come true. Her family, whom she most expected to perceive and appreciate the play's nuances, was unforgiving. And she could not tell Will. He didn't know her faith. Or did he? She did not know how much to trust him, especially with so sensitive a subject. She could hardly afford to alienate him, so she would remain silent. Nobody else could know about her authorship.

"What happened? Why are you so upset?" asked Will.

"I've been castigated mercilessly for—"

"For what?"

"I made a horrific mistake, and Alphonso's parents, who are also my cousins, have reacted heartlessly. I've just come from their home, where they were unrelenting in their criticism."

"But what did you do that was so terrible?"

"It's a family matter and too painful to recount, especially now. Perhaps, someday, I'll be able to explain."

Will persisted, "Amelia, you can trust me."

"Will, I know. You're a dear man."

He didn't look pleased with that characterization, but remained buoyant. "You can take solace, at least, in having composed a truly great play. Audiences in every quarter are praising *Merchant*. One acquaintance said he felt like he had lived through it with the characters and left the theater emotionally wrenched. People are talking unceasingly about it... and recommending it—which makes Burbage euphoric."

"I wish such news would alleviate my hurt, but it's too deep for that. Will, your desire to comfort me is most appreciated. I am grateful for your friendship. Thank you for helping in this moment of despair."

Will stepped behind Amelia's chair and massaged her taut shoulders. "I trust you'll confide in me about your distress when the time is right."

Amelia squeezed her lips tight as Will's fingers pressed soothingly into her skin. Will's kindness and compassion should be all a woman wants, she told herself, yielding to the sensations. Yet she knew she could never go further. Their relationship relied on their mutual love for playwriting and nothing more.

It was curious, Amelia thought, that she could remain celibate for three years in Venice, but having returned home to her loathsome husband she was thinking much more about sex. She needed to find the right benefactor.

39

Months later, still shaken by reactions to *Merchant*, Amelia sought to regain her confidence. The work she and Will did together contributed most to her gradual recovery, along with his friendship and deference. Today she expected to enjoy another stroll with him to discuss plots for each other's scripts and those they decided to compose together. Recently they had focused mostly on Will's project for *Henry IV*, both Parts I and II. Each time they met in different London locales to keep the scenery and hopefully their ideas fresh.

Today, they met in the churchyard in front of Saint Paul's Cathedral. Amelia planned to present her latest concept for *Julius Caesar*. A bare oak with thick branches towered overhead in the shadow of the cathedral's high spire. The frost-rimed grass crunched and crackled underfoot as she approached.

Instead Will announced, "James Burbage has died."

A lump formed in Amelia's throat. Burbage's brusque rejection years earlier when she tried interesting him in *A Comedy of Errors* still rankled. He had dismissed her outright before she could show him the script. Yet he had profited from it. On the other hand, he helped Will become England's premier playwright. His successor will need Will just as much, and might be more open-minded. That thought sparked a surge of hope. "I'm sorry. Was he ill?"

"He caught pneumonia from the bitter cold. He'd been bedridden for days and didn't wake yesterday morning."

"What does that mean for us?" she asked cautiously.

"I doubt much will change. Burbage's son, Cuthbert, will manage The Theatre. I know his brother, Richard, better. He acts in our company."

"What is Cuthbert like?"

Will evinced an ominous uncertainty, uncharacteristic for him. "I know him mostly by reputation. He's handled tough business issues for his father, especially after his partner— John Brayne, a co-owner of The Theatre—died. Cuthbert tried cutting Brayne's widow out of her husband's share of the business, setting off a vicious legal battle. I suspect he's shrewder than his father."

Amelia's momentary hope flickered out as she digested this news. If Cuthbert had tried cheating a dead man's wife, could there be any chance he'd be fairer than his father?

Will reached down and grabbed a clump of frozen leaves and let them fall from his hands. "We have another problem. We aren't making nearly the money we could because of The Theatre's size, and other venues are no better. We're turning droves of people away every day."

"What are our choices? We can't build a larger theater. Neither of us has that much money. In fact, I—" Amelia stopped in mid-sentence as she debated with herself over whether to raise a bothersome subject.

"In fact, what?" asked Will.

Amelia repressed her annoyance, seeking to project calm. She didn't want Will to think she was making an accusation, but she felt he hadn't been forthcoming with her share of the royalties. She gathered herself and managed a neutral tone. "Will, you haven't paid me for some time."

Will seemed discomfited by her demand, although he probably expected it. "I will as soon as Burbage, now Cuthbert, pays me. That's how it works."

"Why hasn't he paid you?"

"Burbage made some bad business investments. He's held back payments to actors and to me as playwright while trying to juggle his debts."

Amelia would not be fobbed off with such an excuse. She knew well that Will's standing in the world had risen considerably. "Will, my arrangement is with you, not Burbage."

"I'm committed to pay you a share of what I receive for your plays," he maintained. "Unfortunately, Burbage's death will delay payments further. I doubt I'll be paid until it's sorted out."

Amelia believed Will had sufficient money of his own and could advance her share if he so desired. He was being tight-fisted, perhaps because of his upbringing. To emphasize her concern, she added, "During my absence, Alphonso helped himself to a large share of my savings and spent it frivolously. My reserves are dwindling and I'll need cash soon. I don't want debt collectors knocking on my door."

Will nodded, showing his understanding. "I'll press Cuthbert again. He dodged my query when I raised the subject yesterday, and with his father's death I didn't pursue it."

"Please do," Amelia said in a softer tone. "After the burial."

"At the right time, I'll also ask about enlarging The Theater," said Will. "But I don't know how it could be done even if the lease were renewed. It's hemmed by streets on two sides and buildings on the others."

"Cuthbert might have ideas. I suspect his ambition is to earn as much money as possible."

"By the way, he asked when I'll finish writing *Much Ado About Nothing*, which he knows is a work-in-progress. Before Burbage died, the two must have talked. Cuthbert said his father complained that we once had too many comedies. But now we have too many dramas."

Amelia pulled her shawl snugly around as the chilly wind picked up. "He wants a mix because they draw different audiences," she said with touch of annoyance. He probably assumes an artist can deliver a product on demand, like buying a bolt of cloth. "Promise it for next year," she said grimly, "if he pays us."

40

T o her surprise, Amelia's relationship with Alphonso improved after being severed from his family. They were united in their antipathy for Lucretia and Nicholas.

"You saw the charming side of my parents when you visited for Jewish holidays," said Alphonso. "They were perfect hosts. But they possess a vicious underside most people don't see. My brother and I could never meet their expectations, because Ellen became their favorite. They didn't hide it."

Amelia and Alphonso were rarely intimate, but today they disclosed their feelings and insecurities. He told her he felt lost. He confessed to being a musician of above average ability but not stellar, in contrast to his description six months earlier. His father constantly reminded him that he didn't measure up to the best in the Queen's recorder consort, and few liked him besides.

Alphonso needed her companionship, but that left her in a dilemma. She desired more than he could offer. He was an empty vessel who brought pain and little joy to their marriage. He couldn't provide the comfort, affection, and love for which Amelia yearned. Alphonso was not intellectual, nor did he have passions for learning and literature. He remained uninterested in her work. They had little in common and little to discuss.

On the following bone-chilling Sunday, after Enid had left for church and Julia had taken Henry outside to play, Alphonso approached Amelia as she sat writing.

"I am making a life change," he announced grandly.

Amelia set down her quill and waited for Alphonso to say more.

"I'm leaving my job as a court musician."

Dumbfounded, Amelia stared at him. Doesn't he know we depend on his wages, even the meager amount he brings home? "But why? What will you do?"

"I'm becoming a gentleman soldier. I'm joining the forces the Earl of Essex is assembling to drive the Portuguese from the Azores. He's leading the invasion with Sir Walter Raleigh."

"Why are you going?"

"To do something important. To get away from my father, whom I can't avoid when I'm playing at the palace. He has not spoken to me since I decided to stay with you."

"Alphonso, you're important to our family and a valued court musician," said Amelia, as the full import of his announcement sank in. "Why put yourself in harm's way?"

"You don't understand. I play the recorder and flute and people are entertained. Nothing significant is accomplished. I want to be more. I want recognition."

"Sailing a thousand miles to islands in the Atlantic Ocean to fight the Portuguese will do that?" Amelia asked incredulously.

Alphonso became belligerent. "I'll be serving my country. We will claim the Azores for England and I'll share in the spoils."

Amelia considered this an imprudent venture for Alphonso. He is not a warrior. He must know the hazards. He's deceiving himself if he believes he'll return with a large bounty. "You expect a share of the plunder?"

"I'm more interested in personal rewards."

"Personal rewards?"

Alphonso smiled. "To be dubbed a knight. When we return victorious, the Queen will recognize all the men aboard."

Amelia stared, stunned. Alphonso was all bluster.

"It's a noble calling. But aren't you ill-suited for such a venture?"

Amelia regretted her last sentence. It slipped out before she could recall it.

"You think I'm not man enough?"

"Not at all. It's your safety I care about."

Alphonso departed for Portsmouth a week later for training. Amelia did not know when she would see him again and worried about the husband she didn't love. Would he survive this foolhardy mission?

Strangely, Alphonso's absence made her feel adrift. The thought that he might die loomed like an omen she could not shake. Her mind meandered to Lady Susan's comments about astrologist Simon Forman and the skills she claimed he possessed. She made an appointment to have her fortune told, knowing she had suspended her better judgment. Yet learning what he might say wasn't the only reason for going.

Forman rippled his wide forehead as Amelia introduced herself. His fingers played with his moustache and his beard formed a wide arc beneath his chin. Amelia took a seat in his dark-paneled office. The curtains had been pulled and oil lanterns cast angular patterns of light and shadow across his oak desk. His manner reminded Amelia of Christopher Marlowe. They looked nothing alike, yet she found herself drawn to his physical presence.

"Since Lady Susan Bertie referred you, you will receive the finest advice I can offer. I'll convey special insights and reveal qualities you have yet to realize about yourself, but upon hearing them you will know they are true," said Forman in a low voice.

"Mister Forman, I know little about astrology, if it actually works, and if it does, why. But I worry about the future. Could you begin by explaining how astrology functions and why it should be believed?"

"You're skeptical. That's good. Astrology is the study of cycles—cycles in your life, the lives of people you know, and in life as a whole, which has no beginning or end. There are cycles in nature such as the seasons. There are celestial cycles in the movement of the sun, moon, and stars. Understanding these and how they interact with our lives is the essence of astrology. Astrologers unlock their mysteries and link them to each person's life."

"But how do you decipher these cycles?" asked Amelia.

"First, when were you born?"

"January 27, 1569."

"You're twenty-eight. You're an Aquarius. What do you know about Aquarians?"

"Very little."

"Aquarians enjoy learning about life's mysteries. They're imaginative. They chart their own course. Does this sound like you?"

"I'm surprised, because it does," said Amelia. "But couldn't that apply to almost anyone?"

Forman's gaze slowly fell from Amelia's face, to her narrow shoulders, and landed on her pewter front-laced bodice. After lingering on her breasts, he looked back into her eyes and smiled. "There is an air of mystery about Aquarians. They're thinkers. They like exploring ideas, especially their own, and pondering. Intellectual pursuits are probably your forte. You may have your own ideas about right and wrong... and a rebellious streak."

"My astrological sign tells you all that?"

Forman leaned across his desk with deliberate ease, closing the space between them. "If most of what I described rings true, you should conclude there's validity to my counsel."

Amelia could not help admiring his suave nature. She decided to test him with one of her concerns. "Unlike the captain of a ship at sea using Polaris, the North Star, to guide his voyage, I don't have a star giving me direction. I'm adrift on the sea of my life. I'm not drowning but worry my destination is forever illusory—like a dream that can't come true."

"Most interesting," said Forman. "Ships navigate by the North Star because it is a constant in the night sky—the celestial universe. I can help you discover your constant." He leaned away for a significant pause. "Tell me, what does your husband think of your quandary?"

"He thinks nothing of the matter. He has joined the Earl of Essex to combat the Portuguese. I won't see him until he returns, months from now."

"So you are without the company of a man. Is that another reason you feel rudderless?"

Amelia flared at the implication. "I might miss my husband, but he is neither my rudder nor my compass."

Foreman stretched his arms across his desk until his fingers almost touched Amelia's. "Do you wish to know what is in your future?"

Despite his oily smoothness, Amelia felt the pull of his personality and his mysterious air. He made no secret of his interest in her. "I doubt you can predict that. Our futures are revealed as we walk life's path. Studying astrological cycles won't matter."

Amelia rose to leave, seeing a glimmer in Forman's eye. Did she prick his curiosity?

He scanned her body from head to toe and smiled before reverting to his professional demeanor. "I would like to continue our discussion. I'll charge no fees. We'll talk as two people who intrigue each other. Will you agree?"

She leaned on the chair back, considering. Forman was an interesting man and she would enjoy his company. "Indeed. I imagine there is much you can teach me. And that I can teach you."

41

LONDON, MAY 1597

Amelia strummed a children's song for four-year-old Henry in her parlor. She sang in harmony with Enid and they laughed at the words.

Amelia's mood had brightened since she began meeting with Simon Forman, finding their discussions during the past month pleasurable and stimulating. He viewed life through a mystical lens, which intrigued her. His unabated flirtations became more suggestive each time and she was flattered—but she held out reciprocating in kind.

Boom! Bang! The three jumped.

"Alphonso Lanier! Open the door. We want our money!" a man howled.

"We know you're in there. Open now!"

Amelia's hand froze over the strings. Oh no! What did Alphonso do? What does he owe? He's gone but his recklessness has darkened our door!

Boom! Boom! The door rattled violently. "Lanier, open or we'll break through. You've got five seconds. One. Two. Three—"

Breaking free of her paralysis, Amelia hurried to unlock the door. Two burly men filled the doorframe. The bigger one's head resembled a pineapple. Gnarled scars marred the left cheek and forehead of the other.

The larger man pushed Amelia aside. "Where is he?"

"He's not here. What do you want?"

"Where is he? He owes us money. We're not leaving without it."

"You'll be waiting a long time—"

"No! Now!"

Amelia inhaled deeply to calm her nerves. She could not help them. "May I explain?"

The big man glared. "So what then?"

Henry cried and Enid gathered him in her arms. "Let's go to your bedroom."

"Alphonso is fighting the Portuguese in the Azores," said Amelia. "He won't return for months."

The man's anger sharpened. "Bert, you hear that? He's a lying cheat. He's run out on us."

"You his wife?" the man named Bert asked.

Amelia stepped back. "I am. What does he owe and why?"

"Eighty pounds sterling. Ain't that right, John?"

"Eighty pounds?" Her voice quavered on his naming such an enormous sum." "What for?"

Panic gripped Amelia. That's all she had left from Lord Hunsdon. They had been living meagerly off her trickle of royalties. Alphonso, even before leaving, brought home little and now nothing at all. If she paid them, she would have to scrape for every pence for rent, food, and clothing.

"Gambling debts, ma'am. He kept thinking he'd get lucky and win some back. But never did. So we cut him off. Now we're demanding what he owes."

The news turned Amelia ice-cold inside. "Alphonso told me nothing of this."

"It doesn't matter. We'll take every stick of furniture and throw you on the street if we're not paid. Think of your boy, missus."

That's exactly who Amelia was thinking about. This demand would cripple them financially. Not paying it could cripple them physically.

"Sirs, what proofs have you that Alphonso owes such a vast sum?"

Bert pulled a stack of papers from his pocket and dropped them on the dining table.

Amelia perused each note, over twenty dated with Alphonso's distinctive signature. Many sloppily penned. Was he drunk when he signed them? She added each note mentally, her hands shaking while restacking them. They added to slightly over eighty pounds. Amelia's jaws tightened as the logic of his actions struck home. Alphonso knew this was coming and joined the armed forces to avoid it. He's a coward! Now I'm being intimidated instead.

"Sirs, I beg for a brief respite," Amelia said, trying to calm these uncouth brutes before they exacted damage on the spot. "The amount owed is not here. I must check our account at the exchange, which will require a day or two. Can you return in three days? I'll have something then."

The two burly men glanced at each other. Bert scoured the room with his dark eyes. John grabbed Amelia around her neck.

"This ain't a game, missus. If you don't have all of it, you'll regret it. I'm sure you want to see your boy grow to a man, not a drunken scoundrel like your husband."

He released her throat and ripped Amelia's gold hamsa from her neck, the chain breaking as he raised it high. "I'll keep this until we get our money."

The men slammed the door upon leaving. Trembling, Amelia listened to their boots tromping down the stairs. Then silence.

Enid emerged from the bedroom with Henry. He looked frightened. "Mama, will those men take all our money?"

Two days later, Amelia, Enid, and Julia hovered over the dining table stacked with coins. "This is all the money I have," Amelia said, discouraged. "It's what remains from Lord Hunsdon and my father. Enid, it's what I use to pay you and buy anything beyond necessities."

"How much is it?" asked Julia.

"Sixty-eight pounds."

"But Alphonso owes eighty."

"Yes, I'm twelve pounds short."

"Could you ask Lady Susan?" suggested Julia.

"If she were well, she might help. But I'm too humiliated to ask."

"What about Alphonso's parents? They hate you but—"

"To them, I'm dead. They won't rescue us, especially if he can't ask personally."

Amelia stepped to the window and peered at the buildings across the street. She instinctively reached for her hamsa, which no longer hung around her neck.

"Enid, if I pay off Alphonso's debts, I'll have no money to pay you. I'll be destitute."

Enid stood behind Amelia and wrapped her arms around her waist. "Amelia, my plight is bound with yours. I've saved a little and can spend it if need be. You, Henry, and Julia are my family more than any I've had."

Amelia placed her hands over Enid's as they rested on her belly. Enid's generous offer cemented in her mind the course she must take. "I have an idea. It's a desperate ploy but—"

"What?" asked Julia.

Amelia directed them back to the table. "Enid, take eighteen pounds. Hide it. Don't tell me where until this has ended. But don't stow it here. Those men might search the place."

Enid looked puzzled. "Then what'll you do? You'll have even less to give them."

"But if I show them the fifty remaining pounds and declare that's all I have, maybe they'll rip up the other notes and leave us alone. You can't take money that doesn't exist and our furniture isn't worth much."

Enid reluctantly placed her hands on the money. "You are taking a big risk."

"How else will we care for Henry and keep this place? That's the greater danger."

Enid looked at her uncertainly.

"Hurry. Take the eighteen and go. Hide it somewhere safe."

Enid counted and gathered the coins. She wrapped them in a towel and bound it tight with cord. She put the bundle in a box and knotted a rope around it. Finally, she applied sealing wax on all sides where the lid and box bottom met, and etched her initials "EF" on each seal. Carrying the box, she fled the apartment.

Harsh raps rattled Amelia's door early the following morning. Enid, Julia, and Henry had already left since Amelia expected the debt collectors to return soon after daybreak. She wanted to confront them alone.

Amelia opened the door. The two imposing figures marched in scowling.

"Good morning," said Amelia cheerily, hoping to set the right tone.

"Have you got our money?" John asked with a snarl.

"Much of it. Let's have a polite discussion?"

"Do you have it or not? There's nothing to discuss."

"Sirs, I'll give you all the money I have to settle my husband's debt. It's not my obligation and I haven't evaded you. After I pay, I'll be penniless except for personal furnishings. Let's have a civilized conversation?"

The men glanced at each other and Amelia appraised their reactions, wondering how amenable they might be. Regardless, she'd forge ahead. She had no choice.

John spoke first. "Ma'am, what have you to say?"

"Please sit. I'll bring cider and crumpets."

A look of suspicion crossed his face. "Ma'am, there's no need. Say what you have to say and give us our money."

"I'll be right back. I have a plate ready. Don't they smell delicious?"

Amelia returned with crumpets and cider. She poured each a cup and sat across the table. The small cups looked puny in the men's large hands. They bit into the crumpets.

"You said you have most of our money. How much?"

"Have you brought my necklace?"

"It's in my pocket," said Bert.

"Please place it on the table so everything we discuss can be seen."

"Where's the money?"

"In a box in the kitchen. You can look at it so you know it's there. Then I'll keep it on my lap. You can count it when we conclude," said Amelia, sounding braver than she felt.

Amelia retrieved a heavy box filled with bags of coins, which she left partially open for the men to view. They nodded, but she didn't think they'd be able to estimate well how much was there.

"I'll take a closer look," John said.

"You can have a longer look but not a closer one," said Amelia. She stood on the far side of the table, opening the box again, her heart pounding. "Satisfied?"

"Not until we count the money," Bert said.

"Understood. But you haven't yet put my necklace on the table."

The man laid it close to the edge near him.

"Let's talk. This is a business transaction. Let's be businesslike. First, I'll be giving you fifty pounds. That's all I have."

"Fifty pounds? Alphonso owes eighty!"

Amelia studied them, noting their bluster but also discomfort in dealing with a woman, especially one not becoming hysterical at the sight of them. "You can beat me or kill me, but you still can't get more than I have. If you do, you'll be called to account."

"Don't threaten us! And you don't know our real names— only the false ones we've used here."

"I know your faces. So do my friends." Amelia paused, gauging their reactions and sensing uncertainty. "I know Alphonso lost this money at an illegal gambling den. Tracking you won't be difficult. I have drawn sketches of you both for the authorities, which they will receive should you strike or murder me. They're well hidden. You won't find them by ransacking these rooms."

"You're bluffing," declared Bert.

I've cracked their armor, thought Amelia. Time to disarm them further. "Will you take that risk? I know people in Queen Elizabeth's court. A letter has been written. It will be sent should anything happen to me."

"Another bluff! Who do you know?" John asked, waving his muscular arms.

Amelia held steady but felt vulnerable. She refused to yield to his intimating gestures or show weakness. She fought to control her ire as the cords of her neck tightened. "I have performed services for the Queen, and William Cecil, Lord Burghley, knows me. I am meeting with them again next week."

"You expect us to believe that?"

Amelia fixed her unblinking eyes on them. "I do. Would you like me to describe the inside of Whitehall Palace? Would you like to know what the Queen wears when not in public? Did you know Alphonso, who owes this money, was a court musician? So was my father."

The men looked enraged, like they wanted to launch themselves at her, but knew it would be a mistake. Amelia gripped the edge of the table. She didn't want them to miscalculate. "I don't wish to go that route. I would rather resolve this matter."

John shook his oversized head. "You are a tough harlot. What are you proposing?"

"A simple exchange. You return my necklace. I give you fifty pounds. Then you tear up the notes my husband signed and leave the scraps behind."

Bert pointed a stubby finger with black crud under his nail. "What about the sketches and letter? Were you holding them back?"

Amelia now knew they were worried. She removed a crimson scarf from around her neck. "When I hang a certain kerchief from the window—not this one—my friends will know we've reached an agreement and concluded our transaction. They will retrieve the letter and sketches and hand them to you. Then we'll be done with each other forever. If you ever attempt to hurt my friends, my son, my husband, or me word will be sent to the palace. I know your faces."

"And if there's no kerchief hanging outside?"

"If none appears or the wrong one, they know what to do. Both are watching this window from where they can't be seen."

The two ruffians looked at each other and nodded glumly. Bert dropped the necklace into Amelia's outstretched hand. She gripped it firmly, feeling a burst of pleasure with her father's hamsa back in her grasp. She took a yellow scarf from a bureau drawer and hung it from the window, closing the pane to affix it.

The men gathered the coins into a leather drawstring purse, counting them as they went.

Amelia peered out the window and saw Enid and Julia in the spots she had selected. She turned toward the thugs. "Enid, my friend, is holding the sketches and letter across the street. When you leave this building, she'll put them on the carriage seat between you and her. Then she'll walk away. And our business is done."

Once the men had left, Amelia sighed with relief, but that did not override her deep resentment of her husband. He had nearly ruined them with his reckless behavior. Emotionally exhausted, she listened as a carriage rattled away on the street below. She then made a decision. She would never let a man govern her again. She would do what she wished. For now, that meant returning Simon Forman's attentions.

42

Amelia fought her way through the throng exiting The Theatre, her resentment growing with each step. She had seen several of her plays this summer and left seething each time, never more so than today. The actors and Will basked in the glow of her work. None of the applause was for her, yet they were using her scripts. She had made her pact with Will and lived with it, but it pained her. She had no real choice, but the unfairness rankled. All because of her gender. More than ever, she felt called to advocate for change, using her talents as best as she could.

Amelia reflected on her upbringing and how Lady Susan had instilled within her the values and principles that now shaped her convictions. Always in her heart, she also carried her father's belief in her—and his hamsa served as a constant reminder. She heard his encouraging voice when she closed her eyes at night, expressing faith in what she could be. That's why upon his death he arranged for Duchess Katherine Willoughby and Lady Susan to take her in and educate her. They were examples for her to follow. They advocated genteelly, if fruitlessly, for equal treatment, literacy, and opportunity for women. Their hearts were in the right place, Amelia thought, but they feared jeopardizing their aristocratic social status—a balancing act even with Queen Elizabeth on the throne. Amelia had no such qualms.

Amelia thought about her scripts, the messages she embedded, and the strong female characters she created. These were wholly insufficient. They were too subtle. She needed to confront the matter pointblank. The new project she had in mind might do that. She sought Lady Susan's counsel and broached the topic after they'd climbed a wooded rise overlooking the River Thames.

"Lady Susan, would you agree that humans are unique because of our intelligence, language, and problem-solving abilities?"

"Of course. And our souls as well. Why raise such a point?"

"Because I believe we are unique in another way. Is there another creature that restricts the capabilities or places arbitrary limits on half its population based solely on gender?"

Lady Susan looked upward as two sparrows flew overhead. "Certainly not birds, nor cats, dogs, horses or pigs. I can't think of a species that does."

"I can't either. It is an unusual trait. One invented by men so they can reign over women." Amelia pointed to a stone church tower across the river. "And men construct monuments like that to symbolize their dominion."

"Possibly," said Lady Susan. "Most girls—and boys for that matter—are raised believing that is the natural order of human life. It's rarely questioned."

Amelia felt more strident than that. "We are taught nonsense not because it's right but because men want it so."

"And refer to us as the weaker sex, using our lesser physical strength as an excuse, though intellectually we are their equals."

"Perhaps even their intellectual betters in some areas," said Amelia, "but we're denied opportunities to exhibit it."

Lady Susan stooped to pluck a wildflower and rolled the stem between her palms, apparently thinking about Amelia's points. "Queen Elizabeth is one of our wisest and most revered monarchs. That provides some evidence."

Amelia stopped by a gristmill and listened to water spill from the paddles on the large waterwheel. "True," agreed Amelia. "Imagine the impact if the aspirations and talents of all women were unleashed, and they could contribute unfettered in all professions."

Lady Susan nodded as Amelia continued. "Most men don't appreciate that suppressing us hurts them too. We should be able to navigate our lives and deploy our abilities as we see fit. That's what I'm driven to write about."

"Amelia, I would contribute, but a woman in my position has much at risk."

Amelia noticed the sadness that turned Lady Susan's mouth. She prayed that her mentor did not think she was judging her. "You have been an inspiration for me. I will write for public approbation what women like you think privately but dare not say. My intention is to spark controversy, precipitate reassessments, and open doors. Even doors opened a crack can admit a stream of sunlight, illuminating a dark room and the thinking therein."

Lady Susan squeezed Amelia's hand, acknowledging her bravery. "If women act in concert, those doors could be pushed fully open someday. But what about the risk you are taking?"

"There's very little," said Amelia. "I am not wealthy in money, possessions, or property. My wealth is in my vitality, talents, imagination, and ideas. I will use them all to advocate and stir passions."

"Who will be your readers?" asked Lady Susan.

"My call to action will be to women, but I want to sway men as well."

Lady Susan coupled her arm with Amelia's. "I believe your primary audience will be devout Christian ladies with whom men use religious teaching and customs to justify their hindrance."

"Why them in particular?"

"Because more of them can read and they're devoted to Our Savior, Jesus Christ. They believe in him. To persuade and enlist them, you must wield the tenets of Christianity in directions supporting your cause."

"That's an ingenious thought. Their current beliefs can form the foundation, and I will present an entirely new perspective—which will give my message power and legitimacy."

Amelia mulled this idea for a few days then decided to write to Christian readers as if she were one of them. *Should they think I'm a Jewess, they'll dismiss everything I say.* She began with a "prefatory" or introductory poem:

I have written this small volume, or little book, for the general use of all virtuous Ladies and Gentlewomen …to make known to the world, that all women deserve not to be blamed… by evil disposed men, who forgetting they were borne of women, nourished of women, and that if it were not by the means of women, they would be quite extinguished out of the world: Such as these, were they that dishonored Christ his Apostles and Prophets, putting them to shameful deaths. Therefore, we are not to regard any imputations that they undeservedly lay upon us, no otherwise than to make use of them to our own benefits, as spurs to virtue.

Amelia felt like a wild horse bucking against corral rails, trying furiously to free itself along with docile companions penned inside. To provoke curiosity and controversy, she chose to name her volume *Salve Deus Rex Judaeorum,* Praise God, King of the Jews.

For the body of her work, she decided to start at the biblical beginning by reinterpreting the story of Adam and Eve. She called this poem "Eve's Apology." Amelia thought deeply about Eve, who had committed the original sin by biting the forbidden fruit. For centuries it had been used as a theological bludgeon to subjugate women, blaming them for humanity's eviction from the Garden of Eden and the world's subsequent chaos and hardship. Men used it to justify their refusal to share power in religious, business, and societal affairs. But what if Eve was not entirely at fault? What if Adam bore responsibility, perhaps more than Eve? He might not have fallen under the serpent's spell and taken the bite:

> But surely Adam cannot be excused,
> Her fault though great, yet he was most to blame;
> What Weakness offered, Strength might have refused,
> Being Lord of all, the greater was his shame:

Amelia felt like her character Portia in *The Merchant of Venice* crafting a courtroom argument. *There is much more to say, more beliefs to dispel, but I have launched my most worthy poetic endeavor. It may take many months, perhaps years to complete as I weave it into my other work. Then I will find a way to publish it under my name. It will be how I am remembered. It will inspire other women to seek independence of their own.*

43

Will sat across the desk from Cuthbert Burbage, a little man with frog-like features and a croaky voice, as he shuffled though papers and desk drawers in his father's former office. He stopped hunting and announced with a scowl, "We have a problem."

As Will waited for him to continue, Cuthbert tossed a sheaf of parchments into a bin. "My father built this theater twenty-one years ago on land leased from Giles Allen. The lease expires at year's end and Allen refuses to renew it. I've gone round and round with him for months. He's a most unreasonable man."

"Refuses? But why?" asked Will.

Cuthbert ran his hand through his hair. "He's a Puritan. Some of our plays offend his sensibilities."

"There's nothing we can do?"

"He'll only renew it for an outlandish sum—an amount greater than the revenue the theater produces."

Will saw the paradox. "So if you find the money, he will prostitute himself?"

"But he knows it's impossible. He threatened to demolish The Theatre and lease the land for something other than vile dramatic performances." Cuthbert glanced around at the disorderly piles on his desk. "In the meantime, I can't find my father's copy of the lease to identify our legal rights."

His grumbling continued while he cast among more documents. Suddenly Cuthbert rose from behind his desk, as if energized by a new idea. "Will, walk with me. I've something important to show you."

The two men strode through London's streets in a southwesterly direction to an area sandwiched between the Ludgate Hill and the River Thames. Broken clouds hung overhead in the brisk morning. They traversed rickety walking planks to avoid street muck, which wasn't always possible, and Will stopped to knock mud from his boots with a resigned frown.

"Where are we going?" he asked.

"To see an old refectory at Blackfriars called Upper Frater Hall. My father bought it for six hundred pounds long before he died. He wanted to convert it into a luxurious playhouse for upper class patrons. Lord Hunsdon also invested before passing but they never started renovations."

Will considered this novel possibility as Cuthbert offered further details. Blackfriars had been constructed in the thirteenth century as a Dominican friary. Richard II used its Upper Frater Hall, a massive stone structure, for Parliament meetings.

"Why didn't we move here before?" asked Will.

"My father never intended it to replace The Theatre because it can't accommodate large audiences, but it might serve as a temporary location."

As the two men continued, Cuthbert explained, "Lord Chamberlain dreamed of constructing a winter playhouse because The Theatre, as an open-air venue, is uncomfortable in cold and damp weather. This auditorium is enclosed and in an aristocratic neighborhood. They'll pay a premium to see shows in a more agreeable setting. But we still need a large theater for the masses."

The men approached a large stone edifice on Water Lane. They entered the empty building and came upon a massive curving staircase. They found a spacious room upstairs resembling an abandoned construction project. The wall between two chambers had been removed, creating a large open area, half of which might once have been a small theater. White dust littered the surfaces. A raised platform ran along one side. Benches, torn from their mountings, were piled haphazardly on the floor. Long boards were stacked in corners and in front of the stage.

Will examined the space, gauging its scale in comparison to The Theatre. "Cuthbert, it'll require months to get this ready. The gallery must be constructed. The old auditorium seated roughly a couple hundred," he speculated. "By combining the two chambers we could double that occupancy, but the stage and backstage areas must be enlarged too. Even then, it'll be half the size of The Theatre."

Cuthbert climbed onto the small stage and surveyed the chambers. "The original idea was to build a prestigious theater for the aristocracy and wealthy merchant class. It would feature more comfortable seats, better sightlines, and appeal to the status conscious—allowing us to double ticket prices to compensate for the lower capacity."

"It can be done," said Will, continuing to assess the possibilities. "But what about commoners? They have been our biggest supporters, creating their din in the pit. This theater would lack one."

"Which would also appeal to the elites."

Will slung his coat over a post and trampled over wooden scraps to the annexed chamber. "We could change the direction of the theater. Imagine if the stage were on the long side rather than the narrow end. There will be fewer but longer gallery rows, and actors would have a wider performance area. We could then build more elaborate sets."

"We'll need an architect's opinion for that," said Cuthbert. "And that orientation would require more time to construct."

Will frowned. "And we'll have nowhere to perform until its ready, which could be months"

"I've solved that problem. Henry Lanman will let us move into The Curtain in the meantime. He needs only to cancel plans with a new playwright slated to stage his first production in January."

"Who?" asked Will.

"A fellow named Dekker. Thomas Dekker, I believe. Have you heard of him?"

Clothed, Amelia lay on Simon's bed with her back spooned against his chest. His warm hands caressed her legs, then wandered to her breasts, tantalizing her. Slowly he hiked up her skirt and massaged her thighs, heightening her desire and passion. He kissed the back of her neck and Amelia's breathing quickened. She felt his hardness against her buttocks. His hand slipped beneath her neckline, seeking her swelling breasts. She let it rest there for a moment, then placed her hand on top, slowing its movement. Her mind still held rein over her desires.

This is odious. Do I loathe myself so much to stoop this low? But I need the warmth and pleasure of a man's arms. I don't prefer this communion with Simon, but he's convenient and willing to be used as long as he can use me.

"Simon," she said coolly, "I crave your embrace, but my marital vows create a quandary. I ask myself, 'What line will I not cross?'"

"Line? You're in my bed. We both have desires."

"But what are the limits? This relationship cannot endure. It will pass when our desires subside or other obstacles intervene. We have other lives and mine is bound with another."

Simon stopped caressing her. "Amelia, what are you saying?"

"I'll go only so far with our intimacy. We can enjoy each other's passion, but you may not enter me. That's my boundary. Will you honor it?"

"What do you fear? We're following our natural desires."

"If we join our bodies sexually, I will have surely sinned."

"You fear having a child by me?"

"My reasons are my own. Will you abide by my wishes?"

Simon growled in frustration. "I will until I can no longer. Then I'll spurn you."

"Is that a promise?"

"It is."

Amelia turned to face Simon. She kissed him with a passion long corked inside. This arrangement would be on her terms. She would control how far she fell.

44

T homas Dekker watched *Henry IV, Part II* from the back of The Theatre's rowdy pit, his suspicions aroused as never before. When it ended, he pushed through the crowd as it cheered the bowing actors. An elbow struck his chest shooting a sharp pain to his ribs as he muscled toward the exit. Upon reaching the street, he pulled an apple from his coat pocket, biting into the crisp fruit.

Never before had Dekker felt so sanguine. Henry Lanman, The Curtain's proprietor, had agreed to stage his first play, *The Shoemaker's Holiday*. Dekker had already created cue scripts to prepare actors for its January 3rd debut, and anticipated competing with the great William Shakespeare.

What rot, Dekker thought as he wended his way through crowded streets. Some feats were not humanly possible. Writing ten plays—four historical dramas, three comedies, a romantic tragedy, a romantic fantasy, and a Venetian drama in four years was one—especially when the "author" performed in some simultaneously. Dekker had been watching

Shakespeare surreptitiously. He observed how he spent his days at The Theatre. Shakespeare wasn't writing when acting or rehearsing. He rarely appeared tired as if he'd spent the night composing scripts. His fingers were rarely ink-stained. Somebody must be composing for him. Dekker was driven to discover who.

Dekker, a short bearded man with close-set eyes and dull brown hair falling in waves over his large ears, was the grandson of a Dutch diplomat who had died suspiciously. Authorities called it an accident when the body emerged in the murky River Thames downstream from London, but the cracked skull appeared to have been struck with something like a blacksmith's hammer.

Dekker aspired to be a playwright but had only collaborated on scripts authored by others, including one about Sir Thomas More that had yet to be performed. His name had appeared nowhere, and that further fueled his envy of Shakespeare. The man penned highly acclaimed scripts with ease. Dekker worked on his own manuscripts endlessly. They required vast amounts of time.

Dekker's suspicions of Shakespeare had deepened in the prior three years during an astonishing run of *Two Gentlemen of Verona, Love's Labour's Lost, Romeo and Juliet, Richard II, A Midsummer Night's Dream, King John,* and finally *The Merchant of Venice*. Most were intricately woven plays requiring a wealth of knowledge he doubted a commoner from some remote village would readily possess. In fact, he considered it impossible. Since nobody else will, he told himself, "I'll uncloak him. I'll prove he's a fraud."

At last Dekker reached The Curtain. Home, he thought with a burst of elation, to my first play.

He went inside to find Henry Lanman in The Curtain's musty office. Lanman had sent a message summoning him.

Dekker's blood boiled upon hearing the news.

"You're replacing my new play with a raft of Shakespeare's old plays? You can't do that! We have an agreement."

"We do indeed," replied Lanman pointing at it. "Read it closely. I can cancel thirty days prior to the first scheduled performance, which isn't until January."

"But Shakespeare's dramas have been playing at The Theatre for months, some for over a year. Mine is fresh," Dekker sputtered.

"His are proven. They make money," Lanman said severely. "I don't know if yours will draw audiences or for how long. Lord Chamberlain's Men will fill the house until Blackfriars is renovated. We'll talk when they depart, but that's months away."

"What if some of Shakespeare's plays aren't his?" Dekker blurted.

Lanman's face turned grave. "I dislike what you're insinuating. Besides, it matters not a whit to me. Crowds flock to them. And, Mr. Dekker, be careful about spreading such rumors. It won't help you and probably won't hurt Shakespeare."

Dekker barged from the office, feeling even more like a victim of another man's success. He promised himself that Shakespeare would rue the day he did this to him.

45

A melia carried her dreary mood through London's bleak weather. A chilly wind funneled between buildings whipping her curly hair. The worry she had borne about Alphonso fighting in the Azores had surfaced today with particular sharpness, though she hardly understood why. Perhaps because she awoke abruptly last night—unnerved and suspecting he had been killed in battle.

Downcast, Amelia climbed the stairs to her rooms. She heard moaning from outside the door. That's strange, she thought, it doesn't sound like Enid, Julia, or Henry. She flung the door open. Alphonso sat slumped at the dining table with his head in his hands.

She gasped, and then felt relief. Her nightmare had been entirely wrong. "Alphonso, you're safe. Are you all right?"

His filthy trousers were ragged and torn. His tattered coat hung unbuttoned from his shoulders and smelled of the sea. Grit caked his unruly red hair.

Alphonso glanced at Amelia then hung his head over the table.

"I'm pleased you're back," said Amelia with forced cheerfulness, swallowing hard. "Why are you so glum?"

"I'm a failure. I turned and ran. I failed my fellows in arms."

Amelia had worried he'd return bitter or chastened, but not humiliated. She'd never seen him so low. Yet despite his shortcomings—and how he left her to the mercy of debt collectors—she pitied him.

Amelia placed her hands gently on his shoulders. "What happened? You're a fine man, you know that."

"Don't patronize me, wife. I know who I am and what I did and didn't do. Leave me alone. I don't want to be with anyone, least of all you, who has known no such ignominy."

Stunned, Amelia jerked her hands from his shoulders and stepped around the table, facing him squarely. "But Alphon—"

"There are no 'buts.' Your embarrassments pale by comparison."

No matter how much compassion I extend, he will seek to open old wounds, to cut me to the quick. In a peremptory voice she demanded, "Have you been paid for your service?"

"My meager earnings are already spent."

Amelia believed Alphonso had been through perdition, but he hadn't changed. He still thought first of himself and little for others, perhaps not at all for her. "I won't ask how. But I suspect on alcohol, games of chance, and women."

Alphonso shrugged his shoulders. Amelia wanted to shake him.

"Alphonso, our savings are depleted because of your ill-fated gambling. Men came demanding the eighty pounds you owed—the debt you hid from me. And you left me to face them without a word of warning. Now we're strapped to support our family."

"*Your* family. Henry is not mine. He's your bastard son."

"I'm your wife. Am I not your family? Does Henry not think you're his father?"

"So you spent the money Lord Hunsdon gave you for being his whore to pay my debt. Aren't you the sainted one?"

Amelia surged toward Alphonso, slapping him hard across the face. Her palm stung from the blow's sharpness. Alphonso's face turned bright red, but he sat impassively.

He taunted, "Feel better now? A little violence always cures a spate of anger. But it doesn't make anything better."

"Isn't that a clever rejoinder?" retorted Amelia. "We have grave problems. We can hardly pay our rent. Henry has nightmares that we'll be thrown onto the street. Enid, out of heartfelt goodness, has relinquished her wages. She seeks only room and board. And my royalty payments have dwindled. We're in trouble."

Amelia, Enid, and Julia had decided not to tell Alphonso about the eighteen pounds they'd retained, so he couldn't gamble or drink it away.

Alphonso did not acknowledge anything she had said.

Amelia pleaded, "Can't you look at me?"

Tears welled in her eyes. Alphonso's return brought only misery.

Finally Alphonso spoke, his breath reeking like spoiled meat. "I'm ashamed. My dream of being knighted was laughable. I let everyone down, myself included. Go! Get out of my sight!"

Furious at his attempt to dismiss her, Amelia fastened her wool jacket and hurried to the street. The frigid wind whirled past, seeping into her bones. She shivered all the way to Simon Forman's office.

"My husband has returned from the Azores in disgrace. He wants nothing to do with me. I'm numb and require invigoration."

46

Will would have preferred arguing with his wife, Anne, who he hadn't seen in months, to confronting fellow actors as desperate as he was once. Today, Lord Chamberlain's Men would move to The Curtain, displacing performers who had been acting in now discontinued plays. Lanman cut all but the most popular show to make room in the facility and play rotation.

At The Theatre, Shakespeare's troupe packed costumes and props into crates. They dismantled sets, loaded horse-drawn wagons under ominous skies, and made several treks to The Curtain, only two hundred yards away.

Actors leaving The Curtain sneered and bumped into arriving ones, causing crates to drop and fragile items to break. They stabbed knives into costume boxes. And their comments cut like a daggers.

"Will, how could you force out your fellow thespians? Have you no heart?" one shouted, passing him on the way out as Will trudged in.

"Bastards, we've got no place to go."

"How will we feed our families?"

Will didn't consider himself a conqueror but knew the departing performers felt like the vanquished.

During the long day, the storm stayed at bay until soaking the last delivery in gray dusk light.

The troupe then spent a week preparing The Curtain for its productions, including Will's new one, *Henry V.*

While Will oversaw rehearsals, Cuthbert met with architects at Blackfriars. They studied Will's sketches, refined the layout, and took measurements. Crews gutted Upper Frater Hall and construction supplies arrived. Over several months the redesigned playhouse would take shape. It would be London's most elegant theater with oak-paneled walls, carved balustrades, and a vaulted ceiling.

Thomas Dekker and Garvan Shaw, a friend and actor who performed often with Lord Chamberlain's Men, waited until dusk before heading for the neighborhood surrounding Blackfriars. Several actors who had lost jobs at The Curtain joined them. They carried satchels loaded with placards, tacks, cords, knives, and hammers. Dekker explained that he sought revenge and the first step was disrupting Shakespeare's plans.

Dekker and Garvan organized their accomplices. Dekker's group canvassed blocks north and east of Blackfriars, and Garvan's covered blocks south and west; then they'd reassemble on Water Lane. The men, dressed in black from head to toe wore hats or hoods to remain anonymous. Dekker admired the first three placards he attached to lampposts. In bold block letters they read:

STOP BLACKFRIARS FROM BECOMING A PUBLIC THEATER!
STOP ROWDY CROWDS FROM INVADING OUR NEIGHBORHOOD!
ACT BEFORE BLARING HORNS ANNOUNCE PLAYS!

The following morning, Will and Cuthbert trotted on their horses to Blackfriars. Will intended to review progress in the backstage areas. He also planned to discuss the space above the stage—heaven, as actors called it.

Cuthbert noticed the first placard when they were three blocks away. He cantered toward it, leaned from his horse, and ripped it from a fence.

Cuthbert frowned, shaking his head. "This will create a furor we'll need to defuse. I have huge sums invested in this project."

They found placards posted on every pole and gate. A boisterous crowd swirled around Blackfriars itself. Men and women waved the signs shouting, "What's going on? We want answers! Not here!"

The mass swarmed around Will and Cuthbert as they drew to a halt. "Is this your theater?" a man in an expensive black coat asked.

"It is," responded Cuthbert. "We'll be pleased to answer questions and show it to you. It's being designed for the comfort of nobility."

"What do you mean?" asked another man.

"I inherited The Theatre, London's first playhouse, from my father, James Burbage. It accommodates aristocrats and commoners. But we've been told by many, such as those gathered here, that you would prefer a theater of your own—one without a pit, with better seats, and where you need not mix with lower classes or tolerate their stench. That is what we are building in Upper Frater Hall."

"An exclusive club?" a man with a well-tended beard asked.

"Not a club. It will be open to the public."

"So commoners can attend. Not like you said," a woman cried.

"Admission will be affordable only to wealthier commoners and gentry, like successful merchants."

"Our streets will be clogged with folks from all over London, who have no other business here," yelled a man from the back.

Will said, using his most charming manner, "The theater is not large and audiences will be like churchgoers. They'll be well-behaved because they'll be people like you."

A primly dressed woman in a high-ruffed collar waved her placard shouting, "It's sacrilege to convert a church into a theater."

Then a tall man waded through the crowd, wagging a finger at Will and Cuthbert. "We'll take this to the Privy Council. They will stop it."

"You won't get away with this!" shouted another.

A priggish woman had the last word as Cuthbert and Will switched their horses around, "Get out! Get out now!"

47

LONDON, JANUARY 1598

Cuthbert flung the Privy Council's declaration onto a gray marble table in his high-ceilinged salon on Halliwell Street in Shoreditch. "Will, we must cease renovations at Blackfriars," he howled. "I will never recover the money I've sunk into it. We have no other plans and I am making a pittance from shows at The Curtain."

"Someone is sabotaging us," said Will, "but who?"

"We'll discover soon enough," Cuthbert replied grimly. "I have people asking around. In the meantime, we must find a suitable theater."

Will had expected this development and had already considered alternatives. "What's our objective?" he asked rhetorically to Cuthbert and his younger brother, Richard. "It's to build a theater—one larger than existing playhouses to earn more per performance. Our revenue rises with the number of spectators."

"We know that," said Cuthbert. "But where, and how do we pay for it? First, let's try to reason with Giles Allen. The

Theatre stands empty. He hasn't re-leased the land and he isn't making money from it. Perhaps we can negotiate another term."

Richard shook his flaming red hair, "He won't budge. He's a cantankerous old man."

Will walked toward the stone fireplace then veered back with a sharp stage cut toward the brothers. "Let's pursue both simultaneously. Richard and I can explore options and costs for building our own theater while you talk with Giles."

"Will makes a good point," said Richard. "As an actor, I've played The Rose, The Swan, and The Theatre. The Rose and Swan are on land leased from the Bishop of Winchester, Thomas Bilson. We should visit him."

"Won't we encounter religious objections again?" asked Cuthbert.

"The other theaters haven't according to Philip Henslowe, The Rose's owner," said Richard. "Will, you know Henslowe since *Romeo and Juliet* plays there."

Will liked this plan. "Cuthbert, try to persuade Giles. Richard and I will inquire with the bishop. There's open land in Southwark, Bankside."

"Isn't there also a prison?" asked Cuthbert.

"Yes, on a section ironically called the 'Liberty of Clink.'"

A month later, Will, Cuthbert and Richard Burbage gathered in The Curtain's pit as Dr. John Dee unrolled plans for a new playhouse.

Cuthbert rapped on the long table to get Will and Richard's attention. "Before Dr. Dee discusses his drawings, you should know my last attempt to reason with Giles Allen has failed. His parting words were, 'I don't need the money and I despise your sinful plays. I'd rather tear the place down, sell the lumber, and build something noble than renew your lease."

"We should knock sense into his head with a timber," remarked Will.

The other men smiled and Cuthbert continued, "Dr. Dee designed The Theatre for my father over twenty years ago. He will now present plans for a new one, hopefully one we can afford."

Dee was short and stooped with a kindly face. Spectacles rested on his slightly curved nose. A few tufts of white hair were swept over his otherwise baldhead.

Dee began in a gravelly voice, "Gentleman, you've selected an excellent site near the south bank of the Thames. It can accommodate a grand playhouse and is near The Rose and Swan theatres."

Dee pointed to a sketch. "I propose erecting a large twenty-sided amphitheater—a polygon—with three floors and two curved balconies. The circular shape will be approximately one hundred feet in diameter. It will hold up to three thousand people."

"Three thousand?" confirmed Will hovering over the drawing. He did quick calculations in his head. With a full house, he could quadruple his earnings per performance.

Dee turned the page, revealing the next sketch. "Yes, three thousand. But not all seated. The plans include an uncovered pit while the stage and gallery will be sheltered."

"How large is the stage?" asked Will.

"Much bigger than other London theaters—approximately forty-five feet wide and thirty feet deep—and five feet higher than the pit floor."

"Astonishing," said Will as he pored over the details, pulling his long hair back from his face. "The actors will have more maneuvering room for elaborate scenes."

Dee expanded on his explanations, and Will, Cuthbert, and Richard asked clarifying questions. They suggested slight modifications, but Dee's overall plan stayed intact.

"We must address two essential questions: How can we pay for it? And who will build it?" asked Richard.

"We have commitments for eighty percent of the amount required," said Cuthbert. "The Theatre cost six hundred and sixty-six pounds to build." He pointed to the plans as he continued, "This one is twice the size. Master carpenter Peter Smith estimates it will cost two thousand pounds."

"That's an enormous sum. Why will it cost three times as much if it is double the size?" asked Will.

"Because of more complex structural issues, a roof that covers a greater area, and higher quality materials. Plus, costs for construction have risen in twenty years."

"How much do we have?" asked Richard.

"From among our six investors, future co-owners, sixteen hundred pounds."

"How is that divided?" asked Will.

Cuthbert put an arm around his brother's shoulder. "Richard and I are putting in four hundred pounds each, fifty percent of the total so far. Will, you agreed to invest two hundred pounds, and so can three fellow actors: Thomas Pope, John Heminges, and Augustine Phillips. As of now, Richard and I will own twenty-five percent each and others will each have a twelve-and-a-half-percent share. Of course, those percentages will change when we acquire additional investors."

Will wondered where they would find the other four hundred pounds. "I, for one, can't invest more. I'm extended far out on a limb already."

Cuthbert paced around the table wringing his hands. "We will need to raise the rest or scale back our plans. Meanwhile, The Theatre has been left to rot."

Will heard rustling on the stage behind him. He turned to see a curtain sway at stage left and someone with curly blond hair making a hasty retreat. *Garvan Shaw?*

Will asked, "Cuthbert, have you found the old lease for The Theatre? You were hunting for it after your father died."

Cuthbert flashed a smile of triumph. "Last week I discovered it buried under papers in his home study. I almost burned it, then thought I'd keep it for our files."

"Could I read it?" asked Will. "I'm not a barrister, but there might be provisions to include or exclude in a new one."

Will had no notion why he said that. He knew only that he had been drawn to the idea of reading the lease since Cuthbert first mentioned it. He had an inkling that buried inside the legal agreement might be something useful, if he could make sense of it.

48

LONDON, MARCH 1598

Amelia longed for love and to sing, dance, and somehow marry her devotion to theater and her desire for a cultured man. Yet, she thought, this had always been elusive. I am an accomplished playwright but with none to my name. I am a shadow. There is no man I truly love. Will, perhaps, comes closest. I've teased him with smiles and gestures but allowed no more. His refusal to credit my work has gnawed deeper. It has kept me from giving him what he seems to want dearly. Now I will satisfy him.

Amelia noticed the yearning in Will's eyes as she approached him in the cobbled courtyard of George Inn, a Southwark establishment that also served as an inn-yard theater. She had made a point of dressing alluringly in a square-necked linen chemise that hinted at the small swell of her breasts, complemented by an open feminine doublet and tight sleeves. She touched her long thin neck and neatly curled hair, tucked under an escoffion headdress, and watched Will's eyes follow her gestures—the effect she had hoped to have.

She knew Will's vulnerabilities, which were especially acute due to the loss of Blackfriars, insufficient funds to build a new theater, an aggrieved wife in distant Stratford, and a dearth of ideas for new plays. It seemed he was going through every King Henry in English history and was dependent on her creativity for other scripts. Today, she had a new one to discuss, a romance comedy that fit her purpose—to persuade him to announce her authorship or co-authorship for all future plays she penned.

"Will, your eyes are gleaming but your shoulders are slumped, a contradiction in posture."

"That's because you bring me cheer but you know well my troubles."

"Well, at least I can be a temporary respite." She coupled her arm in his as they walked inside to a table by the stone fireplace. "I have a merry love tale to discuss, perhaps a script we can write together."

As Amelia discussed the plot for fleeing lovers disguised as other people, and the joyous conclusion reached after much scheming, she continued enticing Will closer to her. She moistened her lips with the delicate tip of her tongue, gazed up at him through her eyelashes, and touched the back of his hand. As daylight faded, they walked through the neighborhood toward his rooms. "Shall we discuss our last few ideas upstairs?" she suggested. "I think more poetry and song will distinguish this play."

A look of surprise and delight came over Will, as if he had hoped for but had not expected this. If he only knew, she thought, how I have longed to marry my love of theater and love of men—my most elusive yearning. She had yet to find a man she truly loved. Perhaps Lord Hundson came closest. Marlowe was pure infatuation. Forman served as a convenient outlet. Will, though unhappily married like her, was her playwriting conduit. Their intellects and interests drew them to each other, but unlike him, her passion went no further. Tonight, like the guise of some of her characters, she would pretend otherwise.

As the candles on Will's writing table burned lower, Amelia removed her doublet and square-toe shoes. She maneuvered her hosen legs and feet until they grazed his under the table. She watched his eyes wash over her breasts, and then she leaned toward him and cupped his cheeks in her hands. Gazing into his eyes, she said, "Shall we proceed with our inevitable destiny?"

With that they padded to his bed. She loosened the laces on her chemise, let it spread open, and pulled him tight to her body as their lips met. His hasty hands squeezed her breasts and slid between her legs. In minutes they were joined. After he calmed, she liked that his touches became more affectionate. He gently touched her face, kissed her forehead, and finger-brushed her hair. She responded in kind until she felt his readiness to make love once again—and she encouraged him onward. Eventually, exhausted, they curled into each other and drifted to sleep.

In the morning, Amelia greeted Will with a shy smile while wrapping bed sheets around her chest. He sat at his table wearing only breeches. As he twisted toward her, tufts of his chest hair brightened from daylight streaming through the window. The moment had come for her plea.

"Will, dear, last night we consummated a new relationship."

"Indeed we did. It came as a surprise, as if you had a sudden altering of feelings."

"Will, could two people be more intellectually suited than we?"

Still sitting, Will turned his chair to face her. "I was referring to your amorous affections."

"For me, it was the affinity of our minds and interests that first attracted me to you. Blinded for years by other matters, I suppressed my feelings. But now, with my passions inflamed, I revel in the bliss of our lovemaking."

Will wiped his quill and put it down. "You sound like you're discussing the plot for a script more than your zeal for me."

Amelia rose from the bed, dragging the sheet and holding it tight to her body. She cradled his head into her chest, wanting him to bask in her scent and the feel of her body. "Will, I've been confused and disheartened by my misfortunes and marriage. I am a musician's daughter raised by nobles since I was seven. To which class do I belong? I am married to a louse. I am invisible to all but a few. And my work is unheralded except to you who gains esteem from it. Is it any wonder I am adrift?"

Will leaned back his head. "What do you want from me?"

Amelia caressed his back and shoulders as he looked up at her. "I want what we're developing...and—"

"And what?" asked Will with unexpected sharpness.

"Oh, Will, I dearly hope you'll present me as a co-author on new scripts. I am deserving."

Will pushed back from her and burst to his feet. "Deserving but at my expense! My reputation will be diminished and all prior plays will be questioned. I won't risk that, especially with the likes of Dekker prowling around."

Amelia, feeling rebuked and defeated, picked up her clothes and dressed without saying a word.

While she buckled her shoes, Will broke the thick silence. "Was that the point of your seduction last night? To induce me to relent?"

"I wish you no harm but you have seen fit to malign my affection. Last night was not a masquerade. I desire only a small measure of respect and recognition, and thought that was within you."

Before closing the door behind her, Amelia stared into his eyes. "Is it because you think so little of me or only of you? We're long past Burbage's ignorance and bias. He is dead, but as England's most admired playwright, you have power. It takes only a grain of courage to exercise it and end this injustice."

She shut the door. The sound of the thud and the squeaky hinges stayed with her long after trudging down the plank steps.

49

Amelia recognized her symptoms. Without question, Will was the father. She had not slept with her husband in months—until last night. Although she had continued seeing Simon Forman covertly, she enforced her limitations, rebuffing his tiresome protests for intercourse. She pledged to take this paternity secret to her grave, foreseeing only painful tribulations should either Will or Alphonso learn the truth.

Yesterday, when Alphonso returned from his first day as a rehired court musician, she decided to reward him and resolve her dilemma. She bestowed her congratulations and showered him with kind words and tender gestures. As night fell, she led him to bed, coupled with him, and ensured that he completed his arousal.

Now with morning light brightening the bedchamber, Amelia watched Alphonso sleep, his naked body beside her on the mattress. His wheezy breaths reminded her of how hard he made everything. As unappealing as she found him, she did love him in a way—perhaps as family members love the least favored among them. But being loving toward him, as a wife should be, was a chore. For a few weeks she would maintain her loving pretense then make her announcement.

$$\mathcal{Q}$$

A month later, Amelia opened her eyes and looked over at Alphonso. He showed no signs of waking and she decided to put another burden to rest. She dressed, brushed her hair and tucked it beneath a coif headdress. When ready to leave, she leaned over their bed, kissed his cheek, and ruffled his hair.

"Alphonso, I must see to some business but have something important to tell you. I'm pregnant. And the baby is ours...*ours*...yours and mine!"

His eyes sprang open and his mouth wide—as stunned an expression as Amelia had seen. Her heart skipped. Then he smiled. "Are you sure?"

"I am."

She kissed his forehead and waved on her way out the door, trusting her enthusiasm masked her deception. "I'll return later."

She realized the time had come to conclude her affair with Simon Forman. She assumed the conversation would be difficult but she felt lighthearted. On the way she thought back over the last few years, realizing that her creativity followed the ebb and flow of turmoil in her life. When tensions were high, her creativity waned, which explained why the last few months were dormant. Now that life had calmed, new ideas were germinating. Themes for a romantic comedy with a Christmas theme took root. Her working title: "What You Will."

She approached Simon Forman's office in a yellow and green dress with a bounce in her step. Spring buds sprouted from trees. Purple crocuses poked through the soil. Her attire was light for the weather, but the chill didn't bother her. She wished to look cheerful and share her happiness, thinking her mood would temper Forman's response. She felt her life turning around.

"Now that you're expecting, you need not worry about being impregnated until after the baby's born," Forman said slyly. "There's no need to hold back from what you know you want."

"I'm sorry, Simon, but no." she said standing on the threshold. "Was I worried about becoming pregnant? Yes. But the other reason hasn't vanished. I won't break my vow further."

Forman came forward, offering Amelia his arms for an embrace. "My lovely paramour, you make no sense sometimes. It should not make a whit of difference now."

"To you, it may not. But it does to me."

"I see," said Forman with a touch of nastiness in his voice. "Then I will be satisfied with your boundary, as you call it. Shall I show you to my bed?"

She steeled herself. "No, I think not."

"Why? Are you here to tease me? To see if I'm interested in an impregnated woman—one who draws arbitrary lines in her relationships with others—including her husband, I suppose?"

"I won't stand here being insulted."

"Would you like to enter my chamber and be insulted? Or do insults go only in one direction?"

His surly behavior fit her purposes. "Goodbye, Simon," she said calmly. "That's why I came today. I've had enough of your bluster." She turned to leave.

He grabbed her arm and spun her around. "Enough, you say. When have you ever offered me enough? Go! Go to whoever it is who now attracts your eye. I'll tolerate you no more."

Amelia glared with contempt. He would not be speaking that way if he could keep pawing her.

"Here's something to consider."

"What might that be?" asked Amelia.

Forman pressed onto the door ledge, forcing Amelia to step down. "You once lamented about drifting between classes in English society. Here's your answer: You were born a commoner. You'll always be one. That won't change no matter whom you know or wish to be. Your aristocratic friends know it too. And I'll give them another reason to spurn you."

50

A larm. Amelia stared at Lady Susan's shaky handwriting and tearstains that had dissolved a few letters. Something dreadful must have happened. She knew it intuitively. The letter shook in her trembling hands. She unsealed it but could barely focus as the shocking words sunk in:

> *I loathe being the bearer of unfavorable news, but rumors are spreading that your relationship with Simon Forman was not fully professional. He is known for his philandering and indiscretion, and is spreading his version of events. Needless to say, he is sullying your reputation."*

Amelia's mouth dried. Her head pounded. Shrill tones pulsated in her ears. Furious, she didn't know what to think yet hundreds of thoughts exploded in her mind all at once. In her rage, she remembered Forman's parting words. That bastard. I trusted him. She could only guess at the enormity he had inflicted on her life. And she hated her own complicity and faulty judgment.

Tears welled in her eyes. She crumpled the note. Painful memories of the abuse she had endured from Marlowe sprang to mind and how she still suffered from it. Are most men's first and last instincts to use women for their personal needs—and exploit our vulnerability?

She went to meet with Lady Susan. Yet once she entered the drawing room at Willoughby House, Susan's pasty pallor dismayed her. The older woman's voice had weakened and she moved unsteadily. A servant had to help her to a cushioned chair. The harpsichord on which Lady Susan had once given Amelia lessons sat silently in a corner beneath an ornately framed family portrait.

"Lady Susan, I'm here to discuss the matter you raised in your message."

Lady Susan spoke slowly with a pained expression, "Those unsavory rumors are so rampant in aristocratic circles that they reached my ears, and I haven't been out in days."

Amelia's cheeks burned. She tried maintaining her composure but a tremor riddled her voice. "Wha…what have you heard? I won't be offended."

"It's scurrilous."

Amelia curled her fingers, wincing as her nails dug into her palms.

"Everything I have heard is secondhand. Simon Forman is claiming he 'felt and kissed all over your body willingly but you would allow no more.' He declared that he ended the affair because you were too needy and demanding, and he wouldn't risk being falsely accused of impregnating you."

Humiliated, Amelia burst into tears, hiding her face in her hands. Who knew about this? Probably everyone she knew at the court. She would be an outcast and the butt of gossip. She imagined being looked upon with vile contempt. "I am so embarrassed. I can hardly hold my head up. I would say it's all a lie, but part of it is true."

"I'm sorry to convey such painful news," said Lady Susan.

Amelia rubbed her bloodshot eyes. "You must be terribly disappointed in me. You raised me to be better."

"You must face this undiminished. Only then will you restore yourself."

Amelia stood trying to control her anger. "How can I show my face again? Forman has ruined me. Or I've ruined myself by trusting him. My reputation is in tatters." She paused and then bitterly continued. "Of course, his conduct is considered acceptable—he's bragging about it—while the gossips are calling mine disgraceful."

"Amelia, I wish I could do more to help, but my health… my vigor…is slipping away."

Amelia felt pangs of remorse, for they should not be worrying about her when her benefactor so clearly was failing. "Lady Susan, how can I give you strength? I am distraught but not so much that I cannot care for you."

"There is nothing to do that my household is not doing already. I take solace knowing I instilled fervor in you. Use it to overcome this. Implant it in your poetry. If your reasoning reaches others, perhaps my legacy will be amplified too."

Amelia leaned over and kissed Lady Susan's soft cheek. "I'm returning home to sequester myself and I'll carry your counsel with me."

Amelia arranged the poems she had so far composed for *Salve Deus Rex Judæorum* on the small desk by her window. "Eve's Apology" put her grievances in a religious historical perspective. It makes compelling points, she thought, but it requires more invective. My hostility is so much greater now. It's venomous. Men like Forman are spared the indignity of sexual immorality. They brag about their conquests and disperse innuendo like wildfire—burnishing their own reputations while ruining the lives of the women they've bedded. Could anything be more unfair or reek more of a double standard? Words could be her weapons. She'd channel her anguish into her writing. She gripped her quill and scrawled:

> *When spiteful men with torments did oppress...*
> *...their malice hath no end,*
> *Their hearts more hard than flint, or marble*
> *stone...*

Women must confront these wrongs, not accept them, and not forsake their sex. She could not let anyone dissuade her from this mission. She would not tell Will. She intended to keep these poetic works a secret until she found a way to publish them. Then she would face the reactions.

After several days of wallowing and writing, Amelia ventured out with Julia's encouragement. She had to rise from her malaise. She needed someone to talk to—not about Simon Forman, she'd keep that to herself—but to occupy her mind in a completely different way. She had yet to fully reconcile with Will. Since leaving his room on that pivotal morning, they had limited their conversations to scripts and business. She missed the jocularity and warmth they once had. Yet, if anyone could lift her spirits, it was her fellow wordsmith.

Upon entering The Curtain, Amelia and Julia heard shouts reverberating through the Henry Lanman's office door.

"When? Just tell me when! You own this theater."

"Thomas, it won't be soon. Stop trying to elbow your way back in! It won't work!"

"It's all about money for you! You refuse to help someone who truly needs it!"

"Get out! Now!"

The office door whipped open and banged against the wall as a stocky bearded man stormed out—running into Amelia and nearly knocking her to the stone floor. She dropped her valise and the final draft of *Much Ado About Nothing* slipped out along with a section for *Julius Caesar.*

The man, about her age, instantly drew back. "My apologies, madam."

Amelia steadied herself and bent down to gather her papers. Julia and the man reached for them as well, each grabbing a few.

Amelia stood straight, squared her shoulders, and appraised the man. She reached for the sheets but he clung to them while glancing at the disarrayed papers she and Julia held. A sly smile creased his face as he began reading the pages in his own hands. Amelia tried tugging them away but he held them fast.

Finally, he looked at her skeptically. "Interesting. And a few clever lines as well."

Amelia again reached for the papers. "I'll take those back now, Mr...."

"Dekker. Thomas Dekker. And you are?"

"Amelia Lanier. This is my cousin, Julia."

Dekker handed her the sheets as his gaze shifted from the two women to the gallery behind them. He clenched his jaw and Amelia followed his sightline. In the sweep of her eyes she noticed a man with curly blond hair watching from the shadows of an offstage wing.

"Will, is that you?" Amelia called, peering into the gallery.

Will raised his head. It had been buried in a document. "Amelia, Julia," Will shouted excitedly, "do come up."

Suddenly nervous, Amelia's hands started shaking. She pressed the pages to her chest. "We will indeed."

She swung back to look Dekker in the eyes. "Mr. Shakespeare, you may know, is an excellent playwright."

"Evidently," he replied with an incredulous snarl. He tarried a moment longer and turned to leave, then looked back as if taking Amelia's measure.

Will began coming their way, and Dekker shot him a malevolent glare before turning on his heel and marching from the theater.

The cousins advanced toward Will, meeting him half-way. "Why was Dekker so upset?" asked Amelia.

"He's a novice playwright, and indignant that Lanman revoked their agreement to stage his first play after we negotiated temporary use of The Curtain. So Dekker resents me, especially since we don't know how long we will be here."

"That explains his hostile glare."

"He's also been a thorn in my side, but that was years ago."

"How so?" asked Amelia.

"After a performance of *The Taming of the Shrew*, when you were in Venice, he asked a few suspicion-laden questions. With Lord Hunsdon's help, we diffused them ably."

Will now had Amelia's rapt attention. Dekker's name sounded familiar but she had not connected it with anything specific. Now she recalled Lord Hunsdon writing about Dekker's inquiries regarding Will's shift from writing English historical dramas to marital comedies set elsewhere. Dekker clearly had suspicions and now a motive for denouncing him. "Will, he could still create problems."

"All he has is conjecture. There's nothing he can do."

Suddenly Amelia was distracted by a figure lurking in the shadows backstage. "Don't look deliberately, but there's a lanky blond man watching us from the left wing. Who is he?"

Will did not turn his head, but asked, "Is he wearing a white shirt with sleeves too short for his long arms?"

"Yes, that's him."

"He's Garvan Shaw, an actor," Will said, annoyed. "He spends more time here than necessary—and he's curious about my work. He inquires frequently about scripts I am writing, how I get ideas, and where I find the time to do everything."

Alarmed even more, Amelia wondered about Garvan's motives—which could not be good. "That's highly suspicious, isn't it?"

"I didn't think so at first, but I do now. He loiters surreptitiously, observing me, and those I meet with. He's a strange man."

Amelia's uneasiness grew as she made an association that Will, perhaps familiar with both men, did not see. "Could Dekker and Garvan be conspiring? If they suspect others are composing your scripts and intend to expose you—"

"But what would they gain? My plays—our plays—give Garvan work. They have nothing to do with Dekker. We would be occupying The Curtain regardless. We're the most renowned troupe in London."

Amelia decided to forgo the subject for now, believing it unwise to pursue it with Garvan slinking around. She'd raise it another time, and soon.

Amelia noticed the papers on Will's hand. "What's that? It's not a script."

Will regarded the papers with distaste. "It's the lease Burbage signed for the land on which he built The Theater. I don't know why anyone would hire a barrister to compose such an incomprehensible document."

"Why are you studying it? Burbage and the company were evicted months ago when it expired."

"Since we'll need to sign another lease with the Bishop of Winchester, once we raise enough money to build the new theater on church land, I wanted to understand it. It's mind-numbing."

"May I look?" asked Amelia, extending her hand.

"Read it while I check something backstage," he replied, handing it to her.

Will marched across the stage and through the shadows in the rear.

As Julia looked on, Amelia pored through the lease, scorning at the minutia that anticipated circumstances that might never come to pass. Yet buried in a paragraph on the third page were phrases that stopped her eye. She reread them a second time to make sure she understood, using her index finger to not miss a word.

Will bounded back and she raised her hand, signaling him to not break her concentration. He restrained himself for a few seconds and studied her closely, looking intently at the emerging bump in her waist.

Amelia glanced up and read his worried expression. "Yes, I'm with child. Alphonso and I feel blessed."

Amelia watched his worry turn to relief. She then waved the lease vaguely in the direction of the building it discussed in such detail. "The last time I walked by The Theatre, it stood abandoned. Does it still?"

"Yes. Why?"

"Apparently, parts of this lease remain in force even though it has expired."

"Such as?" asked Will.

She stabbed her finger at the clause she had spotted. "As I interpret it, Burbage or his heirs, as the building's owner, have the right to dismantle the theater and reclaim all material parts when the lease expires."

Will's reached for the document with a burst of energy. "Show me!"

Amelia pointed. "Look. It says they own and can remove everything, inside and out, if the lease is not renewed."

"Do you know what this means?" yelped Will jumping from his seat. "Will, stop!" She reached into her valise and clutched a wad of papers. "Before dashing off, take the script for *Much Ado About Nothing*. And the first act of *Julius Caesar*."

Will grabbed them as he raced away.

She heard the theater gate clap shut then straightened the remaining papers in her valise. Her heart stopped upon realizing the pages for *Julius Caesar* were still inside but not the poems she had written for *Salve Deus*.

Garvan Shaw receded from view. Before Dekker met with Lanman, he had asked Garvan, as his eyes and ears at The Curtain, if he had seen or heard anything new. He hadn't until now. Dekker paid for useful intelligence and Garvan's rewards depended on piecing patterns together.

He had seen that olive-skinned woman before, but where? After searching his memory, it came to him. Today her brownish hair with glints of red was partially covered by a black and beige caul. She had worn it under a fashionable feathered hat when he first saw her—the day she delivered a flat package to Shakespeare during a rehearsal for *A Midsummer Night's Dream*. And she was familiar with the script, even answering his nuanced question. He had mentioned it in passing to Dekker, but they thought little of it. But today Dekker saw what she had—scripts must likely—and he saw her hand them to Shakespeare, like before. A distinct pattern had emerged.

Will met with Cuthbert and Richard in the cramped office Cuthbert used a block from The Curtain. Will pointed to the lease's right-to-dismantle clause, and the two men looked at each other in wonder.

"My eyes must have glossed over it before," said Cuthbert.

"It's buried in a dense paragraph and may have been inserted hastily," suggested Will, judging from the crimped handwriting.

Cuthbert clapped his hands together. "This means we can take down The Theatre piece by piece, remove every scrap, and reuse the materials for our new theater. That will save us considerable sums, perhaps enough to close the gap between the funds we have to invest and the projected cost."

"Who else knows of this?" asked Richard.

"Only my friend Amelia Lanier. It's she who found it."

"We must keep it a secret, informing only those who need to know," declared Cuthbert. "We'll tell only our other investors, architect John Dee, and our construction carpenter, Peter Smith. I'll ask John and Peter to estimate how much of The Theatre is reusable and how much it will save us."

"I would not be surprised," Will said, envisioning the potentially reusable material, "if it amounts to over four hundred pounds."

51

Five months pregnant and feeling ponderous, Amelia rubbed the protrusion beneath her loose-fitting dress while waiting in Will's cluttered office. He charged in and slammed her poetry on his desk, pounding it with his fist.

"You believe this?" he asked angrily. "Look at me! Who has been helping you for years? Me! A man! And you boil us all in the same pot?"

He picked out a few incendiary lines from her *Salve Deus* treatise, glaring as he read each one contemptuously. "You wrote all this and didn't bother to tell me!"

Amelia stared back. She would not yield to his tantrum, nor apologize for defending women and arguing for fair treatment and equality. She had expected Will to react unfavorably to the poems she had mistakenly handed him, but did not think he would be quite so enraged. "Will, I'm not attacking you or any particular man. I'm challenging the institutions, culture, and customs men have created and perpetuated over the centuries, and which serve to keep them in power and keep women contained. I thought you, of all men, would see that."

"You'll never get this published, so what's the point? It's little more than the bombast of a shunned woman."

Amelia vaulted from her chair, hurled the first act of *Julius Caesar* at Will, and snatched her poetry from his desk. "And you are not the enlightened man you pretend to be!"

She rushed out the door feeling deceived and betrayed— getting a small measure of satisfaction upon looking back at the shocked expression on Will's face.

52

Contractions. Unbearable pain. Amelia's emotional distress gave way to the physical agony of childbirth. With the exception of seeing Will occasionally, she had remained cloistered in her rooms through the long summer days that flowed into autumn. Temperatures had dropped with winter's approach but Forman's maliciousness still burned. She still could not bear facing the aristocratic gossipmongers who had undoubtedly passed judgment on her.

"Push. Push," the midwife instructed.

Amelia pushed, wincing in waves of pain and drenched in sweat with her legs spread wide. Enid held Amelia's hand and wiped a moist towel over her forehead. Amelia prayed that this midwife with stringy hair and thick arms knew her craft. Between contractions, Amelia heard faint sounds of Alphonso, Henry, and Julia beyond the bedchamber door.

Amelia grimaced as her contractions grew in intensity. The pain sharpened. She gritted her teeth.

The midwife again put her hand inside Amelia. The first time she had used a barbed thimble to break the membrane enveloping the baby. Searing pangs jolted through Amelia and suddenly fluid gushed forth.

"I feel its head," announced the midwife. "You push. I'll tug."

Amelia felt her insides stretching and widening with each thrust.

"I have the head in my hands. Push harder."

Amelia felt the infant squeeze through her and into life on its own. She gasped at the baby's first cry.

"A girl!" shouted Enid.

Amelia squirmed as the midwife severed the umbilical cord and removed the placenta. The midwife cleansed the infant with water and a damp towel, then dried and swaddled her with strips of linen and placed her in Amelia's arms.

"What'll you name her?" asked Enid.

"Odillya," replied Amelia, spelling the name.

"Odillya?" said Enid. "Pretty, but not one I've heard before."

"The beginning is for the word *ode*—a melodic poem. The rest is a variation of the end of my name. Our names will rhyme, and hers will honor the musical and poetic heritage of her family."

Amelia looked up from the baby to Enid hovering over the bed. "Invite in my boys and Julia to meet her."

Three days later, Will visited Amelia with a twinkle in his eye. Since their confrontation months ago about her poetry, neither had mentioned it. Over a series of script meetings, the tension between them had dissipated—much to Will's relief and he believed to Amelia's as well.

As the father of three, Will recognized a healthy baby when he saw one. Odillya's pale skin and incessant crying suggested otherwise. Amelia appeared exhausted with dark smudges beneath her eyes.

"I don't know what's wrong," she said. "Enid thinks she's colicky. But she doesn't have gas or apparent stomach pain."

Will tickled Odillya. She stopped crying momentarily then continued her wails. He made a slight face; glad he was only a well-wisher. "Where's the little lad?"

"Henry's with Alphonso," Enid informed. "They'll return this afternoon."

"Enid and Julia are more patient with Odillya than I," said Amelia. "Will, I apologize for my moodiness. I've had little sleep."

Enid lifted Odillya, kissed her downy coxcomb hair, and swayed her gently. The infant calmed and closed her eyes. "I'll rock her to sleep, so the two of you can talk."

When Enid left the room, Will said, "Amelia, I have been worried about you and I'm relieved you've come through childbirth safely. Odillya will get better."

"Will, you're very kind and thoughtful," Amelia replied, rising out of her torpor. "I'll be better when Odillya is."

"Soon, I hope. But you must attend our secret event on Monday night, December 28th."

Amelia roused herself and walked to the window, cracking it open to let in a stream of fresh air. "What is it? Why December 28th?"

"Because Giles Allen will be still be away for Christmas. He is not expected back until January 4th. On the 28th we will begin dismantling The Theater. We'll haul the lumber and anything reusable to the Bankside construction site."

Amelia smiled, happy the clause she'd discovered in the lease had been useful. "Allen will be furious."

"No doubt. He'd try to stop us by legal means or intimidation if he knew our plans beforehand. But once the deed is done, there will be little he can do."

"Will the salvaged materials close the money gap?"

"Most likely, according to Peter Smith, our carpenter, and architect John Dee."

Amelia thought about her royalties, which would grow substantially with a much larger venue. She would have more money to buy fresh fruits and vegetables for Odillya and Henry. And maybe have enough for more fashionable gowns and bodices. "I am pleased for you, Will. Who will take it apart?"

"Peter will instruct his crew, currently laying the new playhouse's foundation, to report for work at four o'clock that day."

The odd hour struck her. She wasn't sure if he meant morning or afternoon. "Why four o'clock?"

"We're beginning at dusk to be as secretive as possible," explained Will. "We'll work through the night, although it will take a few days."

"But the word will go out when they swing the first hammer."

"True. But Giles will be a two-days' ride from London. By the time he hears and returns, we'll be done."

Odillya started crying again and Amelia's eyelids drooped further. "Will, I hate cutting this conversation short, but I must tend to Odillya and get some sleep."

"Do what you must," Will said, seemingly eager to escape the wailing from the other room. "Amelia, our problems are being solved. The new theater will be superior and more popular than all others in London. We will have exceptional plays ready to debut when it opens. The future promises to brim with good fortune."

When alone with Odillya, Amelia rocked her baby in her lap. Odillya soon drifted to sleep. Her angelic face warmed Amelia's heart. Holding her daughter, stroking her tender skin, watching her tiny breaths, and imagining her future infused Amelia with peaceful joy. "There is so much I want for you…and that I will teach you, show you, and love with you."

Amelia placed Odillya in her crib and covered her with a soft blanket. She then curled up in her own bed and dreamed of the grand future that beckoned to her daughter.

53

Amelia rushed to finish feeding Odillya so she could get to The Theatre before darkness fell. She reflected on its significance in her life. It was there that Burbage had rejected her and where *A Comedy of Errors* had debuted—with Will named as the playwright. She watched *Merchant* from its balcony and fretted over the audience's reaction. *Midsummer* triumphed on its stage along with *Shrew* and other plays. Soon the dismantling would begin and a piece of her past would disappear.

Odillya's cheeks showed more color and her tiny hands flailed less. As Amelia re-buttoned her blouse, she reveled at Odillya's toothless expression feeling an incredible bond. Yet she worried. Odillya remained weak and sickly. Her skin often looked too pale and her moods alternated between fussiness and lethargy.

Amelia swabbed drops of breast milk, smelling like buttered crumpets, from around Odillya's lips then prepared to leave. She dressed warmly in a wool tunic, bodice, and sleeves. She slipped on her black-hooded coat and headed across the city to The Theatre.

A fine mist hung in the moist winter air and a few sprinkles followed. Horses and carriages splattered mud on Londoners who hurried along the walkways. The city's gray buildings looked mysterious and gloomy in the pall. But by the time Amelia reached The Theatre, the darkest clouds had moved on, leaving a thin layer illuminated by the rising moon.

Work had already begun when Amelia arrived. A crowd, watching and murmuring, had formed an arc around the building. The front doors had been removed and men carried planks, stage rigging, and benches to waiting wagons under torchlight. Letters were painted on each wagon and materials with the same letters loaded on each one, allowing materials to be efficiently organized. Some items were labeled with one or two words such as "stage floorboard," "balcony rail," and "trapdoor lid."

Will spotted Amelia as he exited the old playhouse to give instructions to a worker. He slapped dust from his hands and waved, then stared at someone behind her before remaking eye contact—as if trying to communicate something before reentering the building. Amelia twisted around but saw only a wall of onlookers.

When she had seen enough, Amelia forged her way back through the crowd. Once through the mass, she detected Garvan and Dekker standing across the street. That, she realized, was what Will was trying to say. Both spotted her instantly.

"Amelia Lanier, is it?" called Dekker. "Remember me? We unfortunately collided at The Curtain when you entered and I attempted to leave."

"You were upset about something, if I recall," said Amelia, trying to pass without taking the conversation further.

"Just in a hurry. What brings you to this theater-wrecking drama?"

He enjoyed asking questions, she noticed. "Curiosity. Like you, I suppose."

"How did you learn of it?"

"I hear many things."

"You're a coy one, aren't you?"

"Call it what you will, Mr. Dekker, is it?"

"It is indeed."

"I must go. I have an infant who needs me," she said striding swiftly beyond them.

"Giles Allen was madder than a hornet with its nest afire," snickered Will as Amelia met with him a week later in his workroom at The Curtain. "When he returned from the countryside and saw only rubble where The Theatre once stood, he went berserk."

Amelia laughed, tapping a scrolled parchment on the desk. "Can he do anything?"

"He's threatening to sue Peter Smith because his crew dismantled it."

"Giles probably forgot about that clause in the lease or thought it would go undetected after Burbage died," Amelia speculated.

"He's embarrassed. He's lost face. He's fuming about that as much as the demolition."

"When will the new theater be completed?"

"September, if we have fair weather and few unexpected problems," said Will.

"That's fast."

"Peter knows we're in a hurry. He's doubled his crew. When it's finished, it will be the finest and largest playhouse in London."

He had crowed about this before, and Amelia turned to the reason she had come in the first place. She untied the scrolled pages and flattened them on the desk. "Will, let's discuss Act III for *Julius Caesar.*"

"Indeed," Will said, proud of how it had turned out. "The dueling funeral soliloquies define the turning point in the play. First Brutus praises the man he murdered while claiming he slayed him for Rome's greater good."

"Then Antony dissects Brutus' justifications, turning them around with sarcastic vengeance and winning over the assembly," said Amelia, knowing what Will was about to say.

Amelia pointed to where the orations appeared in the script. "Read their speeches back-to-back. Does it work? Does Antony tip the balance?"

Will studied the script, his lips twisting back and forth with his rapt concentration. In the quiet, Amelia heard a floorboard creak behind her and twisted to look. A man appeared beyond the costume racks.

"Oh, Will," interrupted Garvin Shaw, "I didn't know you had a guest. I'll return later. I came to discuss one of my scenes."

"I'll find you when we finish," replied Will.

Will glanced at Amelia then back at Garvan, whose raised eyebrows seemed to ask an unspoken question. "We're discussing cue scripts for *Henry V,*" Will lied.

"I'll be in the prop room," said Garvan, turning to leave.

Garvan's interruption and Will's awkward excuse for her presence heightened Amelia's suspicions. Garvan keeps re-appearing at unexpected times. His interest exceeded idle curiosity.

"Where were we?" asked Will.

"I was waiting for your reactions to Brutus' and Antony's soliloquies," whispered Amelia, leaning across the desk. "Let's keep our voices down."

"In a word, eloquent."

Amelia smiled as Will proceeded. "Let's split the work for Act IV. I'll compose the scenes in which Brutus and Cassius disagree on how to defeat their enemies." Then in a voice projecting like a stage whisper, Will continued. "Will you write the scene in which Brutus is haunted by Caesar's ghost?"

Amelia's ears perked up again as costumes rustled on the racks behind her. She heard receding footsteps then a door close from down the hallway.

Panic seized Amelia. Had Garvan been hiding and listening from behind the racks? She assumed Will had the same thought. How much had Garvan overheard?

In the tense silence that ensued, Amelia realized that despite wishing to be known as a great playwright, she also wanted to protect Will. She had entered into their pact reluctantly, out of a sense of futility. Then she regretted it and resented Will for accumulating credit and adulation for her creative works, and then for refusing her requests for acknowledgement. Recently she had come to accept the arrangement. She now had a vested interest. If her role were exposed, it could destroy him and leave her practically destitute.

54

With Will's permission, Julia sat alone writing in The Curtain's balcony with parchments spread on the seat beside her and stacked on her lap. No performances were scheduled and she expected the venue would be quiet. She tried imagining stage action as she reviewed notes and sketched scenes. Her quill scratched across the pages. She dipped it repeatedly in her ink jar as ideas sprang to mind. She had trouble writing as fast as her thoughts and switched to Vèneto to make it easier. She had hastily dipped her quill again when interrupted by a loud male voice.

"Hey, who's up there? The theater is closed," shouted a man from below.

Startled, Julia's hand jerked with her quill still inside in the jar. It tipped over. Black ink spilled over the corners of her papers and dripped off the chair, staining her forest-green smock, and puddling onto the floor.

"No! Oh, no!" screamed Julia as she shot to her feet.

STEVE WEITZENKORN

"What happened? Are you all right?" the man asked with urgency as he rushed to her.

Julia recognized him. Garvan Shaw. She scurried to gather her compositions as he approached, jaunty in manner with his bony hands sticking out well beyond his shirtsleeves. Curly blond hair fell over his ears. But, she thought, he hadn't always been handsome. His oily skin was pockmarked, apparently from adolescent blemishes.

"I knocked over my ink jar. That's all."

Garvan smiled. "I'll get a towel to mop it."

He veered to leave then turned back. "Didn't I see you here once with Will Shakespeare and another woman?"

"Yes, with my cousin. We were discussing costume sketches," she lied.

"Is that what you're working on now?"

Julia glanced at the pages on her lap, which she attempted to hide with her arms. The top sheet was in Vèneto. "Not today. I'm writing a letter home."

"Where is home? You have an interesting accent."

"Venice."

"Is that page in Italian?"

"No, it's Vèneto."

"May I see it?"

"Not today," said Julia. "I should clean this mess and leave."

"Oh, I didn't introduce myself. How rude of me. I'm Garvan Shaw."

"I'm Julia."

"Julia, have you a surname?"

"Garvan, I must wipe up this ink and leave. I don't have time for extended conversation."

"I'll be right back."

Garvan jogged down and disappeared backstage. Julia grabbed blank sheets of paper and quickly blotted as much black ink as she could. She stuffed everything into her satchel and raced out of the theater—relieved she escaped before Garvan returned.

A royal guard escorted Amelia to Whitehall Palace's Great Hall, where high mullioned windows bathed the room in natural light, while crystal candelabras flickered high above the stage set for *A Midsummer Night's Dream*. Amelia's invitation claimed *Midsummer* was Queen Elizabeth's favorite play, which she had first seen three years earlier.

Twelve years ago, Amelia remembered watching *Knight in the Burning Rock* here with Lady Susan and meeting Lord Hunsdon and Will afterward. Then Amelia was a spirited eighteen-year old who imagined a resplendent future. Now, over thirty, she felt more truculent than fiery, unrewarded, and resented the ill treatment of women— even as she had resolved to accept her arrangement with Shakespeare.

Amelia's escort encouraged her forward, but she stopped to soak in the elegance and pomp. Men outnumbered women by half, many wearing black doublets with heavy necklaces or brightly colored sashes. Matching breeches were tucked inside tall leather boots. Cloaks fell from their shoulders beneath white neck ruffs. Women wore high-necked gowns in bright colors—scarlet, royal blue, white, and gold. Many were adorned with gold broaches embedded with precious stones. Others wore long pearl strands that draped from ruffed necklines.

Amelia's black and gray satin gown stood in sharp contrast. Nobility wore vivid colors. Commoners dressed in muted tones in accordance with English Sumptuary Laws—especially at official functions.

In the wide corridor outside the Great Hall, Lady Susan signaled with a head nod that she would like to speak with Amelia. The aristocrat's pale skin and fragility alarmed her. Susan now required a staff for walking support and to stay upright. Taking tiny steps, they edged into a side room for privacy, Amelia held Lady Susan's arm to keep her steady. Winded from the exertion, Lady Susan settled heavily into a velvet-cushioned chair. Her staff slipped from her hand, clattering on the stone floor.

"Amelia, I will not belabor this topic, but we must discuss it. The damage to your reputation inflicted by Simon Forman has been considerable."

Amelia knew better than anyone. "I have lost more sleep over those rumors than imaginable. I acted shamefully. I should not have trusted Forman's discretion."

"Any of us would have regrets. Forman is vengeful when he does not get his way."

"Lady Susan, with my unhappy marriage, I hungered for affection like Lord Hunsdon once provided. I did not expect such calumny."

"If it is any consolation, Forman has done this before. Those gossiping at the court know that. But they still derive an unsavory pleasure from discussing the misfortune of others. Many would have little to do if they weren't entertaining themselves so feebly."

Amelia fingered her hamsa. "I learned too late of Forman's reputation and dread seeing these people again—which is why, at this very moment, I am trembling."

Lady Susan leaned toward Amelia. "Buttress yourself. Stop sequestering yourself. You're adding to the misery imposed by others."

"But how?"

Lady Susan pointed a shaky finger. "You've given them a victory."

"I hadn't considered it that way. What should I do?"

"Amelia, dear, you must face them. Hold your head high. Not haughtily, but with composure. Some will feel small. Others are impervious. But that will speed putting this misadventure behind you."

The escort led Amelia and Lady Susan into the Great Hall. A tall man, immaculately dressed in a black waistcoat and white ruffled shirt, stood near the throne scanning the room. Even from a distance, he captured Amelia's attention.

The escort introduced them. "Lord Stafford, may I present Lady Susan Bertie and Mrs. Amelia Lanier. They will sit with you and the Queen today."

"I am pleased to meet you," said Lord Stafford. He bowed slightly from the neck, lifted Lady Susan's hand and then Amelia's, kissing them both.

Amelia tried to hide the shiver his touch spawned in her. "Lord Stafford, I am honored. Please call me Amelia. I am more comfortable with familiar names."

He rewarded the gesture with a slight bow. "In that case, call me Edward."

The lord had a practiced charm and courtesy, but acted as if he were out of place, thought Amelia. She guessed he hailed from the countryside and in his late twenties, a couple years younger than she. He had watery blue eyes, a strong jaw, thin waist, and sandy hair that curled around his ears. His easygoing mien reminded her of Henry Carey.

"The Queen must think highly of you to invite you to sit with her. May I inquire as to why she has bestowed this honor?" asked Amelia.

"I am also surprised. This is my first visit to Whitehall Palace. My father usually attends theatrical events, but due to illness I am carrying his responsibilities."

"Which are?"

"He's a patron of a traveling theatrical troupe called Lord Stafford's Company. It lacks the prestige of Lord Chamberlain's Men, but is well known among communities in Staffordshire and central England."

"I've heard of them," said Lady Susan. "Occasionally they perform near my country castle."

"How interesting," said Amelia, wondering if Will knew of the troupe. "Are you knowledgeable about theater?"

"Less than my father, I'm afraid. I believe he is entrusting—"

A trumpet blared with high-pitched notes, drawing everyone's attention: "Hear ye, nobles and royal guests, it is my great honor to present Her Majesty, Queen Elizabeth, Ruler of All England."

Queen Elizabeth, in regal splendor, strode gracefully through the center aisle in a glittering midnight blue and silver gown with billowed shoulders. Guests stood and bowed. She acknowledged her advisors and friends as she passed their rows. Her white facial makeup drew attention to her dancing eyes and red-painted lips. Attendants helped her as she settled into the oversized chair.

"It appears you have introduced yourselves," she said to Lady Susan, Amelia, and Lord Stafford.

"Your Majesty, we have," said Amelia. "We have learned we all share an interest in theater."

The Queen conveyed a polite interest before waggling her fingers in a shooing motion. "Edward, Susan, excuse me while I speak privately with Mrs. Lanier."

Amelia was as surprised as the puzzled expression on Edward's face as he retreated to the other side of the throne.

Queen Elizabeth placed her open palm by her face, covering it from the audience. "Amelia," she whispered, "I understand you have created this play. Correct?"

Amelia felt her face grow warm, not anticipating a reprise of the conversation they had shortly after her return from Venice.

"Yes, Your Majesty, I have written much of it. My cousin helped."

"Splendid," the Queen said. "Then you can answer any questions I have about it. I do not believe I absorbed all the nuances before."

Amelia nodded. "I would be honored."

Queen Elizabeth signaled for the comedy to commence. Amelia's head spun. The Queen's special favor was dizzying. She bent forward, attempting to concentrate on the performance and noticed Edward looking her way with intense curiosity. He radiated elegance, she decided, as the actor playing Egeus projected: "Full of vexation come I..."

The Queen's private conversation, Amelia reflected, must have piqued Edward's curiosity about her. That pleased her. She sensed a natural attraction, a pull quite unlike her unseemly decision to use Simon Forman out of frustration with her husband. Several times during the performance he glanced her way, interestingly after some of her favorite lines, such as, "The course of true love never did run smooth" and "Love looks not with the eyes but with the mind." Then a troubling thought struck Amelia: Did he know about her authorship? How could he?

During intermissions, Edward stayed close by Amelia's side. She liked the way he looked at her, without Forman's naked lust but rather with esteem. He sought her opinion, and that of Lady Susan, on whether Shakespeare intended to depict the fairies as light or dark spirits. And how much of the play might reflect the fantasies of real lovers. His questions stimulated vigorous discussions and, in the course of them, raised Lady Susan spirits above her physical maladies. Amelia observed her newfound energy and admired Edward for coaxing it forth. He genuinely seemed interested in their insights and she found herself attracted to his good nature and intellectual curiosity.

Afterward, Edward escorted them to their awaiting carriage. He lifted a shaking Lady Susan in first and then helped Amelia. His touch on her elbow once again sent shivers through her, and he let his fingers linger a moment longer than necessary. "I am very pleased to have made your acquaintance."

He tipped his hat as the carriage rolled forward. Amelia resisted the temptation to gaze back. Yet she was already planning to ask Will what he knew about the man. She wanted to see him again.

The joy in Amelia's heart evaporated in an instant. Lady Susan's eyelids drooped over her filmy eyes. Her face lost its last traces of color. She parted her blue lips and tried to speak but instead slumped onto Amelia's arm and stopped breathing.

55

Garvan crept silently through the hall to Will's office door in The Curtain and pressed his back to the wall. Cuthbert had left the door ajar after entering and the voices inside carried into the corridor.

"Will, until *Much Ado* opened, your last four plays had been serious dramatic works. Audiences were clearly thirsty for comedy, and it's drawing better than *Henry V*. Do you think that the monarchial plays have lost favor?"

A few moments lapsed until Will responded cautiously. "Possibly, for now. Three strong scripts will be ready when the new theater opens, and two are comedies: *As You Like it,* with a comedic court jester, and *Twelfth Night, or What You Will*—a boisterous romantic comedy for the close of Christmas."

"What play have you selected for the new theatre's opening?"

"*Julius Caesar.* It's a stirring historical drama about conspiracy, intrigue, and murder in ancient Rome. Audiences will flock to it, I assure you."

When the conversation drifted to other topics, Garvan slipped quietly away. He had heard enough.

Thomas Dekker ranted, pacing his rooming house floor. "First, I thought writing five plays in two years was impossible. Then eight new plays were produced in the following four years. Now three more will debut this year when their new theater opens! That's sixteen plays in seven years."

"And they're a mix of historical dramas, tragedies, and comedies set in several different countries," said Garvan, "and take place at different points in time."

"How does he do it? What role do these mysterious women play?" asked Dekker.

"I'm uncertain. The older one, Amelia, speaks with an aristocratic English cadence. Julia, the younger one, has a foreign accent."

"And they're pretending to write cue scripts?"

"And sketch costumes." Garvan scratched his head. "It's a masquerade. But we have no proof."

"Trail these women. Learn what they're doing. They're the key to solving this mystery."

For the first time Garvan pulled back. "I will raise suspicions if I inquire too much. I may have already. I'll wait until I see them again."

"Remember, Garvan, I'm paying you for information. No information, no money."

Amelia waited in the Queen's anteroom at Whitehall Palace, peering through diamond-paned windows to the lawn below. The Queen's latest call for her presence mystified her. None of her plays were being performed at the palace and she could not imagine that the Queen had more questions about her and Shakespeare.

The door opened and Amelia entered the Queen's opulent presence chamber, surprised to see Edward Stafford standing before Elizabeth. He nodded as Amelia stepped forward.

Amelia, feeling the heat of his presence, performed a deep curtsey. "Your Majesty, I am honored to appear before you."

Amelia turned toward Edward. "Lord Stafford, it's a pleasure seeing you again."

Although delighted by this coincidence, Amelia wondered why Queen Elizabeth had invited him.

"You have a common interest in theater," said Elizabeth, "and Lord Stafford desires good scripts for his productions."

"Mrs. Lanier," he said, turning toward her, "the plays my company has staged are beneath the caliber of those performed by Lord Chamberlain's Men. I'm seeking higher quality scripts. I understand you might be able to assist."

Amelia's words caught in her throat. "I would like to… but Mr. Shakespeare is…the playwright. I'll confer with him. I am confident he will agree to some."

"Amelia, I am sure you will persuade him," the Queen intoned. "The secret to Mr. Shakespeare's success is well known to you."

Amelia smiled awkwardly. "Perhaps he will relinquish scripts that have completed their run. Of course, Mr. Shakespeare will require royalties."

"Naturally, I would expect that," said Edward.

"You two negotiate details," the Queen said, seeming bored by such a trifling matter. "Lord Stafford, if you please, I want a private conversation with Mrs. Lanier."

"Yes, Your Majesty. I will take my leave."

Yet Amelia did not want him to leave immediately. "Lord Stafford, if you wait in the anteroom, we can discuss your request before going our separate ways."

After Edward left, Elizabeth said, "Amelia, don't fret. I have not disclosed your clandestine work with Mr. Shakespeare. I am simply returning a favor for Lord Stafford's father."

Relief swept through Amelia. "Thank you, Your Majesty. I never dreamed you would do anything of the sort."

Amelia walked backward toward the exit, since proper decorum required that one's back not turn toward the Queen. Her thoughts, though, turned to how this fortunate chance had thrown her and Edward together. Yes, she would grant permission to use the scripts. Only she would arrange several conferences to help him make the choices.

56

LONDON, APRIL 1599

Amelia prayed for a more sympathetic portrayal of Shylock as she sat in The Curtain's balcony with Julia. She had entreated Will, and he allowed her to be his assistant during rehearsals for a new production of *The Merchant of Venice*. She coached the cast on intonation, especially emphasis of key words in Shylock's lines to convey his deeper motives and emphasize his quest for long-overdue justice for Antonio's bouts of character assassination and intolerance. She wanted the audience to see Shylock's humanity and identify with his plight.

When the performance concluded, Amelia believed she had succeeded. Julia smiled at her reassuringly and was about to speak when two men approached them.

"Ladies, did you enjoy the performance?" asked Garvan Shaw. "I noticed during rehearsals, Mrs. Lanier, that you instructed some actors on their portrayals."

"Yes," chimed in Thomas Dekker, "Garvan said it seemed as though you had a stake in the play's interpretation."

Before Amelia could reply, Garvan confronted Julia. "You were quite impolite. While I ran to get towels to wipe up you're your spilled ink, you hurried away."

"Remember, I explained I was pressed for time?"

Amelia wanted to cut off these insinuations. "Gentlemen, what's the purpose of this conversation?"

"Need there be one, Mrs. Lanier?"

"Lanier doesn't sound English, nor do you look English," contended Dekker.

"The origin is French, but I'm as English as you fellows. I was born and raised here," she replied with strained politeness.

Dekker rubbed his hands together, as thought he had secret knowledge. "Julia, what is your surname?"

Julia hesitated. "Bassano."

"Bassano," repeated Dekker quizzically. "Like the character in the play?"

Julia's face turned crimson. "I believe that was Bassanio. A coincidence, I suppose."

Garvan asked, "Didn't you say you are from Venice?"

"I am. I am visiting."

"I see," said Dekker as he shifted his gaze to Amelia. "Did you bring her back with you? I understand you lived there for a few years."

Amelia glared at Dekker, her exasperation mounting. "Our pasts are not your business. We do not appreciate such personal inquiries from men with whom we are so little acquainted and don't wish to know better."

"Don't take offense. We are only engaging in friendly conversation," claimed Garvan.

Dekker folded his arms smugly. "But I note some troubling coincidences."

Amelia tried sliding past Garvan and Dekker in the row. "Excuse us."

Dekker sidestepped in front of Amelia, blocking her path. "Amelia, you have a distinctly Semitic appearance, with the shade of your skin and the slope of your nose. Are you Jewish? Are you both Jewish perchance?"

"We must leave," said Amelia as she glanced back at Julia. She raised her hands to push Dekker aside.

"Are you in a rush because you're hiding something? Judaism is outlawed in England, is it not? Consider the fate of Rodrigo Lopez. He was the Queen's physician but his life was not spared."

"Will, yesterday Thomas Dekker and Garvan Shaw confronted us," Amelia declared as she and Julia sat with him at a worn table in The Horn.

Will did not seem vexed by this news. "They ask questions and imply more than they know. There's little cause to worry. Garvan is an actor with limited range who could be discharged at any moment. Dekker is annoying like a fly you can't swat. He can't even get *The Shoemaker's Holiday* staged."

Will's quip did nothing to allay Amelia's concerns. "He and Garvan can still threaten our arrangement."

"There is something sinister about them," asserted Julia. "Garvan dug for information, pretending it was idle conversation. And Dekker, reminds me of the villains in our scripts. Did you see him wringing his hands?"

"Amelia, Julia, they're guessing. They have no evidence."

Amelia waited until some workingmen in grease-stained shirts squeezed past their table. "Will, he can damage you through innuendo alone. I have known such men. He will keep burrowing until he finds something scandalous."

Will finger-combed his hair, apparently struck by Amelia angst. "But what can we do?"

Amelia reached across the table and pulled Will's arms toward her until their faces were inches apart. "We must be careful. I am sure Garvan is Dekker's spy within Lord Chamberlain's Men. We cannot meet at The Curtain or anywhere he frequents. We cannot be seen together."

Will considered that idea, drumming his fingers on the table. "I don't know if you're right about Dekker and Garvan," he said, "but I can't chance that you're wrong. From now on, let's meet in remote locations."

Amelia breathed in, grateful for his concession. After yesterday, she feared those two parasites were drawing close. Her attention strayed until caught by the sight of a man coming toward them. "Oh no! I don't believe it."

"What?" asked Julia.

"Turn around."

Garvan Shaw sauntered toward their table, grinning like he had gambled big and won. "What have we here?" he asked with a smirk. "Discussing cue scripts again? But where are the scripts?"

57

LONDON, APRIL 1599

Amelia met Edward in the parlor of Bloomington Manor, a boarding house in central London, situated between Westminster Abbey and the Houses of Parliament. Surrounded by dark walnut panels and gild-framed paintings of English pastoral life, Amelia watched Edward stride gracefully into the room wearing a dark gray doublet with black breeches and hose. During earlier meetings, Amelia had admired how he exuded both confidence and humility. Unlike Simon Forman, Edward did not project arrogance or guile.

Upon seeing him in his casual finery, though, Amelia felt inadequately dressed. She had carefully brushed her burnished red hair and selected a beaded hat, but her shiny black-satin skirt and plain bodice showed signs of wear. She could no longer afford the latest fashions and had become self-conscious about her attire.

Edward's eyes swept over her as he approached with a friendly smile. He seemed pleased to see her, warming her inside.

"Good to see you again, Lord Stafford," greeted Amelia, as she pressed her leather valise to her chest and patted it, suggesting she had something of interest inside.

"Remember, it's Edward."

Amelia liked his amiable manner and lack of pretense. He had a way of putting her at ease.

"Shall we sit and take some wine and bread?"

"I would like that," replied Amelia, feeling sparks flying between them. "I have three scripts to show you."

Amelia withdrew the scripts from her valise while Edward placed their order.

Amelia said, "Mr. Shakespeare has proposed productions no longer playing in London, so we won't compete with each other."

"I understand, though that's unlikely. Stafford and the surrounding country are nearly a three days' ride from London."

"One condition," said Amelia, "is that you make copies for your company and return the original scripts to us."

"Of course. They're valuable and I'm grateful to you for making them available."

"Of these three scripts, I suggest choosing two. They are quite different and you 'll need to judge which ones best suit your audiences."

Edward leaned over the table as Amelia put *A Comedy of Errors* between them. His head inched close to hers and she enjoyed his fresh, clean scent—just from soap and water, she supposed. His regard for cleanliness appealed to her, setting him apart from most English men. She turned the script pages, briefly explaining the plot and characters. She extended her fingers to places in the script that were tantalizingly close to his arm, occasionally grazing it. The delicious mixture of seduction and intelligent commentary brought back memories of Henry Carey, Lord Hunsdon. As with Henry, Edward's fastidious grooming enticed her. Only Edward was nearly her age, perhaps younger.

Next, Amelia showed Edward *Titus Andronicus* and *The Taming of the Shrew*. He promised to read each one in the next few days, then they would meet again.

Amelia pushed back her chair now that they had concluded their business.

He laid his hand on her forearm, circling her narrow wrist. "Amelia, please stay longer. So far we've spoken only about scripts and the theater, but otherwise we know little of each other." Only then did he withdraw his grasp.

Amelia pretended not to notice. "Like me, you are married. Correct?"

"Yes, but to the wrong woman, if you ask my parents, and I have concluded that they've been right all along"

"How interesting. I am married to the wrong man. Why are you displeased with your betrothed?"

"I fell in love with my mother's chambermaid, Isabel. My parents had arranged for me to marry the daughter of a wealthy landowner in Cheshire, the county northwest of Staffordshire. But her haughtiness repelled me. Isabel, however, was beautiful with a genial manner."

"Did your interest in Isabel upset your parents?" asked Amelia.

"When they discovered it. They did not know at first."

"You kept your desires hidden?"

"I did. Isabel mesmerized me. She delighted me in all the ways a young man could desire, and acted disinterested in my considerable possessions. Because she was a few years older, she seemed wise. Her smile melted me. I wanted to marry her—not because I had to but because I saw her as the woman of my dreams."

Amelia knew how this tale went. "Ah, let me guess. Once you married she became less than you expected?"

"In part. She wished to marry into wealth. My parents warned me, but I paid no heed. Once we were married, Isabel lost interest in the marital bed and everywhere else besides. She became cold, selfish, and demanding."

"She took advantage of your naiveté," said Amelia.

"She is also illiterate," Edward lamented, "creating a gulf between us that cannot be bridged. So, I spend as little time as possible at home."

That also sounded like Henry Carey, except to make babies in his younger years. "Where do you go?"

"I enjoy London and travel with my theater troupe. Over half the performances are in small towns rather than Stafford, keeping me on the road. When my father asked me to manage Lord Stafford's Company in his stead, he knew the job offered an escape from Isabel."

Amelia's thoughts swirled with all this information. Where was this man, she wondered, when she was free to fall in love?

She told Edward the sad tale of how she came to marry Alphonso, omitting details about Christopher Marlowe. "Now I have a baby daughter, to whom I am devoted."

Edward touched the back of Amelia's hand. "May she grow to be as lovely as her mother."

Amelia felt her face blush. It had been years since a man complimented her quite that way. Normally, she might brush it off, but Edward seemed genuine. She liked his openness and sincerity. They connected like kindred spirits. But her circumstances stopped her. She would not repeat her past mistakes with men, yet she felt the tug of her heart and head pulling in different directions...and this relationship she fervently desired.

She gazed longingly at Edward's handsome face. She had to find a way out of her quandary. The route had to go through Alphonso, her husband in name only, since their marriage could not be broken legally. Until then, she would retain some distance.

"I am flattered, Edward," she said softly. "You are a kind man and I have enjoyed our conversations." She stood abruptly, returning to her businesslike manner. "When will you have the scripts read?"

"Shall we meet again in two days? And I hope we'll continue our conversation."

Amelia's heart leapt at the thought, entranced by Edward's mesmerizing blue eyes and evident interest in her. She had to figure something out.

58

Amelia weaved her way to the new theater's construction site, south of the River Thames near Maiden Lane and several paces east of a putrid drainage gully. The building rose three stories high and spanned nearly one hundred feet. Exterior walls had been erected and inside workmen were constructing the lower balcony. Chalk lines mapped the backstage areas. The space rattled with the pounding of hammers and cutting of lumber.

Amelia spotted Will inspecting the stage flooring. She sought his collaboration for a script rife with court intrigue and conspiracies over monarchal succession. He excelled at them and she wanted to corral his genius.

"They have made great progress," observed Amelia.

"They're working quickly," Will acknowledged. He pointed to the raised platform slanting upward from the pit and spoke to be heard over the clamor. "That's where the first floor seats will be installed. The posts along the front will support two covered balconies. Pillars on either side of the stage will support the roof above it."

Amelia looked around, imagining the finished playhouse.

"What will you call it?" asked Amelia.

"We're unsure. But we've chosen a motto to be inscribed above the main entrance—'*Totus mundus agit histrionem*' which is Latin for—"

"The whole world is a playhouse," translated Amelia. "A nice variation of one of our lines."

"Indeed, it was inspired from dialogue you and Julia penned for *As You Like It*."

"It is still fresh in my mind. Jaques, the downhearted lord proclaims, 'All the world's a stage. And all the men and women merely players: They have their exits and their entrances; And one man in his time plays many parts.'"

"That's it."

"The original idea came from the Roman courtier Petronius. He said, '*Quod fere totus mundus exerceat histrionem,*' which translates to 'because all the world plays the actor.'"

"Then our version is in good company," said Will.

"With that motto, why not name the playhouse The World?" asked Amelia.

Will repeated her suggestion as if considering how it resonated in his ears. "Or The Globe. It sounds more modern since cultivated people believe the Earth is round like a ball—although skeptics remain."

Amelia smiled. "That is even better."

She pulled a few papers from her valise. "Now, for what I came to discuss, a captivating new play I am calling 'The Prince of Denmark.'"

"The Prince of Denmark?"

Amelia waved her outline. "Yes. It's a riveting tale about court conspiracies, moral dilemmas, revenge, humor, and troubled personalities. Shortly after I returned from Venice, Peregrine Bertie, Lady Susan's brother and England's former ambassador to Denmark, conveyed the story. It's fictional, so we can tap our creativity all we like."

"We?"

"Yes, we. This will be a great one to write together."

Will beamed at the prospect.

The hammering stopped as workmen broke for lunch.

Amelia pointed to the open area behind Will and spread her arms wide, waving her papers. "Will, imagine the stage that will be here." She aimed her finger toward the sky. "Look up. It is a cold moonless night. It's dark on the ramparts of Kronborg Castle in Elsinore, Denmark. Two shivering watchmen making their rounds can't see far ahead or beyond the castle wall…"

Amelia jumped to the other side of Will and raised her hands high in the air. "Suddenly, a ghost appears resembling the dead king…"

Amelia continued dramatizing the story. Will looked transfixed. She finished by extending her arm and stabbing her finger in the air like a sword, enacting playfully the deaths of the king, queen, and prince. "What do you think?"

Will laughed. "The plot is terrific. But your acting…You were adorable but should stick to writing."

Amelia laughed. "I tried to make telling the tale fun, and for you to visualize it as I see it."

"In that you succeeded."

"Thank you. And I'll take your advice. Don't expect me at auditions."

"May I see your outline?" asked Will.

Will studied it for a while. "You have names for every character but the prince and deceased king. Why?"

"That's my next topic."

"You want to use family names again?"

"Your family this time—by naming the prince after your son, Hamnet, to honor his memory."

"Prince Hamnet?"

"Actually, I propose a variation: Hamlet rather than Hamnet."

"Why change the N to an L?"

"First, it's easier to pronounce. Second, that is the word Lord Peregrine used to describe Elsinore—a small town. The word also comes from the French 'hamelet' where 'ham' refers to fenced land. At the end, the prince is hemmed by events."

"Hamnet. Hamlet. Hamnet. Hamlet," repeated Will, letting the names roll from his tongue, while emphasizing the different consonant to see which would be easier to say. "I see your point. And I would like to honor Hamnet. His death at so young an age pains me still." Will lowered his head, took a deep breath, and then raised it again. "Are there any Amelias in this script?"

"Not yet. But there's still time," said Amelia, chuckling as she repacked her valise.

Will reached for her hand. His expression turned serious. "Are we beyond our disputes over authorship credit and your poetic volume?"

She pressed his hand between her palms, touched by his warmth and care. She closed her eyes to contain unbidden tears as she sought to subdue welling emotions. After a few moments she looked deeply into his eyes. "I won't raise the topics again, but your obstinate and hostile reaction to *Salve Deus* did gall." She took a heartfelt breath. "But I have chosen not to let them taint our otherwise fruitful collaboration. I know what I have contributed to our enterprise, as do you. In the spirit of the philosopher Maimonides, I find joy in knowing I have endowed you with a gift, which in turn brings pleasure, and perhaps a dose of wisdom, to others. I need not be known, except in my heart. I am now happy with that."

Will kissed Amelia softly on her forehead, gratitude apparent in his tender mien and embrace.

Upon stepping back, he said, "I believe you'll be pleased with our initial rotation for the new theater. Your work is prominently featured. We will open with *Julius Caesar*, which will be followed by *As You Like It* and *Twelfth Night*. Then we will add *Hamlet* when it's finished.

Amelia kissed Will's cheek. "It will be grand."

A chill streaked down Amelia's spine as she trudged through the muggy July heat on her way home. She had just passed the Gothic Southwark Cathedral half a mile east of the new theater when she turned and looked behind. She sensed danger but saw nothing unusual, only other pedestrians going about their business. After crossing the London Bridge over The Thames she pivoted again, this time noticing two bearded men in dark clothing. They stopped in mid-stride but kept their gaze on her. She quickened her pace, figuring she would be home in thirty minutes.

Nearing her building, Amelia saw Enid stretch her head through an open window, waving both hands and pointing to two other men stationed in front.

"Bailiff! Bailiff!" Enid screamed.

Amelia swung back, set to run. The constables were upon her. One grabbed her arm as she tried rushing past. The others surrounded her, binding her hands.

"What's this about? I've done nothing wrong?" Amelia protested.

The beefiest of the constables announced, "A warrant has been sworn out against you. We're to make the arrest."

Amelia struggled to free herself from one bailiff's grip but to no avail. "For what?" she demanded.

"For being a Jew! A religious offense." he said, spittle flying from his lips. "We are taking you to the Clink."

Amelia shuddered upon hearing the name. She had walked near the dreaded prison, known for its horrors, on her way to London Bridge.

She twisted her neck and screamed toward Enid, still watching aghast from the second floor window, "Tell Alphonso! Tell him to tell the Queen! She can help me!"

As the constables led Amelia into the gloom of the Clink in the Bankside section of Southwark, she turned for one last glimpse of daylight. Her heart sank upon seeing Thomas Dekker lurking across the street with a look of heartless satisfaction.

Alphonso listened while Enid described Amelia's arrest, unsure how to broach the subject with the Queen or if she would agree to see him. As a court musician, he lacked standing. He had not fought bravely in the Azores. Did he have the courage for this, especially as a Jew himself? What could he say? How would he say it? Might he be arrested as well?

Julia paced by the window, glancing outside. Enid had asked her to announce anything suspicious, for constables could return to apprehend both her and Alphonso.

Enid said, "I know nothing of these matters. But you must do something. You're Amelia's husband."

Julia pointed at Alphonso. "If you're afraid, recruit Shakespeare to go with you. He owes Amelia favors."

"But what can he do? Does he know we're Jewish?"

"It doesn't matter. He'll learn soon enough.

Guards pushed Amelia through a narrow brick hall to a stone-block cell and forced her into a sturdy wooden armchair. Irons with heavy chains were hammered onto her wrists and ankles.

Another guard hovered over her until his face perched inches away. "How do you plead?"

She smelled his foul breath. "Plead to what?" Her voice cracked.

"To being a Jew! Do you confess?"

Her mouth dry, she held her head erect to project bravery. "I was baptized in the Church of England at Saint Botolph's in Bishopsgate. My parents are buried in its churchyard. I was married there."

"That's all meaningless. That's what imposters do!"

"I'm a Christian. How else can I prove it?"

The interrogator snarled. "You've been accused of being a Jew. Confess your guilt or I'll press it from you?"

Amelia's frightened eyes saw the plank and large stones heaped in a corner. "I have nothing more to say."

The interrogator backed toward the heavy iron door. "You'll not be so stubborn when you feel the weight on your chest. You have three hours to change your mind." He turned abruptly and left, followed by the other guards. The door clanged shut. The latch clanked into place. In eerie silence, chained to the hard chair, she stared blankly at the bleak cell walls.

"My petition to see the Queen on Amelia's behalf was quickly granted," Alphonso told Will as they strode to Whitehall Palace. "Robert Cecil, Earl of Salisbury, her principal advisor understood the urgency, although I said nothing about Amelia's alleged faith."

"Surely they inquired and the Clink informed them of the accusation," Will postulated, nervous at having been pulled into this matter but feeling obliged to participate. "The Queen must favor Amelia to accede to your request."

"We'll discover how much once she hears our plea."

Alphonso accelerated his pace as the palace came into view, stepping around horses tied to posts and over manure in the street. Will stayed with him, shoulder to shoulder, as they approached the gate.

Guards escorted the two men to the Queen's presence chamber where she sat elevated on her gilded throne. Long, narrow windows stretched up toward the high ceiling, bathing the room in light.

They bowed upon approaching her. "Your Majesty," said Alphonso, "thank you for seeing us. We have come because my wife, Amelia, has been arrested. We seek her release."

Elizabeth looked from Alphonso to Will. "I understand Mr. Lanier's interest in this, but Mr. Shakespeare, what is yours?"

"Your Majesty, as Mrs. Lanier's friend, I wish for her good welfare. I can testify to her virtuous character."

The Queen shook her head, as if knowing there was more to Amelia's relationship with Shakespeare than he had disclosed. "Are the accusations true, that she is a Jewess?"

Alphonso swallowed hard and stretched his neck upward. "As you may know, Amelia's father, Baptista Bassano, born a Jew in Venice, was invited to England by King Henry VIII to perform as a musician in his court, and after his death played in yours. In England, Mr. Bassano was baptized and lived his life according to Christian precepts. Amelia's mother, Margaret Johnson, was born and raised as a Christian and died as one. Amelia was baptized in her parish church on January 27th, 1569. Her son and daughter were baptized after their births. Nobody disputes these facts. There is no evidence of Amelia practicing any other faith."

The Queen nodded, giving no hint as to what she believed. "Mr. Shakespeare, what do you know?"

Will bowed again, sweeping his arm across his knees. "The accusation is scurrilous. I know little of Amelia's family history, but the duchesses Katherine Willoughby and Susan Bertie, both devout Christians, raised her following her father's death. I believe both were well known to Your Majesty. They gave Amelia a Christian education and ensured she accepted Jesus Christ as her Lord and Savior. Amelia became as devout as they."

Alone, shivering with fright in the dark chamber, Amelia consumed herself with terrifying thoughts while listening to the distant moans of prisoners in nearby cells and guards trudging through the hall. She could only imagine the agony that might befall her if she failed to confess. Yet the horror of being hanged and disemboweled while still partially alive—as was the fate of Rodrigo Lopez—seemed far worse. Were the last sounds he heard those of a cheering crowd while executioners castrated him and sliced open his chest? Could there be a more painful and humiliating death? She could not stop envisioning the worst while praying that Alphonso, despite their deep differences, sought her rescue. Was he brave enough to be so merciful?

The cell door banged open. The burly interrogator and two guards marched in.

The interrogator held a candle close to her face and pulled roughly on the lace fastening her bodice. "We know you're a Jew! Ready to confess?"

"A Jew? What is a Jew? Was Jesus not a Jew?"

"Jesus has nothing to do with this?"

"He is not the Savior who died on the cross for our sins? He has everything to do with this."

The interrogator jerked again on her bodice lace, pulling her upward and spitting into her face. "But you don't believe in him! You're a Jew!"

"How could I not? Would the merciful Jesus treat a lady this way, especially a fellow Christian?"

He flung her back into the chair. "I have no patience for this! Chain her to the floor!"

The guards unlocked her from the chair, forced her back to the floor, and shackled her down.

"Get the plank and weights. She won't bear it for long."

The guards laid the board across her chest and dropped three heavy rocks on top. Amelia felt her ribs compress and air rush from of her lungs with each jolt. She coughed. She could hardly breathe and the pain grew with each passing second.

"That should be enough for now. We'll give her a couple hours and see if she comes to her senses."

Again they left her in darkness, this time staring at the vaulted brick ceiling. She closed her eyes and tried taking her mind elsewhere, but could not escape the throes of the moment. The stones seemed to grow heavier as time wore on.

Amelia believed she must have lost consciousness. Her next awareness was hearing gruff voices shouting at her. She opened her eyes to see the interrogator and guards glowering above.

"Had enough? It's easy to die this way but I won't allow it to be quick. Ready to confess? We know your guilty but I must hear it from your lips."

Amelia stared up at him. She licked her dry, cracked lips but her tongue and mouth were parched as well. Her weak voice squeaked out, "I believe in the same God as you."

"Liar!"

"Sir, that is the truth."

"You refuse to confess?"

"I prefer to speak the truth. I have been accused but not shown any proof? Is there any? Or only hearsay?"

To the guards the interrogator commanded, "Put a jagged stone under her and fourth large rock on top."

A thickset guard lifted her back off the hard floor while his comrade slipped a sharp-edged stone beneath her spine. The guard released her shoulders and she slumped on top of it, screaming in excruciating pain. The other guard held another heavy rock aloft, as if giving her time to anticipate the crushing, stabbing pain it was sure to cause when he dropped it on the plank.

"One last chance to confess," declared the interrogator.

She squeezed her eyes shut bracing for the inevitable, expecting the searing pain to be unbearable.

"Halt! Do no more!" boomed a voice from the hall.

Amelia raised her head as far as possible to see two soldiers in the cell doorway, each gripping the hilt of his sword. One held high a scrolled document.

"On orders from the Queen. This prisoner is to be released into our custody."

Stooped over, her chest and back throbbing, Amelia plodded wearily up the steps to her rooms, leaning on Alphonso for support. Julia and Enid embraced her tenderly as she reached the top. Never had she been so glad to be home.

"Alphonso, thank you. You saved me from a tortuous death."

"Enid and Julia must also be thanked. And Mr. Shakespeare too."

Startled, Amelia asked, "Will? But why?"

"At Julia's urging, I enlisted his help. We met with the Queen together."

"What does he know?"

Please sit," suggested Alphonso as he eased her into a chair. "Will knows the accusation but not the truth of it. I believe the Queen's intervention put his suspicions to rest."

"I'll see him soon and judge that then. Now, all I want is to bathe, breathe, and sleep. Everything else can wait."

59

Amelia slept for the greater part of three days after
returning from the Clink and had done little beyond thinking for several days after that. Grateful
for the Queen's rescue, she would find a way to show her
gratitude in addition to the note she sent on her second
day home. Although still sore and shaken, she prepared
to meet Edward Stafford. She had a new script for him but
mostly she wanted his company. In her traumatized state,
she had forgotten about a meeting and imagined his dismay when she didn't appear. She hoped he did not think
less of her or feel spurned. Upon realizing her oversight,
Amelia dispatched Julia to apologize and arrange another
meeting.

In an unadorned charcoal smock and feeling unlovely,
Amelia stepped hesitantly into Bloomington Manor where
Edward waited in a black doublet and white ruffled shirt. She
had trouble meeting his sparkling blue eyes, as much as she
wanted to peer into them. Finally she lifted her downward

gaze with a weak smile. Her vivacity had been wrest from her soul and she lacked the energy to revitalize it.

"I'm delighted to see you," she said faintly.

Edward strode toward her and reached for her hands. "Come, you've been through an ordeal. Allow me to help you recover."

Amelia stiffened, "But...but what did Julia tell you."

"She only apologized for you and arranged this meeting."

"Then...then how do you know I've been through an ordeal?"

Edward pulled out a chair by a table for her to sit. "I asked the Queen, through an intermediary, if she knew what had become of you."

Trembling, Amelia asked, "And how did she respond?"

"I was told you were arrested in error and spent some difficult time in the Clink."

Amelia dropped her head into her hands and started sobbing. She did not know what she felt...whether it was chastened, relieved, disgraced, grateful, fearful, confused, or some stew of them all. She looked up at Edward and saw compassion and love.

At that moment, she decided to tell him everything except about her pact with Shakespeare. If he still loved her after that...

She reached across the table for his hands. "Edward, sweetling, I will tell you the truth about me—about my flaws, my faith, my delusions, my infidelity, my fears, my fights, and what I want and need. Then decide the kind of relationship you would like to have with me, if any. If you walk away, I won't fault or think less of you—but I hope you stay by my side."

Edward squeezed her hands. "I'm listening. I believe I am a good judge of people, so I doubt what you are about to say will change my opinion much."

Amelia drew her hands back. "First, I was not arrested by mistake. I am a Jew. My father was a Jew, born in Venice. It's a family secret for obvious reasons…"

Amelia watched Edward closely as she continued. He kept his eyes on hers. She occasionally swept tears away when she spoke of her father's death, being raised by the duchesses, her affairs with Lord Hunsdon and Marlowe and Forman, her forced marriage to Alphonso after becoming pregnant, her travails in Venice with Julia, the torching of the instrument-making studio, fearing discovery of her Jewishness while pretending to be Protestant, Alphonso gambling away her savings, the agony of her arrest and imprisonment, and more. It seemed like she had talked for hours until she could say no more. Somehow she felt cleansed, that she had stripped away her pretense but for the anonymous script writing—which was a big part of her life. She prayed she had not scared him away.

Edward moved his chair so he sat next to Amelia and clasped her hands in his. "It took enormous courage to disclose so much. You have placed great trust in me. I assure you, it has not been misplaced."

"Is that your only reaction?"

"Indeed not. I understand much better the woman beside me, who until today has been an enigma. You are the most interesting person I know. I respect who you are and how you became that way. And the vulnerable little girl that lives inside you. And I love you for making her visible to me. Indeed, that is a high compliment."

It had been ages since Amelia had seen such sincerity in a man's eyes. "I have not disillusioned you?"

"Are there any illusions left?"

Amelia swallowed hard and kissed the back of Edward's hand. She yearned to devote herself to him but a big secret remained. If he discovered it, would he consider it a sign of distrust? Would it destroy his faith in her and deny her the happiness she foresaw? "Only one I am duty-bound to keep confidential."

"Someday, perhaps, you will tell me. But I surmise it involves your relationship with Mr. Shakespeare and the Queen."

Amelia felt her heart lighten and freer now that a huge burden had been unlade. She loved this man. She wanted him in her arms and saw promise in her future. The fear and torment of prison seemed to be receding. She had almost forgotten about her residual aches and sense of doom. Since Edward had mentioned Will, she used the opening to shift the conversation.

For the first time since her incarceration, and perhaps well before, she felt the sparks of her youthful spontaneity, which she thought had been lost forever. "Your reference to Shakespeare reminds me that the new theater will open in September. I'll show it to you if you don't mind stepping through construction debris."

Edward reacted with astonishment. "You must have a close relationship with Shakespeare to allow that. It's been wrapped in secrecy since they enclosed the building."

"Will and I have been friends for a long while. He won't mind." Amelia believed Will was performing at The Curtain, and since she had once been a familiar face at the to-be-named Globe they would have no trouble gaining access.

Amelia fluttered her eyelashes. "Want to go there now?"

"I'd be delighted," responded Edward, clearly pleased.

Amelia sprang to her feet, grabbed her valise, and pulled Edward's arm to coax him up. She noticed a slight blush overtaking his face. "Shall we?"

Amelia relished the effect she had on Edward, reinforcing her desire to break free of Alphonso. She coupled her arm with his when they reached the street and ensured their shoulders brushed as they walked in tandem.

When they passed through the theater's construction entrance, Edward scanned its vast interior. "It's enormous. My company plays in modest facilities that hold but a couple hundred people. Nothing like this."

Workmen were installing seats in the first-floor gallery and affixing railings. Amelia pointed to the middle of the lower balcony, which had yet to be completed. "That is where I will be sitting on opening night, in the first row."

Edward looked at her in surprise. "That will be the best seat in the house."

She turned toward him and traced her finger lightly along his jawline. "Would you like to have the seat next to mine?"

Edward's fair face reddened, seemingly unaccustomed to such romantic gestures. He placed his hands gently on Amelia's waist, "I would be honored."

"Come, I'll show you the backstage areas too," said Amelia, as she grabbed her valise with one hand and grasped Edward's palm with the other, leading him across the pit and around the stage. She wished to know if he truly loved her or if everything she sensed was a mirage. She had to believe it was pure and true and right for her—and more than friendly adoration. She had to experience it bursting naturally from inside her and from Edward to be sure. And she needed to see his reaction to the strongest of her beliefs. Only then would she approach her husband.

When they were alone in the room that would soon house costumes, they looked deeply into each other's eyes. Edward folded his arms around her and she leaned into him. He pulled her closer. She felt their hearts beating in unison. She reveled in his warmth, his touch, his strength, his affection, his love. Never had she felt so secure. Then she gently pushed him away and pointed to a stack of lumber. "Please sit. I'd like to show you something, to get your opinion."

Amelia's heart fluttered seeing the disappointment on Edward's face. He wanted what she wanted. He felt what she felt. Yet there was something else she needed to know. She opened her valise and showed him a raft of her most polemical poetry from *Salve Deus*.

He read with rapt attention, smiling and nodding as he turned the pages. "You wrote this?" he asked with an air of amusement—one of the traits she liked about him.

"She nodded."

He chuckled. "I thought so."

"What does that mean?" she asked cautiously.

"I'm not laughing at the sentiments. Expressing them takes courage and many people might agree after due consideration."

"Then why were you laughing?"

"I was envisioning priests fuming from their pulpits, defending Adam and disparaging the sinfulness of Eve. And the confounding reactions of the pious whose life-long assumptions have been pricked. I can see heated discussions between wife and husband, since you might have burst the beliefs of one but not the other on matters they took as the settled order of life. Women might think you're an enlightened prophet while men call you a heretic—and dispute your contention that the achievements of great men hinged on the contributions of women. If seen from a distance, the quarrels might be amusing and, perhaps, create some good. But first your poetry will ignite a furor, like a torch to a hornet's nest."

Amelia stared at him, disbelieving, astonished such thoughts came from a man. Her biggest question had been answered. Ecstatic, her heart throbbing, she folded herself onto his lap, draped her arms around his neck, and pressed her body into his. Without another thought, she pressed her lips to his, conscious only of her joy and the passion of their kisses. Her love flowed up from her heart through her lips and into his. And his cascaded through her like a sparkling waterfall. Finally she had found the love for which she had always longed.

60

G arvan Shaw hid in the prop room as other actors changed to street clothes and left The Curtain. He was not performing today but had sneaked through a back door. He waited behind shelves stacked with crates labeled with names of various plays. He heard muffled banter from actors complaining about flubbed lines, missed cues, and audience responses to favorite puns and scenes. When thirty minutes passed without a sound, he slipped cautiously into the hallway. Like a prowler, he tiptoed to avoid making noise, checking to ensure he was alone.

The dark theater had become eerily quiet. When certain everyone else had left, he opened the rear gate. Thomas Dekker slid in silently, carrying a rucksack.

"We're alone?" whispered Dekker.

Garvan nodded.

"Where's Shakespeare's office?"

"Follow me. It's in a backstage corner."

Garvan checked the door. Locked. "Are you sure you can pick it?"

"I have been practicing but I'll need more light."

Garvan lit a candle in a tarnished brass holder. Dekker removed keys and lock-picking tools from his bag. One by one he tried several keys. None worked.

"This old lock will test my skills," said Dekker.

He inserted a combination of picks into the keyhole until he could nudge the tumbler. Sweat beaded on his brow until the bolt clucked open. He pushed open the office door.

Stacks of beige and brown papers cluttered Will's desk. Garvan and Dekker riffled through them. One pile included detailed notes for the new theater design. In another they found the script for *Henry V.* A few sheets contained a scene for a play about Julius Caesar. Dekker raised an eyebrow.

Garvan frowned. "I see nothing suspicious or incriminating."

"All for naught," said Dekker, turning to leave.

Garvan jerked his hand up, signaling him to stop.

"What is it? Did you hear something?"

Garvan pointed under the desk. "There is a trunk underneath."

Dekker stooped to look. "So there is. Pull it out."

Garvan scraped the oak trunk into the open. It was reinforced with brass slats and secured with an old padlock.

"Can you pick it?" asked Garvan.

Dekker grabbed his tools and worked as Garvan shined candlelight on the proceedings. Minutes later the shackle creaked open. Dekker yanked off the lock and lifted the lid, staring at haphazard piles of old scripts.

"What have we here?" asked Garvan, leaning over Dekker's shoulder.

They snatched documents and held them to the candlelight. A bundle on top included scripts and cue scripts for *King John* and *Henry IV Parts I and II*. Another stack bound with a cord was labeled *Merchant of Venice*. Scrawls across another stuffed to the side read *Original Draft: Midsummer Night's Dream*. Tucked against the back they discovered a dog-eared script for *Richard II*. Dekker placed them side-by-side on Will's desk.

Garvan set the candleholder on the desk. Together they leafed through scripts.

"The handwriting for the two *Henry IV* scripts, *Richard II*, *King John*, and *Henry V* are identical," said Garvan.

"But the script for *The Merchant of Venice* is in a different hand," said Dekker. "That's telling."

Garvan turned the pages of *A Midsummer Night's Dream*. "Whoever wrote *The Merchant of Venice* also penned parts of this script along with somebody else."

"It must be those girls, Amelia and Julia—sometimes writing separately and sometimes together." said Dekker. He smirked slyly. "This is all the implicating evidence we need."

"But it's not proof," countered Garvan. "We have nothing, like letters they signed, to use for comparison."

"But it's more than circumstantial." Dekker pointed. "Look, there are marginal notes in a foreign language. Aren't they similar to—"

The jarring slam of a door echoed through the hallway.

Garvan tensed to an erect posture. "What was that?" he whispered.

"Douse the candle," hissed Dekker. "Shut the office door quietly and press hard against it, so it seems locked if someone tests it."

Garvan leaned his shoulder against the door and pressed his ear to the wood. He heard voices. He mouthed "Cuthbert" to Dekker.

"Who else?" mouthed Dekker back.

"Don't know."

The footsteps stopped short of Will's door. Garvan listened but could not decipher the muffled words. He held his breath, not making a sound. They waited silently without hearing anything for several minutes, which seemed like an eternity. Garvan then heard Cuthbert's voice again, which came through clearly this time. "We have what we need. Let's go."

The patter of footsteps receded until the outside gate banged shut.

"Let's put these scripts back in the trunk and slip out," suggested Garvan as he lifted a stack.

"Wait. Not yet," said Dekker, holding his hand up. "Let's rip incriminating pages from each one. They won't be missed."

This idea panicked Garvan. "What for? It's an unnecessary risk. We can't show them without implicating ourselves."

"I want them. They're proof Shakespeare is a fraud. He is putting his name on someone else's work."

Dekker grabbed the papers from Garvan's hands and flipped through them. He tore sheets from each script and from two others still on Shakespeare's desk, stuffing them inside his bag. "Now let's put everything back, so nothing looks touched."

Upon finishing, Dekker fitted the padlock through the rungs and pushed the trunk back under the desk. They re-locked the office door, crept to the theater's rear exit, and disappeared into the night.

Dekker now knew he could ruin Shakespeare. He had only one question: *How can I use this evidence to discredit him without revealing how I got it?*

61

Amelia rushed to get ready for The Globe's opening and the debut of *Julius Caesar*. She had devoted more time to her makeup and hair than planned. She wished to impress those scandalized by the rumors Simon Forman had spread and look her best for Edward. With him by her side, she would feel more confident and protected. She attached her double-stranded pearl choker, accentuating her long neck and complementing her cranberry silk gown.

The opening performance had been sold out for weeks, and the two center seats Will had reserved for Amelia would be in the midst of London's wealthiest aristocracy. Amelia intended to apply Lady Susan's advice: look the gossipers straight in the eye, keep her head high, and maintain a serene composure.

Amelia tied on her pearl-studded French hood, inspected her appearance in the mirror, kissed Henry, and went to check on the napping Odillya. She planned to meet Edward at The Globe's main entrance.

※

Edward arrived early. He scanned the gathering festively-attired assembly seeking Amelia's distinctive visage— her caramel complexion, coiled chestnut hair, and petite build. As he examined every face, he considered the brilliance of opening The Globe with *Julius Caesar*. He knew the story, if not how Shakespeare would dramatize it. This tale concerned the succession of power in ancient Rome, and the English were uneasy about succession. Few expected Queen Elizabeth, at sixty-six, to live much longer. Since she had not married and had no natural heir, would the succession be orderly or violent? Nobody knew. *Julius Caesar* would resonate with the angst of the times.

Edward kept waiting, growing worried. The performance was about to commence, but Amelia had yet to appear.

※

Will stared at the first row of The Globe's lower balcony. Amelia's reserved seats remained empty and the play would begin soon. The audience was buzzing. *Where's Amelia?*

Garvan Shaw, cast as Flavius, a Roman official elected by lower classes as their advocate, would be the first actor speaking onstage. Backstage, he paced nervously. "Will, it's time. Are we starting?"

"Not yet. I'm waiting for someone."

Will searched the aisles and doorways. No Amelia. The hum from the audience grew louder. He sensed their impatience.

"Will, why are we waiting? The audience is about to revolt," urged Cuthbert.

He had to consume more time. He decided to begin his speech and keep talking until Amelia arrived.

Will advanced to center stage. "Ladies and gentlemen, Lord Chamberlain's Men welcome you to the magnificent Globe Theatre and our first production in this new playhouse…"

Still no Amelia. *Where is she?*

"You are about to witness the debut of our newest play, *Julius Caesar*…a story of ancient Rome…forty-four years before the birth of Our Lord Jesus Christ…"

Where can she be? Amelia, what's the hindrance?

"We hope you will return tomorrow when we will perform another new play…a love story and court comedy… called *As You Like It*…"

Amelia, please walk through the door. I can't delay much longer.

A man in the pit barked, "Start the play. That's what we come for."

A restless murmur rippled through the crowd.

Amelia, I cannot hold the performance any longer. Where are you? This is your play.

"…and now without further ado…I present for your pleasure…*Julius Caesar.*"

As Will stalked offstage, he continued gazing at the empty seats. *Why isn't she here?*

Amelia approached Odillya's crib, pleased to see her calm after another restless night. But her relief turned to horror upon inspecting her daughter's ashen face and bluish lips.

"Enid, come quick!" screamed Amelia, lifting her nine-month-old baby from the crib. The child's body felt unnaturally cold and flaccid.

"What's wrong?" asked Enid, bursting into the room.

"She's not breathing."

With a finger, Amelia forced Odillya's lips open and covered her daughter's mouth with her own. She exhaled a long stream, trying desperately to breathe life back into the infant. Deep inhale. Heavy exhale. Over and over again, but to no avail. Odillya's little body did not respond.

Stricken by a blind wave of grief, Amelia hugged Odillya to her chest, not wanting to let go. "My dear God, she's gone!"

Amelia heart plunged. She collapsed into a chair, sobbing, still clutching Odillya. "My precious baby girl is dead," she said softly. "How could you die? You were just sleeping."

Amelia had never imagined her daughter dying. She had dreamt about encouraging her first steps, teaching her to play the lute, watching her frolic with girlfriends, seeing her laugh and dance with boyfriends then fall in love and marry, and helping her pursue her passions to accomplish something notable—but never crying over her lifeless body. Never this! Amelia had envisioned a wondrous life for Odillya—a better and more lighthearted one than her own. None of it would come to pass. How could she fathom it? How could she continue on? A deep dark void grew inside her, like a weight she could not put down.

Edward Stafford reluctantly took his seat beside the other one reserved for Amelia, hoping she would soon arrive. His mind went numb and his heart heavy, not understanding why she had not shown. He could barely concentrate on the performance.

When Act Five neared its climax, Edward watched as Brutus, Julius Caesar's one-time friend turned mortal enemy, prepared to commit suicide with his sword. Brutus announced that his motives were more righteous now than when he had murdered Caesar, who could rest peacefully with his death avenged: "Caesar, now be still. I killed not thee with half so good a will."

Restless, Edward decided to leave before the play ended. He had thought constantly of Amelia throughout the performance, continually craning his neck for a sight of her. Dejected, he rose from his seat and strode toward the exit.

The festive atmosphere surrounding The Globe before the show had dissipated. In the quiet, carriage drivers stood by their horses and conveyances for their employers to exit. Loud bangs pierced the calm. Edward pivoted, seeing a dark-haired man hammering papers to the theater's outer wall. The man rapidly affixed three documents and started posting a placard above them as Edward drew nigh. In large block letters it read: "DID SHAKESPEARE WRITE ALL THESE PLAYS? CAN YOU IDENTIFY THE 3 HANDWRITINGS?"

Edward studied them. The barrel-chested man with a long nose and brown beard who had posted the items stood to the side.

"Recognize anything?" he asked pointedly. "I'm seeking to settle a matter."

Edward inspected the three pages taken from different scripts. Each had been penned by a different hand and one apparently by two people. Curious, thought Edward, Shakespeare could not have written all three. The handwritings were too different, but this matter was not his concern. He stepped away, then angled back abruptly to reexamine the papers. He looked from one to the next to the next. He recalled the poetry she had showed him. He was certain. Handwriting on two sheets belonged to her.

Edward directed his attention back to the barrel-chested man who was watching theatergoers trickle out as applause from inside ebbed. Edward lifted his coat flap and unsheathed the dagger strapped to his belt. Without warning, he rushed the man, jammed his shoulder into his chest, and knocked him to the ground. Edward raced back to the posted documents and sliced them free.

"Wait! Stop! You can't do that!"

A crowd began encircling them. Edward ignored the onlookers and glared at the man. He folded the sheets and stuffed them into his coat pocket. "I already have."

"Return them! They belong to me!"

Edward jabbed his dagger toward the man, stopping short of his rounded chest. "I think not. I doubt those sheets are rightfully yours—and probably stolen. I will tell you only once. Turn slowly and walk away from the theater. I will be following. My blade will be an inch from the small of your back."

The man paused, shifting his eyes both ways as if searching for an escape or a sympathetic face. Edward touched the soft underside of the man's chin with the sharp tip of his knife. "Now!" he commanded in a harsh whisper.

The man turned and took a few deliberate steps away. Edward pricked his back.

"Hey! Why did you do that?"

"To convince you I'm serious and won't hesitate to mete out justice. My blade is razor sharp. Now who are you?"

"My name is…Dekker. Thomas Dekker. Who are you?"

"Mr. Dekker, I'm asking the questions."

"Where should I go?"

"Where you have the rest of these scripts. I want everything."

Will fretted about Amelia throughout the performance. He wondered why one of her seats remained empty while a man sat in the other. *Julius Caesar* was her masterpiece more than his. He had given it scant attention during the past few months while concentrating on innumerable details for The Globe's opening. Why hadn't Amelia attended its debut and The Globe's premiere—the most important day of his career? Something was amiss, perhaps terribly so.

Pushing Amelia from his mind, Will hurried from the confines of The Globe to gauge reactions to the new theater and play. While overhearing enthusiastic comments, he noticed a commotion from the corner of his eye. Two men were arguing off to one side. He saw the flash of a dagger through an opening in the surrounding crowd.

Will raced over, anxious to avoid an incident that could draw unpleasant attention to the new theater. A tall sandy-haired man was forcing another away at knifepoint. "What's the meaning of this?" Will asked, breathing heavily as he caught up to them, then suddenly recognizing one. "Dekker! What's this man doing to you?"

Dekker scowled back mutinously. The tall man extended his arm, jabbing Dekker's back with the blade tip to spur him on. Dekker flinched as he staggered forward.

"The better question," the man said, "is what was Dekker doing to you?"

"Who are you?" demanded Will, now recognizing him as the man who had occupied one of Amelia's seats.

"Edward Stafford, a friend of Amelia Lanier."

Will looked him over, appraising him carefully as if he were an adversary.

"Mr. Shakespeare, we've not met, but these materials should be of interest," Stafford declared with controlled calm as he handed the placard and script pages to Will. "Your friend Dekker posted them on The Globe's exterior wall."

Will examined the sign and script pages in the late afternoon haze, realizing how devastating they would be if brought to light. "Thank you for your prudence. I don't know how Mr. Dekker came into possession of these documents, but they don't belong to him."

Dekker's eyes flared with contempt. "I've been caught but it's too late to stop Garvan Shaw. At this moment, he's grabbing that Jew, Amelia Bassano Lanier—who lacked the nerve to attend your spectacle. He'll punish her as he sees fit!"

Will spun on his heels and raced toward London Bridge, and then to Westminster and Amelia's home.

Amelia clung to Julia, tears falling on her cousin's shoulders after taking her last look at Odillya, kissing her cold forehead, hand-brushing her wispy hair, laying her lovingly in her crib, and covering her with a sheet and blanket.

Dear beloved Odillya, did I love you all that I might have in life? I did, but I devoted too much time away from you with my writing, and pursuing relationships that did me little good. Oh, the foolish things I sought in desperation. How did that affect you? My belated realization makes my sorrow more agonizing. I ache in my heart, and mind, and every limb. I should have cherished you and Henry above all else.

A loud clattering of boots on the wooden staircase outside the door jarred Amelia from her somber introspection. Then came a thunderous pounding on the door.

"Bassano! Amelia Lanier! Open before I smash through!"

Amelia jumped, her heart hammering. She backed toward the window and seized a kitchen knife. Enid grabbed a stone pestle and held it aloft, ready to thrust it toward whoever came through the door.

"Garvan! Stop!" Amelia recognized Will's panicky voice.

Will charged up the steps and launched into Garvan, ramming the assailant against the door. Garvan pushed back, shoving Will with his long arms toward the steep staircase. Will stumbled down a few steps. Garvan leapt after him but Will clutched his wrists and pulled the actor into him. They crashed down the stairs with Garvan landing on top of Will. He straddled the playwright and pinned his shoulders to the stone floor.

"William Shakespeare, master playwright, where's your nerve and conceit now?" asked Garvan mockingly.

"Where's yours?" asked Edward as he collared Garvan's neck with one arm and pressed his dagger against his throat with his other hand.

Will gazed up at Stafford, grateful twice in one hour for the man's intervention.

"Edward, Will! What's this fight about? Shouldn't you be at The Globe?"

Will crawled out from beneath Garvan as Edward held him in place. He looked up to see Amelia standing at the top of the stairs in her scarlet gown, her face streaked from tears and hair straggling to her shoulders.

"That's a question Mr. Shaw should answer," replied Edward. "Will and I were battling to stop him."

Garvan stared up at her as Edward pulled him to his feet and bound his hands with a rope.

"If you're curious, Shaw, Mr. Dekker is already bound, gagged, and tied to a post in an abandoned building a block from The Globe. Once I ensure Amelia is unharmed you will join him. And should you attempt to hurt her again, you will be contending with me as well."

Edward peered up at Amelia. "Has he been holding you captive?"

"No, no," Amelia cried, tears pouring forth. Something far worse has happened. Odillya...Odillya has passed and I am bereft."

Amelia swept tears from her eyes and cheeks while Julia explained the tragedy to Will and Edward.

Edward forced Garvan down to his knees and asked Will to watch him. He climbed the stairs and enfolded Amelia in his arms. Her heaving chest pressed into his warm body, absorbing his comfort. She couldn't speak. No words could capture her sorrow and regret.

Once Edward escorted Garvan away, Will embraced her as well. Will, she thought, has come here on the day of his greatest triumph. And wants only to see me through my anguish.

Will whispered into Amelia's ear as he held her close. "Don't let this loss tarnish your hopes for the future. You… we… can rise above tragedy."

I don't care about the future, Amelia thought miserably. Yet she could not be ungrateful. He simply wanted to help. She tilted her head upward and kissed Will on the forehead. She squeezed herself against his chest. "I hope we can. But there is a secret you must know."

Will leaned back his head and brushed a tear from beneath her eye. "A secret?"

"Odillya was your daughter too. I did not know how to tell you…or anyone."

Amelia saw Will's look of surprise but also his compassion and understanding. They knew each other so well. He kissed her cheek and hugged her warmly as he never had before.

Then Amelia remembered something Lady Susan had told her when she was seven or eight. She could picture herself, sad and complaining about the unfairness of her father's death—and how her art and poetry sparkled with joy when he was alive but had turned dull and gloomy. Lady Susan explained that happy people sought sunshine no matter their misfortunes—and the sun always shines beyond the clouds. Amelia was about to get down from her lap when

Lady Susan added, "Great artistic expression—whether with words or paint or acting—can spring from a grieving soul. From pain, you can create something beautiful."

EPILOGUE

London, September 1599

For seven days following Odillya's death, Amelia received friends, neighbors, Will, Edward, and Lord Peregrine Bertie, along with musicians who played at the court with Alphonso in her modest home. They all expressed sympathy and comfort. Over the week, their faces had blurred before her eyes as they conveyed similar but no less sincere offers of condolence. Amelia's mind kept drifting. Many families lost children in the first year of life. But this was her daughter. The child she wanted to nurture to self-sufficiency, and whom she hoped would achieve success in her own right and own name. Those aspirations vanished with Odillya's last breath, leaving behind only emptiness—a deep chasm Amelia could not imagine filling. She blamed herself, convinced she had failed as a mother.

When Amelia emerged from the blur, she became aware of Alphonso's shallow assertions of grief, as if he only pretended to mourn his daughter for appearance's sake. She indicted him in her mind for such falsity and an irrevocable change overtook her soul. She felt freer—less bound to convention and the opinions of others.

As the last group of friends voiced their final words of sympathy, Amelia reflected more on Odillya's brief life, her own, and the world in which she lived. Most people, she realized, accept with few questions or challenges the imposed burdens, predetermined roles and rules, constraints, conditions, and customs of their cultures. They rejoice in moments of gratification, perhaps because they are so few. Their hearts leap at rare unexpected joys. They cling to precious relationships but often fail to invest sufficiently in new ones that could add greater light to life. With those thoughts, Amelia chose to change her life. Her dreams for Odillya would inspire her. She would embrace them as her own. They'd instill her with courage. She'd see Odillya sparkle in the stars at night, a reminder to aspire, pursue her own convictions, seek the bright and let go of the dark, and nurture the relationships that meant the most to her.

The next morning she confronted Alphonso. "Dear husband, only two matters have bound us together. The first was our marriage born from my out-of-wedlock pregnancy. It rescued me from disgrace and provided you with a spouse who met your parents' approval. But they have since rejected me, and you by extension. That bond is broken."

Alphonso stared blankly at Amelia. He tightened his lips as if preparing to say something disagreeable but she barged on, "Allow me to finish."

He nodded with a look of skepticism.

"Odillya also bound us to one another. Now she is gone."

"What's your point?"

"That there is nothing left to hold us together. We can live our lives free of one another. You can go your way and I can go mine, seeing each other only by mutual choice. We need not weigh each other down."

"You'll take Henry?"

"Yes. He'll no longer be a burden to you. You can enjoy life as you choose."

Alphonso picked up his flute. He tapped his fingers over the holes as if silently playing a melody. Finally, a small smile creased his lips. "We never were suited."

Amelia nodded. "Let's then release each other from our marital vows, so you can act without remorse as can I."

Edward lent Amelia his arm as they strolled into the Globe Theatre early the next morning. Seeing it completed for the first time, she marveled at the cavernous structure. It dwarfed all other London playhouses. The gleaming gallery rails reflected sunlight pouring in from overhead. The pitched roof drew the eye to the stage, which jutted toward the large pit. Amelia climbed onto the platform and scanned the magnificent performance area.

While Edward stepped outside, Amelia strode through a wing and found Will in his vastly larger office. "Will, have you a few minutes?"

Amelia placed her draft of *Hamlet* on his polished desk. "Remember how we named the prince of Denmark Hamlet?"

"I do. You suggested it."

Amelia blinked back a tear. Her grief and emotions welled inside. She choked getting her words out. "I'd like to do the same for Odillya. It would be fitting to re-name Hamlet's lover for her. I suggest Ophelia."

Will came from around his desk and embraced Amelia. His warmth and compassion soothed her. "Both lives ended tragically. And the final scene you created for…Ophelia, in its poetic beauty, will stand as a testimony of your love."

Will gazed into Amelia's velvety brown eyes and took her hand. In a complete change of tone, with a bounce in his voice, he said, "Come with me." He playfully pulled her backstage. "I'll take you where you've never been."

He grabbed a folded red banner and took three steps up a wooden ladder. "Follow me to the top."

Amelia climbed behind. They ascended high above the stage and into a narrow tower. Will pushed open a trapdoor and daylight flooded in. He clambered through and extended his arm to lift Amelia up.

"This is the theater's highest point," announced Will as Amelia steadied herself on the steeply pitched roof. She gripped one of his hands as he grabbed the flagpole rising from the roof's apex with the other. She stood behind him as he attached the banner to ropes and hoisted it to the top.

Edward shaded his eyes and observed the scene from ground level. He saw Will's silhouette as he raised the red flag. It unfurled in the brisk breeze revealing an image of Hercules holding a globe over his shoulder. Then Amelia climbed beside Will atop the tower. Their silhouettes joined as one with Amelia's curls streaming in the wind. With the bright rising sun behind their shoulders, they peered into the distance, across The Thames and beyond, with the banner waving majestically between them.

ACKNOWLEDGEMENTS

Many people contributed to the creation of *Shakespeare's Conspirator*. I extend a very special thank you to:

Bonnie Kabin—my wife, love, and life partner—who encouraged me and offered many suggestions in addition to accommodating my obsession with this project.

Christine DeSmet of the University of Wisconsin, who coached, critiqued, and offered incredible advice.

John Paine, who edited and offered continual guidance.

Andrée Aelion Brooks, an expert on Amelia Bassano Lanier, who helped improve historical accuracy and terminology.

Lee W. Haas, who identified inconsistencies and researched Jewish customs.

Victoria L. Martin, who provided feedback and advised on revisions.

I am also grateful for the assistance of David Basch, Rabbi Robin Damsky, Rabbi Yosef Garcia, Pam Gardner, Rabbi Peter J. Haas, Leslie Lerman, Hannah Lurie, Michelle Seagull, Ilene Singer, Fulvia Tognati, Linda Toomer, Benjamin Kabin Weitzenkorn, Helene Weitzenkorn, Ruth Yip, and many others who helped along the way.

From the Author:
I hope you enjoyed reading
SHAKESPEARE'S CONSPIRATOR
The Woman, The Writer, The Clues.

To learn more about Amelia Bassano Lanier and delve
deeper into this fascinating mystery, visit:
ShakespearesConspirator.com

You will find details about:

- The Premise and Supporting Research
- The Characters (both real and imagined)
- Other Hidden Clues and Mysteries in Shakespeare's Scripts
- Amelia's Jewish Lineage
- The Blog
- The Author (and how to contact for questions, insights, and speaking engagements)
- References and Other Sources
- Discussion Questions
- Inquiries

All the best,
Steve Weitzenkorn
February, 2016

Made in the USA
San Bernardino, CA
04 February 2016